A MATCH of WITS

Books by Jen Turano

A Change of Fortune
A Most Peculiar Circumstance
A Talent for Trouble
A Match of Wits

A MATCH of WITS

JEN TURANO

BETHANYHOUSE
a division of Baker Publishing Group
Minneapolis, Minnesota

© 2014 by Jennifer L. Turano

Published by Bethany House Publishers
11400 Hampshire Avenue South
Bloomington, Minnesota 55438
www.bethanyhouse.com

Bethany House Publishers is a division of
Baker Publishing Group, Grand Rapids, Michigan

Printed in the United States of America

Library of Congress Cataloging-in-Publication Data
Turano, Jen.
   A match of wits / Jen Turano.
     pages cm
   Summary: "Zayne and Agatha have always been a match in wits, but will
unlikely circumstances convince them they could also be a match made in
heaven as they return home to 1880s New York City?"— Provided by publisher.
    ISBN 978-0-7642-1127-0 (pbk. : alk. paper)
    1. Couples—Fiction. 2. New York (N.Y.)—History—1865–1898—Fiction.
I. Title.
PS3620.U7455M38 2014
  813'.6—dc23   2014003688

Cover design by John Hamilton Design

Author represented by The Seymour Agency

14 15 16 17 18 19 20   7 6 5 4 3 2 1

For Dominic
I've watched you turn into an
extraordinary young man, Dom,
which, quite honestly, has surprised me
upon occasion given that you were
such a terror in your youth.
Since I know you loathe anything of a
mushy nature, I'll keep this simple—
I'm incredibly proud to call you my son.

Love you always,
Mom

COLORADO—LATE SEPTEMBER 1883

Sometimes, no matter how independent and self-assured a young lady believes herself to be, certain situations demand a good dose of screaming.

Dropping her traveling bag to the floor, Miss Agatha Watson snapped her mouth shut when she realized her shrieks were hurting her ears and took a hesitant step forward. For some reason, there was a blanket scooting her way, but what was underneath that blanket, well, she couldn't actually say.

Her heart continued pounding in her chest when the blanket moved closer, but when an adorable little pig popped out her lips curled into a grin.

"Aren't you just the most darling thing ever, but . . . good heavens, is that foam dripping from your snout?" Backing up a step, she considered the pig, and her eyes widened when it began pawing the ground, right before it charged directly at her. Spinning on her heel, she raced out the door, fresh screams erupting from her lips.

The hallway soon filled with employees of the Antlers Hotel. But rather than coming to her aid, they thundered past with barely a glance tossed her way. Stopping in her tracks, she turned and watched in dumbfounded amazement as the employees hovered around the pig.

It was an odd circumstance to be sure.

"What did you do to poor Matilda?" one of the hotel maids demanded as she straightened and sent Agatha a glare.

"I think a more pertinent question would be what Matilda did to me. There I was, tired from my journey and looking forward . . ." Agatha's words trailed off when she glanced to the pig and found that the fierce beast of only a moment before was nowhere to be found. In its place was a quivering mass of pink cuteness that was emitting noises that almost sounded like sobs.

Edging back down the hallway, Agatha stopped a few feet away from the gathered employees but far enough from the pig that, if it decided to attack, she'd have enough room to bolt. "As I was saying, I really didn't do anything to the pig other than open my door and take it by surprise."

"Better watch the P-I-G word, Miss," a lanky man with rather bad skin said as he rose to his feet. "Matilda doesn't react very well when people call her that."

"I highly doubt she understands the meaning of words."

Shaking his head, the man lowered his voice. "Strange as this may seem, she does, at least the P-I-G word. I think someone must have abused her mightily in the past, and she thinks bad things are going to happen to her when that word is used."

"How unusual. I—" Agatha began, but a loud clearing of a throat distracted her from the numerous questions she'd immediately longed to ask regarding the pig and its ability to comprehend words. Knowing all too well who was responsible for that particular clearing of a throat—something she'd heard on an alarmingly frequent basis over the past year—she squared her shoulders and swung around. Her gaze reluctantly locked with that of Mr. Blackheart, the gentleman who'd been hired to protect her.

Unfortunately, he was not gazing back at her with understanding on his face. His expression was filled with nothing less than clear disapproval, a look she was becoming quite accustomed to viewing. The thought flashed to mind that she just might have to send a telegram to Mr. Theodore Wilder, the most reputable private investigator in all of New York and Mr. Blackheart's employer, requesting a change of guard. The months she'd spent in Mr. Blackheart's company were beginning to take a toll on her. And even though she knew full well she needed someone by her side as she traveled around the West in pursuit of articles for the *New-York Tribune*, Mr. Blackheart's time with her might need to come to an end.

There was only so much disapproval a lady should be expected to experience.

"Miss Watson," Mr. Blackheart began, "explain to me, if you please, how you've managed to become embroiled in yet another bout of calamity. I left you alone for only a miniscule amount of time while I saw Mrs. Swanson settled, and yet here you are in trouble again."

"Honestly, Mr. Blackheart, it's not as if every calamity that occurs is of my making. If it has escaped your notice, there seems to be a mad pig in our midst, one that I'm fairly certain was intent on harming my person."

Mr. Blackheart switched his attention to Matilda. "It's only a small pig. What did you expect it to do to you—gnaw off a toe or perhaps nuzzle you with its snout?"

Agatha lifted her chin. "It's frothing at the mouth."

"You naughty girl," the man with splotchy skin crooned as he shook his finger at Matilda. "You've been in the chalk again I see."

Agatha blinked. "She's been eating chalk, as in blackboard chalk?"

The maid who was still hovering over Matilda nodded. "We were concerned when we learned the teacher staying in your room was allowing Matilda to eat it, but the little darling seems to love it. Once it became clear she wasn't getting sick, we stopped fussing about it. They seemed to be getting along so well, but the teacher up and departed this morning, and she actually balked at our suggestion she take Matilda with her."

"I wonder why?" Agatha asked, glancing down at the drooling pig that was now rooting around the floor, obviously searching for something else to eat.

"I have no idea," the maid replied before she gave a sad shake of her head. "But if someone doesn't offer to take her soon, I'm afraid she's destined for the slaughterhouse."

At that pronouncement, Matilda stopped rooting, began quivering harder than ever, let out a mournful squeal, and promptly scampered back into Agatha's room.

"I take it she has an issue with the word *slaughterhouse* as well?" Agatha asked, and the employees nodded back at her. Curiosity sent her after the pig, and she grinned when she spotted a wiggly pig tail sticking out from under the bed. Finding herself charmed in spite of the fact the pig had scared her senseless only moments before, she moved farther into the room but came to an abrupt halt when a distinctly disgruntled voice sounded from behind her.

"Do not even tell me that pig is still here."

She looked up and discovered Mr. Farrington, the manager of the hotel, marching her way. He brushed past her and seemed to swell on the spot when he caught sight of Matilda's backside, which had stopped wiggling. He turned around and narrowed his eyes at his employees.

"Well?" he demanded. "Would someone care to explain why that pig is not yet off to a farm?"

"Matilda doesn't actually care for farms," a maid mumbled.

"Did she tell you of her dislike?" Mr. Farrington asked.

"Not exactly, but you see, I tried to take her out to old Mr. Galloway's homestead, sir, but . . ."

"But what?"

"She turned up back here a few hours later." The woman's eyes grew round. "It was truly remarkable that a little thing like Matilda was even up for such a long journey."

A tic began throbbing on Mr. Farrington's temple before he looked back at Agatha. "You must accept my deepest apologies, Miss Watson. Pigs are not a normal occurrence here, but I'm certain it was quite the shock to find a pig in your room. I'll have another room readied straightaway. And while that's being taken care of, I'd like to offer you a complimentary meal in our fine dining room. By the time you're finished eating, I can guarantee your new room will be perfect, and I assure you, you'll not see that abomination again."

Noticing the telling glare Mr. Farrington was sending Matilda's way, Agatha's heart gave a tiny lurch. The poor pig was now trying to squeeze under the bed—a futile attempt if there ever was one, because its backside was much too large. "Forgive me, but I have to ask, what are your intentions for the pig?"

A snort of obvious protest erupted from under the bed.

Mr. Farrington licked his lips. "I enjoy a nice slice of ham upon occasion, and since no one seems to want to take responsibility for the pig, well . . ."

Matilda let out a high-pitched squeal right as she finally managed to disappear from view.

Uncomfortable with the thought of Mr. Farrington serving Matilda for dinner, Agatha opened her mouth, but before she could utter a single word, Mr. Blackheart gripped her arm. He pulled her across the room at a rapid clip, pausing for only a second to scoop up her bag from the floor with his free hand. Tugging her past the employees, who were now muttering not very nice things about her under their breaths, Mr. Blackheart hustled her down the long hallway without speaking so much as a single word. Digging in her heels right before they reached the stairs, she forced the infuriating gentleman to a stop.

"Mr. Blackheart, after all the time we've been forced to spend together over the past year I understand that you're the strong, silent type, but what has gotten into you? Those people must believe you've taken leave of your senses, hauling me away in such a roughshod fashion."

Mr. Blackheart fixed his piercing blue eyes on her and released a grunt.

That was it—a single grunt.

Why in the world did so many gentlemen who spent time in her company resort to that particular response? Did they assume she understood the language of grunting, and if so, was it expected she'd respond in kind?

She shook out of his hold, crossed her arms over her chest, let out a grunt of her own, and began tapping her toe against the wooden floor.

Mr. Blackheart looked at the floor, watched her feet as she

began tapping faster, and then raised his gaze before he rolled his eyes—an action that sufficiently summed up their relationship.

It was quickly becoming evident she'd annoyed the gentleman once again, but she truly couldn't think of anything she'd done that warranted his displeasure. Besides, even if she *had* done something—which, again, she hadn't—he was paid well to watch over her. Sending annoyance her way on a regular basis wasn't in his job description.

Why, he was beginning to remind her more and more of Zayne Beckett. . . . No, she was not going to allow herself to travel down *that* memory lane.

" . . . it was yet another disaster waiting to happen."

Blinking, Agatha realized that, while she'd been reminiscing on matters best left forgotten, Mr. Blackheart had evidently put his grunting aside and was now voicing another complaint.

"I beg your pardon?" she forced herself to ask, earning a scowl from Mr. Blackheart in the process.

"I *said* we barely averted another disaster. I saw the expression on your face when you heard that pig was about to get served up for supper. I'm telling you right now, I did not sign up to look after you, Mrs. Swanson, *and* a pig."

"I don't cause disasters on a regular basis," she said before she swept past him and began moving down the stairs.

Mr. Blackheart caught up with her all too quickly. "What about the cattle wranglers?"

"Complete misunderstanding."

"You set their chuck wagon on fire."

"I didn't do it on purpose." Agatha reached the bottom step and paused to get her bearings.

"Be that as it may, your actions caused a flaming catastrophe."

Agatha bit her lip. "I don't think I've ever ridden a horse so fast in my life."

"Having twenty hungry and enraged cowboys chasing you does lend a certain motivation for spurring a horse forward."

"At least I got a riveting story out of the ordeal, one that was incredibly well received by the readers and earned me an award from the *New-York Tribune*."

Mr. Blackheart arched a brow. "We almost lost our lives."

"But we didn't, so winning the award was delightful for me."

"What did I get from the fiasco?"

"I would think you got satisfaction from the mere fact you were able to keep me alive. There's nothing quite like a job well done to give a person a deep sense of contentment."

Mr. Blackheart's other brow joined the first, and he stared at her for a moment before taking a firm grip of her arm and prodding her faster than necessary down the hallway. They entered a large room filled with tables draped in fine linen, and Agatha looked around in surprise.

"I was expecting rustic with perhaps a few spurs tossed around for decoration," she said. "This is a dining room one might see in a big city."

"And you're disappointed about that, aren't you?" Mr. Blackheart didn't bother to wait for her to respond and began walking around the room, giving the patrons who were dining there a quick once-over before he rejoined her. "It looks relatively safe, but I'm hesitant to leave you by yourself. It's unfortunate that Mrs. Swanson is feeling poorly and can't join you."

"Really, Mr. Blackheart, you're being overly protective, and while it's true that Mrs. Swanson normally joins me to dine, she is only my companion. She is paid to accompany me, not protect me. I hardly believe if a troubling situation were to occur, she'd be much assistance." She gestured around the room. "As you said, it seems perfectly respectable here, and I'll be fine. It's not as if I'll be dining alone in one of those questionable establishments down in Colorado City."

Mr. Blackheart stiffened right before he narrowed his eyes. "We are *not* going to Colorado City."

Agatha narrowed her eyes right back at him. "I don't see why not. From what I've been told, it's a seedy town, and the brothels alone would make wonderful fodder for an article. Why, I could tie in the information I uncovered regarding the New York brothels and write a story comparing the brothels in the East and those in the West."

"Have you forgotten that the major reason you were forced to leave New York and go on this *delightful* western journey was because someone wants to see you dead, someone who might be connected with the New York brothels?"

"My memory is fine, thank you very much, and I wasn't forced out of New York. If you'll recall, my editor was already making plans for someone to travel out here to gather feature stories. He thought I was exactly the right journalist for the job."

"No, he didn't. He only suggested you take on the assignment after the threats to you began to escalate. If *I* remember correctly, another journalist was supposed to make the trip—a Mr. Pitkin, I think, who was not exactly happy to have been replaced by you."

Giving an airy wave of her hand, Agatha smiled. "Mr. Pitkin was perfectly fine with the decision, especially after he learned how dangerous the environment can be out here. He never struck me as an overly brave sort."

"Then it was probably to his benefit to remain behind, but

that has nothing to do with your getting it into your head to travel to Colorado City. It's much too dangerous. And since I *have* been hired to keep you alive, I'm going to have to put my foot down and tell you here and now that we won't be traveling there . . . ever."

"It's not like I intentionally seek out dangerous situations."

"Miss Watson, intentional or not, you have a concerning ability to land in dangerous predicaments, and those predicaments are indeed the reasoning behind our taking this extended western journey. Not only are the madams of all the brothels furious with you, you've also incurred the wrath of a shirtwaist factory owner, the tenement slum lords, the sewage disposal authorities, the men who've taken issue over your support of laws concerning the power husbands hold over their wives, and . . . Well, I could go on and on. I'd prefer not to ignite those particular bad feelings toward you out here. My job of keeping you alive will become incredibly difficult if the entire country wants to see you dead."

"Don't you think you're exaggerating a touch?"

"No."

Agatha lifted her chin. "It's not as if all of those people are aware I'm the person behind the Alfred Wallenstate articles. Most readers assume my stories are penned by a man."

"Someone evidently figured it out, since threats started showing up at your New York residence." Mr. Blackheart looked over her shoulder. "Ah, here comes the waiter. I suppose this lovely conversation we're having will have to come to an end, and just when I was beginning to enjoy myself immensely."

"May I show you to a table for two?" the waiter asked with a glare at Agatha.

"I think everyone might be blaming me for Matilda's fate,"

she muttered. "Which means it might not be a good idea for me to eat here."

"Nonsense," Mr. Blackheart replied. "No one blames you for Matilda's fate. And just so we're clear, we're not going to rush in and save her."

He looked at the waiter and scowled. "I expect Miss Watson to be served a delicious meal, without a side of guilt, if you please, but since I won't be joining her, she'll only need a table for one. I need to ascertain no other farm animals will be showing up in her room and check on Mrs. Swanson, who seems to be suffering from the altitude, but do know that I will be stopping by every so often to make sure Miss Watson is staying out of trouble."

The waiter turned pale and nodded.

"There's no need to intimidate the poor man, Mr. Blackheart. And if you're so concerned about my getting into trouble, perhaps you should join me."

"While that does sound truly enjoyable, I prefer to dine alone . . . in my room, after I get you settled for the night." He turned around and strode away, leaving her standing beside the waiter, who was looking a little sulky.

"I wouldn't mind a table by the window," she finally said.

A minute later, she wasn't sitting at a table by the window or even at a table in the dining room. Instead, she was squished into a less-than-comfortable seat in a darkened corner of what appeared to be the hotel's pub. She looked around, delighted that the waiter had left her in a much more interesting spot than the dining room—not that he probably intended that result.

When her gaze settled on what appeared to be a mountain man sitting at the bar, her delight increased. Two ladies were sitting on either side of him with another leaning across the bar, all three ladies giving the man their undivided attention as they laughed uproariously over something he'd just said.

Her writer instincts kicked in.

Why would a man who was garbed in ratty old clothing and certainly hadn't seen a barber in the recent past attract the attention of ladies, and what was he doing in a reputable hotel?

A panicked squeal immediately distracted her from the mountain man. Leaning forward, she peered through an open door and watched as little Matilda scurried into view, running as fast as her stumpy legs would allow, with Mr. Farrington's yells sounding in the distance.

The sight of the obviously frantic pig caused Agatha's stomach to clench, and she simply couldn't sit idly by and watch what she knew was about to happen. "Matilda, over here," she called, and the pig barreled rapidly in her direction. Not giving herself a moment to think through what she was about to do, she hitched up her skirt. Matilda needed no other encouragement to scurry underneath it. She'd just managed to drop her skirt into place when Mr. Farrington darted into the room. Picking up a menu from the table, she breathed a sigh of relief when he rushed past her.

The question that remained was how to proceed?

The decision was made for her when Matilda plopped her solid body down on Agatha's shoes and seemed to settle in for the duration. Trying to shift in her seat, but finding that next to impossible with a pig lounging on her feet, Agatha ducked her head under the table. "Would it be possible for you to move just the tiniest bit, because . . ." Her words died in her throat when the sound of a gentleman's voice unexpectedly captured her attention.

"We need another round over here when you get a minute."

Lifting her head, she winced when she hit it against the edge of the table. She knew that voice as well as she knew her own, but . . . it made no sense.

Zayne Beckett would have no reason to be in Colorado Springs. He was supposed to be happily married by now and living with his lovely if overly delicate wife, Helena, in California.

Rubbing the sore spot on her head, she glanced around, breathing a sigh of relief when none of the gentlemen sitting at the other tables turned out to be Zayne. The only gentleman whose face she couldn't see was that of the mountain man, but he certainly wasn't cause for concern. Zayne had always been a meticulous dresser, something that couldn't be said for the man hunched over the bar. That man was dressed in a jacket covered with bits of what looked like dirt and leaves, his boots were caked with mud, and there was a ratty old cane perched by his side, giving testimony to the fact that he probably was not in the best of health. He also possessed a headful of matted and incredibly long dark hair, while Zayne's hair had always been perfectly groomed, except for the occasional times she'd gotten him involved in something . . . messy.

Forcing her attention back to the menu, she perused her options, wondering if she should choose the buffalo soup or . . .

"Ladies, after this drink, I'm calling it a night," the man at the bar proclaimed. His words sounded just the tiniest bit slurred, but . . . he sounded exactly like Zayne.

He dug his hand into his pocket and pulled out a wad of bills, which he promptly thrust at the employee tending the bar. "Here's to settle the bill, and keep the change for your efforts,"

The money certainly explained the ladies surrounding him,

but she was at a loss as to why the man sounded so eerily like Zayne.

Curiosity kept her watching the man. He lifted his arm, tilted his head back, and downed a glass of what appeared to be whiskey in one gulp. Releasing a loud belch, he turned.

All the breath squeezed out of Agatha's lungs as her gaze met his. She wouldn't have recognized him if it weren't for his eyes, but those eyes were something Agatha had never been able to forget. They were a distinctive shade of green, much like the grass in springtime, and they were usually filled with mischief.

But there was no mischief in the eyes currently narrowed on her.

Mr. Zayne Beckett stared at her for what seemed like forever, and then he smiled a lopsided smile. "Aggie."

He'd never once, in all the time she'd known him, called her Aggie.

Before she could summon up a single word of response, he lurched off the stool, his leg seemed to give out, and Zayne Beckett—the one gentleman who plagued her thoughts on an almost daily basis—plummeted to the ground even as his eyes rolled back in his head, and a cloud of dirt puffed up from his clothing.

2

Something strange swept over Zayne's face, and oddly enough, it felt remarkably like a tickle. When he turned his head into the pillow, the tickling went away, but then something rough and wet began assaulting his ear, and alarm coursed through him.

The thought came that the prudent action would be to open his eyes in order to see who or what was assaulting his ear, but he immediately disregarded that idea. If he opened his eyes, he'd wake up for good, and it was always so depressing to face another day, always so very disappointing.

Deciding he was probably imagining—the imagining brought on no doubt by the whiskey he'd taken to enjoying a little too much—he began counting sheep in the hope of going back to sleep. Unfortunately, his counting was interrupted by the distinct sound of snuffling.

Stiffening, he realized he was not imagining anything and sorted through his jumbled thoughts to come up with a plausible explanation as to what could possibly be snuffling in his ear.

Surely one of the women he vaguely remembered talking with at the pub hadn't followed him back to his room, and if one had, was it a normal occurrence for women to grunt in that particular fashion?

Knowing there was no help for it, he forced his eyes open and found himself staring up at two moist holes.

It was a rather peculiar thing to see.

The two holes lifted, and he blinked and then blinked again when a pink tongue began edging ever closer until it made contact with his mouth.

"Ugh," he yelled before he began flailing around on the bed, trying to escape the covers that were holding him hostage.

He rolled over and slipped off the bed, landing with a loud *woof* on the hard floor, his fall knocking the breath from him.

"Ah, lovely. I see you've finally decided to rejoin the living."

He heard the sound of heels tapping across the floor, and then the hem of a lady's dress came into view. Lifting his gaze, recognition mixed with disbelief caused his mouth to drop open.

Miss Agatha Watson was standing above him, there in the midst of his hotel room, smiling down at him, but . . . that couldn't be right. He obviously really was imaging things. Agatha would have no reason to be in Colorado. Everything she held near and dear was back in New York. He forced his mouth shut, shook his head, and then peered through gritty eyes at the woman who, strangely enough, hadn't disappeared.

It really was Agatha, and she looked . . . wonderful. Her inky-black hair was caught up in some kind of twist on her head, but curly strands of it had escaped her pins—something he clearly remembered them doing frequently in the past. Agatha had always been a lady in perpetual motion, that motion causing her hair and clothing to occasionally be in disarray, not that she'd ever been concerned about that. She'd once told him there were too many adventures waiting for her to take time lingering over her appearance, but even in disarray, she'd always looked lovely.

"What are you doing here?" he finally asked, wincing when her smile disappeared to be replaced with a frown.

"That's how you greet me after we haven't seen each other in two years?"

His head began throbbing from the loudness of her voice, but before he could ask her to keep it down, he caught sight of something pink flying through the air. That something landed squarely on his chest and began to squeal, causing the throbbing in his head to intensify. All the breath left him again when the creature began prancing around on top of his body. Nausea, brought on by the prancing, and probably also from the large amount of whiskey he'd indulged in the night before, had a moan slipping out. "I could use a little help here," he managed to mutter, praying he wasn't about to get sick all over the floor.

"Matilda, enough," Agatha said with a snap of her fingers, which had the animal scurrying off him and scampering to her side. She tilted her head. "You're looking a bit green."

Struggling into a sitting position, he pressed a hand against his stomach. "And you find that surprising, given the manner in which I've been woken?" He narrowed his eyes. "Is that a pig?"

The animal disappeared underneath Agatha's skirt.

"Yes, she is, but Matilda doesn't care for that particular word."

"Huh, interesting, but what's it doing in my room?"

"I let her in."

"Because . . . ?"

"It's nearly noon."

Zayne lifted a hand and rubbed at the throbbing in his head that was steadily growing. "May I assume you decided it was past time I woke up?"

"Exactly."

"Why didn't you just wake me up, and how did you get the key to my room, and . . . what are you doing here?"

"I've been up since six and I've tried numerous times to wake you, but you wouldn't budge." Agatha sighed. "I even took to singing, quite loudly at that, and you must recall, even if it has been over *two* years since we've spoken, that I don't exactly sing well, but even my attempts at a song didn't have you stirring."

"So you sent a pig to do the job?"

"Patience has never been one of my virtues, Zayne. I thought it would be interesting to see what would happen if I set Matilda on you."

"She almost gave me a heart attack, and I'm bound to have bruises on my backside from falling to the floor." He struggled to sit up straighter. "It was hardly friendly of you to sic your pig on me."

Giving a dainty shrug, Agatha began strolling around the room, until she stumbled to a stop. Peering down, she lifted her skirt a few inches and grinned. "I beg your pardon, Matilda. I forgot you were under there." She dropped the skirt back into place, covering the pig. "I do hope my little darling doesn't get a stomach upset from gnawing on that mess you've got covering your face. You might be offended by what I'm about to say, but you look like you have a porcupine hanging from your cheeks."

"It's a beard and I've been told it lends me a distinguished appearance."

"Distinguished compared to what?"

Seeing absolutely no point in continuing the conversation, Zayne summoned up what he hoped was a credible scowl. "Getting back to your pig, why did you allow her to gnaw on me? I thought we were friends."

"Friends don't ignore one another for years, Zayne, and I didn't know Matilda was gnawing on you at first, not until she gagged. Do be careful though with calling her a P-I-G. She's remarkably sensitive and intelligent but does seem prone to sulking."

"How in the world did you come into possession of a sulking, er, Matilda?"

"Quite by accident, I assure you. I rescued her yesterday from an unpleasant fate, but she's a charming creature, even if she does have a strong aversion to men."

"And yet you put her in bed with me."

"Hmm, so I did."

His lips tugged into a reluctant smile. Agatha had been one of his closest friends before he'd moved out west, and she'd always been different. She was strong-willed, independent, and perpetually getting herself into trouble, but . . . he'd missed her. He just hadn't realized that until now.

"What are you doing in Colorado?" he finally asked.

Giving an airy wave of her hand, Agatha moved closer to him, her steps hampered by the pig still underneath her skirt. She wobbled to a halt right beside him. "We'll have plenty of time to discuss me and what I've been up to of late, but I think it's more important right now to talk about you. You're a mess."

"I see you haven't abandoned your preference for getting straight to the point."

"Saves time." Agatha hitched up her skirt again. "You're

going to have to come out now, Matilda. I'm feeling the need to have a bit of a chat with Zayne. It's probably going to turn into a lengthy chat, which means I'll need to get comfortable."

Zayne watched as Matilda scooted out from underneath the skirt and hurried to hide behind a chair.

"She obviously knows you're about to interrogate me," he said right as Agatha plopped down beside him and rolled her eyes.

"Interrogating sounds menacing, Zayne. I'm simply going to ask you a few questions."

"That's comforting."

Leaning forward, Agatha patted his leg, his bad leg, causing him to wince. Her patting came to a rapid end.

"Did I hurt you?"

"Of course not."

"I distinctly saw you grimace."

"You claimed I have a porcupine on my face, which I'm fairly certain makes it next to impossible for you to notice me grimacing."

"A valid point, but if I did hurt you, I'm sorry."

Zayne felt his teeth clink together. "I'm fine."

Looking him over with blue eyes that saw entirely too much, Agatha's lips thinned. "Clearly, you're not, which begs the question of what happened to you?"

"Nothing that you need to concern yourself with. It's a long and dreary story, and I don't really care to talk about it, especially not before breakfast."

"We are long past breakfast, but I'll go get you some eggs."

"Now that I think about it, I'm not very hungry."

"Suit yourself, but you must know I'm not going anywhere until you give me some answers."

The two years they'd been apart disappeared in a flash,

and Zayne felt as if he were once again back in New York with Agatha being her usual tenacious, nagging self. The memories came rapidly—one with her being held behind bars, another with her insisting he dress in a gown to travel to an opium den, along with convincing him to shave all the hair from his chest.

His lips began to curve until he also remembered that Agatha truly wasn't one to let her questions go unanswered, but he, unfortunately, was in no state to engage in any type of bantering with her. His thoughts were jumbled from having had too much whiskey the night before, his mouth was parched, and dealing with Agatha could leave even the most clear-thinking gentleman a bit bemused. There was no way in his current state he'd even be able to keep up with her rapid train of thought. He rubbed his temple and peered around the room, stalling for time.

"Can you tell me how I came to be here?"

"Are we talking about how you came to be in Colorado or how you came to be in your room?"

"I know how I got to Colorado, but I have no idea how I got to my room last night."

Agatha's nose wrinkled. "You really don't remember?"

"The last moment I remember was sitting at the bar last night, having a drink."

"I think we can both agree you had more than one drink."

Zayne tilted his head. "Were *you* there?"

"I was, but I wasn't sitting with you. You were surrounded by three ladies who seemed to find you absolutely fascinating, even given the fact you were looking rather, well . . . we'll get into that later. As I was saying, you were conversing rather enthusiastically with these women before you proclaimed in a very loud and, I must add, slurred voice, that you were calling it a night. You got up from your stool, saw me, called me *Aggie*, which I'm going to encourage you never to do again, and then promptly passed out." She shook her head. "It was not one of your finer moments."

"I must have passed out over the shock of seeing you after all this time."

Agatha placed her hand over his. "You know that's not what happened."

The heat from her skin sent real shock traveling up his arm.

He'd always refused to acknowledge the fact Agatha had the ability to do peculiar things to his pulse, his heart, his . . . No, he would not dwell on that.

He'd made a decision to swear off women forever after the disaster with Helena, and he was determined to remain true to that decision. There was absolutely no reason to think of Agatha as anything other than an old friend, even if her touch did—

"Tell me about your leg."

Zayne pulled his hand back. "I told you, I don't care to discuss it."

"Why are you in Colorado?"

"I needed some time alone."

"Because of your leg?"

He sighed. "You're still very annoying."

"Thank you."

He blew out a breath. "Can we just leave it that I'm in Colorado because I really do need to be alone right now?"

"You once told me when we were having one of our philo-sophical talks—although I think this particular talk might have happened in jail—that a person is never truly alone."

The pounding in his head immediately increased. "I re-member that talk, Agatha, but I was wrong. God certainly wasn't with me when I suffered the injury to my leg. That has caused me to decide that He's not the caring God I once thought Him to be. He allowed me to become a cripple, and I must admit that I really have little faith in Him anymore."

Agatha opened her mouth, but he shook his head, causing her to close it. He knew she longed to argue with him, especially since she was a lady who believed deeply in God and all that went with that, but he no longer shared her beliefs, and he wasn't in the right frame of mind to argue anything at the moment.

Forcing a smile, he edged a few inches away from her. "Now then, while I've enjoyed catching up with you, as you mentioned before, it's past noon, and I really must head off to work."

"We haven't caught up on anything yet."

"Of course we have. Would you mind fetching my cane for me? It's over there against the window."

"I'm well aware of where your cane is, since I put it there last night, and . . ." She rose to her feet, but instead of going to fetch his cane, she moved to his bed, lifting the mattress up before she pulled out a ratty-old bag that resembled a stuffed sock. "Good thing I didn't forget about this, or you would have been hard-pressed to find where I hid it." She moved back to stand over him and handed him the sack. "There's a bunch of gold nuggets in there, but I have yet to figure out what that sack was doing attached to your belt."

"All the prospectors out here use these sacks to store some of their finds. It's convenient."

"Or idiotic," Agatha countered. "Aren't you worried about getting robbed?"

"Not really. Most people out here think I'm a little insane, so they keep their distance."

"I saw three ladies with you last night, and none of them were keeping their distance, but . . . Wait a minute. Surely you're not telling me you're a gold prospector now, are you?"

"So what if I am?"

"I'd have to say you truly are insane then. It can't be good for that injured leg of yours to be stuck in a stream all day while you pan for gold."

"I don't pan for gold in a stream, I have my own mine."

"Why would you purchase a mine when your family owns a very lucrative railroad business?"

"I needed a change—and no, I don't want to discuss all the reasons behind that because I need to get to work."

Agatha nodded, just once. "Fine, I'll come with you."

"I don't recall asking you to join me."

"And I don't recall you ever having such a surly attitude before. Why, your mother would be absolutely appalled if she heard you now. And . . . speaking of your mother, if you don't let me come with you today, I'll send her a telegram straight away, telling her of your situation."

She began to inspect her nails. "I wouldn't put it past Gloria to jump on the first available train and come out here to take you in hand."

"You wouldn't."

She stopped inspecting her nails and quirked a brow. "Wouldn't I?"

Zayne's shoulders sagged as he realized this was going to be one of those battles he wasn't going to win. "Fine, you can come with me, but it's filthy out at the mine and you'll ruin that pretty dress you're wearing."

"I'll change," she said before she walked over to his cane and brought it back to him. "Would you like assistance getting to your feet?"

It would have been helpful to have a hand up, but the last vestiges of his pride roared to life, and he found himself shaking his head even as he disregarded the hand Agatha was holding out to him. He tightened his grip around the cane and struggled to his feet, refusing to groan when his leg protested the movement. He wobbled for a moment, and when he was finally certain he wasn't going to plunge to the floor, he looked at Agatha, who was watching him closely. "The mornings are always the worst, because my leg stiffens up during the night."

"And yet instead of pampering that leg, you take it off to a mine."

"I've made some adjustments out there that make it easier for me to get around."

"I'll be the judge of that." She snapped her fingers, and Matilda hurried to her side. "How long before we leave?"

"It won't take me long to call for my wagon."

"You're not going to bathe?"

"We're going to a mine, Agatha, not a tea party." Zayne hobbled over to where his boots were lying on the floor. "And I'll leave without you if you're not outside when the wagon shows up."

"Then I'll just have Mr. Blackheart dig up directions to your mine and escort me there. In fact, maybe that's what I should do anyway. He's certain to be a more pleasant riding companion than you."

Zayne paused mid-hobble. "Are you talking about Mr. Blackheart, as in Theodore Wilder's right-hand man?"

"One and the same. He's the one who carried you up here last night after it became clear you weren't going to come to your senses and stagger to your room on your own."

His stomach began to feel queasy. "I never knew you found Mr. Blackheart interesting."

31

"What?"

"Granted, he's a somewhat handsome gentleman—if a lady goes for that strong, brooding, silent type—but I would have never thought the two of you would form an alliance."

"I have no idea what you're suggesting."

"I suppose I'll have to get used to calling you Mrs. Blackheart instead of Agatha. Gentlemen don't take kindly to other gentlemen calling their wives by their given names."

Agatha scrunched up her nose. "You should've told me you suffered an injury to your head as well as to your leg."

"You're *not* married to Mr. Blackheart?"

"Don't be ridiculous. Mr. Blackheart is the last gentleman I'd marry—well, except for you, of course. He's been hired to guard me as I collect information for articles for the *New-York Tribune*."

For some reason, a slice of what felt like relief stole over him, but he shoved that relief aside as something concerning struck him. "Don't you think it's slightly improper to be traveling around the country with a gentleman you're not married to?"

"It's 1883, Zayne, not the Dark Ages, but if it'll make you feel better, I'm also traveling with a paid companion, Mrs. Drusilla Swanson." She headed for the door. "Now then, since you seem eager to get out to your mine, I'm off to change. And know that I won't be too long. I certainly don't want to give you a reason to leave without me." With that, she disappeared out of his room, her little pig prancing right behind her.

⁘ ⁘

One hour later, Zayne sat on the seat of his wagon, not exactly certain why he hadn't taken off for the mine yet, or why he'd changed his clothes and washed his face.

"What I'd like to know is what you were thinking, agreeing to allow Miss Watson to travel with you to some mine of questionable safety you've gotten yourself involved with."

Blinking the sun out of his eyes, he turned and found himself pinned under the rather daunting glare of Mr. Blackheart. It was immediately evident that during the two years since he'd last seen the man, Mr. Blackheart had not mellowed with age. "I didn't *agree* to Agatha's accompanying me. She just invited herself and refused to listen when I objected."

"She told me you neglected to answer her questions, and surely you must remember that when Miss Watson has questions, nothing can stand in the way of her getting answers." Mr. Blackheart stepped closer to the wagon, his gaze turning downright menacing. "I'm telling you now, Mr. Beckett, if anything of an unpleasant nature occurs while we're visiting this mine, I'm holding you responsible."

"It would be refreshing if I ever found you not intimidating people, Mr. Blackheart," Agatha said, drawing Zayne's attention as she approached them. "And, since *you're* not coming with us today, if there is any 'unpleasant' business to be found, you won't have to see it." She stopped and took a moment to readjust the huge hat on her head, pulling down a layer of what appeared to be veiling over her face.

"You'd better hope we don't encounter a stiff breeze," Zayne said. "I'm fairly sure you'll blow away, given the size of that hat."

"Highly doubtful," Agatha argued. "Besides, the sun is much too hot out here. I need to protect my skin."

"Why the veil though?"

"I thought it lent a rather dramatic touch, and it'll keep the bugs away." She stepped closer. "So, shall we get on our way?"

Zayne ignored the question. "What are you wearing?"

"May I remind you that you're concerned about the time, but if you really want to discuss fashion, fine." She gestured to her clothing. "Today I'm wearing a practical pair of trousers paired with a lovely billowing shirt. To add an extra dash of flair, I've thrown chaps over my trousers and included a vest so that I'll fit in with my western surroundings. And before you begin arguing with me, I've seen numerous women wearing trousers out here, so my attire is completely appropriate."

Zayne swallowed the protest he'd been about to make, knowing Agatha spoke nothing less than the truth. While women were in short supply throughout the West, the few who roamed around did dress in trousers more often than not, especially those who worked beside their husbands panning for gold. And it wasn't as if he'd never seen Agatha in trousers, but he'd forgotten how incredibly attractive she was, and chances were he'd get little work done today since she was certainly going to be a distraction.

Even though he'd sworn off women for good, he was still a man, after all, and men did tend to notice beautiful women. "It'll be hot in the mine, so maybe you'd be more comfortable in a dress," he settled on saying.

"And isn't it just so unfortunate that I won't have time to change since the day is quickly getting away from us?" Agatha hopped up on the seat next to him and glanced around. "Where's Matilda? I thought she was right behind me."

"Don't think for a minute we're going to take your pig."

"She gets lonely when I'm not around," Agatha replied before she smiled. "Ah, here she comes now."

Zayne swiveled around and found a lady marching toward them, holding a picnic basket in one hand and a leash with Matilda attached to it in the other. Just like Agatha, she was dressed in trousers and a plain shirt, but her trousers appeared to be freshly ironed, whereas Agatha's were a little wrinkled. The woman was wearing a small hat that afforded her a bit of shade, but her hat wasn't outlandish in the least. A trace of amusement flowed over him when he noticed that every brown hair under that hat seemed to be perfectly in place, and she was holding herself as if she'd grown up with a book attached to her head.

"Mrs. Swanson," Agatha exclaimed, "it's wonderful to see you up and about and obviously feeling better, but there's really no need for you to join me today."

Mrs. Swanson deposited the basket in the back of the wagon, handed the leash to Mr. Blackheart, who looked taken aback, and then lifted her chin. "Of course I'm going to join you today, Miss Watson. That's what we paid companions do, not rest in our rooms while our employers go off into the mountains unescorted." She turned to Zayne. "If you don't remember me, Mr. Beckett, I'm Mrs. Swanson, Drusilla Swanson, and I'm great friends with your sister, Arabella Wilder."

Zayne peered at the lady, thought she looked somewhat familiar, but before he could even acknowledge her, Mr. Blackheart stepped forward.

"I was telling Mr. Beckett that I think taking Agatha with him to this mine is a bad idea."

Mrs. Swanson pursed her lips. "I couldn't agree with you more, Mr. Blackheart, but at least Miss Watson will have the two of us to watch out for her, and the poor dear has been fretting lately over a new story idea. Perhaps this will give her some inspiration."

"That's what I'm afraid of," Mr. Blackheart mumbled before he turned his attention back to Zayne. "What were you planning on doing at this mine today?"

"I set some dynamite up yesterday, and I'm intending to

blow out a new portion of a tunnel today." As soon as the words left his mouth, Zayne knew he'd made a huge mistake. Agatha was suddenly bristling with excitement, while Mr. Blackheart and Mrs. Swanson had both turned a little pale.

"You need to get out of the wagon," Mr. Blackheart demanded, shoving the leash back at Mrs. Swanson before he began moving in Agatha's direction.

Agatha, being Agatha, shook her head and gripped the seat with both hands. "Not on your life, Mr. Blackheart. I've never been around dynamite before and I've always been curious as to how it would feel to blow something up."

"Don't make me cause a scene," Mr. Blackheart growled, his lips barely moving.

Agatha's eyes turned stormy. "I don't appreciate the assumption that I'm going to blow *myself* up."

"It's not an assumption, Miss Watson—it's what will most likely happen."

An uncomfortable silence settled over them, broken only by the snorts of Matilda as she rooted around in the dirt, until Agatha finally released a huff. "Fine, I promise I'll try not to touch any dynamite."

Mr. Blackheart quirked a brow. "Try?"

"It's all I'm willing to offer."

"You might as well give in gracefully," Mrs. Swanson said as she handed the leash back to Mr. Blackheart. "You know she'll just figure out a way to get out to the mine on her own if we stand in her way."

"We could lock her in her room," Mr. Blackheart suggested.

Mrs. Swanson's lips pursed again. "I believe you tried that before, and with unfortunate results, so just be a dear and get Matilda into the wagon, won't you?"

Mr. Blackheart sent Zayne another scowl, as if the situation were his fault, before he bent over, scooped Matilda up, plopped the pig in the back of the wagon, and began to walk toward another wagon parked a few feet away. "Just remember that I warned you about the danger of this," he tossed over his shoulder as he waited for Mrs. Swanson to join him, helped her up on the wagon seat, and then climbed up beside her.

"He's so dramatic," Agatha exclaimed with a cheery wave to Mr. Blackheart before she turned her attention to Zayne. "So, tell me, exactly how *does* one get dynamite to explode?"

Deciding it would be in his best interest to ignore that ominous question, Zayne flicked the reins over the mules. The wagon lurched into motion, and as they picked up speed, he felt an unusual desire to say a prayer, one that would request assistance from God in helping him retain the use of his remaining good limbs. Remembering the troubling fact that he was at distinct odds with God at the moment, he pushed the desire aside and settled for keeping his attention fixed on the road. He could only hope Agatha would get the hint and realize he wasn't in the mood for answering questions, especially those concerning dynamite.

3

Peering through the veil that distorted her view, Agatha considered Zayne as they plodded along, her concern for his well-being growing the longer he remained unusually silent.

The Zayne of her past would have been trying his very best to distract her from the dynamite situation, not calmly driving along as if . . .

"You haven't asked about Helena."

Horror immediately replaced the concern.

How could she have been so remiss?

Helena was the answer to everything.

She swallowed past the lump that had formed in her throat. "I never even considered Helena in all this, Zayne, but do know that you have my deepest sympathies."

"Why do I need your sympathy?"

Agatha shoved the veil aside. "Because losing your true love had to have been remarkably difficult on you."

"Helena was never my true love."

"That's hardly an appropriate way to speak of the deceased."

Zayne pulled on the reins, bringing the mules to a stop before he turned in the seat. "What are you talking about?"

"What are *you* talking about?"

"Helena isn't dead."

"What do you mean, she isn't dead?"

"I think that's fairly self-explanatory. One is either dead or one is not, and believe me when I say Helena is not amongst the deceased."

"She didn't die in the accident that damaged your leg?"

Zayne's jaw clenched. "My accident was caused when Helena insisted on taking her horse up a steep hill that was beyond her abilities. When I realized she was in danger, I tried to pull her off her struggling mount. Helena, for some unknown reason, balked at my assistance. She kicked out at me, missed, and kicked my horse. The horse took issue with that and reared. I was thrown to the ground, the horse fell on top of me, and my leg was crushed in the process."

"You're lucky you weren't killed."

"Was I?" he countered. "My leg suffered an extensive break. Since Helena and I, along with her parents, were on holiday well away from progressive cities, I was left at the mercy of an incapable hack who managed to reset the bone, but not cleanly. Now I'm forced to hobble around on a leg that's barely usable."

"Have you consulted a different doctor, one who might be more proficient in the art of setting bones?"

"Of course I have, but the only option available to me is to have the surgeon rebreak the leg in order to reset it. There's no guarantee that will work, and I'm not exactly keen to go through that type of trauma again."

"But if it would allow you to walk better and, perhaps, ease the pain, don't you think you should consider it?"

"No." He held up his hand when Agatha opened her mouth, effectively cutting off the argument she'd been about to make. "Why did you believe Helena was dead?"

Agatha blew out a breath. "That was the only conclusion I could come up with to explain your appearance and your somewhat disagreeable attitude. I assumed you'd suffered a tremendous shock. Death is one of the greatest shocks of all, hence the reasoning behind believing Helena to be dead." She tapped her finger against her chin. "Although, now that I think about it, Helena's demise probably wouldn't be a huge shock to anyone since she always possessed such a delicate nature."

"Helena's delicate nature seems to have been a figment of her imagination."

"I beg your pardon?"

Zayne's eyes turned a little stormy. "When I arrived out west two years ago, I was delighted to discover Helena had put her fragile ways behind her. I foolishly believed we'd finally be able to embrace an active future together, but then I began to realize Helena was different. She was no longer the girl I'd known since childhood."

"And that's why you broke off your engagement—because she was different, or . . . because you were furious with her for causing your injury?"

"We never got around to getting officially engaged, and I didn't break off our association—she did."

"I'm afraid I don't understand."

"Quite honestly, neither did I at first, but I'm growing weary of this topic and no longer care to discuss Helena."

Agatha's teeth clinked together. "You're the one who brought her into the conversation, so we're going to continue discussing her until I'm satisfied I understand exactly what caused me to find you in such a sorry state."

"You're beginning to irritate me."

She arched a brow.

Zayne glared at her for a moment before he shrugged. "Fine, if you must know, Helena wasn't happy to see me when I arrived out west."

"Wasn't it always the plan for you to join her?"

"*I* thought it was, but apparently I was wrong, because she appeared downright surprised when she came to the door and found me standing on the other side."

"Didn't you let her know you were coming?"

"I sent her a telegram, but . . . if you'll recall, I'd sent her numerous telegrams stating I was leaving New York, but events kept happening that delayed my departure. It might have been that she didn't believe me anymore. Truth be told, the only people who greeted me with any enthusiasm at all in California were Helena's parents."

"I'm sure Mr. and Mrs. Collins were delighted to see you. Every parent with unmarried daughters dreams of adding a son from the illustrious Beckett family to their household. Even my parents pushed me quite diligently in the path of your brother before he made the acquaintance of Eliza."

"You and Hamilton would never have made a match of it, even if Eliza hadn't entered the scene."

"True, but my mother didn't see it that way." She smiled. "But enough about me and your brother and the courtship that never was. We need to return to the Helena situation."

"There really isn't much more to say about the lady."

"I beg to differ. What happened after Helena got over her surprise at finding you in California? Did you ever discuss a wedding?"

"She was rather evasive about the matter."

"Didn't that concern you?"

"I didn't give it much thought."

"Were you still considering marrying her at that point?"

"Of course I was. I'd told her back when we were six years old we'd marry someday."

"I don't think any gentleman can be held to a promise he made when he was all of six years old."

"True, but Helena brought up my old promise when we were seventeen." Zayne looked down and began fiddling with the reins. "She asked me if I still intended to honor what I'd promised her in our youth. Since she broached the matter right after her doctor told her she'd have to abandon her desire to have a debut, I didn't have the heart to disappoint her. I was her only hope of obtaining a secure future, and I couldn't deny her that. We were friends, you see, or at least I thought we were."

Agatha's heart gave a tiny lurch. Here was the reason why she'd never been exactly successful pushing Zayne out of her mind. Though seemingly oblivious to the nature of some women, he was inherently honorable and chivalrous. He'd been willing to set aside his own desires, not that he'd ever spoken of those to her, in order to ease the distress of a friend, even if that friend didn't deserve him or—

"Maybe things *would* have turned out differently if I'd gotten around to formally proposing to Helena once I landed in California."

Agatha felt the oddest urge to laugh. "You truly never proposed to her?"

"Well, yes, when I was six, but again, it wasn't exactly what anyone could call a formal proposal." He frowned. "I don't think I even proposed when we were seventeen. I was at that awkward stage, and wasn't really sure what to do around girls."

"From the sound of it, I'm not certain you've grown out of that awkward stage," she muttered.

"Nonsense, I'm a connoisseur when it comes to the ladies."

"Hmm . . . if you say so, but getting back to the whole proposal situation. Do you really believe Helena left you because you didn't get down on bended knee?"

"It's hard to say at this point, although I'm fairly certain her decision to leave me had something to do with that other man."

"Other man?"

"Indeed."

"You might have mentioned that a little sooner, Zayne. It puts a whole different perspective on your situation."

"Really?"

Resisting the urge to roll her eyes, Agatha nodded instead. "You're not very good at explaining this mess, so I'm afraid you need to back up a bit and give me better details. When did this other man come along, and how did Helena get involved with him in the first place?"

"Do we really have to continue with this discussion? It's not a particularly happy period in my life."

"We can always discuss dynamite instead. As I mentioned before, I'm very interested in learning how to ignite it."

"I started to get a few suspicions when Helena and I left to go on holiday," Zayne began quickly. "She wasn't exactly excited about leaving town with me and was somewhat sulky up until my accident. After I began to slowly recover, I couldn't dismiss the idea any longer that something was definitely amiss between us."

"Don't tell me she brought up this other gentleman while you were recovering?"

"Not right away, but she was crying more than usual, and

I assumed that stemmed from the fact she felt obligated to stay by my side as I healed. Helena's never been one to put the needs of others before hers." He reached out and began rubbing his bad leg.

"Once my cast was removed and it became clear I wasn't going to regain the full use of my leg, events quickly turned dismal. Helena's weeping intensified, and then, one day, out of the blue, she blurted out the little tidbit that she'd made a horrible mistake. She didn't love me, and could not stay and nurse me another second because the stress of it was causing her to lose her hair. Then there was the pesky matter of her true love. She told me she couldn't bear to be parted from her secret beau another second."

"And?"

"And nothing. She raced off to join her love, and I never saw her again. Her parents did, however, visit me to profess their extreme disappointment with their daughter. They tried to convince me she'd change her mind, but by that point I'd had enough of Helena to last me a lifetime. I packed my bags and left California."

A sharp whistle suddenly sounded from behind them. Turning, Agatha settled her attention on Mr. Blackheart and Mrs. Swanson. They'd stopped a few yards away from Zayne's wagon, and both of them were looking decidedly put out.

"I do beg your pardon for interrupting," Mr. Blackheart drawled as he, strangely enough, reached over and slapped Mrs. Swanson's arm before he looked back at Agatha. "But Mrs. Swanson and I are getting eaten alive out here. Do you think it might be possible for us to move along?"

Agatha winced. "Forgive me. Zayne and I were just catching up, and I'm afraid I forgot you were following us."

"That certainly makes me feel all fuzzy inside, but I'm

going to suggest you catch up while you're moving. It's hot out here, and I think my nose is beginning to blister."

"You could always borrow Agatha's hat," Zayne called, but he turned back and flicked the reins over the mules when Mr. Blackheart sent him a glare. "Charming man, your Mr. Blackheart."

"He's not *my* Mr. Blackheart, and *charming* is certainly not an adjective I've ever used when describing him," Agatha retorted. "Besides, I didn't have a choice about bringing him out west with me."

"Ah, wonderful. We can finally turn the conversation to you," Zayne said. "I've been waiting with bated breath to discover exactly why Mr. Blackheart has been hired to guard you. You haven't done anything crazy lately, have you?"

"Define *crazy*."

A rusty laugh escaped Zayne's mouth. "Strange as this may sound, I'm delighted to learn you haven't changed a bit since we last saw each other." He returned his attention to the road, a small grin teasing his lips.

The sight of that grin sent another ache through Agatha's heart. The Zayne she'd adored, even though she'd resigned herself to the idea they were only meant to be friends, was still there, albeit buried beneath layers of pain and disappointment.

From out of nowhere, as she sat in the midst of the evergreen trees, she suddenly knew what she was meant to do—knew it as if God had leaned over and whispered explicit instructions in her ear.

She'd been sent west to save Zayne, to bring him back to the man he'd been before he'd left New York to join Helena.

Zayne was a social gentleman. He thrived when he was in the midst of *good* company, and it was going to be her

45

new mission in life to help him reclaim his affable self. Her compulsion to explore Colorado had obviously been God's way of sending Zayne the assistance he so desperately needed.

However, she had the sneaky suspicion Zayne wouldn't appreciate her racing to his rescue. That would injure his pride and offend his chivalrous nature, but . . . perhaps she could use that nature to her advantage.

He'd never once disappointed her when she'd requested his participation in some of her madcap plans. She'd always known his agreement had stemmed from a desire to keep her safe, which meant all she had to do was stir up that old desire.

Garnering his cooperation would be difficult though. He'd always been stubborn, and if he realized what she was trying to do, he'd probably turn difficult. Turning her head away from him, she practiced a few flutters of her lashes before she turned back to him, placed her hand on his arm, released what she thought was a credible sigh of distress, and—with eyes she'd forced as wide as they would go—batted her lashes at him.

"I'm hesitant to tell you this, given your troubles at the moment, but . . . someone back in New York wants me dead."

She felt his arm stiffen under her hand. "Dead?"

Sending him another flutter of lashes, she added a small sniff for good measure. "Indeed. I'm beyond distressed about it."

He held her gaze for what seemed like forever, and then, to her complete disgust, he began to laugh . . . uproariously.

Her eyes went from wide to mere slits in a flash. "Did you not comprehend what I just divulged?"

Swiping a hand over eyes that were watering, Zayne let out a snort. "It's a good thing you're a talented writer, Agatha, because you'd never find success on the stage."

"I'm sure I have no idea what you're suggesting."

He grinned. "I know you, my dear, know exactly how you like to manage people. You've decided I need saving, but you might as well put that idea right out of your diabolical mind."

Annoyance chugged through her veins, and not all of it directed at Zayne. She *had* forgotten how well he knew her, which meant this whole "saving him" idea had just gotten remarkably tricky.

"What gave me away?"

"The innocent look and, well, the wide eyes." He laughed again. "Oh, and the ridiculous distressed business. I don't think you've ever been distressed a day in your life. You also could have come up with something better than the whole someone-wants-me-dead nonsense."

"I knew as soon as that distressed part came out of my mouth I'd made a mistake," she muttered before she brightened. "But someone really does want me dead. I wasn't making that up."

Zayne's lips immediately thinned into a straight line. "Who?"

"If I knew that, I wouldn't have been forced out of the city."

"You really were forced out of the city?"

"*Forced* might be a bit of an exaggeration, since my editor was looking for someone to write articles about the West right about the time the threats began to escalate. Theodore brought Mr. Blackheart on board to travel with me and keep me safe while he's been continuing to investigate the threats back in New York. I've been traveling longer than anticipated because there's been little progress made in tracking down the culprit who wants to see me harmed."

"And the reason it's been so difficult would be . . . ?"

"I've annoyed quite a few people," Agatha admitted. "It's

amazing how testy people get when I write articles that don't show them in a favorable light."

"Maybe it's time you stopped writing."

Her mouth opened, but no words came out for a few seconds. "Writing is my life."

"It sounds to me like it might become your death."

"Which is exactly why you should offer to assist Mr. Blackheart with keeping me alive, especially since my journey out here has become somewhat tedious and I long to return to New York."

"I'm not going back to New York."

"Why not?"

Ignoring her question, Zayne turned the wagon off the dirt road and onto a path so rutted it made speech next to impossible.

"Our discussion is not over," she yelled through teeth that were clinking together with every rut, trying to be heard over Matilda's sudden squeals of terror. She tightened her grip on the seat, and just when she felt she couldn't hang on for another second, Zayne pulled on the reins and the mules stopped. She heard Mr. Blackheart's wagon rumbling up behind them and turned to watch as her bodyguard and companion pulled up beside them. Mrs. Swanson was sitting stiff as a poker on the wagon seat, not a single hair out of place and looking completely composed.

"That was enjoyable," Mrs. Swanson exclaimed, stepping lightly to the ground before she strolled over mounds of dirt, stopping beside Agatha. "You're looking a little peaked, dear, and . . . annoyed."

Taking Mrs. Swanson's offered hand, Agatha stepped from the wagon on shaky legs. "I'm looking peaked because I thought I was about to come to a rapid end due to Zayne's abysmal driving skills. And I'm annoyed because he had the audacity to suggest I give up my writing *and* he refuses to consider helping Mr. Blackheart protect me."

"You're being overly dramatic," Zayne said as he accepted Mr. Blackheart's assistance from the wagon, although he seemed to do so rather reluctantly. He wobbled for a moment as he grabbed a cane from under his seat and steadied himself. "It was due to my *exceptional* driving skills that we were able to make it up here alive."

Mr. Blackheart's brow furrowed. "Forgive me, but I think you're both being overly dramatic. We have mules pulling the wagons, not stallions, so in actuality, our lives were never in danger given the plodding nature of the beasts."

"It didn't feel like plodding to me," Agatha retorted before Matilda's whimpers caught her attention. "And it evidently didn't feel like plodding to poor Matilda." Hurrying to the back of the wagon, she snagged the pig's leash and gave it a tug, but Matilda wouldn't budge. "Come on, darling, it's time to get you out of there."

Matilda let out another whimper and staunchly refused to move.

"How about if I promise that we won't ride back with nasty old Zayne, but with Mr. Blackheart? He won't try to kill us."

"I wouldn't be so certain about that," Mr. Blackheart muttered, brushing Agatha aside as he climbed into the wagon, plucked Matilda up in his arms as if she weighed nothing at all, jumped out, and placed the pig in a pile of dirt.

Matilda squealed, scurried out of the dirt as fast as her stumpy legs would carry her, and didn't stop until she found a miniscule patch of grass. She plopped down, wiggled for a moment, and closed her eyes.

"Hmm . . . imagine that, she doesn't care for dirt, which

certainly explains why she doesn't like farms," Agatha began. "But I—"

"Matilda's preferences aside," Mr. Blackheart interrupted, "I'm afraid I'm going to have to insist we take our immediate leave. This place, while certainly *charming* with all its loose rocks and wild animals probably lurking just out of sight, is a certain recipe for disaster, especially for someone like you, Miss Watson."

Not giving her an opportunity to refute that incredibly insulting statement, he gestured up the mountain to where jutting timbers marked the entrance of the mine. "I hope you won't take offense at this, Mr. Beckett, but you are, without a shadow of a doubt, an idiot."

To Agatha's surprise, one corner of Zayne's mouth tugged up. "Since you've suddenly taken to insulting me, Mr. Blackheart, don't you think you should call me Zayne?"

Mr. Blackheart nodded. "Fine. Zayne, then, but you're still an idiot."

"And?" Zayne prompted.

"And what? I believe calling you an idiot sums everything up nicely."

"What's your name?"

"You may call me Mr. Blackheart."

"You're not going to give me your first name?"

"Boys, enough," Mrs. Swanson said, stepping in between them. "This is hardly the time to engage in such nonsense when there are more important matters to discuss. But, in the interest of retaining a small semblance of peace, we'll continue to call Mr. Blackheart by his preferred *Mr. Blackheart* since he seems to have an aversion to his given name. I am, however, perfectly comfortable with everyone calling me Drusilla."

She sent Zayne a smile. "Now then, since that's settled, on to those important matters. . . . What in the world possessed you to become involved with this venture given the harsh environment that currently surrounds us? Making your way out here every day can't be good for that leg of yours."

"Forgive me, but I don't really see where it's any concern of yours what ventures I become involved with," Zayne returned.

Drusilla drew herself up. "I'm making it my concern because, again, I'm good friends with your sister, Arabella. You and I know she'll be peppering me with questions once she discovers I've seen you, and I'm the type of lady who likes to be informed before I answer anything."

Zayne's mouth suddenly went a little slack. "Good heavens, Drusilla, I must beg your pardon. You and I *have* been introduced before, and it was extremely ill-mannered of me not to immediately remember you. But what are you doing out here with Agatha? Shouldn't you be with your husband, Edward?"

What seemed to be anguish flickered through Drusilla's eyes, but then she blinked and the anguish was gone. "Edward passed away almost two years ago. Arabella thought I needed a change of scenery, and when Miss Watson began to make plans to travel west, I decided to apply for the position of her chaperone—or paid companion, if you will, since she's too old for a chaperone."

"That was brave of you."

Before Agatha could smack Zayne over the head, Drusilla laughed. "Agatha has certainly kept me busy and taken my mind off my loss, so for that, I'll be forever grateful to her."

Zayne smiled but then sobered. "I'm sorry about Edward. He was a fine man."

"Yes, he was," Drusilla agreed. "But, he had a dangerous

. . . er . . . Well, no need to delve into that at the moment. You have a mining venture to explain."

Leaning heavily on his cane, Zayne released a sigh. "Since it's becoming clear I won't get any work done until I give at least a brief explanation, we might as well make ourselves comfortable."

He hobbled over to a pile of large boulders, took a seat on one, and waited for everyone to join him. Setting his cane aside, he began his story.

"I ended up in Colorado about seven months ago. Stopped here to see if one of the natural hot springs I'd heard about would help my leg. It was of no help, so I made plans to leave, but an unexpected blizzard delayed my departure, and it was during this blizzard I met a man by the name of Willie Higgins.

"He'd come out west to seek his fortune in order to support his family back in New York. We got to talking, and I discovered Willie had found next to nothing in his mine and was desperate to go home. He was a proud man and refused to accept charity from me, so in exchange for a ticket back east, he signed over this mountain."

Agatha frowned. "You got an entire mountain for the price of a railroad ticket?"

"As I said," Zayne said, "Willie was very clear regarding the fact he'd been completely unsuccessful finding anything of value in the mine he'd purchased."

Agatha lifted her chin. "It's still a lot of land, and since Colorado Springs is growing at a rapid rate, I'd say poor Willie got swindled."

"If I told you I gave him a hundred dollars for good measure and signed the deed without ever seeing the land I was purchasing because, again, we were in the midst of a blizzard, would you feel better?"

"No, because I saw that sack of yours filled with gold nuggets. And it didn't escape my notice that you said what was in that sack was only *some* of what you'd discovered."

"I'm not going to apologize for uncovering gold Willie didn't find, or for the fact that I've come to believe my mine is going to earn me a rather nice fortune sometime in the near future."

"But that's not fair to poor Willie," Agatha argued.

"Life isn't always fair."

"You don't mean that."

Zayne's eyes began to glint. "Don't I? Was it fair to me that I ended up a cripple just because I tried to save Helena?"

"Well, no, but that was an accident."

"It was an accident that I just happened to find gold, which is rightfully mine, and—"

"It might be rightfully yours," Agatha interrupted, "but it's hardly honorable for you to not at least consider Willie still has a legitimate stake in this mine."

"Willie isn't here, Agatha, nor do I know where to look for him."

"You said he wanted to go back to New York, so it wouldn't be that difficult to find him if you put the effort into a search."

"It would be difficult for me to search for him since I have no desire to return to New York."

"What I haven't been able to figure out yet is how you're able to search for gold," Mr. Blackheart said before Agatha could argue her point further. "Have you hired a crew to help you blast and secure beams?"

"Willie did a lot of blasting before he gave me the mine, and he created a remarkably stable tunnel system. I've only recently started using dynamite to uncover more of the gold veins I found." Zayne struggled to his feet. "Speaking of gold,

I would like to get to work. Fall is a tricky time out here, and from what I've been told, snow should have already arrived, since it's late September. Once the snow hits, my mining efforts will be severely limited."

"Which is an excellent reason to consider traveling back to New York." Agatha rose from the boulder and brushed dirt from her trousers. "You could stay in the city for the fall and winter, and then return here in the spring."

"I'm certainly not going to New York in the midst of the social season."

"You love the social season, what with all the parties and balls, and . . . danci . . ." Her voice trailed off when she noticed that Zayne's face had darkened. She forced a smile and tried again. "Besides, since I'll probably end up in the city sooner than later, I'm sure Mr. Blackheart would be only too happy to accept any assistance you might be willing to give him by escorting me to a few of those society events. It would be fun, just like old times."

"Mr. Blackheart would have no reason to appreciate any assistance from me, given that I'm less than a man these days and would only complicate his mission of keeping you alive."

"I think that's the most ridiculous thing you've—"

"And as for dancing, I think my leg speaks for itself." With that, Zayne turned his back on her and began picking his way across the dirt, coming to a stop beside a large basket attached to cables.

Not willing to be dismissed so easily, Agatha charged after him. "You're not being reasonable, Zayne, and I . . ." She stumbled over a pile of dirt, but caught herself before she plunged to the ground by grabbing hold of the basket. Straightening, she looked it over. "This is an interesting contraption."

"Humph."

She ignored his less-than-charming remark. "Do you use this to get up to the mine, and if so, how does the contraption work, and how did you even come up with the idea for the basket gadget thing in the first place?"

Zayne began rubbing his head. "No offense, Agatha, but all of your questions are causing my head to throb harder than ever. What I really need right now is some peace and quiet, which means you need to stop talking, and I'd also enjoy some time completely alone."

She waved that piece of nonsense away with a flick of her wrist. "You loathe being alone, and I'm getting tired of your surly attitude." She nodded to the basket. "What exactly is that?"

"If I explain what this is, will you leave me in peace?"

"Probably not, and besides, I'm in need of a good story. I'll bet my readers would love hearing how you've overcome you're, er . . ." The rest of her words stuck in her throat when Zayne's eyes turned glacial.

"You will not write a story with me as the featured invalid."

"I wasn't going to portray you as an—"

"I have to get to work."

"But you haven't explained what that is yet," she said, pointing to the contraption in front of her.

"It's a basket attached to a pulley."

"Well, clearly, but . . . how did you come up with the idea and why?"

"I would think that's obvious. Necessity is a great motivator for coming up with ideas. I tried to climb up to the mine once but it didn't work out very well for me, hence the pulley system."

"It's ingenious."

"No, it isn't, and I don't want to talk about it anymore. You may sit down here and write to your heart's content about pulleys, but don't bother me."

"I'd be able to write a more fascinating account of your pulley system if you'd let me ride up the mountain with you. That way I'd be able to describe how it feels to hang over jutting rocks with only a cable saving me from certain death."

"Maybe acting wouldn't be such a stretch for you after all, but tell me, do you really expect me, an invalid, to be able to pull not only myself but you as well up the mountain?"

"I don't really like it when you use that particular tone of voice with me."

"Then stop annoying me and I'll stop using this tone." With that, Zayne yanked on the door leading into the basket, stepped in, pulled the door shut, and began cranking a wheel, which caused the basket to slowly ascend up the steep slope.

4

Infuriating man," Agatha grumbled as she watched Zayne make his way up the mountain without her.

"He may be infuriating," Drusilla said, coming to stand beside Agatha, "but I must say, even though he claims he's an invalid, he looks to be in rather fine form to me."

Squinting against the glare of the sun, Agatha found she couldn't disagree. Muscles strained against his shirt with every crank, causing her traitorous heart to beat a touch faster than was strictly necessary. It was unacceptable, this irritating reaction she had to the man, especially since he was being less than cooperative at the moment.

Didn't he remember that she hated being thwarted and that, when she was, she almost always resorted to something of a drastic nature?

Did he really want to put himself smack in the midst of—

"I find it somewhat distasteful, observing the two of you ogling the poor man."

Dragging her gaze away from Zayne and all his muscles, she felt her face heat when she turned and found Mr. Blackheart scowling back at her. Why he was scowling was beyond her. After all, she hadn't been ogling *him*.

"There's no harm in ogling," Drusilla proclaimed, sparing Agatha a response. "Why, a lady would have to be dead not to notice such an impressive display of muscles."

Mr. Blackheart turned his scowl on Drusilla. "Yes, well, Zayne's muscles aside, we have more pressing matters to deal with at the moment."

"Oh?" Drusilla asked.

"Indeed, which is why I'm going to follow Zayne and have a bit of a gentlemanly chat with him. The two of you will stay down here."

"Why do we have to stay down here?" Agatha demanded. "And why do you have to have a 'gentlemanly chat' with him? What's wrong with having a normal chat, one where ladies are included?"

"Must you always be so difficult?"

"It's part of my charm."

A vein began to throb on Mr. Blackheart's forehead. "This is exactly why Zayne and I need to speak privately. Gentlemen occasionally need to distance themselves from ladies—especially when said ladies unintentionally hurt our pride."

"Surely you're not implying that I injured Zayne's pride, are you?"

"I'm not implying anything. I'm telling you that you did." He held up a hand when Agatha began to sputter. "You didn't mean to, of course, but you brought attention to his weakness by suggesting he return to New York for the social season. He obviously can't dance, and what were you thinking, suggesting he should assist me with keeping you alive? You're a nightmare to guard, which Zayne knows full well, and he also knows he'd never be up for that daunting task given his bad leg.

"While it may appear that Zayne is somewhat nonchalant about his injury, I assure you, he's not. That's why I'm going to go speak with him, man to man. And since neither you nor Drusilla are men, you'll need to stay down here until I call for you."

"What if we have an emergency?"

"I'm going to encourage you to avoid emergencies at all costs." Sending her another one of his all-too-familiar glares, Mr. Blackheart turned and began climbing up the mountain.

Drusilla released a huff. "Gentlemen are such peculiar creatures. I cannot believe Mr. Blackheart expects us to twiddle our thumbs down here while he goes off to soothe Zayne's tender feelings. If you ask me, Zayne needs a kick in his rather nice behind, not coddling."

"I can't argue with you there," Agatha said as she moved to the back of the wagon. Pulling the picnic basket out, she set it on the ground. Plucking out two apples, she barely had a moment to straighten before Matilda was beside her, looking hopeful. Giving an apple to the little pig, she grinned as Matilda scampered back to her grassy spot and immediately began to chomp on her treat.

"Interesting pet you've managed to acquire," Drusilla said.

"True, but I don't think Mr. Blackheart is thrilled with my acquisition."

"I'm not sure Mr. Blackheart is capable of experiencing a thrilling emotion, but now is not the time to delve into his odd ways." Drusilla lifted her chin. "We need to discuss Zayne. I couldn't help but notice the animated conversation the two of you were sharing on the ride out here, which made me realize you're probably up to something."

"I'm sure I should take offense at your reasoning, but annoyingly enough, you're right," Agatha said. She took a few minutes to explain everything Zayne had told her, finishing with, "So Helena left him right when he needed her the most."

"And you're determined to sort him out."

"He's my friend."

"Rumor had it back in New York that the two of you were more than friends."

"That's exactly why one shouldn't put much stock in rumors, Drusilla. Zayne and I have always been just friends."

"You spoke about him almost nonstop when we first started out on this adventure."

"Did I?"

"Indeed. Non . . . stop."

A flash of heat swept over Agatha's face. "Oh, very well, if you must know, I did, once upon a time, hold Zayne in a small bit of affection. But after he learned of that affection, he very nicely explained to me that he was beholden to Helena and that I mustn't ever believe he'd abandon her to form a relationship with me."

"Helena doesn't seem to be an issue anymore."

Agatha wrinkled her nose. "You're supposed to be my companion, Drusilla, not a matchmaker. Besides, you've spent an entire year with me. Surely you've realized by now that I'm perfectly content being an independent lady. I enjoy the success I've achieved as a writer, and I'm not ready, nor will I probably ever be, to give that independence up for a man."

"Zayne was raised by one of the most progressive ladies I've ever known," Drusilla countered. "I would have to imagine Gloria Beckett was more than successful with teaching her son tolerance for independent ladies. I'm sure Zayne wouldn't be bothered in the least if you continued on with your writing, if you *were* to form an attachment to him."

"Zayne's a mess at the moment, and the last thing I need is more messiness in my life."

"He's an enticing mess."

"*Anyway*, since I still consider myself his friend, I'll do whatever I can to help him recover. However, much to my disgust, he's already figured out what I'm up to, which means it's going to be remarkably difficult to get him to cooperate." She smiled at Drusilla. "I think I'm going to need your assistance formulating a plan."

"No."

"Why not?"

"Because the only way you'll have the slightest chance of helping Zayne get better is if you somehow manage to convince him to go back to New York. He's not going to agree to that, which means you'll get it into your head to somehow drag him back there. Have you forgotten you're not safe in the city?"

"Have you forgotten I haven't exactly been safe out *here*?"

"True, but at least out here the danger is random, while in New York there's a very specific and troubling threat waiting for you."

"Theodore's certain to find some leads soon. Maybe he's already run the culprit to ground and just hasn't had a chance to send us a telegram."

"I received a telegram from Theodore a week ago. There are no new leads."

"Why would *you* receive a telegram from Theodore Wilder?"

"Did I say *I* received the telegram? How silly of me, I meant Mr. Blackheart received a telegram, and . . ." Drusilla's voice trailed off as she looked past Agatha's shoulder. "Hmm . . . Now that's interesting," was all she said before she started rummaging through a satchel that was attached to her hip. She pulled out a pair of opera glasses and immediately began peering off into the distance.

"I know I should ask why you have opera glasses stashed in your satchel, but since that's somewhat self-explanatory because you're always so annoyingly prepared for anything, what are you looking at?"

"I'm not sure, but . . . Oh dear." Drusilla passed the opera glasses to Agatha. "Take a look."

Pressing the opera glasses to her eyes, Agatha frowned. "Are those *women* riding this way?"

"Indeed, and do notice the rifles attached to their saddles."

Agatha took another look. "I'll bet those are soon going to prove to be problematic."

"Exactly," Drusilla said crisply before she took the glasses back from Agatha and quickly stowed them away. "I think we're about to be held up, and I swear, if we get out of this latest calamity alive, I'm going to strangle Zayne. Only an idiot would flaunt his finds in a silly sack hanging from his belt."

"You saw that?"

"I'm very observant." Drusilla reached back in her satchel and pulled out a pistol, holding it with what seemed to be a practiced hand.

"I didn't know you carried that."

"Forgive me, Agatha, but this is no time for a pleasant chat regarding what you do and don't know about me. We need to get up to the mine and warn the gentlemen. Plus, if those ladies begin shooting at us, we'll have the better advantage if we're higher." Taking a firm hold of Agatha's arm, Drusilla began to prod her up the mountain.

Agatha slipped on some loose dirt, which had Drusilla

tightening her hold and hauling her upright. "I'll bet Mr. Blackheart never imagined when he told us to avoid emergencies that one would really happen."

Drusilla's brows drew together. "He should have remembered you attract emergencies like honey attracts bees, but enough about that. You need to stop dawdling."

"I'm not dawdling. I slipped, and I'd be able to move faster if you weren't dragging me along."

"Stop being difficult," Drusilla said, even as she released Agatha's arm and scrambled up a few feet. "Honestly, if I'd known exactly what I was getting into, I might have hesitated briefly before I swore to protect you, because . . ."

Agatha stopped moving. "Swore to protect me?"

Drusilla let out a grunt, which was unusual in and of itself, and glared at Agatha, looking slightly like Mr. Blackheart. "I'm your paid companion. Of course I'm expected to protect you."

"Protect my *virtue*," Agatha clarified, "and forgive me, but I don't believe that's in jeopardy at the moment. Nor—just so we're clear—are you actually responsible for my reputation, since I'm rapidly becoming a lady of a certain age."

"You're twenty-two, hardly ancient, but this is not the time to discuss such matters. We're soon to be set upon by a motley-looking group of outlaws."

"They didn't look motley to me. I thought they—"

"Would you come on?"

Snapping her mouth shut even though she still had plenty to say, Agatha climbed a few steps, then stopped. "I forgot Matilda."

"Don't even think about going back for her."

"What if they shoot her?"

"Why would they do that? They're after gold, not lunch."

"It's a good thing Matilda can't hear you, otherwise, she'd be very upset."

The next second, Drusilla had another very firm grip on her arm, and Agatha had no choice but to continue upward. "I don't like being manhandled."

"Since I'm a woman, that makes absolutely no sense," Drusilla said. "But in order to alleviate your distress, I saw Matilda making a dash for the wagon. She's a smart little thing. She'll hide until the danger passes."

"Or until she's dead."

Apparently, Drusilla didn't feel the need to address that particular statement, because she tightened her hold and increased her pace, dragging Agatha up the mountain. They finally reached the entrance to the mine, and Drusilla promptly pushed Agatha toward the opening. "Go find Mr. Blackheart. I'll stay here and try to dissuade those ladies from climbing after us."

Reaching beneath her shirt, Agatha pulled a pistol from the waistband of her trousers. "I'm armed as well, so perhaps both of us should stay here and hold the ladies off."

Drusilla's mouth thinned, and she looked rather fierce, nothing at all like the pleasant companion Agatha had grown accustomed to. "We have limited ammunition. They have rifles and I'm going to assume pistols as well. Go get Mr. Blackheart." She took up a position right inside the entrance of the mine and gestured to Agatha. "Go."

"Fine, but don't think we're not going to have a long discussion about this later." Agatha turned on her heel and marched into the mine, pausing for a moment as her eyes adjusted to the dimness of the space. Seeing a tunnel right in front of her, she scooped up one of the numerous lit lanterns on the floor and barreled through the tunnel, yelling for Mr.

Blackheart at the top of her lungs. Her voice echoed eerily around her, but to her annoyance neither Mr. Blackheart nor Zayne bothered to answer her.

She darted down a narrow passageway as irritation began to replace the anxiety flowing through her veins. Leave it to gentlemen to ignore a lady when danger was nipping at their heels. She was forced to stop when she reached a dead end, turned and raced back the way she'd come, pausing as she considered the two tunnels in front of her. The distant sound of voices met her ears, and she moved into motion once again.

" . . . and if you'll notice, I've carefully placed dynamite in precise locations so that I can increase the size of this tunnel without having all the walls collapse. I've attached the dynamite to that fuse line right over there, and I've already taken the end of that line out to the main tunnel. All I need to do is light it and—"

She skidded to a halt right in front of them. "Didn't you hear me yelling for you?"

Zayne lifted up a lantern and peered back at her, his face looking oddly green in the light. "I don't believe what you were doing constitutes a yell, Agatha. It sounded more like screaming to me, and of course we heard you. I'm certain people in England heard you, but you'll need to wait a moment before explaining your dramatics. I'm right in the middle of telling Mr. Blackheart how I placed this dynamite so that no unforeseen problems will—"

"There are three women riding this way. Drusilla and I believe they're doing so in order to hold us up." She drew in a breath. "They're armed, heavily we think."

Zayne tilted his head and, to her annoyance, barely batted an eye. "Three women you say? How odd, unless . . . I vaguely remember spending time last night with three women, but . . . no, they'd have no reason to track me down out here."

"You probably let them see that stash of gold you keep attached to your belt since you were, well, drunk," Agatha snapped. "I would hazard a guess they're here to divest you of it, and—" A shot suddenly rang out, and Agatha forgot what she'd been about to say.

"Stay here," Mr. Blackheart ordered before he disappeared, a pistol gripped in his hand.

"Stay here," Zayne repeated, his nonchalant attitude of a moment before gone. Before she had a chance to protest, he snatched the pistol out of her hand and hobbled away as fast as his bad leg would allow.

She stood frozen in place for a second, completely furious. It wasn't as if she were some wilting flower who couldn't handle herself in dangerous situations, but that dangerous situation would be easier to handle if Zayne hadn't just made off with her favorite gun. Bending over, she set down the lantern, yanked up the leg of her trouser and pulled her second-favorite gun from the strap attached to her ankle and straightened. Snatching up the lantern again, she headed in the direction Zayne and Mr. Blackheart had disappeared, stopping abruptly when another shot rang out.

It sounded so close that Agatha had the unwelcome suspicion the ladies might have gotten past Drusilla and were now in the mine. Knowing she might have to make use of the element of surprise, she turned the knob on the lantern, shutting off the flame before she set it on the ground. Edging slowly through the dark, she bit back a yelp when she hit her head on something hard. Rubbing it for a second, she started forward again, slowing to another stop when she heard a lady's voice echo down the tunnel.

"Gentlemen, I encourage you to put down those guns or this woman will definitely not like what we do to her."

Pulse racing, Agatha inched ahead, using her hand against the roughhewn tunnel to guide her until the light from the main entrance finally made it possible for her to see. She stopped in the shadows right as Mr. Blackheart began to speak.

"What do you want?"

"Now, now, watch your tone, sir. I don't care for aggressive men, and I've been known to shoot men who've aggravated me in the past."

"Who are you?" Zayne demanded.

"Why, Mr. Beckett, how cruel that you don't remember me, especially after we shared such a lovely time last night. I'm Mary, and that is Jessie, and the other lady is Hannah." Mary laughed, the sound making the hair on the back of Agatha's neck stand up. "We've come to relieve you of that delightful bag of gold we noticed you had last night."

"You are more than welcome to it."

A second later, a thump sounded, and then the woman laughed again. "I must say, that was easier than I expected."

"I always try to be accommodating," Zayne returned. "And since I've cooperated and given you what you came for, I see no reason for you to linger."

"Ah, but that's where you're wrong. Me and the girls don't like to leave any loose ends, which is why I didn't hesitate to give you our names. But speaking of loose ends, where's Agatha Watson?"

"What do you want with Agatha, and how did you learn her name?" Drusilla asked.

"Everyone was only too willing to talk about the odd lady journalist who rode into town. I watched her drive away from the hotel with you, Mr. Beckett, and, well, sadly for her, the last person I need to leave alive is a journalist."

"She's not here," Zayne said. "Miss Watson and I suffered a slight misunderstanding on the ride over, and I'm afraid she got annoyed with me and jumped off the wagon. She's probably back at the hotel by now."

"You're hardly the type of gentleman to leave a lady on her own out here in the wild, Mr. Beckett, and besides, I watched her climb up the mountain." Mary's voice got considerably louder. "We know you're here, Miss Watson. You might as well come out of hiding and save all of us a great deal of trouble."

Agatha took a second to consider her options. If she showed herself, she'd lose any hint of a surprise attack, but if she didn't . . .

"We don't have time for this, Mary," one of the other ladies snapped. "And it doesn't matter if she comes out or not. Once we dynamite the place, no one will be left alive to identify us, and we'll finally be able to collect that fee we've been promised for—"

"Shut up," Mary snarled. "Miss Watson, if you don't stop this game immediately, I'm going to start shooting your friends, starting with the lady who tried to kill me. It really was a shame when her gun jammed, depriving her of my death."

Agatha took a small step forward but tripped on something and fell to her knees, ripping her trousers in the process. Pushing upright, she glanced down and smiled when her gaze settled on Zayne's fuse line, a line that just happened to be attached to . . . dynamite.

Plucking it off the ground, she straightened, but before she could consider how to proceed, squeals split the air.

"Oh no, not Matilda," she whispered as the squeals changed

to threatening-sounding grunts, something Matilda seemed to do right before she was getting ready to charge.

"Stupid pig, stop trying to bite me," Mary shrieked before another shot sounded and Matilda's grunts turned to terrified whimpers.

Agatha rushed into the room. "Stop shooting," she yelled, dropping the fuse line to the floor as she aimed her pistol at the woman who was chasing after Matilda.

The woman stopped chasing Matilda, which allowed the pig to disappear behind a large crate that seemed to be filled with dynamite. Swinging her pistol around to face Agatha, the woman had the audacity to smile. "Ah, Miss Watson, I presume?"

"Indeed, and you must be Mary."

"But of course I am," Mary agreed. "And now, since we've gotten the pleasantries out of the way, I'm going to have to insist you drop that little weapon of yours and place your hands over your head."

"I don't think I'm going to do that, Mary," Agatha drawled as she glanced to the right and found Zayne, Mr. Blackheart, and Drusilla being held at gunpoint by another lady, one who looked remarkably mean. She looked back to Mary. "The only thing standing between me, my friends, and death is this pistol, so you and I are going to have to come to some type of compromise."

Mary considered her for a long moment and then smiled again. "Shoot her, Jessie."

Agatha dropped to the ground right as another pistol went off. Rolling to her side, she squeezed the trigger and her pistol fired, but instead of hitting the woman who'd just tried to kill her, her shot went wide and hit a lantern attached to a heavy beam. Kerosene went everywhere, followed immediately by flames, and some of those flames were heading directly for the fuse line she'd dropped, while others were traveling toward the crate filled with dynamite.

"Run," she yelled as she scrambled to her feet.

No one seemed to need any prodding.

Mary and her girls rushed from the tunnel first, without a backward glance, followed by Drusilla and Mr. Blackheart. As she ran, terror struck Agatha and brought her stumbling to a stop.

Zayne's leg would never be up for the task of carrying him to safety fast enough.

Mr. Blackheart must have been of the same mind, because he rushed back into the tunnel, ran to Zayne, bent down, flung Zayne over his shoulder, and raced back the way he'd just come.

Her feet swept into motion, and she pounded after them, breathing a sigh of relief when fresh air hit her and she ran through the entrance of the mine. Her relief was cut short when an explosion split the air, hurting her ears, and then the mountain began to tremble as more and more explosions erupted.

She lost her balance and pitched forward, unable to stop herself as she tumbled over and over down the steep mountain, barely feeling the rough rocks tearing her clothing and skin. She finally came to a stop and could only lie there as dirt and debris settled over her and the air turned dark with dust.

The air gradually began clearing around her, and she pushed aside a mound of dirt that was covering her, but before she could sit up, the mountain gave another shudder and more explosions erupted, sending an avalanche of dirt her way. She covered her head and began choking as dirt clogged her airway.

The trembling seemed to go on forever, and every time she thought it was finished, it began again. Minutes dragged by, and then, the mountain stilled, the dust in the air thinned, and she began to unbury herself.

How long it took, she couldn't really say, but as she pushed dirt away, panic settled deep in her bones.

She needed to find the others—see if they were hurt, or more importantly, alive. Finally managing to free herself, she sat up, frowning when she couldn't hear a thing. She patted her ears and patted them again before she finally heard what sounded like horses in the distance. Squinting in that direction, she saw three horses racing away, ridden by none other than Mary and her girls.

"Good riddance," she said before she stumbled to her feet, looking around for any sign of movement.

The first thing she saw was Matilda trembling a few feet away from her, bleeding from the snout, not a hint of her pink skin in sight. "It's all right, darling," she said softly, moving to squat down beside the pig. "Where are the others?"

Matilda let out a mournful whine and began walking over to a large pile of dirt, Agatha following a step behind. What met her gaze on the other side of the pile took her completely by surprise.

Three pairs of outraged eyes peered back at her from blackened faces, the sight causing relief, mixed with a surprising touch of amusement, to rush through her. Only people who weren't suffering dire injuries would be remotely capable of summoning up that particular amount of outrage.

Mr. Blackheart coughed and then coughed again. "Where's Mary?"

"She's gone. I saw her riding away with the other two women."

"Must've thought we were dead," Drusilla muttered before she began wheezing.

"We should be dead," Zayne rasped as he pulled a clump of dirt out of his beard before he scowled at her. "Why, pray tell, did you think it was a good idea to bring that fuse line out to the main entrance?"

Agatha stiffened. "I didn't actually think about it, Zayne, and it certainly wasn't my intention to blow your mine up. It was an accident, but one that brought positive consequences."

"Positive consequences?" he thundered. "You destroyed my mine and almost killed all of us in the process. What exactly do you consider positive about that?"

"We're still alive, and . . ." She cleared her throat. "Since it seems I did do a rather good job of demolishing your mine—*unintentionally,* of course—and you mentioned it's about to snow soon . . ." She brushed dirt from her sleeve and summoned up a smile. "You won't have enough time to build new tunnels, at least not until the spring, which means you have absolutely no reason to resist returning home to New York."

Zayne's mouth dropped open, he peered at her through dirt-encrusted lashes, and then . . . the yelling began.

5

Zayne stretched out his legs and leaned back against the plush seat as a distinct sense of disgruntlement settled over him. That disgruntlement made it next to impossible for him to enjoy the opulence of the private Pullman car on the train his family had sent for him. And that gave him yet another reason to be annoyed with Agatha.

She'd always been a meddler, but this time she'd gone too far.

Not only had she blown up his mine, she'd somehow decided—even though he thought he'd been more than clear about the matter—she needed to take him in hand. She'd been spending almost every minute of the past two weeks since the *unfortunate incident* as she liked to call it, ordering him around. She'd even gone so far as to personally pack up his meager belongings before they'd boarded the train to head east.

He was beginning to lose patience with her.

His foul mood increased when the door to the train car opened. Knowing the morsel of quiet he'd finally been able to obtain was soon to disappear, he narrowed his eyes at the door but sighed in relief when only Mr. Blackheart strode into view. His lips curled just a bit when he got a good look at the man. Mr. Blackheart was wearing his ever-present scowl, but his normally well-groomed hair was slightly untidy, giving clear testimony that something was bothering him—something that probably went by the name of Agatha.

"What's wrong with you?" Zayne asked.

"The ladies are what's wrong with me, or more specifically, Miss Watson." Mr. Blackheart dropped into a chair next to Zayne and began rubbing his temple. "I swear, once we reach New York, I'm off to my club—one that, thankfully, doesn't admit ladies and one where peace and quiet is the order of the day." He stopped rubbing his head and looked around. "Although, this setup you have here is very nice, very peaceful at the moment." His gaze sharpened. "Is that Matilda's tail sticking out from under your bed?"

"It is. She seems to have taken a peculiar liking to me."

"Highly doubtful, since it's become clear she doesn't like men. If I were to hazard a guess, I'd say she likes sleeping in here because it's never quiet in the ladies' Pullman car." Mr. Blackheart eased his head back against the chair. "But do be sure to thank your family for me for sending us this train. I certainly wasn't expecting to travel back east in such luxury. It's made it easier to watch Miss Watson with no other passengers onboard, only highly competent members of the staff." He considered Zayne for a second. "Why do you think your family sent us our own train?"

A tiny trace of remorse stole through Zayne's dark mood. He knew full well he'd been horribly negligent when it came to his family after the accident. His mother and father had come to see him while he'd been recovering, but they'd left before Helena had abandoned him. He'd sent them a letter, explaining briefly that he and Helena were through. He'd also let them know he needed to be by himself for a while, but he'd never bothered to tell them anything about the mining venture.

A monthly telegram telling them he was still alive was all he'd managed. It had been a very telling statement of how much his parents wanted him home when, after sending them word he was coming back to New York, they'd immediately arranged for this train.

"Are you feeling unwell?"

Zayne forced a smile. "I'm fine, simply lost in thought."

"Those must have been some thoughts."

"Perhaps, but I don't care to discuss them." His smile dimmed. "I'd offer you a drink, but Agatha poured out every drop of alcohol I tried to bring with me."

"I'm fairly sure, if you're really thirsty, the staff should be able to provide you with whatever you want."

"Agatha got her greedy hands on their supply as well, and told them she'd be very disappointed if they purchased additional quantities during the route to New York."

"She is thorough when she gets her mind set on something."

"She's irritating. It wasn't her place to dump out my whiskey."

"Whiskey rots your insides."

Zayne shrugged. "I use it to numb the pain in my leg."

"Understandable, but at least now your insides won't start giving you trouble." Mr. Blackheart tilted his head. "I did find it interesting, though, that you didn't protest too strenuously when Miss Watson insisted you stop drinking. Makes me wonder why you gave in so easily."

"*Is* there a reason you sought me out?"

Mr. Blackheart's lips twitched, but then he coughed behind his hand, and when he lowered his hand, he looked as grouchy as ever. "I've been trying to eavesdrop on the ladies."

"Brave of you."

"Indeed, especially since I keep getting caught. . . . But I am concerned about Miss Watson. I get the distinct impression she's not going to stay behind closed doors once we reach New York."

"And that surprises you?"

"Given that her life is in danger in the city, yes. I was hoping she'd be reasonable and agree to lay low until I have time to assess the situation."

Even though he was incredibly irritated with Agatha, Zayne couldn't stop the worry that began trickling through him, worry that was distinctly mixed with guilt. "You do realize that I didn't *want* her to accompany me back to the city, don't you?"

"You were quite vocal with your protests. Although, I have to tell you, the more you protested, the more determined Miss Watson became to see you safely home." He released a snort. "You turned into a challenge for her, and unfortunately, Miss Watson views a challenge the way most ladies view a delicious tart. Even if she hadn't blown up your mine, she'd have found a way to get you back to the city."

Fresh irritation replaced the guilt. "But she *did* blow up my mine."

"You may not appreciate my reminding you of this fact, but I did warn you that putting her in the direct vicinity of dynamite wasn't exactly a stellar idea. It shouldn't surprise you in the least that something of a dastardly nature occurred. Although, I suppose we do owe Miss Watson our thanks for getting us away from Mary alive."

"That was completely unintentional."

"Everything is with Miss Watson."

"Exactly my point," Zayne said before he folded his hands over his stomach. "Do you know that I stored a whole cache of gold in that mine? It's gone now, buried under an entire mountain of dirt, and it will take months of hard work to unbury it again—if I can even find it."

"That explains why you've been a bit sulky of late, but . . . don't you think it would have been more prudent to store your gold in a bank?"

"And let everyone know how much I was uncovering? Certainly not."

"You're supposed to be a businessman, Mr. Beckett, but burying your fortune in a mountain is hardly good business, which makes me question your mental capabilities at the moment. I would have thought you'd have invested your profits in the market, earning you additional, and probably substantial, money."

"Weren't we talking about the ladies?"

"You're the one who brought up the mine and your loss of what seems to be a fortune."

"I still have a fortune, one I earned working in the family business, and then there's the trust I received from my grandparents."

"Then you have absolutely no reason to sulk. Most people never acquire one fortune in a lifetime, let alone several."

"Getting back to Agatha," Zayne said loudly. "Any ideas on how you're going to keep her safe?"

"Not a one. She's unpredictable, fearless, and doesn't enjoy being told what to do. Quite frankly, I have no idea how I'm going to keep her alive once we reach New York."

"The threats to her are really that severe?"

Mr. Blackheart's almost pleasant expression immediately changed to menacing. "Forgive me, Mr. Beckett, but you've spent a great deal of time with Miss Watson during the past two weeks. Surely she explained the threats that have been made against her."

"She did mention that someone wants to kill her."

"And?"

"Well, that was about it."

"You didn't press her for details?"

"No, I didn't, because right after she mentioned the threats I realized she was trying to manage me, and . . . I suppose I didn't take the time to sufficiently sort out the idea that she truly is in serious danger."

"You do remember, even though Miss Watson is a progressive sort, that she's a lady, don't you?"

"What's your point?"

"Even if you realized she was trying to manage you, Miss Watson, as I'm sure you remember, doesn't lie. She might exaggerate the details of a situation, but she puts her dainty foot down at speaking an untruth."

"I have no idea where you're going with this."

"You should have shown her concern. Ladies, whether they be independent or not, like to know we gentlemen will do everything in our power to keep them safe."

"Our conversation went downhill rapidly when I started laughing and she got testy, but . . . " Zayne paused as an intriguing thought sprang to mind. "You're right. Agatha is a lady, which means"—he caught Mr. Blackheart's gaze—"we need to find her a man."

Mr. Blackheart blinked, just once. "I beg your pardon?"

Pushing himself up in the chair, Zayne rubbed his hands together. "A man, that's exactly what Agatha needs. Someone strong, possessed of a great deal of patience, and . . . well . . . I suppose he'll have to be somewhat attractive."

He looked Mr. Blackheart up and down. "Hmm . . . you're a man, and you've put up with Agatha for an entire year and haven't killed her yet, so . . . you'll do nicely."

"I don't think I like the direction this conversation is taking."

Zayne ignored him. "It's genius, sheer genius. If Agatha settled down to a more traditional life, she'd no longer be running amok looking for riveting stories or trying to save wounded gentlemen. The danger that constantly seems to stalk her would simply go away."

"Miss Watson has never been traditional, nor do I think she has any desire to become so."

"That is exactly why you'd be a perfect candidate. You understand her, but you're a strong man, so you wouldn't get browbeaten into agreeing to her madcap plans."

"Really, Mr. Beckett, you've heard some of the adventures we've had on our trip this past year. They should show you that I have little to no control over the woman."

"She's still alive though."

Mr. Blackheart began drumming his fingers against the arm of the chair. "She's still alive because it's my job to keep her that way. But I'm paid to protect her, not court her. Becoming overly familiar with Miss Watson would be a serious breach of ethics."

"Ah, but if you were to tell Theodore you wished to be released from the case because your feelings for Agatha have changed, there'd be no problem, would there?"

"I don't have feelings for Miss Watson."

Zayne arched a brow. "Everyone has feelings for Agatha. She's very beautiful, and you have to admit, life would never be boring with her by your side."

"I like boring."

"But you do find Agatha beautiful, don't you?"

"Mr. Beckett . . ."

"I thought we agreed you'd call me Zayne."

"Fine. Zayne then, but I have to . . ."

"And don't you think you should allow me the privilege of your given name, given the personal direction this conversation is taking?" Zayne pressed.

"No."

"Come now, Mr. Blackheart. What is it?"

"None of your business."

"That's an unusual first name."

Mr. Blackheart rose from his chair. "I think I'll go check on the ladies."

"I thought they were annoying you, which was why you sought me out in the first place."

"*You're* annoying me, so I'll take my chances with the ladies. I vastly prefer trying to eavesdrop on the women over this ridiculous conversation we're having."

"We're not actually having much of a conversation, since you're being stubborn and won't agree to go along with my idea."

Mr. Blackheart let out what sounded remarkably like a huff and slowly resumed his seat. "Fine, we'll discuss this further, but know that I'm in no way interested in pursuing Miss Watson in a romantic fashion. Though I find her to be very beautiful and intelligent, which has always appealed to me, she's much too young and . . ."

Mr. Blackheart continued speaking, but Zayne barely heard him. For some reason, the moment the man had admitted he found Agatha beautiful, a sour taste began filling Zayne's mouth and his stomach had taken to clenching.

It was rather disconcerting and made absolutely no sense, because it wasn't as if he thought of Agatha *that* way. He . . .

". . . given that Miss Watson does seem to hold you in a slight bit of affection, you should be the one to court her."

Zayne's mouth dropped open. "Me?"

"But of course. I remember noticing the two of you back in New York before you left for California, and I always thought you made a lovely couple."

"We were never a couple."

"But you could have been, if not for Helena."

Zayne paused for a moment in order to formulate an adequate response. Had he spent most of his time with Agatha when he'd been in New York? Certainly, but they'd been friends—good friends, but friends.

Had he ever considered more with her?

"Zayne?"

Pushing aside his troubling thoughts, Zayne lifted his head. "I'm afraid I'm not the man for Agatha either, Mr. Blackheart. I've sworn off women for good. After the fiasco with Helena, I think bachelorhood is the only life for me."

"But you *do* find Miss Watson beautiful, don't you?" Mr. Blackheart asked, throwing Zayne's own words back at him.

"I've already admitted as much. A man would have to be blind not to see how beautiful she is, what with those amazing blue eyes of hers and all that unruly black hair. Not to mention her form, which is . . ." Zayne stuttered to a stop when he realized Mr. Blackheart was watching him with clear speculation in his eyes. "But, that's neither here nor there, since I'm not in the market for a lady."

"You enjoy sparring with her."

"No, I don't. If you haven't noticed, Agatha and I have been arguing almost constantly since she blew up my mine—arguing, not sparring, and I certainly don't enjoy it."

"You smile when you think she's not watching, especially after the two of you trade heated exchanges."

Zayne rolled his eyes. "Since *you* don't seem keen to pursue her, and I know *I'm* not, can you think of any other gentleman who might be interested?"

"I can't think of any gentleman who *wouldn't* be interested."

The sour taste returned to his mouth, causing Zayne to pick up the glass of lemonade—the only drink Agatha seemed to approve of—from the small table beside him and take a gulp. Setting the glass aside, he frowned. "I suppose I could make a list of eligible men once we get back to New York."

"You could indeed. But remember, Miss Watson has a mind of her own, and I doubt she'll take kindly to us, or rather you, playing matchmaker. Besides, finding a gentleman to suit her will take time, something we don't have, since we're almost to the city, where I expect the threat will resume."

"Is there any hope that the threat to her has diminished since you've been gone?"

"Probably not, given the escalating nature of the threats to her right before we left. I've tried to talk her into leaving the city after we deposit you back with your family, but she's adamant about keeping an eye on you."

"I'm perfectly capable of seeing after myself. I've been doing it for quite some time now."

"Yes, and doing a remarkable job of it."

Zayne pretended he hadn't heard that sarcastic remark. "Agatha has absolutely no reason to feel responsible for me."

"I agree, but she does, so . . . Hmm . . . perhaps we could use that to our advantage."

"Meaning?"

82

"Miss Watson has a very caring heart underneath her annoying demeanor. If you were to assume the role of a true invalid, we could keep her by your bedside. That would allow me an opportunity to work on flushing out whoever wants her dead without worrying about her."

"But I've been feeling better lately."

"I'm not surprised, given that you're no longer crawling around a mine and have been forced to give up whiskey, but . . ."

Whatever else Mr. Blackheart was about to say came to an abrupt end when the door burst open and Agatha, followed by Drusilla, breezed into the train car, both ladies looking remarkably smug, which was an immediate cause for concern.

"Ah, lovely," Agatha exclaimed, walking up to stand beside his chair. "I was hoping I'd find you in here, Zayne."

"Where else would I be?"

She waved his comment aside. "Drusilla and I were just in the kitchen car."

"Learning to cook, are we?" Mr. Blackheart asked in a wary tone.

"Don't be silly, I'll never learn to cook, although Drusilla told me she is a proficient cook, which doesn't surprise me in the least." Agatha sent Drusilla a fond look and then returned her attention to Zayne, even as she brandished a sharp-looking pair of scissors in his direction. "Look what the chef gave me. They're supposed to be used to cut up fish, but they'll do in a pinch."

"They'll do what in a pinch?" Zayne asked slowly.

"Hack off that hair of yours, of course."

"Well, I must be off," Mr. Blackheart suddenly exclaimed, rising to his feet so quickly Zayne barely had a moment to blink. "Mrs. Swanson, would you care to join me in the dining car? I feel the most unusual urge for some refreshment."

Drusilla caught Zayne's gaze, then looked to Agatha, who was still waving the scissors. "You know, I do believe I'm a little hungry as well, Mr. Blackheart." She hurried for the door, Mr. Blackheart a step behind her. The door slammed shut a moment later, and Zayne was left with only Agatha standing beside him, brandishing her scissors.

"You might as well put those down," he said. "I'm not letting you anywhere near my hair. I well remember what you've done to me in the past."

"I've never cut your hair, Zayne."

"You made me shave my chest one time."

"True, but only because that gown I needed you to wear was somewhat low-cut, and, well, you'd have looked silly with chest hair." She took a step closer, and as she did so, a wonderful scent of lilacs tickled his nose. "Now then, be a good boy and let me get on with this. We can't very well allow your mother to see you looking like a wild man." She waved the scissors in front of his face. "There's really no need to worry. I'm certain I'll do a more than credible job."

Zayne narrowed his eyes. "You don't have any brothers, so how can you make that claim? Whose hair have you cut?"

"I've never cut a man's hair before, but I did have the opportunity to sheer a sheep in Nebraska, and how much different can it be?"

"You know, Agatha, the truth of the matter is that my mother will be thrilled to simply have me returned back to New York. I don't think there's any need for you to touch my hair."

"You also need to lose the beard."

Zayne shuddered. "You're not shaving me. Putting a razor in your hand would be almost as foolish as giving you a piece of dynamite."

Agatha's eyes turned chilly. "I don't recall offering to shave you, and really, I would have thought that by now you'd be over the whole dynamite thing."

"I don't think I'll ever recover from that. You do remember the troubling little fact that you destroyed my livelihood, don't you?"

Agatha moved closer, the skirt of her gown brushing against his leg. He felt the strangest heat flash through him but consoled himself with the idea he was only getting nervous because scissors in Agatha's hands could be construed as a weapon.

"Your family is one of the richest families in the country. Why, up until you had your accident, you were perfectly content to work by your father's side, as well as Hamilton's, growing your railroading business. I certainly didn't destroy your only means of securing a living."

"Since our railroad reached the West Coast a few years ago, there's not that much more growing to do."

A sharp rap on his head had him gritting his teeth.

"Stop being so surly. It's unbecoming, and I know for a fact—given all the traveling I've done of late—that there's still plenty of need for new railroad lines."

"Maybe *you* should join my father and brother, then. I'm sure they'd love working with you every day."

"Sarcasm is almost as unbecoming as surliness," she said before he heard a snip and saw a long piece of matted hair plop to the ground.

"This is a bad idea," he muttered.

"It's not. You're just being difficult, but . . . Good heavens."

"Good heavens, what?"

Agatha moved closer. "The scissors are stuck."

"I guess you'll have to stop."

"Nonsense, I can't just leave them there. I'll have to use the knife."

Before Zayne could protest, Agatha pulled a shiny and lethal-looking knife out of her pocket and proceeded to saw off more of his hair. "This is so matted and dirty, it almost looks black instead of dark brown."

"I probably should have sought out a barber sometime during the past several months, but there wasn't much need to worry about my appearance up in the mine."

Agatha stopped sawing, stepped away from him, and caught his eye. "I don't think I've actually said this out loud to you yet, but I really am sorry I blew up your mine."

He opened his mouth to argue but noticed the true sincerity in her eyes. Agatha was, and had always been, impulsive, annoying, and far too much trouble, but she really was a kind woman at heart, something he seemed to have forgotten.

"I know," he finally said.

She grinned back at him. "That was hard for you, wasn't it?"

He returned the grin. "Incredibly."

"You're considering forgiving me though, aren't you?"

His grin faded. "I don't know if I'd go that far, Agatha. You did lose me a fortune in gold."

"I had nothing to do with Mary robbing you."

"I'm not talking about the pittance I kept on my belt, but what I'd stored in the mine."

"You stored your gold in that mine instead of in a bank?"

Not caring to discuss that subject again, since Mr. Blackheart had already made him feel slightly less than intelligent, Zayne dropped his gaze. "If you're going to finish my hair before we reach New York, you'd better have at it."

She stepped closer, the scent of her perfume tickling his

nose again. He wasn't positive, but he thought he detected the slightest trace of violets mixed in with the lilacs.

He'd forgotten how she always smelled rather delicious.

A jolt of something disturbing slid down his back, and for a moment he thought it was a reaction to his troubling thoughts, until he realized Agatha had dumped half a pot of water over his head.

"Was that really necessary? I'm soaked to the skin."

"You'll dry by the time we reach New York, and I thought the water would help with the matting. I still can't get the scissors out because the tangles are so thick the knife won't go through that part."

As Agatha struggled to remove the scissors, Zayne tried to ignore the warmth that was seeping into his skin from the closeness of her body. Deciding he needed something to distract him, he searched his mind for a safe topic of conversation.

"Did I mention to you that Matilda's sleeping under the bed in here?"

A grunt was Agatha's only reply before there was an ominous snap. She stumbled backward, righted herself, and smiled as she waved the newly freed scissors at him. "Got them, but I do think I took out a huge chunk of your hair in the process." She reached out and ruffled his hair right before she began attacking it again. "Not to worry though. I'm sure I can blend it in so no one can tell. Now, what were you saying about Matilda?"

"Ah, well, she's sleeping under my bed, but . . . let's get back to my hair. I'm not going to be bald, am I?"

"You'd look very handsome bald, because you have such a strong face. And if you were missing a large chunk of hair—not that I'm saying that's the case—well, it would just draw more attention to your eyes. They're a very nice shade of green, unusual even." She let out what sounded remarkably like a giggle. "Did I ever tell you about the time I overheard some ladies sighing over how long your lashes are?"

Zayne frowned. Agatha never giggled, nor did she flirt, which is exactly what she seemed to be trying to do at the moment, which meant . . . His eyes widened. "I really do have a bald spot, don't I?"

"I wouldn't go so far as to say it's completely bald." Agatha cut off another piece of his hair. "But baldness aside, I have something else I need to discuss with you, because Drusilla and I have been mulling over your situation."

All thoughts of flirting immediately disappeared. "What situation?"

"The mess you've made of your life."

"My life is hardly a mess."

"I understand it's easy for a person to embrace denial, but it's time for you to stop that. You need a purpose, Zayne, and Drusilla and I have very kindly found one for you."

"You've found me a purpose?"

"Indeed, and it's a very noble one."

He refused to groan out loud. "And . . . ?"

"Drusilla and I are going to help you track down that Willie person—you know, the man you bought the mine from—once we get settled and all."

"And why exactly would we track Willie down?"

"So that you can return his mine to him."

"What makes you so certain I'd be willing to turn over a lucrative mining venture to a man I legitimately purchased it from?"

For just a brief second, he felt Agatha stiffen, but then she started cutting his hair again, although she did so rather too enthusiastically. "I'm going to pretend you didn't just ask that question."

"It was a legitimate question, Agatha."

"It's too late. I'm not going to be able to help you," she mumbled.

"For the millionth time, I don't need you to save me."

She completely ignored his statement. "The Zayne I used to know was a compassionate man. A man who wouldn't have blinked at what I just suggested because it's the right thing to do."

"I don't know many businessmen who'd willingly turn over a profitable venture simply because of a compassionate nature."

Another handful of his hair fell to the ground. "You could at least try to find Willie and offer him some type of partnership with you."

"We've been over this before, Agatha. I *purchased* the mine from him, sight unseen."

"True, but since I blew it up, it's going to take a lot of time and money to get it up and running again. If we could find Willie, maybe he'd be willing to go back to Colorado and get things moving. You told me he was responsible for making those tunnels. You're in no shape to do it, so . . ."

As Agatha continued speaking, Zayne couldn't help but conclude she had a very good idea. He had no intention of completely abandoning his mine, had only agreed to go back to New York because she'd been so demanding . . . and he'd wanted to see his family . . . and the snow would soon start falling in Colorado, if it hadn't already. But . . . Willie had done a fine job setting up the tunnels, and if he could be found, he would be the perfect man for the job.

"I think you might be right."

Agatha froze. "Did you just say you think I'm right?"

"Well, I wasn't actually listening to *everything* you were saying, but I think you're right about finding Willie."

"And you'll turn over the mine to him?"

"No, but I wouldn't be opposed to bringing him on as some type of partner."

"Why won't you just give him the mine?"

"Because as *you* said, it'll take money to get it running again, and I'm pretty certain Willie doesn't have any of that."

"Oh, good point." Agatha leaned down, smiled, and caught his gaze. "Thank you."

His breath caught in his throat. Why, he couldn't really say, but before he could think of a response, or even get a sound out of his mouth, the door opened and Mr. Blackheart walked back into the room.

"We're about an hour out of the city," he said. "I thought I'd see how Mr. Beckett's transformation is coming along." He walked across the room and winced. "Hmm . . ."

"It's not that bad," Agatha argued.

"Give me the scissors," Mr. Blackheart demanded.

"But I'm not finished, and Zayne and I were right in the middle of an important conversation."

"It'll have to wait. His mother will be appalled if she sees her favorite son looking like this."

"You think I'm my mother's favorite son?" Zayne asked.

"Of course you are," Agatha said before Mr. Blackheart could reply. "But that has nothing to do with Drusilla and me helping you find Willie."

"Shouldn't you go collect the rest of your belongings since we're almost to New York?" Mr. Blackheart asked.

"Are you trying to get rid of me?" Agatha countered.

"Yes."

"Why?"

"Because I'm going to have to give Mr. Beckett a mirror soon so he can begin shaving, and once he sees what you've done to him, your life will be in danger. Since it's my job to keep you alive, I'm going to suggest you leave this room, immediately."

Agatha considered Zayne's head for a moment, wrinkled her nose, and let out a whistle as she began to walk toward the door. Pausing to wait for Matilda to scamper to her side, she looked up and winced when she caught his eye. "Just remember, you look better than you did thirty minutes ago, although that might not really be saying much." With that, she opened the door and disappeared.

"How bad is it?" he asked.

"Oh, it's not that bad," Mr. Blackheart said. "Nothing I can't fix."

"Why did you make me think it was, then?"

"Don't get me wrong—at the moment your hair looks hideous. But again, I can fix it, because I'm somewhat talented when it comes to cutting hair."

"Why didn't you offer to cut it in the first place?"

"Hmm . . . that'll give you something to think about, but not right now. Now we need to discuss a situation that's arisen, and I've come to the conclusion I'm going to need your help."

"A situation?"

"Indeed." Mr. Blackheart eyed Zayne's hair. "After speaking a few minutes ago with Drusilla, not that she was overly generous giving me many details, I think we're going to have to move forward with the idea of you playing the invalid."

"Why?"

"Because I can't protect Agatha if she's roaming around

derelict parts of the city trying to find that Willie character."
He blew out a breath. "From what Drusilla disclosed, Agatha
believes if you make matters right with Willie it'll help you
recover, which means she's focused now on finding the man
and won't be easily dissuaded."

"But there's nothing wrong with me, except my leg, of
course, and Agatha has no reason to believe I need help recovering."

Mr. Blackheart quirked a brow. "Right, because it's completely normal for a gentleman to turn his back on everything
he cares about and dig in the dirt for months on end with
only his sulky attitude for company."

"I wouldn't go so far as to say I've been sulking. And my
digging in the dirt, as you so quaintly put it, was beginning
to turn profitable before Agatha blew everything up."

"Be that as it may, Agatha's determined to save you."

Zayne frowned. "So what exactly do you expect me to do?"

"Let her."

6

Agatha looked around Grand Central Depot, relishing the sight of so many people bustling past her. She'd missed the city, missed the energy it held, but now, finally, she was home. She tugged Matilda's leash and pulled the pig away from something she was trying to eat off the ground before turning to Drusilla. "It's wonderful to be back, isn't it?"

Drusilla, for some unknown reason, had once again pulled out her opera glasses and was peering off into the distance. "Yes, ah, wonderful."

"What are you doing?"

"I'm looking for Zayne and Mr. Blackheart. I have no idea what could possibly be keeping them so long."

"I told you, Mr. Blackheart informed me when I went to fetch them after the train stopped that he had yet to make Zayne presentable and that they'd be along directly."

"We'll be waiting forever, then, because . . ." Drusilla's lips suddenly thinned as her scanning stopped. "Oh, for the love of . . ."

"What?"

Handing over the opera glasses, Drusilla rolled her eyes. "Take a look for yourself."

Lifting the glasses, Agatha turned in the direction Drusilla had been gazing and caught sight of Mr. Blackheart and Zayne in the distance. Frowning, she pressed the glasses closer to her eyes, as if that might change the image she was seeing. "Good heavens, what happened to Zayne? Mr. Blackheart seems to be holding him up and . . ." She lowered the glasses, wiped the lenses on her sleeve, and looked through them once again. "Hmm . . . I wasn't seeing things. Zayne's freshly shaven face looks like it's soaking wet and it's very pale."

"It's pale because his face hasn't seen the sun for months, buried as it was underneath all that hair."

"But . . . why do you suppose he looks so wet? You don't think Mr. Blackheart encouraged him to bathe, do you? But . . . no, that doesn't make any sense because surely he'd have dried off before leaving the train, wouldn't he?"

Drusilla suddenly let out a snort, a sound Agatha had never once heard come out of the woman's mouth. Pulling her attention away from Zayne, she settled it on her companion. "What?"

"I think Zayne's supposed to be perspiring—profusely."

"*Supposed* to be perspiring?"

"Gentlemen have no subtlety when it comes to matters of a devious nature, and these particular gentlemen are definitely abysmal plotters."

"Well that certainly clears everything up for me."

Drusilla waved her hand impatiently toward the men. "I'm reluctant to admit that I think this fresh bout of madness might be my fault."

"You're still being annoyingly vague."

Drusilla took hold of Agatha's arm. "I hope you won't be

too distressed with me, dear, but I was beginning to have some concerns regarding the business of tracking Willie down, and . . . I made mention of my concerns to Mr. Blackheart."

"You're consorting with the enemy now?"

"Really, Agatha, Mr. Blackheart isn't exactly the enemy. He's been charged with the daunting task of keeping you alive, and setting you loose on New York to search for Willie isn't exactly the best way to help him achieve that goal."

"And you believe voicing those concerns is what's behind Zayne's fragile and wet appearance?"

"I have to admit I do." Drusilla shrugged. "Given the fact that Mr. Blackheart didn't have much time before we reached New York, I imagine what we're seeing now is the only plan he was able to come up with on such short notice." She patted Agatha's arm. "Since you've been rather vocal regarding the idea you want to see Zayne recover, I think Mr. Blackheart has convinced him to assume a fragile demeanor in order to persuade you to offer to look after him until he gets better."

"That's a horrible plan."

"True, but it would keep you off the streets if you were to agree."

Agatha lifted her chin. "I have no intention of agreeing. I didn't travel back to the city in order to hide away from whatever danger might still be stalking me."

"You don't *want* to spend more time in Zayne's company?"

"I thought we agreed you'd cease your attempts at matchmaking, Drusilla."

"I don't recall agreeing to that."

Lifting the glasses once again, Agatha found Zayne and Mr. Blackheart still standing in the same spot. Her lips curled as she watched Zayne raise a hand and wipe his brow in a dramatic gesture. His wiping suddenly stopped when Mr.

Blackheart shook his head and dropped his hold on him. Agatha couldn't help but notice the telling fact that Zayne seemed to have no trouble standing on his own, especially since he began walking backward without the use of the cane he held in one hand when Mr. Blackheart plucked a towel out of the sack he was holding. Her mouth dropped open when the man then proceeded to try and wring water out of the towel, right over Zayne's head. Heated words seemed to be exchanged as the men struggled for possession of the towel, but then both of them stilled, looked her way, leaned forward as if they were trying to ascertain whether or not she was watching them, and waved rather feebly back at her.

Lowering the glasses, she caught Drusilla's eye. "I might have to go along with this nonsense if only to see how far those two are willing to go in order to retain my cooperation."

"That's a wonderful idea, and while you're catering to Zayne and his nonexistent illness, I'll start looking for Willie."

"Forgive me, Drusilla, but you're hardly qualified to search the slums for a man."

"You'd be surprised by what I'm qualified to do."

Before Agatha had an opportunity to respond to that telling, yet slightly confusing, statement, someone called out her name.

Turning, she found none other than Mr. Hamilton Beckett, Zayne's older brother, striding through the crowd toward her, a welcoming smile on his handsome face. Passing Matilda's leash over to Drusilla, Agatha hurried to meet him. "Hamilton, this is a delightful surprise."

Hamilton grinned right before he swept her into a strong embrace, lifted her off her feet, gave her a good squeeze, and finally returned her to the ground. "I don't know why you'd be surprised to see me, Agatha. I knew to the minute when the train was due, and I wasn't going to miss the opportunity of welcoming you and my brother back to New York." He looked over her shoulder. "Where's Zayne?"

"He'll be along soon. He's plotting, er, talking with Mr. Blackheart at the moment."

Hamilton moved a little closer to her. "Since he's not here yet, tell me, how is he?"

Agatha bit her lip. "He's . . . different."

"Because of his leg?"

"While his leg is certainly damaged, it's more his spirit I was referring to."

"That's what I've been afraid of, but I do hope you realize how grateful I am, along with the rest of my family, for your having convinced Zayne to come home. You've done us a great service, although"—he narrowed his eyes—"you must know you've put yourself in danger by bringing him back to us."

Waving his concern away, Agatha smiled. "I was getting tired of traveling, so I would have come home soon even if I hadn't run into Zayne. And, just so you know, I didn't really convince Zayne to come home. It was a case of my blowing up his reason for being in Colorado that prompted his return to the city."

"You blew something up?"

"With dynamite," Drusilla added as she joined them, tugging an obviously reluctant Matilda beside her. She handed the leash to Agatha. "It's good to see you, Hamilton."

Hamilton smiled at Drusilla, but his smile dimmed when he glanced down. "Is that a pig?"

Matilda let out a grunt right before she disappeared under Agatha's skirt. Lifting her head, Agatha grinned. "She is a P-I-G, but she's sensitive about that word, so you probably should stick to calling her Matilda."

"And you have this Matilda because . . . ?" Hamilton pressed.

"It's a long story," Agatha admitted.

Hamilton considered her for a second, and then his eyes widened as he turned to Drusilla. "Did you say something about dynamite?"

"I'm afraid I did, and I'm afraid dynamite ignited by our very own Agatha was what put a rapid end to your brother's mining venture." Drusilla smiled. "Although, to be fair, it was an accident, because she certainly didn't intend to blow up that mine with all of us in it."

Hamilton looked from Drusilla, to Agatha, and then back to Drusilla again. "You let her near dynamite?"

Drusilla narrowed her eyes. "If you'll recall, I was hired to provide her with extra protection, but protecting her from dynamite was never part of the . . ." Her voice trailed off, she sent Agatha a guilty look, and then promptly gestured to a lady wearing an extraordinarily large hat. "My goodness, would you look at that. I have to wonder if we've missed some new fashion trend while we traveled around the West. And if that's the case, I'm going—"

"What do you mean, you were hired to provide me with extra protection?" Agatha interrupted. "I was under the impression you were simply my paid companion."

Drusilla stopped watching the hat lady and frowned at Agatha. "There's nothing simple about being your companion, Agatha."

Hamilton cleared his throat. "Forgive me, Drusilla, if I've allowed something to slip, but I simply can't believe you never got around to telling her."

"I didn't think she'd take it well," Drusilla reluctantly admitted.

"Take what well?" Agatha demanded.

"Yes, take what well?" Mr. Blackheart asked as he stopped right beside her, handing Zayne his cane before he turned and glared at Drusilla.

All thoughts of questioning Drusilla further about her obvious duplicity slipped right out of Agatha's mind as she got a good look at Zayne. His face, refreshingly devoid of hair, thereby bringing attention to his classic features, was now drenched, as if Mr. Blackheart had stumbled upon a basin of water and had dumped that water directly over Zayne's head. Zayne was trying, not very successfully, to pretend he wasn't sopping wet, while Mr. Blackheart had apparently forgotten all about Zayne as he glared rather menacingly at Drusilla.

"What didn't you get around to telling Miss Watson?" Mr. Blackheart demanded.

"I don't care for your tone of voice, Mr. Blackheart," Drusilla said with a sniff. "And . . . you're disrupting what is certain to be a very touching reunion between Hamilton and Zayne." She stepped aside and waved a hand at the two brothers. "Well, get on with it."

Reluctant admiration over the gumption of her companion had Agatha's annoyance with the woman disappearing in a flash. She, having all too often found herself in the middle of the frying pan, had frequently employed such diversion tactics, and—

"Why are you all wet?" Hamilton asked, pulling Agatha abruptly from her thoughts.

A rather pained expression crossed Zayne's face as he sent a furtive look to Mr. Blackheart, who completely missed the look since that man was still glaring at Drusilla. Zayne swiped a hand over his face and winced. "Ah, well, I'm perspiring." He glanced over at her, then back at Hamilton, and then . . . he wiggled his brow.

Hamilton's eyes narrowed for just a second before he spun around but not fast enough for Agatha to miss the grin on his face.

Hamilton and Zayne had always shared an incredibly close bond, one that, apparently, was still intact even given the amount of time they'd been apart.

The last vestiges of the concern she'd had regarding coercing Zayne back to the city melted away.

It didn't matter if someone was still out there, intending to do her harm. Mr. Blackheart, along with Drusilla, by the sound of it, would work diligently to see her kept safe. What mattered was Zayne was back where he belonged, and once he was surrounded by his family, his healing really would begin.

Hamilton finally turned back, his grin firmly under control, and took a step closer to Zayne. He paused, looking as if he didn't really know what to do next. To Agatha's surprise, Zayne moved forward and threw his arms around his brother, hugging Hamilton tightly to him for a long moment before he stepped back and smiled. "Sorry."

It was so like a gentleman to sum up the whole of his transgressions with one simple word.

"There's no need for you to apologize, Zayne," Hamilton said, his voice gruff. "I'm simply glad you've come to your senses and returned home. We've missed you."

"I should have kept in better contact."

"Yes, you should have, although we did appreciate your monthly telegrams, but again, you've decided to come home, and that's what matters."

"Agatha didn't give me a choice," Zayne said.

Hamilton smiled. "So I've been told, but you really should have known better than to allow her in the vicinity of dynamite."

Not particularly wanting to delve into the whole dynamite fiasco again, Agatha tugged Matilda out from under her skirt and looked around. "Where's everyone else?"

"In the interest of your safety, we decided it would be best not to have a crowd waiting here to greet you," Hamilton said. "Your mother is waiting for you at your home, along with my mother. My father was called out of town just yesterday, so he won't be around for a few weeks. But he did want me to make certain to welcome both of you back and to mention that he'd appreciate it if both of you would remain in town for the foreseeable future."

"I've always found your father to be absolutely delightful," Agatha said, "but since my mother and yours are apparently together at the moment, we really shouldn't leave them that way long. Who knows what mischief they might get into."

Hamilton grinned, looked at her, then Zayne, and shook his head. "I'm afraid they've already taken to plotting. They haven't had an opportunity to do any matchmaking since Felicia got married two years ago."

Eyes widening, Agatha prodded Matilda forward. "There's no time to waste."

Making her way through the station, Agatha continued chatting with Hamilton while Matilda pranced beside her, letting out squeals of excitement every other minute.

"You do know you're drawing a lot of attention with your Matilda, don't you?" Hamilton asked as they reached the exit and he held open the door for her.

"I didn't really think about the attention we'd garner, but yes, I've seen the looks," Agatha admitted, stepping out into a blustery wind. "It's a good thing no one knew I was coming back to the city besides the family."

"Don't be too sure about that," Mr. Blackheart said, taking

her arm as he joined her. "Motivated people are dangerous, so now that we're back in the city, you're going to have to be careful. And speaking of being careful, poor Zayne is not at his best at the moment, and *someone* is going to have to watch over him."

It took everything she had to keep from rolling her eyes. "Then it's fortunate we've returned to the city where his mother resides. Knowing Gloria, she'll pull up a chair and hand-feed the poor man soup while he struggles to recover from whatever's plaguing him. But . . . speaking of Zayne, where is he?"

"He claimed to need a bit of a rest," Drusilla said, strolling up to Agatha's side. "He'll be along soon I'm sure, once he figures out what's exactly wrong with him, and what symptoms he's supposed to be displaying at the moment." She smiled. "Shall we go get the carriage and have it ready to pick him up right at the entrance when he finally decides to leave the station?"

"That sounds like a wonderful idea, but Miss Watson needs to stay put in order to keep Matilda out of all the traffic," Mr. Blackheart said. "I'll come with you, Drusilla, because I've been dying to chat with you, and what better time than right now, as we go to fetch the carriage?"

"While that does sound like a splendid idea, Mr. Blackheart, I would think, given that your main purpose in life these days is to keep dear Agatha alive, that your time would be better spent looking out for her than trying to discern the extent of my secrets."

"So you do have secrets?"

"Ah, would you look at that, here comes my carriage," Hamilton said rather loudly, speaking over Drusilla and Mr. Blackheart, who'd begun to argue. "My coachman must have seen us and took matters into his own hands." He turned to

Agatha as the carriage pulled to a stop right in front of them. "May I help you inside?"

"Since my bodyguard and my . . . well, whatever Drusilla actually is, don't seem to be paying the least bit of attention to me, I would be grateful for a hand up, and even more grateful if you'd somehow get Matilda in the carriage. She doesn't really like confined spaces."

Three minutes later, Agatha was sitting on the seat, Matilda lying on top of her feet, while Hamilton sat on the opposite side of the carriage, nursing the bloody lip he'd gotten when Matilda had turned feisty and caused him to fall face-first into the carriage. Drusilla fished in her ever-present satchel, pulled out a handkerchief, and gave it to Hamilton, while Mr. Blackheart continued to glare at Drusilla without speaking, even as Drusilla pretended not to notice his glare.

"I wonder if someone should go check on Zayne?" Agatha asked, breaking the silence that surrounded them.

"I'll go," Mr. Blackheart said with a grunt, disappearing out the carriage door a second later.

"Well, this is pleasant," Drusilla remarked.

Agatha rolled her eyes. "You're deliberately avoiding Mr. Blackheart's questions, but I'm beginning to lose patience with you as well, so you really do need to start talking."

Drusilla smiled, turned to Hamilton, and asked, "How is your darling sister doing these days?"

Hamilton smiled back at her around the handkerchief he still had pressed to his lip and ignored Agatha's huff of frustration. "Arabella is well, thank you for asking. Are you aware she's expecting?"

"Why, I had no idea," Drusilla returned with a bat of her lashes. "Theodore neglected to mention anything at all about that in his many telegrams."

"Arabella probably wanted to tell you in person, although once you see her, her condition will be obvious, since she's huge. . . . But don't tell her I said that. She's a little emotional at the moment."

"This was *not* what I meant when I said I wanted Drusilla to start talking," Agatha began, but stopped in mid-rant. "Arabella's expecting?"

"Indeed she is," Hamilton said with a smile before he glanced out the window and frowned. "Is it my imagination or does it seem like it's taking Mr. Blackheart forever to fetch Zayne?"

"I, for one, am enjoying Mr. Blackheart's absence," Drusilla said.

"I'm sure you are." Hamilton reached for the door. "I'll be right back." He stepped from the carriage and began walking toward the train station.

Agatha watched him go. "You don't think something happened, do you?"

"Zayne and Mr. Blackheart are probably just putting some finishing touches on their plan."

"Perhaps, but I should go check on them." Agatha scooted forward on the seat but paused when Drusilla took hold of her arm.

"You need to remember that you can't dash about the city unescorted."

"I doubt I'll be in much danger simply by walking back into the . . ." Her voice trailed off when she looked out the window and saw Zayne being held up by Mr. Blackheart and Hamilton, his cane nowhere in sight, trying to make it down the small flight of steps leading out of the station. She knew without a doubt that the grimace on his face was genuine, and concern had her leaping from the carriage and rushing toward him.

"What happened?" she demanded.

"He fell," Hamilton said.

"I'm fine," Zayne countered. "I tripped over a piece of luggage, but again, I'm fine."

Sweat, this time genuine, rolled down his face, and his color was paler than it'd been before. Agatha moved closer to him. "You don't look fine, Zayne. Is it your bad leg?"

Without bothering to answer her, Zayne allowed Hamilton and Mr. Blackheart to get him down the steps and into the carriage as Agatha stayed right behind him. She felt tears sting her eyes when a telltale moan escaped Zayne's lips when his leg smacked against the side of the seat, right before he fell back against it and closed his eyes. She hurried in and settled down on the seat beside him.

"Is there anything I can do for you?" she whispered.

"Stop hovering."

Folding her hands into her lap so she wouldn't feel the urge to pat him on the arm—because Zayne would certainly take that as hovering—Agatha kept her lips pressed tightly together and watched as Hamilton, followed by Mr. Blackheart, climbed into the carriage and took their seats. An uncomfortable silence settled over the interior as the carriage lurched into motion.

"Would you like us to take you to the doctor?" Hamilton finally asked.

"I don't need a doctor."

"I beg to differ, Zayne. You're clearly in pain, and we should get that leg checked out."

Opening his eyes, Zayne glared at his brother. "There's nothing any doctor can do for this leg, Hamilton, so just leave it alone."

A flash of heat flickered through Hamilton's eyes, but then

he shrugged. "Very well, but we're not going to linger at Agatha's house. We'll fetch Mother and take you straight back to her house to get you settled."

"Fine," was all Zayne said before he closed his eyes again and began rubbing his leg.

Wanting to break some of the tension that now seeped through the carriage, Agatha summoned a smile and nodded to Hamilton. "You were telling me about how Arabella's expecting soon. I imagine Theodore's thrilled he's about to become a father, and—"

"Arabella's going to have a baby?" Zayne interrupted as his eyes flashed open and he scowled at Hamilton.

Hamilton smiled. "I'm delighted to admit she is."

"And why wasn't I informed about that?"

"Ah, well, we didn't want to burden you with family news unless it was news of an urgent sort, and you were crystal clear in your telegrams that you wanted to be left alone."

"Arabella expecting a baby is urgent news," Zayne said, his voice holding a trace of irritation. "And the fact I wanted to be left alone didn't mean I wanted to sever all ties with the family." Color began to seep back into his face. "What else wasn't I told?"

Hamilton considered his brother for a moment. "Quite a bit, but I suppose the information that's going to annoy you the most is that Eliza and I have a new daughter. Her name is Viola—and before you ask, I didn't send you a telegram telling you of her birth because I didn't want guilt to be the reason you returned home."

Instead of turning the anger that was now evident in his eyes on Hamilton, Zayne directed it straight at Agatha. "This is exactly why I didn't want to come home."

"I'm afraid I'm not following you."

"I'm going to be smothered with coddling."

"Families are supposed to coddle, Zayne," she said slowly.

"And pitied," he added with a grunt of clear disgust.

Agatha bit her lip as understanding settled in. Here it was—the real reason Zayne had distanced himself from the people he loved.

He detested the very thought of anyone pitying him, would apparently rather stay by himself than experience it. But . . . what in the world was she supposed to do with this newly discovered knowledge?

She'd known he was damaged but hadn't realized the extent of his emotional distress. Here she'd blithely decided she was going to help him recover his former self without even considering how extremely difficult the task she'd set for herself was going to be.

Closing her eyes, she turned to God, hoping He would be able to send her the assistance she so desperately needed. She prayed for guidance and then prayed for healing for Zayne. When she was done, she opened her eyes and found Zayne watching her.

"What?"

Some of the temper left his eyes. "I forgot you make a habit of doing that."

"Praying?"

He nodded.

"You used to make a habit of it as well, but—"

"I don't need a lecture, Agatha."

Snapping her mouth shut, Agatha turned toward the window and ignored the fact another silence had descended over them. Finally, after what felt like forever, the carriage began to slow, and Agatha felt a sharp sense of relief when she caught sight of her home. Four stories of a white stone façade rose up to greet her gaze, and if she wasn't much mistaken, one of the curtains on the second floor gave a telling twitch, as if her mother had been watching for her arrival.

As soon as the carriage came to a stop, she wrenched open the door and jumped out, not bothering to wait for the groom. "I'll go get Gloria for you," she said with a nod to Zayne as she reached back into the carriage to fetch Matilda, who was trying to hide under Drusilla's skirt.

"I'll walk you to the door," Zayne said.

Struggling to pull Matilda out of her hiding spot, she lifted her head. "Don't be ridiculous."

"Don't *you* be ridiculous," he countered. "I haven't seen your mother for over two years. She'll find it rude if I don't pay her proper respect."

"I'm sure she'll understand, given the condition you're . . ."

"I'm coming with you." Zayne pushed off from the seat and hovered at the carriage door, forcing her to abandon her attempt to fetch Matilda and move aside. He stepped to the ground, wobbled for a moment, and nodded. The odd thought sprang to mind that she should have asked God for a huge dose of patience while she'd been praying.

Making a silent vow to pray for that later, she held out her arm, which Zayne surprisingly enough took. They made it all of three feet before Matilda let out a high-pitched squeal, launched herself from the carriage, and began running directly toward the middle of the busy street.

"Matilda, stop!" Agatha yelled, dropping her hold on Zayne as she ran after her pig.

The traffic on Fifth Avenue seemed to confuse Matilda and caused her to dash around in clear panic. Continuing to call for her little pet in what she hoped was a soothing tone, although, even to her ears it sounded frantic, Agatha dashed around the carriages. Most of them pulled off to the side as she waved her hands to draw their attention.

"Agatha, look out!" Zayne yelled.

Looking up, Agatha froze on the spot when she caught sight of a carriage barreling her way. She began waving her arms again, but to her horror, the coachman didn't seem to see her, perhaps because his hat was pulled low over his face. For a split second, she thought the man had lost control of the carriage, but then he turned the horses ever so slightly and sent them directly at her.

A hard shove had her flying through the air and falling to the ground, rolling instinctively away from the wheels that missed her by inches. Mr. Blackheart's face suddenly came into focus as he bent over her, but then a loud scream split the air, sending chills down her spine.

Mr. Blackheart jumped to his feet, and she did the same a second later. Sheer horror caused a scream of her own to erupt out of her mouth when she caught sight of Zayne's body lying motionless on the ground.

7

Floating through a pool of darkness, Zayne smiled, enjoying the quiet—and the fact that for the first time in forever, his leg wasn't causing him pain. His body was cushioned against something that felt remarkably like a soft cloud, but then panic stole the very breath from him when he tried to shift his position and realized he couldn't move.

Forcing his eyes open, he winced when light blinded him for a moment, and then a room swam into focus.

It was a nice room, decorated in a masculine style, but . . . nothing looked familiar. Not the dark blue canopy draped over his head or the painting of a battle scene over the marble fireplace, or . . . the bearded man sitting in a chair by that fireplace reading a book.

His eyes snapped shut as his jumbled thoughts rolled around in his mind.

Where was he, and what had happened to him?

An image of an out-of-control carriage flashed beneath his lids.

Frowning, he concentrated on that carriage. It had been

in front of Agatha's house, but she'd been right in the path of it, and . . . His eyes flashed open. "Agatha."

"Yes?"

His attention darted to the bearded man setting aside his book as he got to his feet, but . . . he was wearing a dress and sounded remarkably like Agatha.

It was a very strange sight to see.

"Who are you?" he rasped out of a mouth that felt as if it were filled with cotton.

The gentleman reached the bed and peered down at him. "I'm Agatha, of course." Then he reached out a hand and smoothed it over Zayne's forehead, a hand that seemed entirely too soft to belong to a man. "How are you feeling?"

"Peculiar."

The gentleman smiled. "I'm not surprised, given all the medicine you've been given to keep you sedated over the past few days."

"Does that medicine make me hallucinate?"

"I'm not sure, but it might. Why do you ask?"

"Because you sound just like Agatha, but . . . you have a beard."

A delightful peal of laughter rang out. "Good heavens, Zayne, I do beg your pardon. I completely forgot I was experimenting with whiskers earlier. It's no wonder you're confused, what with waking up and seeing a bearded lady first thing."

From any other woman, that statement might have seemed somewhat unusual, but coming from Agatha, well, it was perfectly normal. "And why are you experimenting with whiskers?"

Agatha gave an airy wave of her hand. "Oh, just passing the time. I ran out of good books until Arabella stopped by a while ago and stocked me up on some romances, even though

I will admit they're really not my cup of tea." She smiled, the action causing her whiskers to twitch, but he couldn't help but notice that the smile didn't quite reach her eyes. "But speaking of tea, I'm sure you'd love a cup right about now."

She turned and began walking to the door, looking back at him over her shoulder. "I'll be right back. I'll order you some tea and toast, but more importantly, I need to tell your mother you're awake. She's been dying to talk to you." With that, Agatha hurried out of the room, leaving him with the distinct smell of violets in his nose but without any answers to the millions of questions he had.

Shaking his head to clear the slight fuzziness that lingered in his brain, a result no doubt of the medicine Agatha had said he'd been given, he glanced around the room again. Relief had his lips curling when he finally realized he was lying in his boyhood room, although it looked nothing at all like how he'd kept it when he'd lived under his mother's roof.

Gone were the collections of dead bugs he'd kept on a shelf, as were the pictures he'd drawn of horses, replaced with obviously priceless works of art, none of which he thought possessed the charm of his horrible attempts at sketching, but . . . he was sure his mother probably had those sketches in a memory book somewhere.

She'd always been sentimental about things like that.

A distinct feeling of guilt began to gnaw at him.

He'd been careless with his mother, with his entire family, now that he thought about it, but—

"Zayne, my darling boy, you've come back to me."

The sound of heels tapping rapidly against the floor came to him first, and then his mother was leaning down and smothering his face with kisses, just as she'd done when he'd been all of five years old and had skinned a knee.

He felt the old desire to protest, just like he'd always done when he was five, but then he remembered the grief he'd caused her over the past year and, instead of resisting her mothering, allowed himself to relish it. She finally pulled back and swiped a hand over eyes dripping with tears.

An ache settled in his heart at that sight.

"You've scared a good few years off my life, young man," Gloria said in a wobbly voice.

"I'm sorry about that, Mother."

She brushed his apology aside. "There's nothing for you to be sorry about, darling. It's not like it was your fault that carriage almost ran you over, and Agatha as well."

"So I was run over by a carriage?"

"Almost."

He glanced past his mother and found Agatha standing by the foot of the bed, evidently unconcerned that she still had a reddish beard attached to her face. His lips curved into a smile as he looked her over. Her delicate face was almost completely covered by the beard, and if he wasn't much mistaken, she'd added mutton chops as well, but they weren't in the right place, since they covered her ears. Her hair was gathered in a messy knot on top of her head, numerous tendrils of it sticking out all over the place, their distinct blackness at complete odds with the red of the beard. A lovely yellow dress trimmed in purple only added to her strange appearance.

"I ordered you some tea and toast, and a maid promised to deliver it shortly," she said, moving to stand by his head. She smiled down at him, her whiskers twitching again. "Would you like me to help you sit up? It might be hard to drink tea in that position, and . . . why are you looking at me like that?"

"I can't seem to help myself. Your whiskers are somewhat distracting."

"Oh dear, I forgot all about them." She began peeling the hair off her face, wincing every other second. She walked over to a large and battered black case, dropped the whiskers into it, and firmly shut the lid before she turned. "Better?"

"Your face is quite red now, but yes."

"At least I didn't use much adhesive. Do you remember the time when I couldn't get my whiskers off after our jaunt to the opium den?"

"I seem to recall you broke out in hives after the remedy you were forced to use to get them off didn't work out as planned."

Agatha grinned. "That was a nightmare, especially since I had to go to your going-away ball covered in unsightly bumps when I wanted so much to look nice for . . ." Eyes widening, she snapped her mouth shut and began inspecting the sleeve of her gown. "Well, now is hardly the moment to dig up ancient memories. We need to get you settled, give you some tea, and I'm sure you have questions, especially about your leg."

He'd forgotten all about his leg, what with all the whiskers, memories, and Agatha looking somewhat adorable at the moment, something he didn't want to notice but didn't seem to have any control over.

The scent of violets tickled his nose again, pulling him back to the situation at hand as Agatha put her arms around him and, in a surprisingly strong move, hauled him upright before she plumped up a pillow behind him. "There, that should be more comfortable. Are you ready to hear about your leg?"

He tried to move the limb in question but found it impossible because something heavy seemed to be weighing it down. Swallowing, he nodded. "How bad is it?"

She took hold of the blanket covering him, and when he realized she was about to yank it off, he grabbed her arm.

"Maybe you should leave the room and I'll do this with my mother."

Agatha rolled her eyes. "Really, Zayne, do you think I'd strip this sheet from you if you weren't decently clothed, especially with your mother standing right next to me?"

Sometimes it was downright eerie how she seemed able to read his mind.

"Good point," he muttered, shooting a glance to his mother, who was grinning back at him. He caught Agatha's eye. "But out of sheer curiosity, would you have pulled down that sheet if I wasn't decent and my mother *wasn't* here?"

A snort slipped out of Agatha's mouth even as she rolled her eyes again. "Don't be ridiculous, and . . . you're stalling."

Taking a deep breath, he slowly released it and braced himself as Agatha pulled back the covers. He forced his attention downward and frowned. He was wearing a pair of large trousers with one of the legs cut off, probably to accommodate the huge something or other that seemed to be wrapped around his leg—a something that was the size of a large log. "What is that, and . . . is my leg still in there?"

Gloria stepped closer to him and patted his cheek. "Of course your leg is still there, darling, and that's simply a cast, albeit an unusually large one. Dr. Gessler wanted to be certain your leg would be held perfectly still, especially when you kept thrashing around the first day after the accident."

Zayne's tongue passed over lips that had suddenly gone bone dry. "But . . . what's wrong with it?"

Agatha pulled up a chair, took a seat and gestured Gloria into the chair right beside her. Apprehension stole over him when both ladies began beaming back at him, their actions causing sweat to bead his forehead.

"How bad am I?"

"Well, I'm sure you've been better," Agatha began. "Especially since Dr. Gessler's been feeding you laudanum to keep you sedated. I've heard that can make a person queasy."

"I'm not queasy, and you're not telling me something. What happened to my leg?"

"It didn't get run over by a carriage, if that's your concern."

He looked Agatha up and down. "You don't look like you got run over either."

"Mr. Blackheart pushed me out of the way, but you, my foolish friend, should never have tried to come after me, not given the poor condition of your leg. If Drusilla hadn't leaped out of the carriage and shoved *you* out of the way, you'd be dead right now."

Agatha's eyes turned suspiciously bright, but then she blinked and squared her shoulders. "And speaking of Drusilla, you're going to have to make certain she knows you don't hold her responsible for the condition of your leg. She saved your life, but in the process you fell and . . . rebroke your leg."

"Drusilla broke my leg?"

"Drusilla saved your life."

"I'll never walk again, will I."

Agatha sat forward, reached out and stroked his arm. "Here's the good news."

"I'm alive?"

"No, we've already covered that. The good news is that, according to Dr. Gessler, your leg broke in exactly the same place it broke before, and because you were under the care of an incredibly proficient doctor this time, your leg has been reset . . . perfectly." Agatha smiled at him. "Dr. Gessler believes you're going to make a complete recovery. He doesn't even think you'll suffer any recurring pain except for, perhaps, an occasional ache when it rains."

Zayne could only stare at Agatha, not really comprehending what she'd just said.

"I don't think I fully understand. . . ."

"You're going to be fine," Gloria said right before fresh tears began flowing freely down her cheeks. "I've been beside myself ever since you had your accident, been praying to God for a miracle, and He finally gave me one—you, back home and with a happy and healthy future waiting for you." She sniffed and turned to Agatha. "You were instrumental in helping this miracle along, my darling, darling girl. You got Zayne home. What with the dynamite and all, it was a rather odd way to go about it, but . . . I'll be forever in your debt."

Agatha muttered something under her breath, and Zayne noticed that she was not looking pleased by what his mother had said but disturbed. She opened her mouth, but a maid walked into the room, pushing a cart. Whatever Agatha had been about to say was lost when his mother got up, helped the maid with the tea, and then sat with him as he drank it and ate some toast.

His mother kept traveling back to the topic of God and how He'd answered her prayers, but strangely enough, even though Zayne had pushed God firmly away from him over the past year, his mother's words didn't bother him in the least.

He'd been so angry with God for allowing his accident in the first place, but now he was on his way to recovering and he couldn't imagine that God *hadn't* had anything to do with that. Why, in all likelihood, God might just have led Agatha to him and—

"Well, I must be off," Gloria said, drawing him out of his thoughts.

"You're leaving me?" he asked.

"Not for long, dear, but I feel the distinct urge to go to

church. After God has blessed me by getting you home and keeping you alive, well, I need to give thanks and . . . a large donation." Gloria nodded to Agatha. "You'll stay with him?"

"Of course."

For some reason, Agatha was suddenly looking somewhat anxious. He cleared his throat. "If you need to get home, Agatha, I'll be fine on my own. I'll probably just take a nap."

"I'm not staying at my home at the moment. I'm staying here."

Something unexpected and warm began to flow through him. "While I truly appreciate you looking out for me while I've been unconscious, I'm fine now, or I will be soon. There's no need for you to continue staying here."

"I'm under strict orders from Mr. Blackheart and Theodore not to leave."

"And the reasoning behind those orders would be . . . ?"

"Someone's already tried to kill her, of course," Gloria answered before Agatha could.

His mouth dropped open. "The carriage?"

Agatha nodded glumly. "I saw the driver steer those horses right at me, as did Mr. Blackheart."

"But we'd only just arrived in the city."

"True, but apparently someone learned of my arrival, and that someone still wants me dead." Agatha blew out a breath. "That's why I'm stuck here, er . . ." She sent him a small smile. "Well, not stuck here exactly, since I really did want to watch over you."

"And it's a good thing you've finally woken up, Zayne," Gloria added as she bent and kissed his cheek before straightening. "It's very important that Agatha stay hidden, but you and I know perfectly well she's not exactly the type to remain idle. Since you're no longer unconscious, which is due to the fact Dr. Gessler took you off your sedative last night, you'll be able to entertain her and make sure she stays in the house."

"I might still be too weak to perform that daunting task," Zayne argued. "Especially since she's already brought out whiskers, which means she's—"

"Which means nothing," Agatha interrupted before she nodded to Gloria. "Go. I'll keep him company."

"Thank you, dear," Gloria said as she made her way for the door, turning around once she reached it. She smiled a misty smile and let out another sniff. "It is so good to have you home, Zayne, and . . ." She nodded to Agatha. "I am truly thankful God sent you into our lives, my lovely girl. Why, without you, I wouldn't have my son back, and I . . ." Gloria suddenly seemed too choked up to speak, and with a wave of her hand, she quit the room, the distinctive sound of additional sniffs trailing after her.

Zayne swallowed past the large lump that had formed in his throat and summoned up a smile. "I think she's happy to have both of us back."

Agatha muttered something once again under her breath before she rose and began cleaning up the tea and toast.

"Agatha, what's the matter?"

She put the teacup on the cart before she resumed her seat and folded her hands in her lap. "Nothing, everything's fine."

He considered her for a moment, taking in blue eyes that were suspiciously wet before she dropped her head and clenched her hands into fists. It hit him then, how very dear she was to him, even though she annoyed him on a remarkably frequent basis. They'd been the best of friends before he'd left to join Helena, and the idea that something was distressing her bothered him more than he could say. Agatha was a lady who rarely kept her thoughts to herself, but at the moment she was being unusually guarded.

Clearing his throat, he struggled for something to say, something that would put a smile on her face. "I have to tell you that my mother was right about it being a fortunate day when you came into our lives," he began, sucking in a sharp breath when her head shot up and a single tear trailed down her cheek.

Alarm was immediate. He'd rarely seen Agatha cry, and he couldn't for the life of him figure out what was causing her to do so now. He leaned toward her. "Agatha, what in the world is wrong?"

Blinking furiously, Agatha opened her mouth, but instead of words coming out, she released a strangled sob right before she buried her head in her hands and began to cry in earnest.

Helena had cried at the drop of a hat, and he'd always known exactly how to soothe her, but this was Agatha, and he had no idea what to do, say, or anything. He looked up when he heard something by the door and caught his mother's appalled gaze. When he opened his mouth to summon her in to help him sort matters out, she placed a finger over her lips, shook her head, and closed the door, leaving him completely alone with Agatha, who was sobbing harder than ever.

It seemed a somewhat peculiar thing for his mother to do.

Realizing he was completely on his own, he swallowed past another pesky lump in his throat. "Are you upset because you don't like people telling you they appreciate you?"

Additional sobs were her only response to that question. He tried again. "You must realize that you've done me a huge favor by getting me home, even if I was somewhat surly about it at the time."

Her head lifted, and with tears pouring down her cheeks,

she shuddered and her eyes looked a little wild. "I didn't do you a favor, Zayne. I almost got you killed. I'm a menace—a menace, I say—and . . . and . . . and . . . you should never forgive me for trying to save you." She shuddered again. "When I saw your body lying there in the street, I thought you were . . . *dead*." Covering her face with her hands, she began sobbing again, the sobs only stopping when she'd gulp in a breath of air every few seconds.

He sat frozen on the bed, watching her cry as if her heart were breaking. His heart, or rather the armor he'd carefully wrapped around it, suddenly cracked, and pain pulsed through his veins. Agatha was infuriating at times, and yes, occasionally she was a menace, but she was the kindest lady he knew and generous to a fault. He couldn't sit by and watch her drown in guilt over something that she shouldn't be feeling guilty about in the first place.

"I knew you'd decided to try and save me, even though I told you I didn't want your assistance," he said softly.

"I wasn't exactly subtle about it," she mumbled through her hands.

"You weren't wrong to try."

The hands fell away, revealing a wet and splotchy face. Agatha was not a lady who cried daintily, and when she let out a watery snort, he pulled at the sheet covering him and held out a corner. "You might want to use this to blow your nose."

Swiping at her nose with her sleeve, she frowned. "I can't use that. We'd have to change the sheets then, and since you're really heavy with that cast on, changing your sheets is not an easy task. Believe me, I've done it."

"You changed my sheets?"

"I've had a lot of time on my hands while you've been sleeping."

Relief settled over him when he realized she'd stopped crying. He snatched up the napkin he'd been using while he ate his toast and held it up. Agatha eyed it for a moment, got up from the chair, and moved to take it. He patted the bed. "Why don't you sit beside me for a moment?"

"You shouldn't even want me in the same room with you, let alone right next to you."

They evidently hadn't moved past her distress. "Come on, Agatha, sit down. I need someone to hold my hand."

"I almost got you killed and you want me to hold your hand?"

"You and I have gotten into too many scrapes to count, that almost saw both of us killed. Why you're allowing this latest incident to bother you so much is beyond me."

To his surprise, she perched on the bed and even allowed him to take her hand. "I thought I really *had* killed you this time, and even though it might seem as if I disregard your life all too often, especially with that dynamite business, well, I never really wanted you dead."

He squeezed her hand. "That's very comforting to know."

"Stop making light of this. I'm a horrible person. I meddle in everything, do so because I always think I know best, but I'm done with that for good."

She sniffed and blew her nose into the napkin, causing one side of his lip to curl when it suddenly became clear that, not only didn't Agatha cry in a dainty fashion, she certainly didn't blow her nose that way either.

"You meddle because you're usually right."

She waved the napkin in the air. "Stop humoring me. I've caused you to suffer tremendous pain. I've sat here day after day while you've moaned in your sleep."

"I don't remember being in pain."

"Well, you were, and that's what matters."

"My leg is going to be better now."

"You told me back in Colorado that you weren't keen to experience the agony of breaking your leg again, but since I dragged you back here, that's exactly what happened." A loud hiccup escaped her mouth.

She was pathetic and adorable, and he couldn't bear to see her in so much distress. "I feel great now."

Arching a brow, she took a moment to blow her nose again. "That's just because you're still under the effects of that medicine. You're going to be stuck in that bed for days, and then you'll be in a cast until Christmas."

"But after that I'll be able to walk, and probably without pain."

"You don't like to be stuck in bed."

"It won't be so bad, and since you're stuck in the house as well, you can keep me company."

"Stop being so nice to me." Fresh tears leaked out of her eyes.

Stifling the urge to laugh, Zayne tilted his head. "Your face gets really blotchy when you cry, and when you blow your nose, you sound like a duck."

"What?"

"You told me to stop being nice to you, but that's the best I can come up with on such short notice."

The tears stopped in an instant as Agatha raised the napkin and blew her nose again, lowering it a moment later. "You're very strange sometimes."

"True, and it seems I'm mistaken sometimes as well. You sound more like a goose than a duck when you blow your nose."

The faintest hint of a grin flickered over Agatha's face. "You really don't have to be nice to me. It's my fault you're lying in that bed. If I'd simply left you back in Colorado, you'd—"

"I'd be digging in the dirt every day, by myself, without your charming company, and I wouldn't be facing an optimistic future." He smiled. "Besides, I like being nice to you occasionally. It makes for a pleasant change of pace."

"You really are still under the effects of that medicine, aren't you?"

Prying the napkin out of her hand, Zayne wiped the last of her tears away and smiled. "I can be nice when I set my mind to it."

"You should hate me right about now."

"We're not discussing this further, and if you keep arguing with me, you're bound to distress me, and I'll have to tell Dr. Gessler, and then you'll be in trouble."

Giving another watery snort, Agatha got off the bed and returned to her chair. "Dr. Gessler really is very hopeful about your leg."

"Which pleases me to no end, but enough about me and my leg. Tell me more about this person who almost killed both of us."

To his relief, that had Agatha squaring her shoulders and color returning to her cheeks. "I don't know anything. Mr. Blackheart has gone undercover, per Theodore's request, and is even now trolling around the slums searching for information. No one on the street at the time of the attack could identify the driver, and no one saw where the carriage went after it almost ran us over. Theodore thinks it was a well-laid-out plan to kill me, even though it wasn't quite successful, since I'm still alive."

Zayne frowned. "What happened to Matilda? I remember the reason you ran into the street was to fetch her."

"She's fine, but she's staying with my mother at the moment. Gloria made the huge mistake of serving ham the other day, and Matilda was inconsolable. When she kept trying to escape the house through any open door, my mother finally offered to take her back to her house."

"You're giving up a lot to stay here with me, aren't you?"

Her red eyes widened. "Of course not. As I've said numerous times, it's my fault you're laid up, and if you really don't mind my company, I'll be more than happy to stay with you while you're awake and help you pass the time."

He refused to groan. "What do you mean, *while I'm awake*?"

"Did I say that?"

"Agatha . . . ?"

His eyes narrowed as she sent an all too obvious glance to the black box containing her whiskers and then looked back at him right before she began batting her wet lashes at him.

"Out with it," he demanded.

"Out with what?"

"If you don't tell me, I'll have Mother summon Theodore, and then I'll tell him you're up to something, *and* I'll have her summon Mr. Blackheart as well."

"I wasn't planning on trying to find who wants to kill me," she said in a small voice.

"But?"

"I just thought, given that I know I'll go crazy if I have to stay inside too long, that I would don a disguise and see if I could run Willie down."

"Have you lost your mind?"

"Well, no, not yet, but again that is a distinct possibility if I'm stuck away here for too much longer." She smiled. "I was planning on taking Drusilla with me, and . . . Did I mention the little fact that Drusilla isn't just a paid companion? In fact, she'd never been a companion at all until she took up that position with me." Her smile widened. "She works for Theodore, and she hasn't admitted this to me yet, but I think she might have been a spy along with her husband when he was alive."

"I had no idea," Zayne began, before he realized exactly what Agatha was trying to do. "But we'll have plenty of time to discuss Drusilla and her sneaky ways right after you promise me you won't go looking for Willie."

"You're the one who said bringing him on to help you repair the mine was a good idea."

"And I still think it's a good idea, but how about if you agree to wait until I'm on my feet and then we'll both go looking for him together."

"That'll be months from now."

"I thought you said my cast might come off by Christmas?"

"Which is still months from now since it's just mid-October."

"I think your math's a little sketchy."

Wrinkling her nose, Agatha smiled. "But it would make such a wonderful *early* Christmas present for Willie if we could find him and you could make him the offer, and . . ."

Agatha continued pointing out all the reasons she should go out on her own to find Willie as Zayne simply stared at her. She was like a dog with a bone when she got something in her head, and she wasn't easy to distract once she had a firm grip of that bone, which meant . . . he really was going to have to step in and save her from herself once and for all.

The only plausible way to do that, the only one that made any sense, was finding her a strong and sensible gentleman to keep her in line.

Swallowing past the sour taste that had immediately filled his mouth the moment his original plan flashed to mind, Zayne sorted through his limited options. Given his current condition, he wasn't exactly able to go to any society events to handpick a beau for Agatha, but he could make use of his mother. Gloria was a fountain of information when it came to society matters. But she'd always been vocal in her desire to see him attached to Agatha, even when Helena had still been around, and that might be problematic. However, even his mother would have to realize, given the danger Agatha was in, that they needed to act quickly, and—

"Are you listening to me?"

He smiled. "Of course."

"What did I just say?"

"Drusilla's a spy."

"That was three topics ago."

"Ah, well, no, I wasn't listening."

"There'll be little point in my keeping you company if you're not going to listen to what I have to say."

By the snippy tone of her voice, it was clear she'd put her distress behind her and had returned to the Agatha he knew and enjoyed. No . . . he really shouldn't dwell on how much he enjoyed her. He knew he wasn't her perfect match, since he'd sworn off ladies forever. The perfect gentleman was out there—a gentleman who would keep her safe, who would shower her with so much attention she'd forget all about her ridiculous plans. All he had to do was locate that gentleman, or . . . maybe he'd already found him.

"Does Mr. Blackheart stop by here often?" he asked, causing her to frown.

"No, I haven't seen him since the day after your accident. Why?"

Even though Mr. Blackheart had vehemently refused to consider forming a relationship other than a professional one with Agatha, he was a strong man, and he might, if Agatha found him somewhat agreeable, be convinced to change his mind about her—because who could resist Agatha?

"What do you think about him?"

"What?"

"Mr. Blackheart—do you find him attractive?"

"Maybe I should ring for the doctor."

"I'm not suffering a relapse, Agatha. I'm just curious."

"What I think of Mr. Blackheart is, well, complicated."

"Ah, so you do find him attractive."

Agatha got up and moved toward the door. "I'm going to go send for Dr. Gessler." Without allowing him another chance to argue, she rushed from the room.

Blowing out a breath, he leaned back against the pillow. She wasn't going to make things easy—that was evident. And since it might take more time than he'd first thought to cultivate his plan properly, he needed a way to distract her once again, a way that would keep her safe.

Satisfaction had him smiling as the perfect solution sprang to mind. She was even now on her way to summon Dr. Gessler because she thought he'd suffered a relapse. It was clear that the only solution available to him was what he and Mr. Blackheart had discussed before his accident. He was going to have to wholeheartedly embrace the role of an invalid.

Leaning forward as far as he could, he held his face close to the gas lamp on his bedside table, his smile widening when he felt his face heat. Footsteps clicking down the hallway had him back against the pillows, but not before he stuck his fingers into a glass of water someone had thoughtfully left for him. He flicked the water over his face and then realized he was still smiling. He'd only just pressed his lips into a firm line when Agatha walked back into the room.

"I sent off a note."

"That might be best," he whispered and then, for good measure, groaned.

Agatha was by his side in a heartbeat. "Zayne, what's the matter?"

Not wanting to speak too much in case Agatha got suspicious, he let out another moan, dropped his head to the side, considered having his tongue loll out but then thought better of that, and settled for slumping into what he hoped would come across as a credible faint.

I must say, Agatha, having you spend every moment with Zayne has made my job incredibly easy. However—" Drusilla paused and took a sip of tea, setting her cup aside before she lowered her voice—"I don't understand why you're going along with his ruse of assuming the role of helpless invalid, especially since he's been at it now for over three days."

Agatha turned her attention to Zayne, who was still in bed, being thoroughly entertained at the moment by his five-year-old nephew, Ben, and eight-year-old niece, Piper, Hamilton and Eliza's children. Ben was sprawled out next to Zayne's new and lighter cast that Dr. Gessler had crafted just that morning, painting pictures on it, while Piper had her nose buried in a newspaper and was reading articles out loud to her uncle.

Zayne was getting better, of that there could be no debate, especially since he was now smiling more often than not, and mischief was almost constantly present in his eyes—mischief that was probably a direct result of his believing he was pulling off the great feat of convincing Agatha he was still occasionally at death's door.

Turning back to Drusilla and keeping her voice no louder than a whisper, Agatha shrugged. "I'm not certain why I'm going along with it."

"You enjoy his company—that's why."

"If you've already come to that conclusion, why bother asking?"

"I like to watch you squirm."

"You're a slightly peculiar lady, aren't you?" Agatha asked.

Drusilla waved Agatha's comment away. "Normal is completely overrated. But getting back to the topic of you and Zayne, may I hope you've been entertaining thoughts of embracing my matchmaking idea in regard to the two of you?"

Her first instinct was to flatly deny Drusilla's question, but then Agatha permitted herself a brief second of honesty. She *had* enjoyed Zayne's company over the past few days. He'd been charming, amusing, and just plain fun. They'd played chess for hours on end, engaged in game after game in an attempt to finally claim a decisive victory, but as of today, they were still evenly matched. She'd also sat by his side, holding his hand, while Dr. Gessler poked and prodded him, trying to figure out what was causing Zayne's odd symptoms. The poking had finally stopped the day before, when Dr. Gessler pulled out an incredibly sharp-looking object from his bag. Zayne's eyes had widened, he'd asked her to leave the room, and when Dr. Gessler finally left the house a few minutes later, trying valiantly not to laugh, it was clear there'd be no more incidents of poking.

When she'd asked him about the doctor's diagnosis, Zayne had smiled an innocent smile, picked up the book they were currently reading out loud to each other—one that had a dastardly villain and a swooning heroine—and proceeded to ignore each and every question she threw at him regarding his health.

With every hour spent in Zayne's company, she found herself drawn to him like a moth to a flame, her vow of remaining an independent and single lady slipping further and further from her mind with each passing day.

"Piper told me you found Zayne foaming at the mouth this morning."

Shoving her disturbing thoughts aside, Agatha grinned. "I made the mistake of saying I was intending on going out for a short walk to get some air—disguised, of course—and the next thing I knew, he had a dribble of white froth coming out of the corner of his mouth." Her grin widened. "He'd obviously taken a page right out of Matilda's book and found himself some chalk, but unfortunately for him, Matilda had gotten a piece of his stash and slipped out from under the bed right as Zayne started gagging. His gagging was interrupted when Matilda let out a squeal, drawing our attention, and she just happened to have an identical trace of the exact same foam ringing her snout. That sight left him floundering for a good long moment."

"What did he do after he finished floundering?"

"Tried to convince me Matilda had picked up the same ailment he was suffering from."

"And yet here you are, still sitting in this chair hour after hour while he comes up with outrageous symptoms every other minute." Drusilla nodded to Zayne, who was scribbling something into a journal he'd taken to keeping as Piper continued reading the paper to him. "He won't be able to continue faking much longer though, which begs the question of what you're going to do when your company isn't demanded here."

"I haven't really thought about it."

"Come now, Agatha, I've spent an entire year with you. Don't think it escaped my notice that you mentioned going out for a walk and in disguise, no less. Where would you be walking to, I wonder, and surely you must realize you can't go out alone?"

Fidgeting in her chair, Agatha blew out a breath. "Caught that, did you?"

Before Drusilla could reply, Matilda scampered into the room, hurried over to Agatha's side and promptly sat down on Agatha's feet. Leaning forward, Agatha gave her a good scratch.

"I take it Gloria has promised to refrain from serving H-A-M?" Drusilla asked dryly.

"She has, and she's agreed not to serve L-A-M-B either. My mother, bless her heart, made the unfortunate choice of serving a rack of L-A-M-B for dinner yesterday, which had Matilda going on a rampage. Since my mother was inordinately fond of the oriental carpet Matilda chewed to pieces, she didn't hesitate to have a servant plop Matilda into a carriage and cart the little dear over here." Agatha smiled down at her pig. "Matilda's been on her best behavior today, probably because she doesn't want to be sent back to an overly dramatic household."

"Because there's no drama going on here," Drusilla said with a pointed look in Zayne's direction.

"The foaming at the mouth might have been rather dramatic, but as we've discussed before, his strange antics are just his way of trying to keep me out of trouble."

"And you find that appealing, don't you."

"Perhaps." Agatha sighed. "He can be irresistible when he puts his mind to it."

"Who can be irresistible?"

Heat immediately traveled up her neck and settled on her face when she realized she'd forgotten to continue whispering. Waving a hand to cool herself, Agatha lifted her head and found Zayne watching her. "What was that?"

"I overheard you say something about someone being irresistible."

"Oh, ah, well, Drusilla and I were talking about . . ."

"Mr. Blackheart," Drusilla said.

Mouth gaping open, Agatha looked at Drusilla, who was calmly taking another sip of tea even as Zayne began sputtering.

"The *two* of you find Mr. Blackheart irresistible?"

"Oh, *I* don't," Drusilla said before she began drinking more tea.

Zayne turned his gaze on Agatha and quirked a brow.

"Don't look at me," was all she could think to respond. She glanced at Piper, who was watching her with a most unusual expression on her face, and decided a diversion was desperately needed. "What are you reading to your uncle, darling?"

Piper shook out the paper and disappeared behind it. "The society page." She peeked over the edge. "I've just read that Mr. Jeffrey Murdock danced twice at a ball held by the Tattler family with Miss Georgiana Tattler."

"Ah, Mr. Murdock's still in town. Wonderful," Zayne said before he scribbled something down in his journal. "I do miss his sister, but from what I've been told, Felicia and Grayson Sumner are enjoying life in England and are soon to add a new bundle of joy to their family."

Agatha frowned. "Felicia's expecting?"

"That's what Arabella told me when she came to visit. She also told me that's the reason behind Felicia and Grayson's not coming to New York this past summer," Zayne said rather absently as he wrote something else in his journal.

"There sure are a lot of babies being born or about to be born these days," Piper said with another odd look sent to Agatha. "Aunt Arabella seems to be getting bigger by the hour, but she doesn't even care."

"That's because she's so excited about the baby," Agatha said with a smile.

"Don't *you* ever want to have a baby?" Piper asked.

Zayne stopped writing and looked at Agatha right as Piper sent a not-so-subtle nod in his direction. And then she actually winked at Agatha.

It suddenly became crystal clear that Piper was following in her grandmother's footsteps, and Drusilla's as well, for that matter. The child had apparently decided that Agatha needed a rather hefty shove in Zayne's direction. It was no wonder the little girl had been sending her strange looks, what with the mention of Mr. Blackheart and all that ridiculous irresistible business.

Piper had always been rather clear regarding the fact she longed for Agatha to join her family, but even though her feelings for Zayne had definitely grown stronger, he had given her absolutely no indication that he saw her as anything other than a friend.

"I suppose someday I'll consider having a baby, Piper," she finally settled on saying.

"And you'll need a husband to make that happen, won't you?" Zayne asked.

Her pulse began to flutter as she caught and held his gaze,

but then he returned his attention to his journal and the fluttering came to an abrupt halt.

"Getting back to Mr. Murdock," Zayne said with a nod to Piper. "Was there anything else mentioned about him and Miss Tattler?"

Looking slightly confused, Piper scanned the newspaper and shook her head. "No, he's not mentioned again."

"Hmm, that's too bad." Zayne added something else in his journal and lifted his head. "What other gentlemen were seen dancing with ladies at the ball?"

Piper returned to the paper, and as she read it, Agatha began to feel a touch of apprehension steal through her. Zayne was behaving more unusually than normal, and she truly had no idea what he was up to or why he seemed to be so interested in the eligible gentlemen dancing around the city at the moment. Granted, he'd spent a great deal of his time when family members had come to call—those being Hamilton, Eliza, Arabella, and Theodore—questioning them about society matters, but Agatha hadn't realized until just now that many of his questions revolved around society gentlemen.

"This is unfortunate," Drusilla whispered before she took another sip of tea and narrowed her eyes on Zayne.

"What's unfortunate?"

"That some gentlemen are so obtuse, of course."

"There you go again, explaining matters to my complete satisfaction."

"I do believe I'll need to take a vow right here and now to abandon all attempts at matchmaking in the future. It's evidently way beyond my capabilities, and I apologize to you most profusely for putting thoughts into your head that would have been best not placed there."

"What?"

Drusilla sighed. "Zayne, my dear, is an idiot, and you would be wise to remember that."

Zayne tapped his pen against his journal, completely oblivious to the fact Drusilla had just called him an idiot, and said, "So in review, here's what I make of this matter, Agatha. . . . You *do* find Mr. Blackheart slightly irresistible, but are hesitant to admit that out loud just yet, at least to me, but I can't help but wonder what it is about him you find so appealing?"

Something unpleasant began to snake down her spine. "Are you taking notes about Mr. Blackheart and my feelings for the man?"

Zayne's hand paused over the page. "Ah, so you do have feelings for him."

"I never said that. In fact, if you'll recall, I wasn't the one who brought Mr. Blackheart into the whole irresistible conversation. That was Drusilla, and . . ." Agatha's sputters came to an abrupt stop as her eyes widened and she turned to Drusilla, who was once again calmly sipping tea as if a huge disagreement, bordering on a real argument, wasn't taking place right in front of her. "Why was it that you mentioned Mr. Blackheart when the conversation turned to matters of irresistibility?"

Drusilla choked on her tea, wheezed for a moment, finally caught her breath, and frowned. "I don't particularly care to be brought into this conversation, dear."

By the telltale stain of pink now covering Drusilla's face, and not a color Agatha believed had come from the choking, it was clear the conversation really was making Drusilla uncomfortable, which meant that . . .

"Good heavens, I didn't see that coming," Agatha said, earning another bout of choking from Drusilla in the process.

"Didn't see what coming?" Zayne demanded.

Agatha gave a breezy wave of her hand. "Nothing."

"Fine, don't tell me. But getting back to Mr. Blackheart and your feelings for the man—would you say these feelings developed while you traveled out west with him?"

"I don't have feelings for the man, at least not the kind you're insinuating," Agatha said through gritted teeth. "And I haven't even seen him since the day after the accident. He hasn't bothered to send me an update regarding his investigation, and because of that obvious slight, I hardly find the gentleman irresistible at the moment."

"Ah, so he's not a very considerate gentleman." Zayne returned his attention to his journal and began to write somewhat furiously.

"Mr. Blackheart is in the midst of an investigation, trying to discover who wants to kill me, so in all fairness to him, I don't think consideration can actually be expected from him at the moment."

"Hmm . . . interesting how quickly you excuse his behavior." Zayne stopped writing and looked at her. "If I were a young lady, I'd find it quite charming that a gentleman was so determined to keep me safe."

She'd *thought* it had been rather charming of Zayne to try his hand at keeping her safe, if through somewhat unorthodox means, but now he was being anything but charming. In fact, she was quickly coming to the conclusion he was plotting something dastardly in regard to her, but she hadn't quite had the time to figure out exactly what that dastardliness was.

"You do realize that we're currently engaged in a most nonsensical conversation, don't you?" she asked, her temper beginning to simmer when he had the audacity to laugh.

"It's a delightful conversation, and I find it rather enthralling. So tell me, what do you think of Mr. Jeffrey Murdock?"

"What?"

"Jeffrey Murdock. I wonder what you think of him."

"I heard you the first time, but I have no understanding of what you're really asking me."

"Do you find him handsome?"

Agatha's mouth gaped open again for a brief second before temper had it snapping shut. "He's a lovely gentleman to look at, and I enjoyed my time tremendously with him when he escorted me to three balls after you left town. But, that has nothing to do with what you're up to at the—"

"Jeffrey escorted you to three balls after I left town?"

"Now we're getting somewhere," Drusilla mumbled behind her hand as her eyes gleamed with what almost seemed to be satisfaction.

"No, we're not," Agatha said before she looked back to Zayne and found him once more writing in his journal. "I want to see what you've written."

To her extreme annoyance, Zayne set aside his pen, shut his journal, and shoved it underneath his bottom, right before he smiled a rather strained smile and then let out a really loud moan.

He was back to his old tricks, but his moan evidently scared poor little Ben, who'd been completely absorbed with painting the cast. Ben sat straight up, scrambled off the bed, and stood looking at his uncle with huge eyes, completely unaware that the paintbrush he was holding was dripping paint onto the expensive rug underneath his feet. "Did I do something to hurt you, Uncle Zayne?"

Rising from her chair after she scooted Matilda off her feet, Agatha hurried over to Ben, took the paintbrush away, set it on a table, and sent Zayne a glare. "You scared Ben."

"I'm sorry, Ben," Zayne said in a voice that was less than

feeble. "I forgot you were on the bed, but I'm fine. Just had a quick jolt of pain hit my, er, arm, but it's fine now."

"There's nothing wrong with your arm," Piper pointed out as she set the paper aside, jumped out of the chair, and moved to stand by the bed. "Your leg's the problem."

"Hmm, so it is," Zayne said cheerfully before he looked over Piper's head and smiled. "Ah, look, there's a footman at the door. What a fortuitous interruption. Do come in, my good man."

The footman stepped into the room looking a little surprised—that surprise probably brought on because Zayne was beaming back at the man as if they'd been best friends for life. He stopped and made a small bow. "Excuse me for interrupting, Mr. Beckett, but I have a . . . ah . . . Well, I'm not sure what it is exactly, but it's been delivered for you." With that, the footman turned and waved toward the door. Another footman entered the room, pulling behind him one of the strangest-looking things on wheels Agatha had ever seen.

Walking over to stand beside it, she looked it over for a long moment and laughed. "Is this from Mrs. St. James?"

Nodding, the first footman held up a letter. "Mrs. St. James sent a note along with her apologies for not being able to deliver her invention to Mr. Beckett in person." Walking over to Zayne, he gave him the note, turned, eyed the gift for a second, shuddered, and then beat a hasty retreat with the second footman following right behind him.

"You should open the letter," Agatha suggested as she continued to eye the invention Charlotte St. James, one of her dear friends and an avid inventor, had apparently designed for Zayne.

When Zayne didn't immediately do as she'd suggested, she

tore her gaze away from the contraption and found Zayne frowning back at her. "Well?"

Releasing a breath, Zayne shrugged. "I do so hate to be the voice of doubt, because it was very kind of Charlotte to think of me and send me that . . . whatever it may be, but . . . don't you remember the, er, questionable nature of most of Charlotte's inventions? I mean, she did fall through the bottom of a boat she tried to patch up one time, and that happened while she was trying to sail it."

"Not all of her inventions are dangerous, Zayne." Agatha began to circle around what was evidently another of Charlotte's masterpieces. "It's very complex, isn't it. I mean, it has a steering column that resembles that of a bicycle, but it has four wheels and an elongated box that I suppose is where you're supposed to sit." She nodded. "It seems she's made it long enough to accommodate your cast." Giving the device a small shove, she blinked when it took off like a shot across the room, coming to a stop when it bounced off the wall. "Ah, it's fast." She bit her lip. "Although that might not be a good thing considering your condition."

Moving across the room, she pulled the cart—for lack of a better word—away from the wall and began to inspect it. "Did Charlotte put any instructions in that letter, such as what all these knobs, sticks, and cranks are for?"

Although it seemed he did so reluctantly, Zayne opened the letter, scanned it, and then turned a little pale. "Charlotte says she made it especially for me after running into Theodore and learning I'd returned home but was stuck with my leg in a cast for a while." He glanced up. "She does apologize for not coming to visit, but it seems she's expecting another child soon and isn't very light on her feet, a condition she claims helped her think up her invention." He regarded the letter again as beads of sweat suddenly popped out on his forehead. "She also added that she's fairly certain she fixed the problem of the wheels falling off, but cautions me to keep my speed in check."

Silence settled over the room, until Drusilla let out a nervous, very un-Drusilla-like laugh. "Ah, well, lovely. I suppose someone should give it a whirl around the room just to make sure it's safe."

"I'll try it," Ben said, puffing out his little chest, only to have it deflate when Agatha shook her head.

"I'm sorry, darling, but this is not a toy. I'll go first."

Drusilla cleared her throat, loudly. "In case you've forgotten, Agatha, I get paid a remarkably handsome salary to watch over you. Because of that, and because I've not had to do much of late to earn that handsome salary, it's my duty to try that death contraption out first."

"Maybe we could just push it in the direction of the fireplace and tell Charlotte that it accidently burned up," Zayne suggested.

"Honestly," Agatha said, "the two of you are being complete ninnies about this. Charlotte St. James is a remarkably gifted inventor, and I have no doubt that this gift she's given you is perfectly safe." She turned the cart around and aimed it for the door. "*I'm* going to be the first to drive it, and since the hallway right outside this room is conveniently long, it'll serve nicely."

Bending over again, she inspected the boards that made up the body of the cart and smiled. "Why, she's even added bolts that allow the sides to come down, which will make it easier for you to slide in and out of this, Zayne."

Pulling up the bolts, she lowered the side, hitched up her skirt, slid onto the smooth seat, and brought the side back up. Gazing over all the knobs, she looked back to Zayne. "Did she happen to mention what this round knob thing is?"

Zayne looked at the letter again and frowned. "She says that you can pull that if you're going uphill and it'll give you an extra boost."

"Excellent," Agatha exclaimed as she reached for the knob, stopping when Zayne let out a grunt. "What?"

"There aren't any hills in the house, so you shouldn't try that."

"Don't be silly. My purpose in testing this out is to make sure it's safe for you."

"But what if it's *not* safe?"

"Then you can tell me you told me so and we can return to the ridiculous conversation we were having before this arrived—the one dealing with eligible gentlemen and why you're so interested in that subject at the moment."

"Really?"

"No," Agatha said firmly. Ignoring the dire predictions Zayne began tossing her way, she gave what she thought was a crank of some sort a good thrust and found herself thrown forward as the cart barreled across the room, directly toward Matilda, who'd woken up from her nap and was ambling her way toward the hall.

"Turn the steering column," Drusilla yelled.

"Put on the brakes," Piper called.

Wrenching the steering column to the right, she barely missed running over Matilda before she shot through the open door and began trundling down the hall. Searching for the braking device, she pulled back a large knob attached to the front of the cart, but instead of stopping, she catapulted forward, the cart traveling faster than ever. She barely had a moment to blink before she realized she was reaching the end of the long hallway. Bracing herself, she hurtled into a decorative pedestal that held a lovely cut-glass vase filled with flowers. With a resounding thud, she came to an immediate stop as the vase tipped, water poured over her head along with the flowers, and then the distinctive sound of breaking glass met her ears.

9

With his heart in his throat, Zayne heard the sound of breaking glass right as Drusilla, followed by Piper and Ben, rushed out of the room. Pushing himself up, he swung his cast over the side of the bed and groped around for a moment, finally finding the crutches he'd stashed behind the headboard, the crutches Dr. Gessler had assured him he was ready to use. Putting them under his arms, he got to his feet and began making his way rather clumsily toward the door. He finally made it into the hallway as sweat rolled from his forehead and stung his eyes, blurring his vision for a second. Stopping, he blinked a few times and then felt temper replace his fear when he spotted Agatha. She was soaking wet and standing next to a rather large hole in the wall at the end of the hall, and . . . she was laughing.

Why she was laughing, he had no idea, because from what he could see, there was a distinct trace of red running down her face, clear testimony that she'd been hurt in the crash. Propelling himself forward, he glanced to the stairs and found his mother racing up them. He reached the stairs right as she finished climbing, but she barely glanced his way as she dashed off to join Agatha.

"My dear, you're bleeding," Gloria exclaimed as she fished a handkerchief out of her pocket and handed it to Agatha.

"It's just a scratch," Agatha said, swiping at her wet face with the handkerchief. She grimaced when she looked at the blood now staining the fine linen. "I'm afraid I might just have ruined this, Gloria."

Gloria waved the comment away. "What happened?"

To his annoyance, Agatha laughed again. "It seems I mistook one of the many knobs Charlotte included on that cart for the brake, when in actuality, the knob I pulled must have had some type of spring attached to it which gave it an extra boost, something I certainly hadn't counted on." She pulled a flower stem off her head and grinned. "It's ingenious, that knob, and I'm going to have to make certain to tell Charlotte that the next time I see her, although I probably should ask her exactly how one is supposed to stop that cart, because . . ." Her voice trailed off as she caught sight of him. "What are you doing out of bed?"

Ignoring her question, he hobbled closer. "You've hurt yourself."

Shrugging, Agatha smiled. "Not really, and besides, better me than you."

His temper kicked up a notch. "This is exactly why I need to find you a good man."

The moment the words slipped out of his mouth, he knew he'd made a grave mistake. Silence was immediate, paired with a distinct air of coolness from Drusilla, Gloria, and even Piper, although little Ben was simply watching him with his mouth open. Agatha, however, given the distinct fire in her eyes, was furious.

"What . . . did . . . you . . . say?" she demanded.

"Children, I believe it's time for some cookies and milk, down in the kitchen," Gloria said firmly. She took Ben by the hand and nodded to Piper, who seemed about to protest but settled for saying something under her breath that sounded like "Uncle Zayne doesn't understand ladies at all" before she took her grandmother's free hand. They began walking quickly to the stairs and then disappeared down them.

Alone now except for Agatha and Drusilla, Zayne shifted on his crutches, but before he could speak, Agatha turned to Drusilla.

"You don't have to stay with me."

"I'm not staying for *your* protection."

Agatha brushed a wet lock of hair out of her face. "I'm not going to hurt him." She shot him a glare. "Well, not too much."

"I don't know why everyone is behaving as if I did something wrong," Zayne said. "You're the lunatic who ran right into the pedestal and almost killed yourself, and once again, you did it in order to keep me safe. I'm the man here, in case everyone's forgotten. I don't need a slip of a lady putting her life on the line time and time again in order to save me from some type of distress or injury."

"I think I'll go find those cookies," Drusilla said before she dashed away.

The sound of crunching glass drew Zayne's attention. Agatha was tapping her toe amidst the broken glass she was still standing in, and the reminder of what had happened to her caused his blood to boil. "You're a complete threat to yourself."

Agatha narrowed her eyes. "I cannot believe you've apparently taken it upon yourself to find me a . . . How did you put it? Oh yes, a *good man*."

"You need someone to look after you."

"I must say, this certainly clears up the whole having Piper read the society page to you and your strange interest in eligible gentlemen. I can't help but wonder who you've decided might suit me, besides Mr. Blackheart, of course."

Before he could summon up so much as a single word, she gathered up her skirt and bolted down the hallway, her intentions only too clear.

"Don't touch my book," he bellowed as he took off at a snail's pace after her.

By the time he reached his room, Agatha was pacing back and forth in front of the fireplace, her lips moving but no sound coming out as she held his journal up to her face.

"Put that down."

She lifted her head. "What did you mean by this—Mr. Arnold Putman . . . nice teeth?"

"Ah, Arabella mentioned the other day that Mr. Putman has a nice smile, and she specifically mentioned his straight teeth."

"So that makes him a viable candidate?"

"Well, you wouldn't want to be married to someone who only has gums and no teeth, would you?"

Letting out a snort, Agatha flipped the page. "Mr. Constable Hefferstenforth. . . ." She rolled her eyes. "Do you really believe I'd like to be known forever after as Mrs. Hefferstenforth? Why, I'm not even certain how to pronounce that name."

"If you'll continue on to the notes I wrote after that name, you'll see I made that exact same observation and also wrote that it wouldn't be a good match."

Sending him another glare, she flipped to a different page. "Ah, and here we have Mr. Jeffrey Murdock, although it looks like you tried to scratch out his name." She released a huff of clear annoyance. "Out of *all* the eligible gentleman I know at the moment, Mr. Murdock would probably make me a more than acceptable husband, but there's just the pesky little problem of me not actually wanting to acquire a mate," she said, her voice having risen to almost a shout.

"You're upset with me."

Pacing back and forth again, Agatha practically sizzled with tension. "I thought we were friends."

"We are, which is why I decided I had to help you."

"By marrying me off to someone else?"

Zayne arched a brow. "What do you mean by 'someone else'?"

Agatha stopped pacing. "Nothing, I meant nothing by that, but tell me . . . why?"

Leaning forward on his crutches, Zayne sighed. "You're always putting yourself at risk trying to save others. If you had a strong and capable man to look after you, you wouldn't have to do that."

"I'm perfectly capable of looking after myself, Zayne. I've been doing it for quite some time now."

"But not doing it well."

For just a second, what looked like hurt flickered through her eyes, but then Agatha squared her shoulders and the look was gone, replaced, unfortunately, with rage. "You are *not* going to find me a husband."

"I'm not?"

"No. If I decide I want one—and I'm not sure I'll ever want a husband now—*I'll* do the selecting. Are we clear?"

"Not really."

"That's too bad." With that, Agatha walked to the fireplace, tossed his journal into the fire, and without another word stalked out of the room.

"Where are you going?" he called.

To his dismay, Agatha didn't bother to answer.

⸎

"You do realize this is completely irresponsible of both of us to be out here, in the open no less, and with Matilda leading the way, don't you?"

Shoving her spectacles farther up her nose, Agatha glanced at Drusilla, who was dressed in a hideous floral gown of lime and pink, her hair stuffed underneath a ratty old white wig, and carrying a fashionable reticule that was at distinct odds with her gown. Strangely enough, Drusilla was looking as composed as ever. "We're both in disguise."

"True, and I do thank you for not insisting we take this jaunt around the neighborhood dressed as men, although I'm still a little confused as to why you insisted I disguise myself."

"I didn't want you to feel left out, and I didn't insist we dress as men because it would have taken us too long to don whiskers. I needed to get out of the house."

"And since I find that to be a completely rational explanation, it's clear I've spent entirely too much time in your company. However, I'm not exactly sure I understand why you chose to dress as a lady who looks about ready to give birth, especially since most ladies in society don't venture out in public when they're in your supposed condition."

"It's 1883, Drusilla, and it's past time someone made the stand while in this condition. It can't be pleasant for ladies to be stuck inside for months on end just because they're expecting, so perhaps I'll start a new trend." She was pulled to an abrupt halt when Matilda suddenly found something worth investigating on the sidewalk and refused to budge. Agatha blew out a breath. "He's an idiot."

"Ah, I take it we're back to discussing Zayne, are we?"

"I don't know what I was thinking, allowing myself to care about him, especially since I vowed after he broke my heart a few years . . ." She stopped speaking when Drusilla stepped closer to her and, in a move that was quite unlike the Drusilla she'd come to know, patted Agatha awkwardly on the arm.

"You never mentioned that Zayne had actually broken your heart."

She shrugged. "Well, he did, and now he's done it again." A yank on the leash pulled her into motion. Matilda was apparently on the trail of something new, and since the little darling was rather strong when she turned determined, Agatha had no choice but to break into a trot, if only to save herself from being dragged down the sidewalk.

"Don't you think it might be best to turn around and go back to the house?" Drusilla asked, panting slightly when she finally caught up to Agatha.

"No."

"You can't hide from Zayne forever."

"I'm not planning on hiding for long. In fact, I think it's about time for me to shed my disguises and walk freely around New York as Miss Agatha Watson."

"Please tell me you're not going to shed your disguise right this moment. I'm afraid we really will draw unwanted attention if you go strolling around in your unmentionables, especially since you're walking a P-I-G."

"Hmm . . . such a display might draw the person who wants me dead out in the open."

"I'm going to pretend I didn't just hear that."

Skidding to a stop because Matilda, for some reason, had changed direction and was now rooting around the sidewalk,

Agatha laughed. "I wouldn't really strip down out here, Drusilla. Honestly, where's your sense of humor?"

"Back at the Beckett house, where it's safer for you."

"But not safer for Zayne."

Drusilla sent her a look filled with sympathy. "I truly am sorry for pushing you toward him, Agatha. I never dreamed in a million years he'd tried to pawn you off on some other gentleman, especially since I was certain he held the same amount of affection for you as you hold for him."

"*Held* for him," Agatha corrected. "I foolishly let my guard down, and he wormed his way right back into my heart, but never again. I'm done with him for good this time, and I'm furious with myself for believing he truly understood me, when in actuality, he doesn't understand me at all."

"I don't think Zayne understands ladies in general."

"Be that as it may," Agatha began, jolting forward when Matilda began scampering down the street. "Some other lady can take over the daunting task of teaching him about women, because I've had quite enough of Zayne Beckett." She lifted her chin. "What's become remarkably clear to me is this—I need to return to work. Writing is my great passion in life, and once I get firmly settled again at the paper, I'll be able to put Zayne behind me once and for all."

"Theodore will never agree with the idea of you going back to work."

"What everyone seems to have forgotten is that Theodore is not in charge of me. I am an independent, successful woman. It's time I remembered that and stopped mooning over a gentleman who clearly has no romantic interest in me at all."

"If Zayne *didn't* have a romantic interest in you, I doubt he would have scratched Mr. Murdock's name out of his journal, something I remember you making sure to point out to me."

"I thought you were going to cease with the whole match-making business."

"Oh, right," Drusilla said. "But I really must voice my concern about you going back to work. Someone truly does want you dead, given that you were almost run down by a carriage the moment we returned to the city, and don't forget all those threats you received before we left to go out west."

"I'm hardly likely to forget that someone left a P-I-G's head on my front porch, Drusilla. It was a grisly scene, made all the more horrific now that I have Matilda, and believe me, I haven't forgotten."

"Have you forgotten that the note attached to that head stated your head would be next?"

Before Agatha could respond, a carriage pulled up next to them. And in the blink of an eye, Drusilla shoved Agatha out of the way even as a pistol appeared almost instantaneously out of her reticule.

"Honestly, Drusilla," Eliza Beckett said as her head poked out the window, her red hair styled to perfection underneath the fashionable hat she wore, "you've knocked poor Agatha to the ground. Is that any way to treat a lady who looks about ready to give birth?"

Picking herself up from the sidewalk, where she'd unfortunately fallen after Drusilla's shove, Agatha rubbed her elbow and grinned. "What are you doing here, Eliza?"

"Hamilton and I were just at Gloria's, taking Viola to see Zayne, and . . . well . . . Gloria thought you might want to talk. Hop in."

Shaking her head, Agatha nodded to Matilda, who was straining against the leash, her interest fixed on something in the distance. "I don't think Matilda's done with her little adventure yet. You should walk with us."

"What a lovely idea, especially since the day is turning downright brisk, what with that wind and all," Eliza said before she grinned. "And while it's apparent you're toasty warm, a condition no doubt brought about by the rage you're currently experiencing due to my annoying brother-in-law, poor Drusilla's shivering."

"Gloria told you about Zayne, did she?" Agatha asked before she turned to Drusilla and noticed that the lady was indeed shivering. "Why didn't you tell me you were cold?"

"Really, Agatha, after spending so much time with me, I'd have thought you'd come to the realization that I'm one of those suffer-in-silence types."

Rolling her eyes, Agatha nodded to Matilda. "I'll grab her head, you take her backside, and, Eliza, you'd better scoot over to the far side of the carriage, because I don't think Matilda's going to like this."

"Why do I have to grab her backside?" Drusilla asked in disgust.

"Ladies, allow me," the coachman said as he jumped down from his seat and gestured them out of the way, sending Agatha a pointed look. "You, Miss Watson, are apparently supposed to be in no condition to hoist a pig into a carriage. Go get settled and I'll see to the beast, but may I add that it's delightful to see that you haven't changed a bit?"

Agatha smiled, but before she could respond, Matilda—evidently taking exception to being called a pig, or perhaps she didn't like the word *beast*—yanked the leash straight out of Agatha's hand and took off like a flash. It took a few minutes to run her down, and by the time they got her into the carriage, Drusilla was no longer shivering but sweating. The coachman was eyeing Agatha in amusement, probably because she'd been the one to catch her pig and had then wrestled the dear up and into the carriage. Finally settling back against the seat, Agatha grinned at the coachman as he shook his head and looked at Eliza. "Where to, Mrs. Beckett?"

"I think a nice ride along Broadway might be in order," Eliza said. "I'll let you know if we decide to stop somewhere along the way."

The coachman nodded and shut the carriage door. A moment later they started down the road.

"So much for remaining inconspicuous," Drusilla muttered as she readjusted her wig.

"If you truly wanted to remain inconspicuous, Drusilla, you should have left Matilda behind," Eliza said with a fond smile at the pig. "She is, after all, the reason I was able to track the two of you down so easily."

Drusilla glanced to Matilda. "I wasn't given a say in the matter, Eliza. I talked Agatha into leaving Matilda behind, but the annoying creature somehow managed to slip out of the house and catch up with us. The moment Agatha saw her, carrying her leash in her mouth no less, she was adamant about letting her pet join us."

"What a bright girl you are," Eliza cooed to Matilda, earning a glare from Drusilla in the process. She cleared her throat. "Anyway, since we're now moving, and toward Broadway, would anyone be opposed to me running a few errands? It's rare I'm infant-free these days, and I need to stop by B. Altman's to check on a special order I placed last week."

"We are not going to B. Altman's," Drusilla said firmly.

Narrowing her eyes, Eliza gestured to Agatha. "Fine, by all means, let's not distract Agatha from her troubles by doing something safe, like shopping. Instead, why don't we just take her back to Zayne's house, where you and I both know she'll do her very best to sneak out and will probably end up in the slums."

Drusilla patted her wig and smiled a rather strained smile. "Shopping sounds delightful."

"I thought you'd see it my way." Eliza settled back against the seat and turned her attention to Agatha. "Now then, before we get to B. Altman's, I'd like to hear your thoughts about Zayne."

"He's clearly turned mentally deficient while he's been away."

"I would love to argue that point, but since Gloria did mention the pesky little fact that Zayne's been trying to find you a man, well, there's really nothing to argue, is there?" She leaned closer. "He's hurt you again, hasn't he?"

Seeing no reason to deny it, because Eliza, out of all Agatha's friends, had always known exactly how she really felt about Zayne, Agatha nodded. "He has."

Pulling her into a tight hug, Eliza blew out a breath. "I'm so sorry, darling, but he'll come around."

"I don't want him to come around, and I don't really want to talk about him right now."

"Fair enough," Eliza said as she released Agatha. "We'll talk about shoes."

Agatha's spirits began to lift as Eliza launched into a ridiculous discussion about the latest styles, most of which Agatha was fairly certain her friend made up on the spot, but time flew as they rumbled down the street, and before she knew it, they'd arrived at B. Altman's.

Cautioning Matilda to behave herself, Agatha rolled up a carriage blanket and put in under the little pig's head before climbing out the door with the help of the coachman. She discreetly rearranged stuffing around her middle that had begun to slip and then followed Eliza and Drusilla into the store. They made their way down a marble-covered aisle, but Agatha stopped when her stuffing slipped again.

"I'll catch up with you two in a moment," she said. "I need to visit the retiring room and make some adjustments before someone notices I'm looking a little lumpy."

Drusilla nodded. "I'll come with you."

"I don't need a nanny, Drusilla. I'm perfectly capable of staying out of trouble for a few minutes."

Pushing down her spectacles, Drusilla glared at her. "I realize you believe I'm paranoid, but someone might have noticed us walking Matilda before and followed us here."

"No one knows about Matilda."

"Mary does."

"And since she's probably still out west, spending her ill-gotten gains, I highly doubt we'll run into her in the midst of this fine department store." Not giving Drusilla time to argue further, Agatha headed off for the retiring room, just making it through the door before her stuffing slid down her legs. Hobbling over to a private stall, she slipped inside, closed the door, and put everything back in place. When she was certain she was again looking expectant and not lumpy, she headed back into the parlor area of the room and paused before the mirror, unable to stop the grin that spread over her face.

She was a sight—of that there could be no debate. She'd tucked her hair under a garish red wig she'd given to Piper to use for dress up before she'd headed out west. Because Piper had apparently used it well, the wig was missing chunks of hair, which was why Agatha had plopped a large hat over top of it, one that tied around the chin with a lovely purple ribbon. Add in the fact she was wearing huge black spectacles and a dress that could almost be considered a circus tent, she was fairly unrecognizable. That meant she'd be able to shop in safety because no one could confuse the image she saw in the mirror with that of Miss Agatha Watson, especially since, her figure being sufficiently stuffed, she was round as a barrel.

Hurrying through the door, anxious now to purchase a few new things, she stumbled to a stop when she spotted Matilda sitting smack dab in the middle of the marble walkway. "How in the world did you get in here?" she asked as she bent over, picked up the leash, and looked around. Not seeing the coachman anywhere in sight, she squared her shoulders. "You're quite sneaky, aren't you, darling, and it was really very clever of you to figure out how to get out of the carriage. But I'm going to have to take you right back there. This is one of those fancy stores, and they won't appreciate you being here."

Matilda sent Agatha a pitiful look.

"Oh, very well, I'll sit with you in the carriage while Eliza finishes her errands, but next time, since it's clear you can't behave, I'm leaving you at home."

Hugging the side of the aisle while pretending it was completely normal to have a prancing pig at her side in the midst of the dress department, Agatha spotted a rather stern-looking gentleman talking with some customers in the millinery department. She yanked Matilda in amongst the dresses. "He's management, which means both of us will be in big trouble if he sees us, so be quiet."

Matilda scampered underneath some gowns hanging on a circular rack, leaving Agatha standing on the other side, holding the leash. Striving for an air of nonchalance, she began to sort through the gowns, stopping when her eye settled on a delicious confection of blue that exactly matched a hat she owned.

A squeal from the middle of the rack had Agatha parting some of the gowns and looking down. Matilda was rooting around under the rack, trying to slurp up what seemed to be some type of sweet from the floor.

"That's going to make you sick," Agatha muttered, pulling on the leash and grimacing when Matilda refused to budge. "Listen here, Matilda. You need to leave that alone. I hate to think what will happen to us if you throw that up in the middle of these lovely gowns."

Matilda continued to slurp, and then she began to make grunting noises, noises that were bound to draw someone's attention.

"I'm going to take you back to my mother," she threatened, to which Matilda paid not the slightest bit of attention. "I'll tell her to serve ham."

Evidently Matilda hadn't yet learned that ham and pig meant the same thing, because she didn't so much as twitch an ear, but continued attacking the sweet.

Knowing there was nothing else to do but drag her pig away from the sweet and out of the store, Agatha shoved some dresses aside and was just bending over when the strong scent of a lady's perfume caused her to sneeze. Straightening, she sneezed several more times and then raised watery eyes to the lady standing on the other side of the dress rack.

"What is that under there?" the lady demanded.

Agatha opened her mouth as she struggled to come up with a plausible explanation, but then the hair on the back of her neck stood straight up, and she narrowed her eyes on the woman in front of her.

Dressed in the first state of fashion in a green gown paired with an ornate hat sporting a variety of exotic feathers, the lady's face was partially obscured by the veiling also attached to the hat, but . . . her voice was, unfortunately, familiar.

Matilda took that moment to wander out from under the rack, a sticky treat a child must have abandoned stuck to her nose; and if Agatha wasn't so furious, she'd have found the sight amusing.

"Is that a pig?"

Agatha narrowed her eyes on the woman she'd determined was none other than Mary and watched as the lady's head shot up and they locked gazes. Mary's eyes widened a second later, when recognition set in.

"You," Mary snarled.

Agatha forced a smile. "Hello, Mary. Spending some of the loot you stole from Zayne, are you?"

"What are you doing here—and dressed in such a ridiculous manner?"

"I could ask you the same question."

Not bothering to answer her, Mary took a step toward her but froze on the spot when Matilda let out a grunt that sounded downright menacing, right before she pawed a foot against the floor and charged, her action stripping the leash out of Agatha's hand.

Letting out a shriek, Mary turned and began to run in the opposite direction, but Matilda was fast for such a little thing, and before Agatha had a chance to move, Matilda had grabbed hold of Mary's hem, which brought the fleeing woman to an abrupt stop.

"Stupid pig, you're tearing my gown. Let go of it," Mary screeched.

To Agatha's astonishment, Matilda did let go of the gown, right before she dashed underneath it and began emitting high-pitched squeals, clear evidence she was probably getting ready to begin gnawing on Mary's leg.

"Get out of there," Mary yelled as she lifted up her skirt and tried to pull Matilda off her leg, smacking the pig's head with her other hand.

"Stop that," Agatha snapped, jolting into motion, the only thought rolling through her mind was that of saving her pig.

Snatching up a wire dress form that was showcasing a lovely gown of purest ivory, she aimed it like a lance and rushed toward Mary, smiling in grim satisfaction when the dress form caught Mary in the stomach and pushed her backward.

Unfortunately, Mary sprang immediately back to her feet and grabbed the other end of the dress form, and a rather strange game of tug-of-war commenced. Just when she thought she was getting the best of Mary, a gentleman's outraged voice rang out.

"Ladies, good heavens, this is hardly acceptable behavior. Brawling is not permitted within the confines of B. Altman's, nor are pigs permitted. And I, Mr. Dowry, as manager of this fine establishment, am going to have to insist you let go of that dress form at once. Authorities have already been summoned, but if you cooperate . . ."

Whatever else Mr. Dowry was about to say was lost when two women suddenly appeared, dressed in charming gowns and looking exactly like proper ladies should look, but on closer inspection, the women turned out to be Mary's cohorts, Jessie and Hannah.

Chaos was immediate as the two ladies entered the brawl.

"Jessie, get the pig. Hannah, get the man," Mary yelled as she shoved the dress form into Agatha's middle, making Agatha immensely glad she was wrapped in stuffing.

Trying to get a better hold, Agatha's fingers curled around

the dress right as she gave a good yank. A distinctive ripping noise sounded, and a second later, she found herself holding a tattered and torn slip of silk that had only moments before been a rather lovely gown. She glanced to Mary and found that woman grinning smugly back at her, the dress form solely in her clutches.

"That was an expensive piece of silk," Mr. Dowry howled, "and you mark my words, one of you will pay me the full cost of the creation, because it was very—" His words were abruptly cut off when Hannah began pelting him with clothing she grabbed from a rack.

Agatha threw the pieces of silk to the ground and took a step toward Mary, only to be stopped dead in her tracks when an arm snaked around her throat.

"Not so fast," Jessie rasped in her ear.

"Let go of her."

Agatha opened her mouth to demand that Eliza, who'd just rushed onto the scene, flee and not get involved, but the arm around her throat took that moment to tighten, and all she was able to get out was a feeble croak.

"Hold on, Agatha. I'm coming," Drusilla shouted.

Fear sliced through her when she heard Eliza let out a yelp, but the fear was immediately replaced with rage. This was her city, these were her friends, and she certainly wasn't going to let someone strangle her in the middle of B. Altman's.

Shoving an elbow into Jessie's ribs, satisfaction mingled with the rage when the arm around her throat disappeared and Jessie stumbled backward and landed on the floor. Pushing her sleeves up, Agatha set her sights on Hannah, who was engaged in what appeared to be a duel with Eliza—both women, oddly enough, using parasols. A strong grip on her arm had Agatha turning as she balled her hand into a fist, but she stopped herself from swinging when she realized it was only Mr. Dowry who was gazing back at her with clear horror in his eyes.

"I don't mean to cause you undue alarm, Madame, but I do believe the shock of all this has caused your . . . umm . . . child . . . to want to make an appearance. Might I suggest you abandon this madness and immediately seek out a doctor, because the dress department at B. Altman's is no place to deliver a baby, and . . . think of the mess."

Glancing down, Agatha felt the strangest desire to laugh. Evidently, in the midst of the ruckus her stuffing had slipped and was even now slowly drifting below her stomach.

It was little wonder Mr. Dowry was looking at her with such concern.

Knowing there was no help for it, because the stuffing was hampering her efforts to help her friends, Agatha shook out of his hold, bent over, lifted her skirts, and yanked out the linens. Ignoring Mr. Dowry's gasp of outrage and deciding she might as well be fully prepared for whatever was ahead, she slipped her pistol out from the garter on her leg and straightened.

"Imposter!" Mr. Dowry bellowed.

Wishing she had a moment to explain matters to the distraught man but knowing now was hardly the time, she dashed past him and headed for Eliza, who was now soundly beating Hannah over the head with a parasol while Hannah yelled at the top of her lungs.

A shot had everyone freezing in their tracks.

Turning, Agatha found Mary and Drusilla facing each other, both ladies holding pistols in their hands, but only Mary's was smoking.

Drusilla had lost her wig somewhere along the way, and

her hair was hanging around her face, but her expression was hard and her eyes were blazing. "You missed," she said in a voice that had turned deadly. "Now put your hands up and we'll end this nicely."

"Shoot, Jessie!" Mary screamed right before she ducked, a shot sounded behind Agatha, Drusilla dropped to the ground, and Matilda began squealing.

Another shot rang out.

"Not the pig, you fool!" Mary screeched from behind a rack. "We'll only get paid if we kill Miss Watson."

Crouching as she ran, Agatha reached Drusilla's side and, to her relief, found Drusilla's eyes open. "How badly are you hurt?"

"I'm not shot," Drusilla whispered. "When I say move, jump to the right."

"What?"

"Move."

Suddenly finding herself on her backside as Drusilla jumped to her feet, Agatha could only stare in amazement at Drusilla, who was once again pointing a pistol at Mary. "Put your hands where I can see them, and tell your friends to stand down."

Slowly raising her hands, Mary nodded to Jessie and Hannah. Hannah dropped the parasol she was holding, while Jessie lowered the pistol she was clutching in her hand.

"Very good," Drusilla drawled. "Now, tell me what you meant when you said you'll only get paid if you kill Miss Watson."

"I don't have to tell you nothing."

"Were you responsible for trying to run Agatha over with a carriage?"

Mary frowned. "I don't have a carriage."

"But someone has hired you to kill Agatha?" Drusilla pressed.

Before Mary could reply, another shot rang out, this one coming from Hannah, and complete insanity took over B. Altman's once again as bits of plaster began to fall from the ceiling, evidence that Hannah's shot had gone wide.

"The ceiling's about to collapse!" Agatha heard someone yell.

"Rogue pig, rogue pig!" another lady screamed.

A loud squeal followed that announcement, and a flash of relief darted through Agatha as she realized Matilda was still alive and apparently running for her life, leaving frantic customers in her wake. Pushing herself to her feet, she looked around for Mary, finally catching sight of the woman rushing down an aisle with Drusilla giving chase, Matilda galloping after them.

Hitching up her skirt, she started forward, her path impeded by ladies scrambling to get out of the store. Darting around a lady screaming something about a pig and the unacceptable shopping experience she was having, Agatha set her sights on the door, but she skidded to a halt when the entrance suddenly filled with policemen. Before she could make a discreet exit, her arm was taken in another firm grip by none other than Mr. Dowry.

"I told you the police had been summoned, missy," he said with a distinct trace of glee in his voice. "Never in all my years of being a manager have I ever had the misfortune to witness such an abhorrent display of behavior, especially from what I assumed were ladies of quality."

He lifted a hand and summoned a policeman. "Here's the lady responsible for this disaster, officer. I expect her to be prosecuted to the full extent of the law."

Sending Agatha a glare and ignoring her sputtered protests, he thrust her directly at the policeman. Letting out a
distinctive sniff, Mr. Dowry drew himself up. "Furthermore,
you are forever, from this moment forward, banned from this
establishment—as is that pig."

10

And then, once you get older, I promise to take you sailing, my darling girl. You'll love the feel of the sea mist in your hair."

"While I find your attention to Viola quite adorable," Gloria said from the chair she'd pulled up next to his bed, "she fell asleep a good thirty minutes ago. I'm really going to have to insist you allow me to take her off to the nursery, because it's past time you and I had a bit of a chat."

Glancing down, Zayne gazed at his brand-new niece, her tiny face peaceful in sleep, her rosy lips puckered ever so slightly. He'd fallen in love with the baby the moment he'd laid eyes on her, but . . . his mother was right. He'd been talking nonstop to his niece ever since Hamilton and Eliza had brought her over for a visit, and he'd been doing so to avoid questions from his obviously annoyed mother.

"We really shouldn't move her," he finally said. "She's sleeping so well at the moment."

"She'll be fine," Hamilton said, driving through the door in Charlotte's invention, which he pulled to a smooth stop before he grinned. "This cart she made for you is amazing, and I found the brakes. You just push the elevated pedal on the floor forward." Climbing out, Hamilton ran his hand over the polished wood. "Agatha probably didn't find it since she's short."

"Ah, I'm so glad you brought up Agatha," Gloria said, getting to her feet. She reached out and gently took Viola straight out of Zayne's arms. "I'm taking Viola to the nursery, and when I get back, the three of us are going to discuss the troubling situation Zayne's landed himself in."

"You can't just drop Viola off in the nursery," Zayne argued. "Hamilton and Eliza didn't bring their nanny with them, and since Eliza has yet to return, well, it wouldn't be safe for the baby."

"Which is why it's such a lucky circumstance that Mrs. Johnson is here today. She's perfectly capable of watching over Viola, considering she used to watch over Piper and Ben."

"But . . ."

"Zayne, enough," Gloria said, stepping around Hamilton as she walked with Viola cradled in her arms to the door. "Your stalling tactics have now come to an end."

Unwilling to be thwarted just yet in his attempt at avoiding what was certainly going to be an unpleasant chat, Zayne summoned up a good moan, one of his best yet, and slumped against the pillows. "I'm feeling faint."

"You should be feeling ridiculous," Gloria said over her shoulder before she disappeared through the door.

"Nice try." Hamilton moved to sit in the chair Gloria had just vacated before he grinned. "If you ask me, Mother's shown a great deal of restraint so far. I was expecting her to take Viola to the nursery an hour ago."

Shifting against the pillows, Zayne blew out a breath.

"Don't think I didn't notice that you conveniently left me alone with her."

"I figured it was in my best interest to do so, but she surprised me by remaining mute the whole time I was fiddling with Charlotte's invention outside the door."

"You could have fiddled in here."

"Now you're just being sulky."

Not caring to address that statement, because he'd clearly heard the sulk in his tone, Zayne gestured to the cart. "What do you think about that? Is it safe?"

Stretching out his legs, Hamilton folded his hands over his stomach. "I don't think I'd go so far as to claim it's safe. Charlotte's gotten a bit too ambitious if you ask me, adding all those levers and cranks. But, if you take the time to learn how to operate it, you shouldn't come to any extensive harm."

"That's reassuring."

Hamilton smiled. "Yes, well, hazardous carts aside, tell me what really happened with Agatha."

Knowing there was no point in refusing his brother's request, Zayne began filling Hamilton in on what had transpired, finishing with, "So Agatha took great exception to the fact I'd written down that one of the gentlemen had nice teeth, and the situation quickly went downhill from there."

"Please tell me you didn't actually think that the state of a gentleman's teeth would make him a good choice for Agatha," Gloria said as she marched back into the room, stepped in front of the chair Hamilton was sitting in, and waved him out of it.

"I just got comfortable," Hamilton grumbled, rising to his feet before Gloria sat down.

"I'm old, and I was sitting there first," Gloria grumbled right back before she set her sights on Zayne. "You know, darling, out of all three of my children, you were the one who never caused me a moment's trouble until recently. You were always pleasant, considerate, and charming to the ladies, even if you were a little naïve when it came to dealing with them. Now, however, it's clear you've decided to make up for that less-than-troublesome past."

"I'm not naïve when it comes to the ladies."

Arching a brow, Gloria rolled her eyes. "You are, and while I always found that to be rather delightful and refreshing, I've now come to the conclusion that I failed you miserably as your mother by not setting you straight."

"I beg your pardon?"

"It's clear you don't understand the least little thing about women, and because of that, I'm afraid you might have just lost Agatha for good this time."

Hamilton got up from the chair he'd just sat down in. "I think I should go check on Viola."

"Sit," Gloria barked with a finger pointed to the chair.

"I don't know why you're being snippy with me, Mother," Hamilton said, lowering back into the chair. "I haven't caused you any trouble since I married Eliza."

Gloria waved that away with a swish of her hand. "You, being Zayne's brother, are going to assist me with his education."

"I left school a long time ago," Zayne said slowly.

"Well, you apparently didn't learn anything of importance there—so listen up."

Zayne opened his mouth, intent on arguing, but then felt it gape open farther when understanding finally set in. "You're up to your old matchmaking tricks."

"So what if I am?"

"That's why you left me alone so much with Agatha, which,

now that I think about it, was somewhat odd and barely appropriate."

"I hardly needed to keep a close eye on the two of you, Zayne," Gloria said. "You've always been very proper, and I know you'd never behave in an untoward manner. Why, look at you and Helena. I don't think the two of you ever got around to stealing so much as the occasional kiss."

Heat began to creep up his neck and settle on his face. "You can't know that for sure."

Gloria gestured to his face. "The proof's right in front of me." She settled back into the chair. "I truly hoped that you'd come to your senses about Helena, but when you didn't and traipsed out to join her in California, well, I could only leave it in God's hands and pray He'd sort the mess out."

"He certainly did that."

"Yes, He did, although in a very unusual way, as He's often prone to do. But, my expectations for you and a happy future increased tremendously after your recent accident, in that it allowed you to spend so much time with Agatha. However, since you're evidently a little dense when it comes to matters of the heart, I've realized I've been completely negligent in leaving you to your own devices, and it's past time I corrected that situation."

"Forgive me, Mother, but did you just call me *dense?*"

"Indeed I did, and so you are." Gloria nodded. "Everyone, except for you, has always known your perfect match is Agatha, and yet you've made a muck of it now."

"I thought I'd been perfectly clear regarding the fact I'm content to remain a bachelor."

"You're the least suited gentleman I know to embrace bachelorhood," Gloria countered. "Why, one only has to look at you and Viola to see you'd make a perfect father, would relish that position, but you're going to need a wife in order to do that."

"Since my siblings seem completely capable of supplying me with an adequate number of nieces and nephews, I can get my fill of babies anytime."

"It's not the same thing," Gloria argued before she turned to Hamilton. "Tell him."

"I would prefer to just remain an observer to this conversation, if you don't mind, Mother."

"I do mind, and you, as Zayne's *older* brother, need to explain to him exactly how he should go about winning the love of his life, who is Agatha, if you've missed that pertinent point."

Hamilton simply sat there until Gloria snapped her fingers in his direction. "Now would be a good time, if you please."

Leaning forward, Hamilton sent Zayne a look that had apology written all over it. "Ah, well, ladies can be tricky, but I found that . . ."

"Let me spare you the embarrassment of this little speech Mother's demanding you make, Hamilton," Zayne said. "I'm hesitant to take any advice from you since I remember all too well the fiasco you went through with Eliza, and . . . again, I'm not looking to get married, which is what prompted me to create that list. Agatha needs a strong and capable gentleman, one who won't hesitate to put an end to her shenanigans in order to keep her safe."

"No truer words have ever been spoken."

Looking up, Zayne found Theodore Wilder standing in the doorway, a smile on his handsome face, but no Arabella by his side.

"Where's my sister?" Zayne asked.

Moving into the room, Theodore nodded to Hamilton, kissed Gloria's hand, which had her blushing, and pulled up a chair. Sitting down, his smile widened. "Arabella is napping, and no, there's nothing wrong with her, she's simply tired, which can be expected these days." He looked around. "Where's Agatha?"

"She's not here at the moment," Gloria said.

Theodore's smile disappeared in a flash. "What do you mean, not here?"

Gloria crossed her arms over her chest. "She got into a huge tiff with Zayne and went out to get a bit of air."

Rising to his feet, Theodore headed for the door but stopped when Hamilton called him back. "She's with Drusilla, and she's in disguise."

"And you think I'm going to find that comforting?" Theodore asked from the doorway.

"Eliza went after them in the carriage, and I'm sure, given that she hasn't returned yet, she found them and the ladies are probably even now chatting up a storm, disparaging gentlemen in general as they drive around the city."

Shaking his head, Theodore returned to his seat, although he seemed to do so reluctantly. "It seems highly irresponsible of Drusilla to allow Agatha to leave the house, even if they did so in disguise. Drusilla knows the danger Agatha's in, and she also knows we're no closer to discovering who wants Agatha dead than we were last year."

"You don't have any leads?" Hamilton asked.

"We have plenty of leads," Theodore corrected. "Agatha's managed the uncommon feat—due to her writing, no doubt—of enraging countless people in the city, but no one is talking. My informants on the streets haven't heard a single whisper about who's behind the threats, which makes the situation all that more disconcerting." He began to drum his fingers on the chair. "That's why I don't understand how Drusilla could have allowed Agatha out of the house."

"She was feeling guilty," Gloria said.

"Guilty?"

"I'm afraid so, dear. I noticed her pushing Agatha in Zayne's direction, and I must admit I didn't do a thing to stop it." She sent Theodore a wink. "Drusilla's meddling allowed me the luxury of not being the annoying matchmaking mother for once. But since things didn't go quite as Drusilla planned, given that Zayne turned ridiculous, well . . . guilt had her donning a disguise and going out with Agatha in the interest of keeping Agatha pacified *and* keeping her out of trouble."

"She pacified Agatha by donning a disguise?" Theodore asked.

Hamilton laughed. "Come now, Theodore, surely you can figure out the reasoning behind that?"

"No, sorry, nothing's coming to me."

Laughing again, Hamilton nodded to Zayne. "Don't you remember when Agatha did the same thing to Zayne, made him dress up as a lady even though there was no need for him to do so and even made him shave his chest in order to get into the true character of the disguise? It was her odd way of venting the annoyance she felt since he'd decided to join Helena. I can guarantee she did the same to Drusilla because she didn't appreciate the lady's matchmaking attempts."

Something uncomfortable began to slither through Zayne. "Agatha always lent me the impression she was perfectly content to simply be my friend."

"There you go, being naïve again," Gloria said.

Zayne opened his mouth to put an end to all the non-sense once and for all, but his words stuck in his throat when Drusilla suddenly darted through the doorway, Eliza a step behind her with a limping Matilda bringing up the rear. He craned his neck but, when Agatha didn't show up, turned his attention back to Drusilla, who was now standing in the middle of the room, looking anything but composed—a condition that was downright disconcerting.

The wig he'd seen her leave the house in was nowhere to be found and her hair was sticking out all over her head. Her face sported streaks of what appeared to be blood, while her nose was red and swollen. Her gown was dirty, she was missing half of her sleeve, and when she moved forward, he noticed the heel from her left shoe seemed wobbly.

Eliza wasn't looking much better. Her red hair was tumbling down her back, her dress was torn in places, and she had a long scratch marring her beautiful face.

"Where's Agatha?" he demanded, right as Matilda walked his way on three legs, tail drooping, and looking more forlorn than he'd ever seen her before, she slipped underneath his bed.

"No need to worry, she's fine," Drusilla said before she looked at Theodore and winced. "We, ah, ran into a little bit of trouble."

Hamilton moved over to Eliza and helped her into the nearest available seat. "Darling, what happened? Did your carriage get attacked, and where exactly is Agatha?"

Grimacing as she settled into the seat, Eliza blew out a breath. "Our carriage didn't get attacked, but we did, and as Drusilla said, Agatha's fine at the moment—completely protected, since the last time we saw her she was surrounded by policemen and they were hauling her off toward a police wagon." She pushed a strand of hair out of her face. "I'm sure, given the time that's elapsed since we last saw her, that she's safely being held behind iron bars. And, because Drusilla and I saw the ladies who attacked us make an unfortunate getaway, well, Agatha's in no immediate danger."

"You need to start at the beginning," Theodore said, taking

Drusilla by the arm and helping her into a chair. "Who attacked you?"

"Mary and her girls, although I don't think they did so
because they'd been following us. It appears to have been an
unusual coincidence.

"However . . . Mary did allow something of concern to
slip," Drusilla said. "Someone's paid her to kill Agatha, which
means we're looking at a determined villain. But enough of
all that. Agatha's probably wondering where we are and why
we're not at the jail yet to bail her out, so perhaps I should
tell you the entire story on the way to rescue her."

"The safest place for Agatha at the moment is behind
bars," Theodore argued. "That means you can take five minutes to explain the basics, which will allow me to formulate
a credible defense in order to get her released."

"Besides," Zayne said, sitting forward, "this latest disaster is no doubt a direct result of something Agatha did, so
perhaps cooling her heels in jail will allow her to think her
situation through to satisfaction. We can only hope she'll
come to a logical conclusion and realize that my idea of finding her a gentleman to keep her in line really wasn't that far
off the mark *and* that a gentleman who has nice teeth really
shouldn't be scoffed at."

Silence met Zayne's declaration. Glancing around the
room, he found Hamilton wincing, Gloria shaking her head,
Theodore watching him with his mouth hanging open, and
Eliza wrinkling her nose back at him. Drusilla, on the other
hand, looked just plain annoyed. "What?" was all Zayne
could think to ask her.

"It wasn't Agatha's fault that we happened upon Mary
and her girls in the middle of B. Altman's."

"She talked you into going shopping when she knows full

176

well how much danger she's in!" Zayne countered, his voice rising with every word.

"*I* talked her into going to B. Altman's," Eliza said, speaking up. "Agatha wanted to continue walking, but it was chilly, and I knew she needed a distraction—no thanks to you, Zayne. Because of that, I suggested we go to B. Altman's. If anyone should be held responsible, it's me."

"No," Drusilla argued, "the fault resides with me. I'm the one who is supposed to be watching out for Agatha, and I should have insisted we remain in the carriage."

"What I want to know," Theodore said, talking over Eliza and Drusilla, who'd begun arguing back and forth, "is what Mary and her girls are doing in New York, and how did they recognize Agatha when she was disguised?"

"I think Agatha being recognized had something to do with Matilda being with her," Drusilla admitted.

Theodore's expression turned incredulous. "Taking Matilda into a fine department store wasn't exactly the most effective method of keeping Agatha safe."

"I should start from the beginning," Drusilla muttered before she began to do just that. Five minutes later, she finished with, "So I had Mary in a headlock and was just about to take her to the ground to join her two friends, whom I'd already taken care of, when police began rushing out of B. Altman's. To my absolute disgust, Hannah, one of Mary's girls, suddenly sat up and began screaming for help as if I were the dastardly villain, and I knew I had no choice but to run for the carriage before I got arrested."

"And I was trying to chase down Matilda," Eliza added, "but then that overly dramatic manager showed up outside and began screaming and pointing toward Matilda. Since the police began to brandish their pistols, I had no choice but to scoop the little darling up and run for both of our lives—well, at least her life. And let me tell you, she's heavy."

She reached out and took Hamilton's hand, patting it absently. "Drusilla and I reached the carriage at about the same time, and as we got settled, we saw Agatha being led away. Since we'd both lost our reticules, we realized we didn't have the means to go rescue her. We also didn't want to take the chance of someone absconding with Matilda and serving her for dinner, so . . . we came back here to regroup."

Theodore moved over to Drusilla and held out his hand. "I suppose, even though I think it might be a little tricky for me to get Agatha released, we should head down to the jail now."

"Let me just get my crutches," Zayne said, swinging his cast over the side of the bed. "And I think we should take Charlotte's cart with us. I'll be able to travel faster through the jail with it than hobbling along on crutches."

"You can't go," Drusilla argued as she took Theodore's hand and allowed him to pull her to her feet.

"Of course I can," he argued right back. "I'm certainly not going to miss a prime opportunity to finally convince Agatha that she has no choice but to go along with my plan of finding her a gentleman." He glanced to the fireplace. "It's unfortunate she burned up my list."

Theodore frowned. "I don't think that's a good idea, Zayne. Agatha, from what I gather, is extremely annoyed with you right now, and as we know, she's unpredictable when she's annoyed."

"Another good point that I'll use to convince her to go along with my plan." Zayne snatched his crutches, rose to his feet, and headed for the door, turning his head to look over his shoulder once he reached it. "Do make sure to bring the cart, Theodore." Ignoring the dire predictions Eliza and his mother began to toss his way, he walked through the door and down the hall.

⟜⟞ ⟞⟜

Thirty minutes later, Zayne sped down a long hallway at the jail, pressing the elevated pedal Hamilton had assured him was the brake, but finding, to his dismay, that the brake was a little . . . temperamental.

"You need to slow down," Drusilla said, panting as she ran by his side.

"Use the brake," Theodore called from behind. "And I don't mean to be an alarmist, but that wheel's looking a bit . . . Ah, too late."

"The brake's not working," Zayne called back right before a wheel suddenly whizzed past him and the cart lurched to the right before it bounced to a stop.

"Smooth," Theodore drawled, grinning down at him even as he held out a hand and helped Zayne to his feet.

"I swear Charlotte's note indicated that she'd fixed that problem, but apparently not," Zayne muttered as he grabbed his crutches from where he'd tied them to the back of the cart. Placing them under his arms, he began to struggle toward a door at the end of the hall, finally reaching it a few minutes later.

Theodore knocked on the door, and it opened almost immediately to reveal an officer on the other side, his expression resigned as he shook Theodore's hand.

"Come to bail out that crazy lady from B. Altman's, have you, Mr. Wilder?"

"How did you know that?" Theodore asked.

"It's become a habit over the past few years with you. But I think you're going to have a rough time of it with this one, Mr. Wilder. She's refusing to tell anyone her name, argued quite vehemently with the guards when they placed her in a single cell, because she apparently wanted to talk to the other female inmates, and has taken to praying . . . loudly, and keeps asking God to send her help."

"Why do I feel like I've been in this exact situation before?" Zayne asked.

"Because you have." Theodore nodded to the officer. "Well, lead the way. I'll talk to her first and then go find a judge to see about getting her released."

"The manager from B. Altman's wants to press charges against the lady, but from what we've been able to gather, she wasn't the only one involved," the officer explained before he smiled. "He's also insisting we send out patrols to round up some rogue pig, although, from what that crazy lady claims, her pig isn't rogue but a pet." He shook his head. "Just goes to show it takes all kinds in this world. You'll find her in the last cell at the end of the hallway."

Thanking the officer, Theodore led the way as Zayne tried to keep up. He finally reached the cell Theodore and Drusilla were standing in front of and looked through the bars, his temper edging up again when he caught sight of Agatha sitting on a lonely bench against the wall.

She was still wearing her wig, although her hat was nowhere in sight and the wig was askew, as was her gown. On closer inspection, Zayne saw that ribbons were dangling from her bodice, her hem was unraveling, and she had a scrape on an arm that was missing not only a glove but a sleeve.

What annoyed him more than anything was the fact her eyes were closed, her face peaceful, and she didn't seem bothered at all that once again she was being held behind bars.

She was a danger to herself, and it was time she was made to see that and correct it.

Clearing his throat loudly and ignoring the looks of warning Theodore and Drusilla were sending his way, he stepped closer to the bars. Agatha's eyes flashed open, and for a brief second he thought he saw relief in them, but then they narrowed as she jumped to her feet and stalked his way.

"What are *you* doing here?"

"Rescuing you, of course."

She looked past his shoulder. "What are *they* doing here, then?"

"Well, because it's you, and you're known to be somewhat obstinate at times, they're my reinforcements. Although I'm supposed to tell you that Eliza really did want to come, as did Hamilton, but Viola woke up and they needed to get her home."

Agatha's gaze flashed back to him. "I'm surprised you didn't try to round up some of those gentlemen you were so keen to push my way and have them help you rescue me as well. Why, since I'm apparently a fragile lady in need of a big, strong man, I just might have fallen at one of your recommendations' feet, especially if he came to get me out of jail and had nice teeth."

"Considering how much of a menace you are, and that's *not* debatable," he said when she began to argue, "it's clear no man will ever step forward to willingly take you in hand, which means . . ."

"What?" she snapped, her blue eyes blazing with heat and her expression furious.

"I'm going to have to marry you."

_11_

O ver the two days since her pesky little jail encounter, Agatha had moved home to her parents' house, but even removing herself from Zayne's vicinity hadn't stopped her from thinking about him. One thought she kept circling back to time and time again was that he was a complete and utter lunatic.

Another troubling idea that continued to plague her was that she was obviously a bit of a loon as well, because when he'd first declared he was going to _have_ to marry her, her heart had given the tiniest lurch. The lurching had come to a rather abrupt end though when she'd realized he was offering to marry her for her own good.

She had been charmed by his damsel-in-distress rescue, until reality set in. No lady, whether or not she was residing behind bars at the time, wanted to hear that the gentleman she'd held in affection for far too long wanted to marry her for reasons other than he held her in great esteem.

As she dunked under the massive amounts of bubbles she'd created in the gigantic marble tub her mother had recently installed in her bathroom, Agatha's thoughts, annoyingly enough, wouldn't stray from Zayne. It was clear he firmly believed he'd extended her a perfectly reasonable offer and that he was even willing to sacrifice his prized bachelorhood in order to see that offer through to fruition, which meant . . .

Sitting straight up in the bathtub, she swiped bubbles out of her face as her mouth gaped open. "I've turned into another Helena." Grabbing the scrub brush, she began attacking her skin, pausing for a moment to let out a loud snort.

"What's going on in there?"

Pausing in midscrub, Agatha glanced to the closed door. "I'm taking a bath, Mr. Blackheart, and there is absolutely no reason for you to lurk right outside my door at this particular moment."

"I heard you talking to someone."

"I was talking to myself."

"You do realize that speaking to oneself is a cause for concern, don't you? It's a clear sign of overwrought nerves."

"Perhaps if you'd leave me alone, I could relax and let the bath dissolve those, er, nerves."

"Relaxing would be much easier for you if you'd stop talking."

"Then go away and I will."

Scooting down in the tub, Agatha listened as Mr. Blackheart's footsteps stomped away.

Her life had gotten very complicated of late, and one of those complications was a direct result of once again being guarded night and day by Mr. Blackheart. Theodore, once he'd gotten her out of and then home from jail, had immediately sent one of his men to fetch Mr. Blackheart, who'd been in the depths of the slums, trying to ferret out information regarding her would-be killer.

Mr. Blackheart had not seemed thrilled to be given the honor of watching over her again, but that less-than-enthusiastic attitude might have come about due to the fact he was completely annoyed with her over her recent arrest.

That annoyance made all the time they were forced to spend together rather . . . trying.

"It's not as if Mary and her girls are going to come after me, since they're now wanted in the city of New York," she said, before she snapped her mouth shut and waited to see if Mr. Blackheart would return to lecture her about talking to herself again. When nothing but the sound of popping bubbles met her ears, she sunk under the bubbles and stayed there for a while, wondering how long it would take to drown her sorrows—or at least her disappointment in Zayne.

From what she'd been able to decipher regarding his relationship with Helena, he'd only agreed to marry her because she'd been so fragile and seemed incapable of taking care of herself. And now it seemed he'd transferred that concern to her. But she was no Helena.

Granted, she did have the propensity to land in rather unusual situations, but she wasn't helpless, and Zayne of all men should realize that.

His misguided idea that he was meant to swoop in and save her from herself was ridiculous.

She was insulted . . . and irritated . . . and completely put out with him at the moment, which was why she'd refused all of his attempts to speak with her over the past two days. Although, if she were honest with herself, her feelings had been somewhat soothed by the fact he was being so diligent in his desire to see her.

He'd taken to driving the contraption Charlotte had built for him past her house numerous times per day.

Lack of air caused her to surge upward from the bath water and gulp in a breath, even as her lips quirked as the memory of Zayne zooming past her house the previous night, seemingly unable to stop, flashed to mind.

She would have almost felt sorry for the man, considering his zooming had ended rather badly when he'd run over her neighbor Mr. Bond. But since he and Mr. Bond had been relatively unharmed, except for a few scrapes and bruises, she'd remained annoyed, not concerned.

He needed to give up and realize she was moving on with her life and that life did not have room for Mr. Zayne Beckett.

It was past time to put her foolish and girlish dreams behind her and get on with things.

If only he would stop infiltrating her thoughts at each and every turn.

A loud bang against the small window over the tub had her practically jumping out of her skin right as she swallowed a huge amount of bubbles.

Before she could catch her breath, the door to the bathroom burst open and Mr. Blackheart rushed in, his pistol drawn and his expression fierce.

"Get down," he snarled as he raced around the room.

Scooting down into the tub so that she was covered all the way up to her neck by bubbles, she peered through still-watering eyes and drew in a ragged breath. "There's no one in here," she finally wheezed.

"What was that noise?"

"Something hit the window."

"Someone was trying to get in?"

Narrowing her eyes, Agatha pulled more bubbles around her. "We are on the third floor. It would be next to impossible for someone to climb in that window—especially since it's so small. And in case you've forgotten, I'm currently in the tub, and I'm not exactly properly dressed to be participating in a friendly chat right now."

Ignoring almost everything she'd said, Mr. Blackheart moved to stand closer to the tub, which had Agatha sinking down until only her nose, ears, and eyes showed above the bubbles while he inspected the window.

"Hmm . . . it is rather small, and being that it is on the third floor, I'll bet . . ." He moved even closer and looked as if he were about to step on the rim of the tub.

"Mr. Blackheart, what in the world are you doing?"

Glancing out of the corner of her eye, Agatha watched as Drusilla rushed into the room, her brow wrinkled and holding a pistol in her hand.

"Something hit the window."

"And you're going to climb up and look out it while Agatha's still in the tub, are you?"

Pausing in the midst of lifting a leg, Mr. Blackheart blinked. "Maybe it would be best if you looked out."

"Maybe it would be best if you took your leave," Drusilla countered.

Mr. Blackheart's expression turned stubborn. "Not until I'm sure she's safe."

Drusilla lifted her chin. "I'm perfectly capable of protecting Agatha."

Cocking a brow, Mr. Blackheart actually smiled, although he appeared less than amused. "And you consider allowing Agatha to get attacked in a department store and then carted off to jail a proper way of protecting her?"

"That could have happened even if you were the one in charge of her, as you very well know," Drusilla said with a sniff. "Now, move out of the way and I'll look out the window.

Although I highly doubt anyone was trying to get in through there, since we're currently on the third floor."

"Someone could have propelled down from the roof."

"In the middle of the afternoon, when anyone could see them?"

Mr. Blackheart frowned. "That is a good point, but maybe someone shot at the window."

"A bullet would have shattered that glass," Drusilla said as she moved to the tub and sent Agatha a look that had exasperation written all over it before she stepped up on the rim and peered out the window. "I can't see much, but if I were to hazard a guess, I'd say the bird that's currently wobbling around down there on the ground is responsible. Oh, and look at that—it's flying away."

"It could have been Mary," Mr. Blackheart argued.

"While this is a riveting conversation," Agatha said. "I can't help but notice that my bubbles are beginning to dissipate, so perhaps you, Mr. Blackheart, should leave before things turn embarrassing for both of us."

Mr. Blackheart's face began to turn an interesting shade of red. "That might be for the best." Turning, he headed for the door, but he spun around again when Drusilla let out a small yelp as she lost her balance and began falling backward.

Rushing to catch her, he managed to grab hold of her before she hit the floor, but then he slipped on the marble floor that was probably wet with bath water, and Agatha could only sit in the tub, at a loss for what to do as he fell. A mere second passed before he disappeared, and when Agatha pulled herself up and looked over the rim, she found the poor man lying on the floor as Drusilla stood over him, her eyes huge. "I say, Mr. Blackheart, are you all right?"

"Now that's an interesting question, and one I can't answer at the moment."

"Well, you can't stay there," Drusilla said.

"I wasn't planning on moving in, Drusilla," he snapped. "I just need a moment to catch my breath and to have the stars I'm currently seeing go away."

"Good heavens, what in the world is going on in here?"

Sinking lower in the tub, Agatha summoned up her sunniest smile. "Hello, Mother, Father. What are you two doing in here?"

"I could ask you the same thing," Roger Watson said as he marched into the room, his wife, Cora, following a step behind. He moved to stand over Mr. Blackheart. "When Theodore and I hired you on to watch over my daughter, Mr. Blackheart, I certainly didn't expect to find you watching her while she's taking a bath."

Cora bent over to shake a finger in Mr. Blackheart's face. "Honestly, sir, we have two other young ladies living under this roof, and finding you in my eldest daughter's bathroom is certainly not setting a good example for them."

"Grace and Lily aren't at home at the moment, Mother," Agatha pointed out.

"So that makes this acceptable, does it?" Cora shot back.

"Well, no, but it's really just another one of those little misunderstandings that I seem to become involved in on an alarmingly frequent basis."

"You think that being in the tub, inappropriately dressed, with a man who is not your husband lying on the floor is a little misunderstanding?" Roger demanded.

"Since I'm in the tub, I'm really dressed—or not, as the case seems to be—appropriately, because who wears clothing while they're taking a bath?"

It soon became evident that her father was in no mood for her odd humor. He seemed to swell on the spot right before he exchanged a look with Cora and then headed for the door. "I'm going to go fetch Reverend Fraser."

Any hint of amusement she'd been feeling disappeared in a flash. "There's no need to fetch Reverend Fraser, Father, because I swear to you, nothing untoward is going on at the moment. Mr. Blackheart was simply doing his job of protecting me."

Turning, Roger arched a brow and gestured around the room. "From what?"

"Ah, well, we think a bird hit the window, but Mr. Blackheart at first thought someone was trying to break into this room."

"We're on the third floor."

"True, and I do believe he finally came to the conclusion he was mistaken about the threat to me, but then he fell, you see, in the process of saving Drusilla, which is why he's still languishing there."

"And have other occurrences of him trying to save you or Drusilla caused him to be a frequent visitor in your bathing chambers?"

"Of course not. Mr. Blackheart has always behaved in a most gentlemanly fashion around me."

"Wonderful," Roger exclaimed, turning for the door again. "Then you won't be opposed to marrying the man since you find him to be a true gentleman."

Gripping the side of the tub, Agatha looked at her mother, hoping for a bit of support, but when Cora let out a sniff and began inspecting the ceiling, she realized she was on her own. "Really, Father," she called after Roger's retreating back, "I can't marry Mr. Blackheart. Why, I don't even know his given name."

Roger spun on his heel and marched back to stand over Mr. Blackheart, who was lying perfectly still, as if he didn't quite know what to do next. "That's easily rectified. What is your name, Mr. Blackheart?"

Raising a hand, Mr. Blackheart rubbed his face. "I don't really care to give out my name, Mr. Watson."

"Your name," Roger demanded between gritted teeth.

Lowering his hand, Mr. Blackheart released a sigh. "Ah, well, what everyone needs to understand is that my mother believed I was going to be a girl. She'd found the perfect name for a girl—that being Francine—and when I showed up, she wasn't exactly keen to abandon it."

"Your name is Francine?" Roger asked as his lips began quivering ever so slightly.

"Well, no. My father did prevail in the end, convincing my mother I'd hardly enjoy living life as a Francine, but she was only willing to modify her preference so much, which is why she named me . . . Francis."

"I think that's a lovely name," Drusilla suddenly said, stepping up to peer down at Mr. Blackheart. "I always told my late husband that if we ever had a son, I'd name him Francis."

"You don't have to humor me, Drusilla," Francis said. "It's a ridiculous name and hardly suits me, which is why I always encourage everyone to address me as Mr. Blackheart."

"I don't humor people, *Francis*," Drusilla said with a shake of her head. "I truly do adore your name. It's honorable, and I think it suits you admirably . . . "

Agatha stared at Drusilla for a long moment, noticing that the lady had a very unusual expression on her face, one that looked quite sappy. It was telling, that sappiness, and also telling that Mr. Blackheart—or Francis, as he'd just disclosed—was looking up at Drusilla as if he'd never seen her before in his life. Or maybe he was looking at her that way because she was still gushing about his name.

" . . . and it has numerous meanings, *free man* being one, but my favorite is *gentle giant*, and that, my dear man, exactly describes you."

"It'll be a good name for Agatha to pass along to her son after she and Francis get married and set up house," Roger said, interrupting Drusilla's speech.

Having had quite enough, Agatha cleared her throat, having to do so twice in order to be heard over Francis's protests. When everyone finally realized she was trying to get their attention and turned her way, she opened her mouth. "I'm not marrying anyone, Father—not Francis, not Zayne, and not some random gentleman who has nice teeth. Now then, if all of you would be so kind as to leave this room, I'd like to get out of the tub, since the water has turned chilly."

"But what about your honor?" Roger demanded.

"My honor is perfectly intact, Father. Although, it might not be for much longer if Francis lingers."

Less than a minute later, Roger had helped Francis to his feet and they'd disappeared through the door—with Roger's threats of continuing the conversation in the library drifting back to her.

"I'd better go make certain Roger doesn't take out his gun," Cora said, making her way to the door. She looked over her shoulder. "Although, maybe I should grab mine. After all the trouble you've caused of late, a shotgun wedding is looking almost appealing." Not bothering to give Agatha an opportunity to respond to that piece of insanity, Cora disappeared, leaving only Drusilla in the bathroom.

Accepting the towel Drusilla handed her after she'd closed the door, Agatha stepped from the tub and wrapped the towel around herself. "I hope you know that my father isn't really considering forcing me to marry Francis," she said when she noticed the frown marring Drusilla's face.

"Francis would make you a more than acceptable husband, and you could do far worse."

"True. I could marry Zayne."

Drusilla's lips curved into a smile. "Zayne, no matter how annoyed you are with him right now, is perfect for you."

"He's delusional."

"Perhaps, but in a very charming way."

"There you go again, up to your old matchmaking tricks, but . . ." Agatha moved out of the bathroom and into her dressing room, waiting until Drusilla joined her before she continued. "Speaking of matchmaking, what in the world is going on between you and Francis?"

"Nothing."

"Why then were you so bothered by the idea my father threatened to make me marry him?"

"I wasn't bothered by that, although I was concerned you would do something rash if your hand was forced, such as run off to investigate some brothel or tenement slum."

"It seems that Zayne's not the only delusional person around at the moment, but since you obviously don't care to delve into your true feelings for Francis, let me distract you by telling you what my intentions are for the rest of the day."

"I knew I shouldn't have brought up the whole brothel idea," Drusilla muttered. "You're planning on doing some investigating, aren't you. And . . . I don't have any feelings for Francis."

"You do, but again, you're delusional, so back to my plan." She opened her wardrobe but jumped back when Matilda barreled out of it. "What are you doing in my closet, darling?"

Sending her a look that had accusation written all over it, Matilda scampered to Drusilla's side and let out a pitiful whine. Bending over, Drusilla gave her a good scratch behind the ears. "You must have shut her in there before you took your bath."

"I think you're right. But in my defense, I've been somewhat distracted of late." Sending Matilda a smile that the pig didn't see since she was now burrowing under Drusilla's skirt, Agatha turned back to her wardrobe and pulled out a pair of trousers.

"Do you honestly believe it's advisable for you to dress as a man when you know full well your father is waiting for you in the library with thoughts of marrying you off to someone on his mind? Why, if he thinks you're up to something impulsive, he really will send for Reverend Fraser."

"Hmm . . . I didn't think about that," Agatha said, stuffing her trousers back into the wardrobe and pulling out the first available gown, a delightful frock of emerald green. "We'll make plans to go tomorrow."

"Go where exactly?"

Taking a moment to slip into undergarments and then the gown, Agatha turned around and waited while Drusilla buttoned her up before replying. "I've decided I need to take a more active role in the investigation of the threats against me."

"That's a horrible idea."

"No, it's not," Agatha said firmly. "What everyone, myself included, has apparently forgotten is that I'm an investigative journalist. I spend my time snooping out stories, and yet, here's the biggest story of my life and I've been content to sit back and allow everyone else to try and puzzle it out."

"Because someone's trying to kill you."

"Which gives me a hefty dose of incentive to locate this person."

"Francis will never agree to this."

"While it's quite interesting to me how quickly you've adopted using his given name, that's a conversation for another time." She moved to the vanity and began twisting her wet hair into a knot. "Francis, being an intelligent gentleman, will realize he has no choice but to agree to help me. He knows full well I'm capable of slipping away from him if I put my mind to it, which means he'll reluctantly offer me his assistance, which I will admit I have come to rely on."

"Francis might eventually agree to help you, knowing he really has no choice, but Zayne will never agree."

"Zayne has no business even being mentioned in this conversation." Tucking a strand of hair behind her ear, Agatha nodded. "There, now I'm ready to face my father."

"I do hope we won't find him holding Francis at gunpoint."

"My father would never resort to that. My mother on the other hand . . . We should hurry."

Taking Drusilla's arm, Agatha exchanged a grin with her before they walked out of the room and down the staircase. Reaching the first floor, she turned toward the library, but her steps slowed when she heard a laugh she knew far too well drift out of the room.

"One would think I'd know better than to continue using Charlotte's invention, especially since those silly wheels keep falling off." Agatha came to a complete stop and began lurking right outside the door, refusing to budge even when Drusilla tried to nudge her forward, and listened as Zayne continued, "I have no idea why I can't seem to fix that little problem, but I do thank you and Mr. Blackheart for coming to my rescue a few minutes ago when I lost a wheel right in the middle of the street. Without your assistance, I might have been run over by a fast-moving carriage."

"Since Mr. Watson was just about to send for Reverend Fraser," Francis said, "if you had been run over, well, at least some last prayers would have been said in a timely manner."

"Why was Reverend Fraser going to be fetched?" Zayne asked slowly.

"He wants the good reverend to marry me to Agatha."

"Oh . . . dear," Drusilla whispered. "Francis has turned ornery."

"And isn't it interesting how well you really do understand that man, although, I just might be able to use that orneriness to my benefit," Agatha said, releasing her hold on Drusilla's arm to breeze into the room.

She glanced around and found Francis casually inspecting his nails, Zayne glaring back at him, and her father sitting in a chair by the fireplace with a clear expression of wariness on his face.

"See what you've done now, Father?" she asked before she pulled up a chair next to Francis and sat down, resisting the urge to lean over and take his hand. "I take it you've told Zayne we're soon to marry?"

Francis stopped inspecting his nails and arched a brow even as the right corner of his mouth curled. "Yes, and he has yet to offer his congratulations."

"He should be offering you his heartfelt thanks since you were one of the gentlemen at the very top of that list he made. Although . . . you might want to show him your teeth."

Francis blinked. "What?"

"He was very concerned about the state of teeth, but if you prove to him yours are in good standing, well, I'm sure he'll give us his blessing."

"What has gotten into the two of you?" Cora asked, stepping

away from where she'd been hidden from view by the window, carrying, of all things, a shotgun.

Agatha wasn't certain if she should laugh or make a dash for the door.

"They're just being ornery," Drusilla said, walking up to take the shotgun firmly out of Cora's hand. "And this can kill or seriously maim a person, Mrs. Watson, which is why I'm going to go hide it now."

"Are you coming back?" Agatha called as Drusilla began marching out of the room.

"Not in a million years."

"What's wrong with her?" Francis asked after Drusilla disappeared from sight.

"I think she's lost patience with us, or . . . she might be annoyed that I'm sitting so close to you."

"I'm sorry?"

Waving Francis's question away with a flick of her wrist, Agatha turned her attention to Zayne, who was sitting in a chair directly across from her, watching her with blazing eyes. "Well, aren't you going to offer us your congratulations?"

"You're not marrying Mr. Blackheart."

"I'm not?"

"After careful deliberation over the past two days, I came to the conclusion that Mr. Blackheart should never have been included on my list. He's much too stodgy for you."

Francis let out a grunt. "I *can* be stodgy."

"I adore stodgy gentlemen," Agatha said, unwilling to part with her charade just yet. "Why, I find stodgy gentlemen absolutely delightful."

"I meant to say dodgy," Zayne said, through lips that were barely moving.

"Dodgy gentlemen are even more delicious to me."

"*I* can be dodgy," Zayne said.

"Indeed," Agatha agreed, "but I find you less than delicious."

"I asked you to marry me, and you know perfectly well that you and I are more suited for each other than you and Mr. Blackheart."

"What you did can in no way be considered a marriage proposal." She lifted her chin. "Besides, Francis was discovered by my father in my bathroom while I bathed, which means we have no choice but to get married."

Zayne frowned. "Who in the world is Francis?"

"Mr. Blackheart, of course. And you must realize, since we've taken to addressing each other by our given names, and again, he was in my bathroom, that we truly are considering marriage . . . to each other," she clarified.

Zayne had the nerve to laugh. "Knowing Mr. Blackheart— or Francis rather—he was probably just doing his job. He most likely thought someone had broken in to your bathroom, which means there's absolutely no need for the two of you to get married. As for using his given name, well, he doesn't exactly look pleased with that turn of events, which means he was coerced into telling you his name is Francis. Besides, you're not going to marry him, because you're going to marry me."

"I think we should leave Zayne and Agatha alone," Roger said, getting to his feet and pulling Cora up beside him. "Francis, I've just noticed that you're soaking wet. I'm sure you'll feel much better if you go and change your clothes."

"While I do have extra clothing here at your house, Mr. Watson, I'm afraid my position as Agatha's bodyguard demands I stay here and see after her welfare."

"I would never hurt her," Zayne argued. He struggled out

of the chair and wobbled for a second. "You insult me by even suggesting that."

Francis rose to his feet. "From what Theodore told me after he had me fetched from the slums, you did indeed hurt Agatha—perhaps not physically, but you've hurt her heart. That's why I intend to stay by her side and make certain you don't do that again."

"I don't see how offering her the protection of my name could have possibly hurt Agatha's heart."

"Clearly you haven't bothered to take the time to see anything at all."

Rising to her feet, Agatha stepped between the two men, who were now bristling with temper. "Gentlemen, enough. I have heard all I want to hear." She nodded to Francis. "You need to go change out of those wet clothes, and you," she said with a nod to Zayne, "need to leave."

"I'm not leaving until I say what I came to say."

"I have no interest in anything else you have to say."

Ignoring her, he continued speaking. "As I mentioned before, I've had quite a bit of time to think lately, and I've realized that, not only is Mr. Blackheart not suited for you, but also that I might not have actually done the whole proposing thing very well."

"You never proposed."

"Didn't I just admit that I hadn't done it well?"

"Well, yes, but you said you'd proposed and you never did that at all."

"Which is why I'm here now," Zayne said around teeth that had taken to clenching.

"You're not being very nice."

Drawing in a deep breath, Zayne released it and smiled. "Better?"

"Not really, because you have this vein on your forehead that always throbs when you're really angry, and it's throbbing up a storm at the moment."

Drawing in another breath, Zayne turned and gestured to Roger, who was standing by the door. "Mr. Watson, would you be so kind as to fetch my crutches? They've fallen behind the chair."

"Why do you want your crutches?" Francis demanded as Roger went to fetch them.

"Why, I was going to whack Agatha over the head with them, of course," Zayne bit out before he took the crutches from Roger, popped them under his arms, and started toward Agatha, his eyes stormy. He stopped in front of her and released a breath right as some of the storminess disappeared. "Agatha, I have no idea why it is that the two of us always find ourselves in peculiar situations, but here we are again." He shook his head, and the last bit of storm in his eyes vanished. "You and I have been friends for a very long time, and I must apologize for hurting you by not giving you the proposal you deserved back at the jail."

"I don't think proposals really should be made in jail," she said slowly even as her treacherous heart gave another one of its pesky lurches. She took a step closer to him. "But, you're right, we have been friends for a very long time."

Zayne smiled. "Yes, we have, and because of that, and because I'm quite fond of you, I'd like to try this whole proposing business again."

Her pulse slowed almost immediately, but before she could speak, Cora stepped forward, her eyes glistening with unshed tears.

"How lovely Zayne, but if I may make a suggestion? You

should get down on one knee, but . . . wait to do that until I go fetch some flowers. They'll add a nice touch."

"Forgive me, Mrs. Watson, but I don't think I'll be able to do the getting down on one knee, considering one of my legs is firmly encased in plaster."

"Good heavens, you're right," Cora exclaimed, "but at least allow me to get you flowers. Roger gave me flowers when he proposed, and . . . it was so very romantic." She turned and began hurrying for the door, but thankfully, Agatha found her voice before her mother disappeared.

"We won't be needing any flowers, Mother."

Shoulders sagging ever so slightly, Cora turned. "We won't?"

"I'm afraid not."

"I thought you liked flowers," Zayne said with a frown.

"I do."

"Then why don't you want your mother to get us some?"

He was so dear, and charmingly oblivious at times, but he'd only proclaimed how fond he was of her, and sadly, even though there was a part of her that wanted to hear his new proposal, she knew he wasn't capable of offering her enough.

She didn't want him to simply be fond of her—she wanted him to love her.

Since it was clear he wasn't ready to profess that particular emotion, might never be ready for that if the truth were told, she knew what she had to do.

"I can't marry you, Zayne," she finally said quietly. "Not like this."

The vein on Zayne's forehead began to throb again. "What do you mean?"

"I thought I was fairly explicit."

"You won't marry me?"

"I'm afraid not."

Zayne's eyes flashed as he stared at her for a long moment. "Fine, that's the last time I'll ask, and now that I think about it, I rescind my offer. I don't want to marry you."

"Fine," Agatha shot back, ignoring the shocked faces of her parents and Francis, "rescind your offer. It was a horrible offer anyway, and I wouldn't marry you if you were the last gentleman on earth."

She spun on her heel, lifted her nose in the air, and stalked out of the room, dead silence following her—until Matilda streaked past her into the library and let out a monstrous squeal. Then Agatha heard what sounded like crutches crash to the floor.

12

Laying aside the book he'd been trying to read, Zayne rubbed a hand over his face and stared into the fire, his mood dismal. In the hours since he'd been knocked off his crutches and then provided a carriage home by a clearly unhappy Mr. Watson, he'd had plenty of time to think, and his thoughts were anything but pleasant.

Agatha had flatly refused him.

Mr. and Mrs. Watson were decidedly put out with him, and he was fairly certain that Mr. Blackheart was contemplating bodily harm, and harm that just might be centered around breaking Zayne's other leg.

Why no one could understand that he'd truly had Agatha's best interests at heart was beyond him. He'd summoned up the courage to tell her how fond he was of her, and she'd thrown that fondness right back in his face, embarrassing him in the process.

Granted, he hadn't even considered bringing flowers, something that Cora seemed to feel was a necessity when a gentleman proposed, but an independent lady of Agatha's nature would surely not have expected flowers, would she?

A knock on the door had him turning his head and finding the butler standing in the library doorway.

"A Mr. Blackheart is here to see you, Mr. Beckett. Shall I show him in?"

The last person, besides Agatha, Zayne wanted to see was Mr. Blackheart. That gentleman had been less than helpful getting him off the floor after Matilda had charged him. In fact, Zayne was fairly sure Mr. Blackheart had deliberately dropped him, not once but twice, in his attempt at helping him to his feet.

"Tell him I'm not at home, Mr. White."

"There's no reason to tell me anything, Mr. White, since I took the liberty of following you and can clearly see that Mr. Beckett is, indeed, at home." Mr. Blackheart brushed past the butler, ignoring the gentleman's sputtered protests.

"Shall I summon the authorities, Mr. Beckett?" Mr. White asked.

"Tempting, but no," Zayne returned as he watched Mr. Blackheart cross over to the windows and begin looking behind the curtains.

"Are you certain?" Mr. White pressed.

"Not really, but I'll call for you if I change my mind," Zayne said absently as Mr. Blackheart pushed aside a large chair and bent down to look under it.

"Forgive me for being forward, Mr. Beckett, but he's acting somewhat peculiar," Mr. White whispered in a voice that carried, even though it didn't distract Mr. Blackheart at all as he went about searching the room.

"He's always peculiar, Mr. White, but he's harmless, at least most of the time, so you may go."

"I'll be right outside the door if you need me, sir, and . . . I have a pistol." With that, Mr. White quit the room, leaving the door wide open.

"What are you looking for, Mr. Blackheart?"

"Please, call me Francis, because everyone else seems to be doing that today, and I wouldn't want you to feel left out." Francis got down on the floor and looked under a table that was pushed against the wall. "Where's Agatha?"

"You don't honestly think she'd be here, do you?"

"She hasn't stopped by in the last hour or two or . . . three?" Francis asked, rising to his feet.

Sitting forward so fast that the book in his lap fell to the ground, Zayne narrowed his eyes. "Don't tell me you've lost her."

"Misplaced, not lost."

"You're supposed to be guarding her."

"I'm perfectly aware of my job description, Zayne, but a man does need to eat upon occasion, and while I went off to the kitchen to fetch a sandwich, Agatha, along with Drusilla, disappeared."

"You should have known better than to go off and get something to eat while she's in a temper."

"Since you're the reason behind that temper, you're as much to blame as I am."

"I asked the woman to marry me."

"What you did could never be mistaken for a proposal."

"Fair enough, but my botched attempt was no reason for Agatha to set her pig on me and allow it to maul me."

"Matilda didn't maul you. She was simply distraught because you'd upset Agatha, and all she did was knock your crutches out from under you. If she'd really been intent on mauling, she would have gone for your good leg."

"I don't understand why everyone believes I upset Agatha so much. She did turn down my proposal after all, and if anyone should be distraught, well . . ."

"You offered her an insult, but we don't have time to get into that right now. Agatha's never been a lady who acts rationally when she's annoyed, which probably means she's out on the streets at the moment. I'm afraid she might be dressed as a man since I found whiskers missing from her black trunk. If you'll recall, every single time Agatha has donned a disguise, especially when she puts on whiskers, she gets into trouble."

"It was hardly proper of you to go through Agatha's belongings."

"I've never claimed to be a proper gentleman." Francis headed for the door. "If Agatha does happen to drop by, tell her I'm looking for her and that I'm not happy."

"I'm coming with you."

"No, you're not."

"I'd like to see you stop me."

Francis's lips curled. "Do you really think it will take much for me to stop you?"

Pushing to his feet and sticking a crutch under his arm, Zayne shrugged. "I know Agatha better than anyone, and I can guarantee you that we'll find her faster if I come with you."

"Why didn't you mention that whole knowing her better than anyone when you asked her to marry you?"

"Do you think that would have made a difference?"

"You really *don't* understand women, do you."

Not bothering to address that ridiculous statement, even though Zayne was rapidly coming to the conclusion he didn't have the slightest understanding of women, he got his other crutch into place and began moving to the door. "I'd love to be able to take Charlotte's cart, but the wheels keep falling off, and I must admit, since Matilda knocked me to the ground, I'm bruised in far too many places."

"You'll just have to wait in the carriage when we make stops then."

"We'll see about that." Zayne headed for the hallway, taking a moment to reassure Mr. White that he was leaving the house on his own accord and not because Francis had threatened him. Stepping through the front door, he paused on the landing, waiting for Francis to join him.

"Ah, Zayne. Going out, are you?"

Lifting his head, Zayne found Theodore walking toward him, a grin on his face, but that grin faded when Francis stepped out of the house.

"What are you doing here, Mr. Blackheart?" Theodore asked. "Where's Agatha?"

"She's missing," Zayne said before Francis could speak. "And do make sure, while you're taking your man to task for misplacing his client once again, to call him Francis. He doesn't want anyone to feel left out."

"I really should have prodded Matilda into a little mauling," Francis muttered before he moved to shake Theodore's hand. "I suppose one could say Agatha's missing, but Drusilla's with her, if that's any comfort. Zayne and I are heading out to search for them now."

"And Agatha would be out at night with only Drusilla because . . . ?"

"Zayne proposed to her again but then had the audacity to rescind that proposal." Francis shuddered. "It was not a pretty sight."

"She'll be back in jail in no time." Theodore spun on his heel and headed toward a carriage that was parked in front of the house. "We'll search together, shall we?" he asked over his shoulder.

Thinking that was a wonderful idea, since he wasn't exactly keen to spend time alone with Francis, Zayne followed Theodore to the carriage. Handing his crutches to the waiting groom, he hoisted himself up and took a seat as Theodore and Francis sat down on the seat opposite him.

"You didn't *actually* rescind your offer, did you?" Theodore asked before Zayne barely had a chance to get settled.

"It was not one of my finer moments, but in my defense, Agatha really annoyed me when she refused my proposal."

"Agatha always annoys you, which begs the question of why you asked her to marry you if you have a problem with her annoying you all the time."

"I decided she needed a man—a husband, to be more specific—to keep her in line. After she got herself thrown into jail yet again, I realized that finding her a gentleman to take her on would be somewhat daunting, so . . . I figured I might as well marry her."

Theodore sent him a rather pitying look. "You've lost your mind. Agatha isn't a lady who can be taken in hand, and marriage certainly won't keep her out of mischief."

"Of course it will. Married women don't run amok. They're content to stay home and mind the children."

"You do remember that Gloria is your mother, don't you? She *still* runs amok upon occasion."

"My mother, bless her heart, has always been rather odd."

"And your sister? Even though Arabella is happily married to me, she continues to enjoy a bit of mischief."

"Oddity runs in the family, at least as pertains to the Beckett women."

"And evidently one man."

"*However*," Zayne continued, "because Agatha turned me down, even though I proclaimed myself quite fond of her, I'm now at a loss as to how to proceed forward with the exasperating lady."

"You told her you were 'quite fond' of her?" Theodore asked weakly.

"Perhaps I should have said *exceedingly fond*." Zayne tapped his finger against his chin but stopped when Francis let out a grunt. "What?"

"I'm *exceedingly fond* of Agatha."

Heat began to curl through him. "If you're so fond of her, why did you balk when I suggested clear back on the train that you should consider forming an alliance with her?"

"Because being fond of a woman isn't enough of a reason to marry her."

"Since when did you become an expert on ladies?" Zayne asked.

"I've spent years guarding one lady after another, and before I entered this business . . . Well, no need to get into that." Francis smiled in a far too condescending manner. "I'm an observer, Zayne, and from what I've observed, ladies expect a certain amount of romance, and they also expect professions of love when a proposal is being made—not a profession of fondness. I highly doubt your declaration caused her heart to go all aflutter."

"Agatha does not have a heart that flutters."

"And that right there is exactly why she turned you down."

Zayne rolled his eyes. "What ever happened to the time when gentlemen simply listened to another gentleman's woes and would shake their heads in commiseration, instead of all this troubling business of wanting to discuss feelings?"

He nodded to Theodore. "Take you, for instance. You did an abysmal job of proposing to Arabella, and"—he nodded to Francis—"no matter that you claim to be an observer of ladies, you're not in a relationship at the moment, nor do I remember you ever being in one, which means you're not exactly qualified to give me advice."

"My not being in a relationship has nothing to do with giving you advice, because I *could* have a lady if I set my mind to it," Francis countered. "Why, with all this talk of Agatha and having admitted I'm exceedingly fond of her, perhaps I should reconsider my role in her life, especially since I *have* seen the lady in her bath and . . . Is something wrong, Zayne?"

Only the glimmer in Francis's eye kept Zayne from flinging himself across the space that separated them and strangling the man, an urge that took him aback.

Why the mere thought of another man witnessing Agatha in her bath upset him so much was a bit of a mystery, especially since he'd just admitted he was merely fond of her, not in love with her, but . . . if he was only fond of her, why feel the compulsion to inflict bodily harm on Francis?

Unwilling to dwell on what such things might mean, especially since both Theodore and Francis were now watching him oddly, Zayne forced himself to relax back against the seat. He didn't even wince when Francis, after Theodore questioned him about it, began speaking about the whole bathing fiasco.

However, when Francis got to the part about almost falling into the tub, Zayne had heard quite enough and decided a change of topic was definitely in order before he really did give in to the whole strangling urge.

"Getting back to the situation at hand, do either of you have any suggestions regarding where we should start our search? It's getting dark, and I, for one, have to admit I'm getting concerned."

Theodore smiled. "If you've forgotten, my friend, I'm

Theodore Wilder, the most sought-after investigator in the state. Do you really doubt my ability to locate two ladies, and find them quickly?"

Three hours later, Zayne definitely doubted Theodore's abilities. They'd traveled to the shirtwaist factory, which had been, surprisingly enough, still operating even though the hour had grown late. Waiting in the carriage while Theodore and Francis ventured inside, Zayne soon found himself disappointed when Theodore climbed back in, stating that no one had noticed anyone unfamiliar moseying around the factory that day. The good news was that Theodore had been able to track down the owner of the factory. He'd learned the previous owner had recently died, which was wonderful news, if one believed that the dead owner had been behind the threats to Agatha. But this was Agatha, and nothing was ever that easy in regard to her, so most likely her nemesis was probably still out there, but at least they could cross one man off the list.

After the shirtwaist factory, they'd traveled through the tenement slums but had no luck, which was why they were currently sitting in a derelict pub, nursing warm ale while trying to come up with another plan.

"They might have gone to the brothels," Francis said as he took a gulp of ale and grimaced before he set the tankard back on the table.

"They wouldn't go there dressed as gentlemen," Zayne argued. "Even they'd realize some of the ladies would try to proposition them."

Theodore smiled. "If that were to happen, you know Agatha would write about it in her next article, pointing out something like how deplorable the lives are of working women since they're forced to give attention to questionable men."

He leaned back in his seat. "Unfortunately, given that Agatha does have a strange compulsion to visit brothels and write stories about them, I can't discount that idea, which means we should go talk to Dot. She might be able to narrow down which brothels we should visit."

"Dot's still in the city?" Zayne asked.

"She's working at the Wild Rose," Theodore said. "Much to my surprise, she's continued to stay off the streets, but she still keeps abreast of the latest scandals brewing."

Francis rose to his feet and fished some coins out of his pocket, laying them on the table. "I suppose that's our only option at this point." He looked at Zayne. "I can go it alone if you're getting tired. After all, you did have a troubling encounter with Matilda, and I'm certain you're a little sore. I know I'm feeling the effects of landing on Agatha's bathroom floor."

Not really caring to revisit the whole bathroom episode again, Zayne was surprised at what came out of his mouth next. "You didn't actually see much of her, did you—while she was in the bath, that is?"

Francis winked. "She has lovely skin, and honestly, I suppose if you get tempted to conjure up another one of those lists with eligible gentlemen on it, you might as well add me to the top." He smiled a very wide smile. "As you can see, I have rather nice teeth."

"Stop baiting him," Theodore said, rising to his feet.

Blinking far too innocent eyes, Francis shrugged. "I can't seem to help myself, but I'd stop if Zayne would simply admit his true feelings for Agatha."

"I did admit my feelings. I admitted that I was fond of her, which translates into I like her."

"But why are you fond of her?" Francis pressed.

Considering the question, Zayne tilted his head. "She's very amusing, very witty."

Francis's lips quirked. "Perhaps that's why Agatha turned you down. I imagine she's looking for a gentleman who shares those same attributes, but you, my friend, are less than amusing at the moment, and in fact, I'd go so far as to claim you're completely witless."

"Really, Francis, now isn't exactly the time to trade insults, with poor witless Zayne—although that was an excellent point." Theodore reached out a hand and helped Zayne to his feet, giving him a pat on the back even as he grinned. "You set yourself up for that one, my friend, but we really do need to get on our way. The Wild Rose isn't far from here, only about a block if we cut through the alley, but do you want me to summon the carriage?"

"I think I can make it a block, but . . . isn't that opium den we visited a few years ago right around the Wild Rose as well? Maybe Agatha went there in search of more information. I don't recall her ever finishing that story she was writing about the place."

"She finished it after you left and even won an award for it. She's very talented at what she does, even though we sometimes forget that because of all her shenanigans."

A shock of something vastly uncomfortable settled over him. Agatha *was* incredibly talented, but he *had* forgotten that, couldn't even recall the last time he'd read one of her articles or even asked her about what she was writing.

She'd been responsible, in her bossy and demanding way, for getting him back to the city, something that had changed his life completely around, and yet . . . all he'd managed to do for her was insult her.

"Let's use the back door," Theodore said, pulling him from his thoughts, although different thoughts came flinging right back to mind after he walked out of the pub and began to follow Theodore and Francis through a rubbish-strewn alley.

It was little wonder she was upset with him.

He'd completely forgotten who she was.

He'd blithely gone about trying to organize her life, when in reality, even though she was constantly getting herself into tricky situations, she was perfectly capable of getting herself out of them.

She was a proud, independent lady of no small success, and yet, he'd been treating her as if she were some fragile young miss in desperate need of his help.

He'd done her a grave disservice and knew in that moment he needed to make amends. Not so that he could convince her to marry him but so that she'd know he'd been foolish about the whole matter, and perhaps they could agree to be friends once again.

He didn't want to lose her friendship, but how was he to proceed forward?

She was obviously miffed with him, and when Agatha was miffed it was pointless to try reasoning with her, but . . . she wasn't one to hold a grudge.

"Ah, Zayne, have you decided you don't want to come with us to this pub?"

Zayne looked up, realizing that while he'd been lost in thought, Theodore and Frances had reached the pub, but he'd walked right past them. Walking back to where they were waiting for him, he moved through the door Francis was holding open. His eyes barely had time to adjust to the dimness of the pub before a woman with brassy dyed hair and a huge smile on her face sidled up next to him and sent him a saucy wink.

"Mr. Beckett, how absolutely delicious to find you back in town," Dot, a woman he'd met numerous times in the past—mostly when he'd been in Agatha's company—purred. She leaned closer to him, prompting him to try and step back, but his crutches seemed to be stuck to the sticky floor. Before he could so much as blink, she'd wrapped her arms around his neck, pulled his head closer, and began kissing his entire face.

Every muscle in his body froze, and he had no idea what to do, but a loud grunt sounded right behind him, causing Dot to pause mid-kiss.

"That will be quite enough of that business."

Dot laughed and released him, just as he spotted a short gentleman with an abundant amount of whiskers attached to his face, a gentleman who just happened to go by the name of *Agatha*.

Considering she'd made the firm decision she was done with Zayne forever, Agatha was amazed by how much fury was currently sizzling through her body as she watched Dot reach up and plant another kiss on Zayne's cheek.

She wasn't quite certain whom she was more furious with, though—Dot, for being Dot, or Zayne, for doing absolutely nothing to discourage the woman.

Opening her mouth, to say . . . what, she really had no idea, she managed to get out, "This is not remotely appropriate . . ." before Dot laughed again, patted Zayne's face, and strangely enough, grabbed one of his crutches away from him. Tucking herself under his arm where his crutch had recently been, she grinned, looking completely delighted with herself.

"How silly of me to greet you so enthusiastically, Mr. Beckett, when it's clear what you really need is a good chair to sit in."

Dot nodded to Agatha. "Shall I take him to our table, Stanley?" Not giving Agatha a chance to respond, Dot began wobbling away on incredibly high heels, leaving Zayne no choice but to step forward as well since Dot seemed remarkably strong and determined to take him with her. He cast Agatha a look that clearly begged for help, right before Dot pushed him past some rowdy patrons and disappeared from view.

Stepping forward to go after them, she found herself pulled to an abrupt stop when someone grabbed hold of her arm.

"Don't even think about it, *Stanley*."

Lifting her gaze, she found Francis glaring back at her, with Theodore glaring in exactly the same way over Francis's shoulder. She summoned up a smile. "Fancy meeting the two of you here—and Zayne, of course. But, ah, speaking of Zayne, I should probably go check on him."

"Not before you explain what you're doing here," Francis said, taking a much firmer grip on her arm than was strictly necessary.

She tried to shake him off. "Zayne doesn't know how to handle Dot."

"Agreed, but I need explanations before you begin hovering over the man, which I know you'll do if only to escape my irritation with you."

"I wasn't planning on hovering."

"Of course you weren't," Francis said before he surprised her by releasing his hold on her, only to pat her arm a second later. "But that has nothing to do with why you left the house without me."

"I needed some air."

"Was there something wrong with the air in the back garden—you know, the garden with the high walls that keep you reasonably safe?"

"I'm sure the air was fine back there, but . . . Oh, very well, if you must know, there's a small matter of business I needed to attend to, a matter that will finally allow me some closure."

"Should I assume you thought I'd stand in the way of this closure?"

"Since I knew I'd have to travel to disreputable places in order to find the answers I need, yes, I thought you would stop me from coming out tonight."

Francis frowned. "My job is, first and foremost, to keep you safe, but I'm not unreasonable, Agatha, nor would I have balked too much about escorting you here tonight. You've become a friend of sorts to me, and while it is my duty to keep you alive, I truly don't want to see you unhappy. I can protect you, but you have to let me know your plans."

Agatha blinked. "What's wrong with you?"

"I was about to ask that very question," Theodore said, stepping around Francis even as he began to scowl at her. "Francis might be willing to appease your every whim at the moment, my dear, which is rather odd, but believe me, I'm not. I expect you to promise me here and now that there'll be no more of this type of business until we figure out who is trying to kill you."

"I'm not promising you any such thing."

Theodore stiffened, but before he could argue, Dot teetered back up to them, sent Theodore a smile, and set her sights on Francis.

"Mr. Blackheart, it's been far too long since I've seen your handsome face," Dot breathed before she launched herself at him and attached her lips to his.

Feeling strangely mollified by the sight of Dot accosting a gentleman other than Zayne, Agatha took a step forward to give Francis some assistance. She stopped when he managed to break away from the now pouting woman and held her at arms' length. "Get ahold of yourself, Dot," he growled.

"Now, now," Dot crooned with a waggle of her fingers,

"there's no need to get stuffy. I was only welcoming you home. Mr. Beckett didn't cause such a fuss."

"Yes, well, Zayne gets a bit bemused when it comes to dealing with ladies, especially unconventional ones, and by the look on his face when you led him away, he appeared to be in shock."

Even though she was exceedingly annoyed with Zayne, she couldn't help grinning just a little over Francis's comment. Zayne really did seem to be bemused by ladies, herself included, but . . . No, she was not going to allow her thoughts to travel in that direction, because then she'd start excusing his behavior. He'd broken her heart too many times now, and she'd vowed that she wasn't going to allow him an opportunity to ever do that again, but he was . . .

Drusilla suddenly brushed past her, interrupting the silent lecture Agatha had been giving herself. Considering her friend was currently sporting elongated mutton chops on her delicate face, she made a rather intimidating picture as she drew herself up and glared at Dot.

"While I certainly understand that your past occasionally comes back to haunt you, Dot," Drusilla began, "we're in the midst of a business meeting. Since it now appears as if our other business associates, if you will, have decided to join us, you're going to have to stop throwing yourself at them so we can continue on with . . . business. If you don't, I'll go elsewhere for information and you won't see a penny of the money I promised you."

"Jealousy is unbecoming in a woman," Dot said with a sniff before she sent Francis a wink, blew a kiss to Theodore, and sashayed her way back to where she'd apparently stashed Zayne.

"What do you think she meant by that?" Francis asked to no one in particular.

Agatha was certain Dot had noticed the clear temper in Drusilla's eyes, brought on no doubt by witnessing Dot launching herself at Francis. But, since this was hardly the time or place to delve into any type of matchmaking, she simply shrugged. "It's Dot. Who knows what she means by most of the things she says."

"She *is* a character," Theodore said before he gestured forward with his hand. "Shall we go join her at the table and continue on with whatever business the three of you are conducting?"

"You're not going to force me out of here?"

"There's no need for such dramatics, Agatha. Because you're here, and there's apparently a reason for that, I'm going to forget that you caused us no small amount of anxiety tonight, but do know that I'm not exactly happy with you."

"I'm not exactly happy with you either, Theodore, especially since you keep calling me Agatha when I'm supposed to be Stanley—and Drusilla's Mort."

"You look nothing like a Stanley," Theodore said before he took her arm, which caused her to roll her eyes and send that arm a pointed look.

"Oh, right." Theodore grinned and dropped his hold on her, although he kept remarkably close to her as they made their way through the pub. Drusilla followed with Francis, mutters of *jealousy* and *crazy ladies* floating between them.

They reached a back table, where Dot was already sitting with Zayne. Agatha took the farthest seat away from them, waiting until everyone sat down before she nodded to Dot. "Why don't you start back at the beginning so everyone will know what we're talking about?"

Dot leaned forward, although she trailed a finger down Zayne's arm as she did so. Taking that finger and using it to stir the drink she had in front of her, she smiled. "Well, to catch everyone up, Stanley and Mort approached me tonight, revealed their true identities— although I'd recognized *Stanley* straight away—and told me they were interested in learning about three ladies—Mary, Jessie, and Hannah—as well as another matter that I'll tell you about later." She paused and took a sip of her drink. "Fortunately for them, and for me since they said they'd pay for good information, I'm acquainted with those women."

"The two of you are trying to track down Mary and her girls?" Zayne asked, shooting a glare Agatha's way, which she staunchly ignored.

"Continue, Dot, if you please," she said.

Dot smiled. "Thank you. As I have just recently told Mort and Stanley, Mary's a hired assassin."

Silence settled over the table, and then Theodore leaned forward. "There's no talk on the streets about an assassin by the name of Mary."

"'Course there's not. She's not from around here, and the only reason I know of her and her girls is because she hid out a few years ago at a brothel I used to work in. I was actually surprised she gave her real name to all of you out in Colorado, but I imagine she must have done so because she didn't think any of you were going to live to tell the tale."

"And you're sure she gets paid to kill people?" Theodore pressed.

"From what I remember, yes, but I have to wonder how good she is at her job since Stanley over there is still alive, even though she's run into Mary twice."

"That's a reassuring thought," Francis muttered.

"Do you know where she is now?" Theodore asked.

"No, but I'll ask around. If I were to hazard a guess though, she's probably long gone. I heard about the ruckus at B. Altman's, and since what happened is all over town, including that bit about the pig, I would think Mary and her girls wouldn't stick around. It'll be too dangerous for them to move throughout the city."

"But they won't get paid if they don't finish their job," Theodore said slowly.

"Excellent observation, Mr. Wilder." Dot winked at Theodore. "That must be why you're such a sought-after investigator."

"I must be losing my touch, because if I'd simply checked in with you sooner, I would've discovered more information than I've uncovered in months."

"I do tend to have a mountain of information at my fingertips, and don't think I haven't noticed that you've been awfully neglectful of late, but I suppose that's due to your delightful Arabella's condition." Dot winked again. "Do make certain you give Arabella my regards. I'm in the midst of knitting a precious baby blanket for her, but that's supposed to be a surprise, so just keep that to yourself."

Agatha leaned across Drusilla, who'd taken the seat right next to her. "The image of you knitting, Dot, is one I truly never imagined, but getting back to the business at hand, would you have any idea who might have hired these women to kill me?"

"I'm afraid there are numerous people in the city right now who might want to see you dead, darling, what with all those brilliant yet all too truthful articles you write," Dot said. "Even though you write under a man's name, I'm afraid people have made it their business to discover your true identity." She smiled. "I've enjoyed everything you've written and really must thank you for bringing to light all the injustices we of the unfortunate class suffer."

"You've read my articles?"

Dot's smile disappeared in a flash. "I do read." Reaching across the table, she patted Agatha's hand. "The article you did about women walking the streets in order to put food on the table is what helped me turn my back on that life. You pointed out, at least to me, that there was a better way, and while working in a pub is still somewhat sketchy, it's more pleasant than my other life. You also helped me realize that I'm not alone in this world, and you did so without preaching. You did it in a way that allowed me to reach out to God through that delightful Reverend Fraser.

"Although I readily admit I'm still a bit of a sinner at times, I'm growing. And for that, you have my thanks." Dot smiled once again. "I believe, and I mean this from the bottom of my heart, that you've been given a gift from God for the written word, and I hope you remember that, even when you're faced with people wanting you dead."

Agatha's vision blurred as Dot's words sunk in. She'd always hoped that her articles would help someone, somewhere, and evidently they had. Wiping eyes that were now leaking, she let out a sniff, which had Dot rolling her eyes.

"Don't get all weepy on me or I'll lose respect for you," Dot said, although she whipped a handkerchief out of the bodice of her dress and passed it over.

Dabbing her eyes with it, Agatha looked up and found Zayne watching her with an expression of complete understanding on his face, that expression making her eyes well up again.

He'd always understood her, but it had been made all too clear that he wasn't ready for the type of commitment she longed from him, even if he had asked her in a peculiar sort of way to marry him.

Tearing her gaze from his, she looked around the table. "Well, I suppose we've made some progress here tonight, at least as pertains to Mary and her girls."

"If she's truly an assassin, you're in more danger than we imagined," Theodore said.

"As Dot said, it's highly unlikely she's still in the city."

"As Theodore mentioned, assassins don't get paid until they complete the job," Francis countered, catching her eye. "You'll have to leave the city."

"I won't leave, not again. Whoever wants me dead has taken too much from me as it is. I was forced to stay away from my family and friends for a year. I missed births and anniversaries and . . . everything." She blew out a breath. "We've been going about it all wrong. I—"

Zayne let out a grunt. "Absolutely not."

"She hasn't said anything yet," Theodore pointed out.

"She doesn't have to," Zayne returned. "She wants to offer herself up as bait."

Agatha's mouth went slack. "How did you know that?"

"Because I know you, and I'm right, aren't I?"

Pushing aside the pesky realization that his knowing her so well had caused her heart to lurch yet again, Agatha forced a shrug. "It's the only way to put an end to this, and since I understand what I'm facing, I'll be prepared."

"You can't be prepared for an assassin, Agatha," Zayne argued. "They're stealthy."

"Mary's not."

"The person who hired her certainly is, since Theodore hasn't been able to track that person down—and he's been trying for over a year."

"Which is exactly why I'm going to stop hiding and go out in the open. I'm not willing to live my life skulking in the shadows for the rest of my days, and this is the only way I'll be able to reclaim it."

"I can't allow it," Theodore said.

"I don't need your permission, Theodore, but I would appreciate your help."

"Is this what you meant when you told me you came out tonight to seek closure?" Francis asked.

"Not exactly," Agatha said, carefully avoiding Zayne's gaze.

"What do you mean, not exactly?" Francis demanded. "What else are you up to?"

"I'd rather not say until the boy we sent out with a message returns." She looked at the watch she'd pinned to the underside of her sleeve. "But he's been gone over an hour, so I hope we'll have an answer soon."

"An answer to what?"

"Why, the answer just walked through the door," Dot said, rising to her feet and gesturing to the dirty boy making his way through the crowd. He pushed his way through the patrons and stopped beside their table.

"Did you have any luck?" Agatha asked.

"I did, and he's right outside," the boy said.

"Who is right outside?" Zayne demanded.

Ignoring the fact that her heart had taken to aching, Agatha squared her shoulders. She'd known the minute Zayne had professed his fondness for her that she had to give up her hopes and dreams of spending her life with the man. She could no longer deny that she was in love with him, but she needed him to return that love, and he . . . didn't.

It was time to firmly put him aside and get on with her life, a life that was meant to be spent pursuing her stories and trying to correct injustices against people like Dot. Dot's words had resonated within her very soul, and she knew God had sent those words to her to remind her that, yes, her heart was broken once again, but her hands and her mind weren't. She needed to move on, move forward, and she was going to have to do that without Zayne.

But she'd promised God clear back in Colorado that she'd help Zayne recover, and this—what was waiting outside the pub—was the last piece he needed to truly heal.

"Would you go invite him in?" she asked the messenger, who nodded and hurried away.

"What are you up to, Agatha?" Zayne asked.

"I think we might have found Willie."

"Who?"

"Willie Higgins, the man you bought your mine from."

"I'd forgotten all about him."

The corners of her mouth curled. "Well, we have been busy of late, and you have been stuck in bed and plagued with mysterious illnesses, but I didn't forget."

For some reason, Zayne's eyes began to blaze. "You have to stop trying to put me and my life to rights, Agatha. Coming here tonight was beyond idiotic, and that you did so because of me . . . Well, I won't stand for it anymore."

"You won't have to," she said softly right as a man with his hat in his hand and looking rather careworn stepped up to the table. His gaze darted around and settled on Zayne.

"Mr. Beckett," the man exclaimed. "Good heavens, sir, what are you doing here?"

Zayne's eyes cooled immediately. "Mr. Higgins, how nice to see you again. I'm apparently here to meet you."

Willie Higgins frowned. "That messenger didn't say anything about you, Mr. Beckett. The boy just told me that there was a matter of business to be discussed, and I thought, given that I let the owner of this pub know I'm in need of a job, that he'd found one for me."

"That's how I knew, when Agatha asked about Willie Higgins, where to find him," Dot said speaking up as she smiled at Agatha.

Willie switched his attention to Agatha and frowned, causing Agatha to grin. "No need to fret, Mr. Higgins. I am indeed Agatha. I'm just in disguise."

"How . . . interesting," Mr. Higgins muttered before he looked back to Zayne and suddenly seemed a little nervous. "I take it the mine turned out to be a bust?"

"He's not here to ask for his money back," Agatha quickly reassured the man. "In fact, since you brought up needing a position, I do think you'll soon find you have no need to continue searching for one." Rising from her chair, she moved to Willie's side, patted his arm, and turned and caught Zayne's eye. "You'll take matters from here?"

Zayne frowned. "You're not staying?"

"There's really no need. I've done what I promised to do, and now it's time for me to leave." She turned and nodded to Francis. "I'm not feeling too well at the moment, Francis, and I'd appreciate it if you'd see me home."

Pretending not to see the looks of concern being sent her way, especially coming from Zayne, she waited for Francis to reach her side, took the arm he offered her, even though she knew they looked rather strange since she was disguised as a man, and with her head held high walked out of the pub.

14

Having woken up incredibly sore the day after Matilda had knocked him to the ground, Zayne had taken Dr. Gessler's advice and retreated to his bed in order to allow his body time to heal. He'd resolutely remained in bed, even though his soreness had disappeared after the first day, hoping that Agatha, since it had been her pig that had landed him in bed in the first place, would pay him a visit and they could clear up matters between them.

That hope, however, had never materialized, and he'd begun to think, since he'd been languishing in bed for over two days, that it probably never would.

Reaching over to grab a stack of papers concerning the new mining deal he was in the midst of completing with Willie, Zayne tried to shove all thoughts of Agatha aside. He began leafing through the pages but gave up a moment later when she continued to plague his every thought.

Why she was still so upset with him, he hadn't a clue. Yes, he'd blundered with the whole marriage situation, but Agatha had never before denied him her company, even when she was irritated with him. And that led him to believe that she might be a touch more than simply irritated with him at the moment.

He had a sneaking suspicion her avoiding him had something to do with that disturbing "closure" business she'd mentioned to Francis. But since he didn't understand what the closure matter involved *and* Francis wasn't responding to any of the messages he'd sent a servant to deliver, he was left with unanswered questions.

The one thing he did know for certain was that he missed Agatha's company quite dreadfully, missed their amusing conversations and the sound of her laughter and . . .

Heels clicking against the floor had him leaning forward, a slice of disappointment stealing through him when only his mother came into view.

"Expecting, or hoping, for someone else?" Gloria asked as she moved to the bed, plucked up some of the papers strewn across it, and began to busy herself with mothering.

Taking a step back after plumping up his pillows, she shook her head. "Honestly, darling, I thought after our last chat that you were determined to fix matters with Agatha. Telling the poor lady you were quite fond of her while you were in the midst of proposing was not really an effective method."

"Fondness is an emotion that most ladies long to receive."

Gloria waved the comment away. "You then, from what Cora explained to me, rescinded your horrible offer."

"I was slightly annoyed over the whole rejecting-me-out-of-hand business."

"Ah, hmm," Gloria muttered before she plopped down in the nearest chair and began, much to Zayne's surprise, to look through the papers she'd scooped off his bed. "Matters going well with Willie?"

"You want to discuss Willie?"

"Until I decide what I want to say about Agatha, yes, I'd like to discuss Willie."

Realizing that whatever his mother finally did decide to say regarding Agatha was not going to be pleasant for him to hear, he leaned back against his recently plumped-up pillows and summoned up a smile. "Willie has agreed to form a partnership with me and help me rebuild the mine. Hamilton's been sitting in on our talks, and he decided that this mining venture should be backed by the Beckett name and funds. Because of that, Willie will soon be leaving to set our plans into motion, and the Beckett family should see, in a year or two, a substantial profit."

"That's lovely, dear," Gloria said. "And how do you feel about Agatha tracking down this poor Willie and allowing you to finally do what's right for the man?"

"I thought you weren't quite ready to discuss Agatha?"

"I've suddenly found my words and organized my thoughts."

"That's a little frightening."

"Yes, it is," Gloria agreed. "So, tell me, what do you have in mind next?"

"As pertains to . . . ?"

"Agatha, of course."

"Since she apparently doesn't want to speak with me, I'm not certain how to proceed."

Gloria nodded. "That's exactly what I thought you'd say, which is why Cora and I have come up with a plan."

"A . . . plan?"

"Indeed. And it's a good one—one of our best, if you must know."

"I was under the impression Cora was put out with me at the moment."

"Oh, she's furious, but she still adores you, dear. That's why she's hosting a intimate dinner party at her house, and we're going to sit you right next to Agatha."

"You do remember that, even though Dr. Gessler proclaimed me recovered, he did caution me against placing myself in dangerous situations."

"He was referring to placing yourself in Matilda's vicinity, not Agatha's, and I highly doubt she'll try to inflict any harm on you while dinner's being served."

"Matilda might though."

"Not if you treat Agatha with the proper amount of respect and don't get annoyed with her again."

"That's a daunting idea, especially since Agatha annoys me frequently."

"Which I've always thought is very telling."

Zayne quirked a brow. "How is that telling?"

"She brings out emotions in you I rarely see."

"I get annoyed with you all the time."

Gloria laughed. "No, you don't, you've only started getting that way since I started meddling in your life, but that has nothing to do with getting Agatha back."

"I don't recall asking you to help me get Agatha back. In fact, if we look at this objectively, it might be best if I simply let her go."

"That's a horrible idea, and of course you need to get her back. The two of you fit each other to perfection."

"I'm not sure I understand."

"You complete each other. You're happiest when you're with her. You smile more, laugh more, and seem more at peace."

His breath stuck in his throat when it suddenly struck him that everything his mother was saying was exactly the truth. Zayne caught her eye, saw the compassion in them, and sighed. "I don't know what to do next."

"Which is why it's a good thing you have me for your mother. I have a few ideas—one of which I'm going to ask you to put into motion at the dinner party."

"And that would be . . . ?"

"You're going to have to grovel."

"I don't think I'm capable of groveling, Mother."

"I'm certain you can summon up a good grovel if you set your mind to it. Consider this—Hamilton groveled, Theodore groveled, and even Grayson groveled. If you want Agatha back, groveling will be required."

"Did I miss anything good?"

Zayne turned his head, his mood immediately improving when Piper skipped into the room, her golden curls bouncing even though they were tied back with a red ribbon that exactly matched her dress. She stopped by the bed, leaned over, kissed his cheek, did the same to Gloria, and then pulled up a chair. Demurely placing her hands in her lap, she tilted her head. "Mama says to give everyone her regards. She and Ben are off to get ice cream. Even though I love ice cream more than anything, after eavesdropping—I mean, overhearing Mama and Aunt Arabella discussing your sad plight this morning, Uncle Zayne—I thought it would be better if I came over here to offer you some much needed assistance."

Smiling, Zayne tilted his head. "While I appreciate your giving up a treat in order to help me, darling, I must point out the fact that you're, well, eight."

Piper's expression turned stubborn. "I helped Uncle Grayson win over Aunt Felicia, and I was only six at that time. Age needn't be taken into account when one is dealing with matters of the heart."

"Good heavens, you've been in your Aunt Arabella's stash of romance novels again, haven't you, dear?" Gloria asked.

Grinning, and not appearing at all abashed, Piper nodded. "I do enjoy a good romance, Grandmother, and because of that, I feel I'm becoming an expert on relationships." She looked at Zayne. "You are a classic case of what a hero should not do to win the affections of the heroine."

"I hate to tell you this, Piper, but Agatha and I have never been involved in a romantic relationship."

"And that is why I insisted Mama let me come over here today. I know I'm young and that you're just humoring me at the moment, but no one has brought up the real problem between you and Agatha."

"And you've figured out what that problem is?" Zayne asked slowly.

"Of course I have. It's all about feelings."

The collar of his shirt suddenly felt a little tight. "Feelings?"

"Exactly," Piper agreed. "I heard Grandmother mention something about groveling, but what should be behind that groveling?"

"Ah . . . feelings?"

"And feelings of the romantic kind," Piper added before she looked at Gloria. "I know everyone seems to think that if Uncle Zayne just tries again and asks Miss Agatha to marry him properly, everything will work out for the best, but it won't, not until Uncle Zayne examines himself and decides why he wants to marry her—and not because of that silly idea he had to save her from herself."

"Saving Agatha wasn't a horrible reason to want to marry her," Zayne argued.

"It *was,* as was your proposal attempt," Piper argued right back. "You should have taken flowers, red roses at that, and a well-prepared speech where you would have proclaimed your undying love and devotion. That would have caused Miss Agatha to swoon at your feet and accept your proposal."

Zayne blinked. "Can you honestly see Agatha swooning at my feet?"

"Well, not with that dismal attempt at proposing you gave her. But it might have happened if you'd approached the matter properly."

"Darling, Miss Agatha is a progressive, independent lady. She's not the type to expect romance."

"I'm an independent lady too, Uncle Zayne—at least I will be when I grow up—but I'm telling you right now, I'll expect romance from the gentleman I decide to marry."

Glancing to Gloria, Zayne arched a brow. "I cannot believe I'm in the midst of this particular conversation with my eight-year-old niece."

"She's always been mature for her age, Zayne," Gloria returned, "and she's right. We adults have missed the obvious."

"Miss Agatha deserves love, Uncle Zayne," Piper said softly. "If you don't love her, you shouldn't have asked her to marry you. And you shouldn't grovel the next time you see her unless you can figure out how you feel about her."

"I'm not certain how I feel," he admitted.

Piper sat up straighter. "Perhaps now would be a good time to examine your feelings."

Heat began to trail up his neck. "I don't really think that's necessary."

"Do you enjoy her company?" Piper continued, ignoring what he'd said.

"Well, yes, most of the time, except when she's being irritating."

"I've seen you when Miss Agatha's irritating you, and most of the time you look amused."

"That might be true, but—"

"Do you miss her when you're not around her?"

"Ah, as to that, I suppose . . . yes, I miss her."

Piper beamed back at him. "Then maybe you really do love her, but since you're a gentleman and gentlemen are known to be rather peculiar with matters of the heart, you just haven't realized that yet."

"I don't know if I'd go so far as to claim I'm in love with her."

"Then you shouldn't ask her to marry you again. It's not fair to Miss Agatha, and even though I really wanted her to be my aunt, much more so than I wanted Helena to be my aunt, you should leave her alone."

It hit him then, hard over the head, completely out of the blue.

Piper was right.

It had taken a child to point out the obvious.

Agatha deserved love, and he certainly wasn't ready, or perhaps even able, to give her what she deserved.

He cared about her, truly he did, but he hadn't *really* considered love.

He'd rushed his proposal because she'd come to his rescue time and time again. He was at heart rather old-fashioned, and her rescuing him instead of the other way around had rankled. That was exactly why he'd proposed to her in the first place, but . . . he'd been completely ridiculous.

Marriage was for life.

He'd forgotten that.

But . . . he wouldn't mind waking up next to Agatha for the rest of his days.

Swallowing, he tried to reign in his unruly thoughts. Dwelling on waking up next to Agatha when he was stuck in a room with a meddling mother and a young niece was bad timing. Piper had seemed rather adamant about him not pursuing Agatha unless he was in love with her, but . . . could it be he might be just the teeniest bit in love?

His head immediately began to throb, but before he could contemplate love and whether or not he was actually experiencing it, Mr. White knocked on the door.

"Begging your pardon, Mr. Beckett, but Mr. Higgins is downstairs, along with his wife and two children. He would like a word with you, but I wasn't certain whether or not you're up for entertaining."

Seeing this unexpected visit as a welcome distraction from discussions of feelings, Zayne smiled. "Show them right up, Mr. White. In fact . . ." He turned to Piper. "Why don't you run down and greet them, Piper? If Mr. Higgins brought his children, they'd probably feel more at ease if you escorted them up here."

"Don't think I don't know what you're doing," Piper muttered before she got to her feet, skipped over to Mr. White's side, and disappeared through the door.

"Have I ever mentioned that I'm glad she's my niece and not my daughter?" Zayne asked, turning to catch Gloria's eye.

"She's certain to cause Hamilton and Eliza no small amount of trouble when she gets older, but she was right about you and Agatha. I never once thought to question you about your deepest feelings in regard to her, having assumed you had more than your fair share of them, but now I'm not so sure."

"I care about her, truly I do, but . . ." His words came to a halt when Piper charged back into the room, a little boy on one side of her and a slightly older girl on the other. Mr. Higgins and his wife followed, and Zayne couldn't help but notice the improved condition of Mr. Higgins's appearance. His hair had been recently cut, his jacket and trousers were new, and his eyes held a trace of excitement instead of worry.

"I must say that you're looking better, Mr. Beckett," Mr. Higgins exclaimed as he moved forward and shook Zayne's hand. "I truly felt sorry for you yesterday when I visited, sir, and appreciated that, though it was clear you weren't feeling well, you still took the time to pull together that deal for me." He stepped back and brought his wife forward. "This is my wife, Lydia, and those are my two blessings, Jared and Alice."

"It's delightful to meet you, Mrs. Higgins," Zayne exclaimed as he introduced his mother to the Higginses. Pleasantries were exchanged, and then Mrs. Higgins moved closer to the bed, her eyes suddenly glistening with tears.

"Willie told me you've been ill of late, Mr. Beckett, so I do apologize for descending on you like this. But since we've decided to leave for the West so quickly, I didn't want to neglect to thank you properly."

"There's no need to thank me," Zayne said. "Willie's the one who started the mine up in the first place, and it was just luck on my part that I happened to discover gold."

"You didn't have to offer him a partnership, or even try to track him down."

"That was actually Miss Watson's idea," he admitted.

Mrs. Higgins smiled. "Of course it was, my dear, because that's what we women do, point our gentlemen in the right direction, but you didn't have to listen to her. Because you did, it tells me you're a man of great character, and you will always have my deepest gratitude for changing our lives forever."

A lump suddenly formed in his throat. He hadn't really

considered how much he would be changing this family's life. Granted, he'd known almost from the moment Agatha had made the suggestion regarding Willie and the mining claim that it was the right thing to do, but he'd never thought the matter through.

The last pieces of the ice surrounding his heart took that moment to shatter, and he felt a sense of peace he hadn't felt for far too long.

It was all Agatha's doing, that peace.

She knew him as no one else did. Knew exactly what he'd needed to make himself whole again, and . . . he didn't want to lose her.

Unfortunately, he'd made a mess of things, but perhaps, just perhaps, he could begin again with her, begin as friends and see where that led.

He swallowed around the lump. "I'm just thankful, Mrs. Higgins, that your husband was so willing to take on this daunting job. The mine's a disaster at the moment, and it'll be slow going until the snow clears in the spring. I do hope you won't regret moving out there with your children."

"We'll be fine, Mr. Beckett," Mrs. Higgins assured. "The children are looking forward to this adventure, and with the more than generous salary you've settled on my Willie and then a stake in the profits in the future, well, our lives will be better than anything we've ever known." She smiled. "The children are especially looking forward to going to one of those frontier schools. Willie told me there's one right in Colorado Springs."

Zayne returned her smile. "Miss Watson will be thrilled to learn of that. She's very adamant regarding children and education."

"Speaking of Miss Watson," Willie began, "we stopped

by her house before we came here. I wanted to thank her as well. She received us graciously, but our visit was cut short when Dot showed up to speak with her."

Zayne felt the smile slide right off his face. "Dot was visiting Agatha?"

Willie nodded. "I must admit I thought it was somewhat odd that Dot would pay a visit to Miss Watson, but then, when I overheard her saying something about finding a Mary, I realized that Dot was simply there to impart some type of information."

A dribble of sweat began to trail down his back. "And was Agatha excited about the information Dot imparted?"

"I suppose she did seem a little excited."

"Wonderful," Zayne muttered before he forced another smile. "You didn't happen to hear anything else, did you?"

"Well, there was mention of a—" Willie shot a look to the children, who were chatting with Piper and Gloria, and then lowered his voice—"brothel and something about someone hiding there."

"I see." Keeping his smile firmly in place, he nodded at the Higginses. "I do hope you'll forgive me, Mr. and Mrs. Higgins, but knowing that Miss Watson has suddenly become apprised of the location of Mary, a woman who is incredibly dangerous, I'm afraid I'm going to have to cut our visit short."

"I do hope I haven't passed on news that's going to make you ill again, Mr. Beckett," Mr. Higgins said slowly.

"I'm sure I'll feel much better once I find Miss Watson."

"Now, Zayne, there's no need to be hasty," Gloria said, her attention no longer centered on the children. "You're in no condition to go chasing after Agatha, and besides, we haven't finished our discussion yet regarding feelings."

"I think it's about time we took our leave," Mr. Higgins

said, taking Mrs. Higgins by the arm. "I'll send you a telegram when we arrive in Colorado. Children, it's time to go."

Before Zayne could even blink, the Higginses had left the room, leaving him with Gloria and Piper.

"I do believe that's the fastest I've ever been able to clear a room," Gloria said. "Do you think it was because I mentioned discussing feelings?"

"Nice try, Mother, but I'm not distractible at the moment." Zayne swung his cast over the edge of the bed. "Would someone mind fetching me my crutches?"

It soon became quite clear that neither Gloria nor Piper were opposed to fetching his crutches—there was just the little problem of their bolting out of the room with crutches in hand after they'd been fetched.

"That's not going to stop me!" he yelled, grabbing hold of the bedpost to pull himself to his feet.

"You'll only make matters worse if you go after Agatha in a temper!" Gloria yelled back.

Pausing for just a second, Zayne realized his mother might have a good point, but Agatha was probably already making plans to investigate brothels. He couldn't sit by and allow her to do that.

She might not be a typical damsel in distress, but she was a damsel who was destined for trouble, and knowing Agatha, she'd find that all too soon. Whether she liked it or not, he was going to rescue her for a change.

15

I know I agreed to the whole coming out from hiding idea,
Agatha, but I really must state yet again that I think bringing Matilda along with us on our first venture outside
without disguises might be a bit much," Drusilla exclaimed.

Taking a firm grip on the bright pink leash she'd attached
to Matilda's matching collar, Agatha pulled the little darling
away from a well-coiffed poodle before she sent the owner
of the poodle a smile. That lady, however, didn't seem to be
receptive to pleasantries, because she let out a sniff, yanked
her poodle to her side, and stormed down the street.

"Nonsense, bringing Matilda was a capital idea," she said
as another lady sent her a scowl and tottered away in the opposite direction as fast as her high heels would allow.

"She's drawing attention."

"Of course she is. It's not every day one sees an adorable pink
P-I-G strolling down Park Row, or anywhere else in New York,
for that matter, which is why I brought her in the first place."

Matilda stopped in her tracks and swung her head around,
sending Agatha a look of deepest reproach.

"Good grief, she's learned how to spell," Drusilla sputtered.

"What a bright girl you are, darling, and I do apologize most profusely for insulting you." Agatha bent over and gave Matilda a good pat. "Perhaps we should find a name you actually like, such as Princess instead of the other P word. Would that be more to your liking?"

Matilda tossed her head, let out a squeal, and then broke into a trot, giving Agatha no other choice but to follow suit as Drusilla kept pace beside her.

"Princess?" Drusilla asked with a snort. "Really, Agatha, you've gone a little nutty of late, especially in regard to your pet."

"Bringing her with us *will* attract attention, which is our goal, if you'll remember. And I couldn't leave her behind. She's been morose of late, ever since she knocked Zayne off his feet, and allowing her to come out today has improved her spirits."

"You've been morose of late as well."

"And I'd rather not discuss that, thank you very much." Agatha stumbled to a stop when Matilda became distracted by a lump of something that might have once been a piece of candy on the sidewalk. "That's revolting," she said when Matilda began slurping it up.

"If you ladies keep stopping, we're never going to reach the *New-York Tribune*, and I would really like to reach that sooner rather than later, because I'm getting edgy out here in the open."

Turning, Agatha smiled. Francis was standing only a few feet away from them, scowling, as he was prone to do, but his scowls no longer rankled, because she'd discovered that underneath his stern and formidable appearance lurked a gentleman with a soft heart and tender sensibilities.

Ever since he'd escorted her home from the pub, he'd taken to asking her about her feelings on a regular basis.

Francis and feelings were somewhat difficult to comprehend.

She'd always known he was a complicated gentleman, but she'd never realized that under his fierce façade was a compassionate and caring soul.

She'd been contemplating a bit of matchmaking of late, when she wasn't occupied with thoughts of who wanted to kill her, what stories she needed to write next, and unwelcome thoughts of Zayne, but . . . No, now was not the time to think of Zayne. She'd been thinking about matchmaking and Francis's soft heart and how well that heart would be paired with Drusilla's soft heart, not that she was certain Drusilla exactly had one of those, but—

"It's not our fault we stopped, Francis," Drusilla said, dragging her from all thoughts of matchmaking. "Matilda found something to eat."

Taking a step closer, Mr. Blackheart frowned. "That's disgusting."

Matilda took that moment to let out a hack, and a glob of something foul erupted out of her mouth.

Agatha released a sigh. "I knew that wasn't good for you."

Before Matilda could snap up the treat again, Francis whipped it off the ground and tossed it over his head, apparently not noticing that the treat immediately attached itself to a lady's hat.

Drusilla's eyes turned huge. "We should get moving."

"Don't you think we should tell that lady she has . . ."

"She already knows, and by the look on her face, if we linger, we're in for a rough time of it." Drusilla pulled Agatha down the street with Matilda scampering to catch up.

"But what happened to Francis?" Agatha swiveled her head and then slowed to a stop when she saw him speaking with the lady in the hat, even as that lady shook her finger at him and then stuck her nose in the air and marched down the sidewalk. Catching her eye, he shrugged and broke into a trot, coming to stop beside her a moment later.

"I knew Matilda was going to be trouble the first time I saw her," Francis said, sending a disgusted look to Matilda, which she blatantly ignored as she rooted around the sidewalk in an obvious attempt to search out more treats.

"He didn't really mean that, Princess," Agatha crooned before she tugged on the leash and began walking again.

"I did mean it, but we have more important matters to discuss, such as why we're going to the *New-York Tribune*." He swung his attention to Drusilla and quirked a brow.

Drusilla quirked a brow of her own. "Don't look at me. I thought we were going to spend the day investigating brothels."

Francis immediately turned grumpy. "Agatha, I thought you and I agreed that, if you decided to do something dodgy, you'd tell me and allow me to come with you."

"Since I'd made plans to travel to the *New-York Tribune* today before Dot imparted the news about Mary, I was determined to follow through with those plans first. So, in all honesty, it's not as if I neglected to tell you anything. And it's hardly my fault Drusilla assumed I'd want to immediately take off to investigate brothels."

"But you *are* planning on investigating Dot's tip?" Francis pressed.

"Of course, but not in broad daylight. And I'll be in disguise, as you will be, so there's absolutely no need for your grouchy attitude."

"Absolutely not," Francis argued. "Being out here is bad

enough, even with all of Theodore's men following us, but going into a brothel knowing Mary and her girls might be there, well, that's just too dangerous."

Agatha craned her neck. "I didn't know we had men following us."

"You're not supposed to."

"Right," Agatha said even as she scanned the crowded sidewalk again, but she couldn't spot a single man she thought might work for Theodore. "I must admit that knowing we have extra eyes on us does make me feel better."

"You're nervous about being out here?" Francis asked slowly.

"I'm not completely oblivious to the danger I'm in," Agatha admitted with a lift of her chin. "I know traveling about the city as myself might cause a, er, situation, but I can't continue to hide for the rest of my life." Her chin lifted another notch. "That's why I've decided to inform my editor that, as of today, I'm no longer going to write under the name of Alfred Wallenstate."

Drusilla narrowed her eyes. "You never told me that you were considering abandoning your pen name."

"Well, now you know." Agatha jerked forward as Matilda began scampering down the street again.

"You'll be dead within a week, two at the most, if you begin writing under your name," Francis said the moment he caught up with her.

"No, I won't."

"I have to agree with Francis on this," Drusilla said, panting slightly when she reached Agatha's side. "You have a very distinctive writing style, and everyone in the city will realize you've been writing as Alfred. Why, you'll be mobbed by all the irate criminals you've written about in the past. Right now we're probably only trying to find one irate person, maybe two, besides Mary and her girls, but if word gets out you're behind all those articles, well, I don't think we'll be able to keep you alive."

Agatha shook her head. "I'm going to respectfully disagree. If I write my articles penned under my real name, I believe all those shady characters I write about will simply disregard what I've written because I'm a woman. They'll just assume I'm some flighty young miss bent on amusement, while others, those like Dot, will still be able to take comfort from the idea someone is writing about their plight in life."

Drusilla sighed. "Strange as it seems, that almost makes sense."

"Good, because we're here, and I'm determined to move forward with my idea." Agatha pulled Matilda to a stop in front of the *New-York Tribune*. Glancing up, she gave herself a moment to simply stand there and appreciate the building's spire tower, a sight that never failed to move her. In the midst of the troubling situation with Zayne, she'd allowed herself to forget that she'd managed to make her way in a profession that catered to men—but no more. She was a journalist, a good journalist. When Zayne had left her two years before, she'd made the decision that she was not meant to live the life of a normal lady—she was meant to sniff out the injustices of the day.

Normal ladies were expected to remain safe inside a house with a brood of children tugging on their skirts while their big, strong husbands kept them safe. She'd never be satisfied living such a life—even if she had occasionally thought about what her children might look like if Zayne just happened to be their father.

She pushed that idea firmly aside and reminded herself that she needed to focus on her career, not a love life, and especially not a life with Zayne. This was the first step in reclaiming her life *and* her ambition.

Pulling Matilda away from the leg of a gentleman the little pig had taken to investigating, she edged off the sidewalk and moved to the front door of the *New-York Tribune*.

"Are you certain about this?" Drusilla asked.

"Fairly certain, and if nothing else, walking through this building with Matilda by my side will certainly draw notice. If we're fortunate, someone will write a story about it, or at least a small posting in the society page."

Francis rolled his eyes. "That's reassuring."

"You don't really want to have to guard me forever, do you?"

"If it means keeping you alive, of course I do."

"You really aren't a horrible man after all."

Before Francis had an opportunity to respond, someone opened the front door of the *New-York Tribune* and Matilda charged through it, leaving Agatha with no option but to follow. Tugging Matilda to a more manageable rate of speed, she nodded to a few of her fellow journalists who were milling around and continued forward.

"You're definitely drawing attention," Drusilla exclaimed when she caught up to her. "And just out of curiosity, how many of these gentlemen actually know who you are?"

"Quite a few."

"What do you mean, quite a few?" Francis demanded.

Agatha pulled Matilda to a stop. "While the public knows me only as Alfred Wallenstate—except for that scoundrel, or two, or maybe three, who wants me dead—there are numerous journalists here who have seen me meeting with my editor from time to time, and . . . because they're journalists, a few of them figured out who I am."

"Why wasn't Theodore or I ever informed of this?"

"I highly doubt someone at the *New-York Tribune* is trying to do me in. They'd have little incentive to do so, since I've never written about them, and—"

"*Pigs* are not allowed in this establishment," a voice suddenly proclaimed, causing Agatha to stop mid-word and glance up. She found herself pinned under the glare of a thin gentleman who looked somewhat familiar. He blinked and then blinked again. "I say, is that you, Miss Watson?"

Before Agatha could speak, let alone remember the gentleman's name, Matilda lurched forward, pulling the leash out of Agatha's hand as she charged directly at the gentleman standing in front of them. The poor man's eyes bulged, he let out a remarkably high shriek, and then spun around and raced away in the opposite direction with Matilda in hot pursuit, Francis a step behind the pig.

Agatha rushed forward but was forced to a stop a second later when a man stepped directly in her path.

"Why am I not surprised to find you responsible for this latest fiasco, Miss Watson?" Mr. George Chambers, her editor at the newspaper, asked, tugging his jacket over his large frame even as he shook his head at her.

Smiling, she shook her head back at him. "Everyone knows it's the mark of a great journalist to be in the midst of fiascos on a regular basis."

"Very prettily said, but tell me, what have you brought for me today? And I'm warning you, it'd better be good."

"My articles are always good, but I don't have a story for you, since I just sent you an entire feature last week regarding gold mines."

Mr. Chambers waved that away with a beefy hand. "Yes, yes, the feature you gave me on the gold mines was fascinating, but I need something new, and I need something now. Mr. Reid has gone off and done the unthinkable, and I'm short a feature story for this weekend."

"What was so unthinkable?"

"He got married. The new wife wanted a honeymoon. He obliged her against his better judgment." He sent her a glare. "That your suitor?"

Agatha turned her attention to where Mr. Chambers had switched his glare to Francis's retreating back. "That's Mr. Blackheart, my bodyguard, remember?"

"Ah, yes, now I do, but you're not planning on marrying the man in the near future, are you?"

"I don't think Mr. Blackheart would have me, Mr. Chambers."

"Excellent. Well, not that the man doesn't return your affections, but that you won't be getting married to him soon."

"I don't hold Mr. Blackheart in affection," she said slowly.

"Then why did you tell me you did?"

"I'm fairly certain I never mentioned anything about affection, but really, sir, my personal life is not actually any of your concern."

"It is if you're planning on abandoning your writing to settle down and bring up a pack of youngsters. I need warning of such events, since I have to make certain I have enough writers. Our readers demand their stories, don't you know?"

"I have no intention of abandoning my writing, nor am I planning on marrying in the foreseeable future. But I must tell you, Mr. Chambers, I find it somewhat offensive you would make such a statement. Do you badger your male writers regarding their marital aspirations?"

At that moment a high-pitched scream split the air. "Good heavens, I completely forgot Matilda is chasing some poor gentleman, and evidently, Mr. Blackheart hasn't met with much success in catching her."

Mr. Chambers' ruddy complexion suddenly wasn't all that ruddy. "Who is Matilda?"

"She's my pig," Agatha said before she dashed in the direction of the scream and caught sight of Drusilla charging down a different aisle. To her amazement, something came huffing up behind her, and that something turned out to be none other than Mr. Chambers. "Run faster, Miss Watson. That's Mr. Horace Pitkin your pig is chasing, and if you've forgotten, he's a nervous sort. The slightest drama sends him into a tizzy, and he has a deadline to meet."

Increasing her speed, she rushed past a row of desks, nodding to writers she knew as she dashed onward and turned down a long hallway only to stop in her tracks at the sight that met her eyes.

Matilda was head-butting a chair Mr. Pitkin was standing on, and with each butt of her head, another high-pitched scream launched out of Mr. Pitkin's mouth. Francis seemed to be trying to talk in a soothing manner to the pig, although why he wasn't trying to grab her leash was a bit of a mystery.

"Get her leash," she called as she started forward again.

"She tried to bite me when I did that."

Agatha skidded to a stop. "Matilda doesn't bite."

"You might want to remind her of that, because she's been trying to get to this gentleman's leg ever since he jumped on that chair."

Prodded into motion when Matilda let out a rather disturbing grunt, Agatha snapped her fingers. "Matilda, enough, you will cease attacking Mr. Pitkin at once."

To her amazement, Matilda didn't stop but continued knocking into the chair as Mr. Pitkin continued screaming.

"Get this demented pig away from me," he shrieked.

"She doesn't like the word P-I-G," Agatha yelled, then snapped her mouth shut when she remembered Matilda had figured out what those letters meant. To her relief, Matilda was grunting so loudly that she didn't seem to hear her. "Try calling her Princess. She adores that word."

Mr. Pitkin sent her a look of utter disbelief, but his disbelief turned to relief when Francis stole up behind Matilda, snatched the leash from the ground, and gave it a firm tug, hauling Matilda over to his side. "Don't even think about biting me," he warned the pig.

Matilda's ears drooped. She let out a whine, sat down, and promptly turned her head toward the wall.

Agatha moved to help Mr. Pitkin, who was trembling, down from the chair. "I must beg your pardon, Mr. Pitkin. I don't know what got into her."

"Apology not accepted, Miss Watson," Mr. Pitkin snapped.

Looking Mr. Pitkin up and down, Agatha was surprised to discover he'd changed his look since the last time she'd seen him, which was probably why she hadn't immediately recognized him. Instead of having incredibly short hair, as he had had before she'd headed out west, his hair brushed against the collar of his shirt. And he was no longer dressing in baggy clothing, but in a jacket that was neatly tailored to his thin frame and trousers that didn't sag over his shoes. The ugly black spectacles she vaguely remembered him wearing had been replaced with a more fashionable style, and overall, he looked better kept than he had the last time they'd seen each other.

"You're looking well," she finally said.

"I looked better before your pig got ahold of me."

"And again, I'm very sorry she chased you, but I—"

"I have no desire to hear your excuses for her behavior. This is the *New-York Tribune*, a reputable establishment and one not meant for farm animals."

Thankfully, Agatha was spared a response to that bit of snippiness when Mr. Chambers finally lumbered up next to them, bent over, and began wheezing.

"Are you all right, Mr. Chambers?"

"I'm fine," he said before he gave another wheeze and straightened. "I think a more important question would be how Mr. Pitkin is doing?"

"I was just attacked by a pig. How do you imagine I am?" Mr. Pitkin returned.

"At least Miss Watson hasn't acquired a tiger for a pet," Mr. Chambers said with a hearty laugh, that laugh dying a rapid death when Mr. Pitkin let out a sniff. "Don't you have a deadline looming, Pitkin?"

Mr. Pitkin released another sniff and then, without a single word, marched away.

"Writers are such a needy lot," Mr. Chambers muttered. "He doesn't mingle well with the rest of the staff, so don't take offense over his behavior, but he's a harmless sort." Mr. Chambers looked over Agatha's shoulder and winced. "Unlike Mr. Jenkins, who, unfortunately, seems to be walking this way."

"So the rumors are true. The prodigal daughter has returned."

Agatha suddenly found herself the recipient of a daunting glare cast her way by a handsome gentleman standing a few feet away from her.

"Do I know you?" she asked.

"I don't believe you've been given that pleasure." The gentleman stepped forward and held out his hand. "Mr. Nicolas

Jenkins, reporter extraordinaire and a *huge* fan of your work, Miss Watson."

Agatha took the offered hand, forcing a smile instead of grimacing when the infuriating gentleman squeezed her hand a bit harder than was strictly necessary. "It's a pleasure to meet you, Mr. Jenkins, but I'm afraid I'm unfamiliar with *your* work. What is it that you write?"

Mr. Jenkins's hand tightened again, and Agatha knew she would probably have bruises, but then Francis stepped forward and let out a growl that had Mr. Jenkins immediately releasing his hold on her. He eyed Francis for a moment, then returned his attention to her, his expression less than friendly. "I took up where you left off, Miss Watson. In fact, Mr. Chambers brought me on from a rival paper right after you departed the city." His eyes narrowed. "And just so we're clear, I cover the tenement slums, the factories, the shipyards, and everything else of a nasty nature, and I intend to continue doing so. However, do feel free to snoop out stories in all those brothels you seem so fond of. I don't actually care to delve into that particular nastiness."

"I'll keep that in mind," Agatha said. "But do know that I have no intention of only writing about brothels. This city is swarming with unpleasantness, and I, for one, enjoy sifting through that unpleasantness to find the perfect story."

"Stick to the brothels, or your bodyguard over there just might find himself out of a job. . . ." With that, Mr. Jenkins sent her another smile, nodded to Francis, who was watching him intently, winked at Drusilla, and stalked away.

Turning to Mr. Chambers, who'd not spoken a single word during the exchange, Agatha arched a brow. "*That's* who you brought on to replace me? You couldn't find someone a bit nicer?"

Mr. Chambers dug a handkerchief out of his pocket and mopped his perspiring brow. "He's a difficult man, Miss Watson, but he writes well. You should probably stay out of his way."

"I think I should go speak further with the man," Francis said before he nodded to Drusilla. "You'll watch over Agatha?"

"I think I'd be more effective with Mr. Jenkins," Drusilla said, her eyes glittering. "He's one of those charmingly chauvinistic types, and he might let something slip. After all, he winked at me."

"Which is why I'll deal with him," Francis argued, holding out Matilda's leash to Drusilla.

"You may stay with Agatha," Drusilla said before she strode away, leaving behind a glaring Francis with leash in hand.

Mr. Chambers' brow furrowed. "What in the world was that about?"

"It's nothing for you to worry about, sir," Francis explained. "We'll handle it."

"Handle what?"

Moving closer to her editor, Agatha summoned up another smile. "Did I mention that I actually have a reason for visiting the paper today?"

"I'm hoping you're going to tell me you were just teasing me about not having a new story ready."

"I rarely tease, Mr. Chambers, and no, I don't have a new story, not just yet. I do have some ideas, but that's not what I wanted to speak with you about."

"Am I going to like what you have to say?"

"I guess we'll soon find out."

Strolling out of Mr. Chambers' office fifteen minutes later, Agatha spotted Francis leaning against the wall, Matilda sound asleep by his feet. She glanced to the left and found Drusilla pacing back and forth, her posture perfect as always even though she was practically sizzling with annoyance.

"May I assume your conversation with Mr. Jenkins didn't go well?" she asked as Drusilla stopped pacing and seemed to be gritting her teeth.

"He's an insufferable man, insulted me at least fifty times, didn't let anything of interest slip, and then, had the audacity to ask me out to dinner. He's lucky I didn't shoot him."

"He asked you out to dinner?" Francis growled, moving forward so quickly he jerked poor Matilda's leash, and the little pig woke up in a flash right before she was pulled a good few feet across the hard floor. She let out a pitiful whine, which had Francis stopping even as he winced. "I do apologize, Matilda. What a rude awakening that must have been for you."

Drusilla grinned. "Nice to see you're still immune to the little darling's charm."

"She has grown on me," Francis admitted. "But getting back to Mr. Jenkins. Shall I go track him down and demand satisfaction from him?"

Drusilla's grin widened. "Since I'm fairly certain duels are considered illegal, no. But I thank you for the offer, even though I'm perfectly capable of seeing after myself. Besides, the man is no longer here. He said something about a story and left rather abruptly, right about the time I mentioned my stellar ability with a pistol."

"We'll have to set someone on him to watch his every move," Francis said.

Agatha nodded. "Agreed, and I have to admit I feel somewhat foolish not realizing my threat could have originated from the paper, but it'll be easy enough to find out if Mr. Jenkins is behind everything."

"Don't let your guard down," Drusilla cautioned. "Mr. Jenkins is a nasty piece of work, but we shouldn't assume he's behind your threats until we find real proof. You need to remain vigilant." She took Agatha's arm. "But enough about that for the moment. How did Mr. Chambers react to your idea about writing under your own name?"

"He didn't balk at all, but that might have been because he was hardly listening to me, was more concerned about trying to puzzle out what had happened with Mr. Jenkins."

"He'll figure that out soon enough," Francis said. "He seems to be an intelligent gentleman, if somewhat harried. Although, since he didn't balk at you writing under your actual name, that might be cause for concern. I suppose I'll need to snoop around his background as well, because no one can be considered innocent at this point."

"I doubt Mr. Chambers wants to do me in considering I provide him with stories readers like to read."

"I'm still going to investigate him. Let's go."

They'd almost reached the door when Agatha noticed Mr. Pitkin standing in the hallway, his back pressed up against the wall, his eyes bulging. Sending him a nod, which he didn't return, she hurried Matilda out of the building, having to exert extra pressure on the leash when Matilda caught sight of Mr. Pitkin and began to grunt. Pulling her pig down the steps, she brushed a gloved hand against her forehead but froze mid-brush when a carriage pulled to a stop directly in front of her.

Francis was blocking her with his body before she could take so much as a single breath, but his body relaxed a second later, and a glance around him explained why.

Getting out of the carriage was none other than her mother, an expression of relief on her face as she set her sights on Agatha.

"Thank goodness you're actually where you told me you'd be today," Cora said before she gestured to the carriage. "I told Zayne you were traveling to the *New-York Tribune* this afternoon, but he didn't believe me." Cora stepped closer and lowered her voice. "He seems to possess a remarkably suspicious nature when it comes to you and keeps going on about brothels for some peculiar reason."

Agatha looked around her mother, and sure enough, Zayne was peering right back at her through the open door of the carriage.

Irritation, mixed with something she didn't want to contemplate, stole through her.

She'd been trying her best to push the man out of her thoughts, but that was slightly difficult to do, especially when he showed up with no warning. Narrowing her eyes, she edged closer to him. "What are you doing here, Zayne, and why are you with my mother?"

"Ah, well . . ."

"He's with me," Cora interrupted when Zayne continued sputtering, "because I certainly couldn't allow him to go searching for you in that dangerous contraption Charlotte made for him. Especially since he'd come up with the crazy idea of attaching the thing to a pony, and, hmm . . . it was a very frightening sight for me to see, him careening down our street, yelling for assistance."

"You attached the cart to a pony?" Agatha demanded, moving even closer. "Why in the world would you have done that? Surely you must have realized it wouldn't be safe."

Zayne's eyes turned stormy. "If memory serves me correctly, Agatha, you're the one who suggested the whole pony idea during one of our many discussions about Charlotte's invention, but I have to say, it was not advisable in the least. The rear wheels fell off due to the speed, I think, and I was then pulled down the street with the back end dragging, and . . . I'm really going to have to add some cushioning to the cart, because my backside will never be the same. I swear I could feel every little rock we ran over."

"He was pathetic," Cora added, "and I couldn't very well allow him to pop the wheels back on and continue looking for you. So I offered him the use of the carriage and decided to come with him."

Reluctant amusement replaced her irritation until she remembered her mother mentioning something about brothels. Handing Matilda's leash to Francis, who'd remained unusually silent, she marched right up to stand directly in front of Zayne. "Why would you think I was off to a brothel?"

Zayne had the audacity to look smug. "Willie told me."

"And that prompted you to attach a pony to Charlotte's invention and come looking for me? Why didn't you simply take your own carriage?"

"Because Gloria and Piper made off with my crutches, leaving me with only Charlotte's cart as a way out of the house, and after I made it outside, I thought I might as well just use the cart, so I had a groom attach a pony to it."

"And why, pray tell, did Gloria and Piper take your crutches?"

"They didn't think I should come after you."

"Which was excellent advice, advice you should have heeded."

"I couldn't very well sit at home, knowing you might be off to a brothel."

"I'm not your responsibility, Zayne, and you need to re-member that." Blood began pounding through her veins. "It's not your job to save me from my silly little self, and besides, what exactly would you have done if you'd found me in a brothel? Extended me another one of your charm-ing proposals?"

Zayne's lips thinned. He opened his mouth, closed it, and suddenly shook his head before he blew out a breath. "I don't want to fight with you, Agatha. And no, I wasn't intending on extending you another proposal."

"What were you planning on extending me?" Agatha asked slowly.

His smile turned into a grin, one that did strange things to her heart. "I'd have probably given you a lecture about the poor choice you'd made by going to a brothel in the first place, but then, well, I would have offered my assistance, just like old times."

"I don't think we can go back to those old times."

"True," Zayne agreed, "but we can go forward, and in order to do that, I need to tell you something."

She drew in a deep breath and tried to steady nerves hum-ming with something troubling . . . but something delicious at the same time. "What is it?"

"I need to apologize to you."

Agatha blinked and lifted her head as Zayne leaned out of the carriage door, his eyes holding a trace of something warm yet disturbing.

"Apologize?"

"Indeed, and you deserve a good one from me, especially since I've come to understand I did you a grave injustice with my botched marriage proposal and then subsequently rescinding that proposal. I never meant to hurt you."

Right there and then, her heart stopped beating, if only for a second or two.

She'd tried to convince herself she could put Zayne behind her, convince herself she didn't really love him. But now, faced with the notion that he seemed to be getting ready to give her everything she'd ever wanted, everything she'd ever dreamed about, which was really just him, she couldn't deny her feelings anymore, especially to herself.

She wanted him.

Wanted to live her life right beside him for the rest of their days.

Wanted to share children with him and enjoy the sunsets with him and . . .

"It is my dearest hope that you and I will be able to resume our friendship."

Her heart started beating again, too fast for comfort as pain washed through her.

"You want to be my friend?" she managed to get out.

"I've always thought of you as one of my dearest friends, and I've missed your companionship ever since we had our falling out."

She would not cry, at least not in front of him.

She drew in a breath, forced it from her body, and summoned up what she could only hope was a convincing smile. "I would love nothing more than to be your *dear friend*." Blinking rapidly as she felt her eyes fill with tears, she turned, and began inching away from the carriage, unwilling to allow him to see her distress.

"Agatha, is something the matter?"

Only everything.

She swallowed a sob, kept her head averted, and let out a laugh, wincing when she heard the shrillness of it.

"There's nothing the matter, Zayne. Now, if you'll excuse me, my editor's demanding a new article from me, and with a deadline looming and no clear idea as of yet what I'm going to write, I must get right to work."

Taking a moment to nudge Matilda awake, she took the leash from Francis even as she ignored his look of concern. Squaring her shoulders, she marched down the sidewalk, waiting until she was certain Zayne wasn't trying to follow her before she allowed her tears to fall.

16

I hate to bring this up, Uncle Zayne, especially since you seem to be in a grouchy mood, but you really should have taken my advice and *not* followed Miss Agatha yesterday. You've made a complete mess of things now."

Pulling his attention away from the passing scenery, even though there wasn't much to see since it was dark outside, he settled it on Piper. She was sitting on the opposite side of the carriage from him, looking adorable in her blue velvet coat, even though her expression was decidedly annoyed. "I believe you might be right."

Her mouth went slack. "You agree with me?"

"Especially about the part regarding my making a mess of things."

Piper grinned. "That's why I love you so much, Uncle Zayne. You're almost always willing to admit when you've been a, well, you know . . . "

"I think the word you're hesitating to say is *idiot*," Zayne finished for her. "And thank you for saying you still love me. It's comforting to know someone does."

"Grandmother loves you, as does Aunt Arabella and my mama, but I have to admit, they're very disappointed with you right now. Aunt Arabella even went so far as to say she thinks you've lost Miss Agatha for good this time."

"She told you that?"

"Not exactly. I was listening outside the door at the time, but I would appreciate it if you didn't make mention of that. I'm not actually supposed to be lurking, er, waiting outside doors when people don't realize I'm there."

"I'll keep it to myself."

"That would be great, Uncle Zayne." Piper blew out a breath. "I also overheard, unintentionally again, that the ladies believe Miss Agatha might not love you anymore."

"Agatha was never in love with me."

"There you go again, being an idiot. Of course she was in love with you. That's why she got so upset when you told her you wanted to resume your friendship with her."

Something that felt like a smidgen of hope slid over him. "Do you really think so?"

"Of course, but again, you might have messed that up."

Leaning back against the seat, Zayne had a feeling Piper had the right of it. He'd seen the sheen of tears in Agatha's eyes the day before, hadn't really known why she'd been close to tears, but had known he'd once again done something to cause her pain. The question was, how was he to proceed forward and right the wrong he'd delivered her?

"I've come up with a plan that might help you get her back, but I'm only going to tell you my plan if you can admit you want more than friendship with Miss Agatha."

"Is that why you insisted on traveling to the Watson dinner party with me instead of your parents?"

Piper grinned. "Well, that's one of the reasons. The other

reason was because you've been looking pathetic all day and I thought you might need cheering up."

He'd been *feeling* pathetic all day, but . . . if Piper had a plan to set that disturbing situation to rights, it would be churlish of him to refuse her assistance.

"What's your plan?" he finally asked.

"What are your true feelings for Miss Agatha?" she countered.

"They're complicated."

"My plan's 'complicated' as well, and since it won't take us that long to get to the Watsons' house, you might want to figure out your feelings quickly if you want to hear what I have to say."

"I'm more than fond of her," he admitted.

"Good, that's a start. How much more than fond of her are you?"

"I'm not certain."

Muttering under her breath, Piper reached in the pocket of her coat and pulled out a crumpled piece of paper that she smoothed out on her lap. "I wrote down some notes that might help you." She bent her head over the paper. "Let me see. . . . Ah, here we go. Do you find Miss Agatha beautiful?"

"Certainly. She's exquisite, in fact."

"That's a good word, and if she does allow you to speak with her tonight, you should tell her that."

"How am I supposed to bring that up in the conversation?"

"I'm eight, Uncle Zayne, I don't have all the answers." Piper returned to her list. "Next question. . . . Hmm, I think I'll just lump these all together. Do you find Miss Agatha amusing, intelligent, irritating, annoying, and just plain good fun?"

"I don't think asking me if I find Agatha irritating is the best way to decipher the extent of the romantic feelings I might hold for her."

"Of course it is. Daddy gets irritated with Mama on a daily basis, but that doesn't stop him from loving her and kissing her all the time. I once overheard him—again, quite by accident—tell her that he finds her absolutely adorable when she's being her most irritating. Why, he told her just the other day, after she got involved in that B. Altman's disaster, that he was annoyed with her for getting into mischief again, but then he pulled her right down on his lap and hugged her."

"Hamilton has always been rather strange."

Piper waved that comment away with a delicate flick of her wrist as she scanned her notes again. "Here it is—the most important question you have to answer." She looked up. "You're going to have to close your eyes for this one."

"What?"

"Why is it gentlemen always seem to ask questions when they really should just do what we ladies tell them to do?"

"You just admitted you're only eight. I don't think that quite puts you in the *lady* category yet, Piper."

"Close your eyes."

"Fine," Zayne said before he closed his eyes and stifled the urge to laugh. "I'm waiting."

"This would be much more effective if we had a piano playing in the background."

"What?"

"I read about this experiment in one of Aunt Arabella's romance novels. In the scene, there was a piano playing in the background. I wonder if it would have the same effect if I hummed a little tune?"

"Piper . . ."

"Oh, very well, but close your eyes tighter. I can see you peering out through those slits from clear over here."

"They're closed. I can't see a thing, but as you pointed out, we're rapidly getting closer to the Watsons', and you're wasting time."

"Don't you think it was so nice of Mrs. Watson to invite me to come over tonight? I mean, not everyone would be that considerate, and even though I won't be able to sit down to dinner with the adults, I'll get to see Lily and Grace, and I just adore Agatha's sisters."

"Was that what you wanted me to picture, Agatha's sisters?"

"Of course not, but it shouldn't escape your notice that Mrs. Watson is a very nice lady and she'd make a wonderful mother-in-law. From what I overheard Grandmother say, Mrs. Watson is holding this dinner party at the unheard hour of seven because she's worried about you getting tired."

"I'm going to open my eyes in five seconds if you don't get on with this."

"You might want to work on that surliness problem you're currently experiencing, Uncle Zayne. Miss Agatha will never come around if you continue being so grouchy."

"One . . ."

Zayne heard Piper rustle her paper. "Are your eyes still closed?"

"They are."

"Good. Then picture this. You're old, rocking on a front porch somewhere out in the country. Can you see that?"

"I can."

"Who is sitting by your side?"

All the breath left him in a split second as an image of Agatha, glorious with white hair, immediately sprang to mind.

She was rocking at a rapid pace—not really surprising given that she approached everything that way, but she was holding his wrinkled hand and laughing.

Everything clicked into place.

Of course he was more than fond of the lady. She was everything he needed and more precious to him than he'd ever realized.

His eyes flashed open, and he found Piper peering back at him with clear expectation on her face.

"So?"

"I saw Agatha."

"I knew it!" Piper exclaimed. "I knew you'd see Miss Agatha, which means . . ."

"I might be in love with her."

Piper narrowed her eyes. "No. Try again."

Drawing in a breath and slowly releasing it, he nodded. "I love her."

"Excellent." Piper beamed back at him before she suddenly folded her hands together, dropped her head, closed her eyes, and went silent, until she muttered an "Amen" and raised her head. She grinned. "I had to tell God thank you."

"Because . . . ?"

"When I got this idea, even though I wasn't sure you'd go along with me, I asked God if He could make sure to let you see the right lady. Since you saw Agatha, I thought it only fair to give Him the credit for that and for showing you exactly who I wanted you to see."

"He certainly did that." Zayne tilted his head. "Maybe I should say a prayer as well."

Scooting off her seat, Piper joined him, placing her small hand in his. "Would you like some help with that?"

Laughing, Zayne bent over and kissed the top of Piper's

head. "While I readily admit I've been put out with God ever since my first accident, I haven't forgotten how to pray, darling, but I would welcome the chance of praying with you."

Bowing his head, he drew in a breath, taking a moment to gather his thoughts. "Heavenly Father, I've been remiss of late in my relationship with you, and for that, please forgive me. I take this opportunity now to thank you for the blessings you've given me, especially the one of giving me my delightful Piper, a girl who is far wiser than her years and who I love more than I can say."

A small sniff from Piper had his lips curling before he continued. "I also need to thank you for allowing me to finally see, even though my eyes were closed, what's been right in front of me for years. I realize now that Agatha is the love of my life, and I ask, most humbly, if you could possibly stay by my side and guide me as I try to correct the wrong I've done her. In Jesus' name I pray. Amen."

"That was a good one, Uncle Zayne," Piper said with another sniff before she removed her hand from his and rubbed her hands together. "And now, on to my plan."

The peace that had settled over him diminished just a bit. "You actually have a plan?"

Piper rolled her eyes. "Of course I do, but . . ." Her expression turned wary. "You have to promise not to get mad at me."

"I don't think I've ever been mad at you, darling, and besides, you're trying to help me."

Blowing out a breath, Piper reached into the pocket of her coat again and withdrew something, reaching out to place that something in his hand.

Looking down, he found a ring nestled there, and not just any ring, but a diamond ring surrounded by rubies—one that had once belonged to his grandmother. "Where did you get this?"

Shifting on the seat, Piper bit her lip. "Out of Grandmother's jewelry box. She showed it to me after you got back from out west and told me you'd given it to her to hold safe until someone else in the family needed it." She lifted her chin. "I thought, if you came around to the idea you loved Miss Agatha, you might need it tonight."

"You think I should give this to Agatha *tonight*, in the middle of the dinner party?"

"She deserves a grand gesture, something to make up for all the horrible gestures you've given her of late. And, oh, I should probably mention that Mrs. Watson's small dinner party has turned into more of a, ah, ball."

"What?"

Piper patted his arm. "Miss Agatha's decided she wants society to know she's returned, so she's doing that by having her mother invite most of society over. Aunt Arabella said Uncle Theodore isn't really too keen about this idea, but Miss Agatha had made up her mind about it, and poor Mrs. Watson had to enlist Grandmother's help in order to pull it off."

"Your grandmother was probably thrilled to do so, but I can't help but wonder why she never mentioned the whole ball idea to me."

"She didn't want you to balk about going," Piper explained. "But back to the plan. You'll need to think up a romantic speech and then present that and the ring to Miss Agatha right after dinner is over, before the dancing. That way you can, after she accepts your proposal, sweep her out on the dance floor and waltz her around the room."

"You really should stop reading Arabella's romance novels,

and I don't think I'm up for the whole sweeping idea since I'm not exactly smooth on my feet right now."

Piper's nose wrinkled. "I forgot about that, but I suppose you'll just have to settle for giving her the ring, and maybe you could kiss her."

"I can't kiss her in front of society—that wouldn't be proper—but . . . I can give her a declaration of my feelings for her, and the ring." He looked down at the ring lying in his hand. "It'll suit her."

"Miss Agatha will love the rubies, but what I don't understand is why Miss Helena gave the ring back to you. She's one of those ladies who adores pretty things, so it's a little confusing to me why she didn't keep it."

"I never gave this ring to Helena."

"Why not?"

Zayne held up the ring. "You never got to meet your great-grandmother because she passed away before you were born, but this was her ring. She always said I was one of her favorite grandchildren, and I used to spend many a happy afternoon visiting her, trading amusing stories, and talking about anything and everything that came to mind. She was a delightful lady, and when her health began to fail, she called me over to her house one day and gave me this ring." He smiled. "It came with instructions, of course, the most important being that this ring was very special and I was only supposed to give it to a lady who could match me wit for wit."

"That's why you didn't give it to Miss Helena," Piper said with a nod. "She wasn't witty and . . . she wasn't very nice."

"You were a mere baby the last time you saw Helena, Piper. How can you say she wasn't nice?"

"I was four, and I clearly remember that she never wanted

to play with me, and she used to pinch me when you weren't in the room."

"What?"

"It's true, although how anyone could pinch an adorable child—which everyone insists I was—is a concern. I think it's possible Miss Helena didn't like me because everyone paid so much attention to me and neglected her when I was around. That's why she waited until she was alone with me to get even."

Something unpleasant settled in his stomach. Helena had been a lady he'd considered a friend and his future wife, but apparently she'd had no difficulty treating a small child in what could only be considered an abhorrent manner. "Why didn't you ever say anything?"

"She told me she'd slip into my room at night and cut off all my hair if I squealed on her."

The unpleasant feeling increased. He'd almost married Helena, had been determined to spend the rest of his life with her for so long.

"If you ask me, it was a good thing, breaking your leg that first time and all. Now you're not stuck with Miss Helena forever." Piper grinned. "And since you never gave that ring to her, you'll be able to fulfill your grandmother's wishes and give it to Miss Agatha, the lady you truly love."

"I'm really sorry I didn't know Helena was treating you poorly, darling."

"It wasn't your fault, Uncle Zayne. You've never been one to understand ladies, so you can't be held responsible. Besides, that was years ago, and I'm quite over it."

"I think you might have just insulted me."

Piper grinned. "*Anyway*, getting back to the plan. . . . I won't be around to help you, so you're going to have to figure out how to go about it on your own."

"You could always peek through the banister, and if I look like I'm floundering, yell some helpful hints down to me."

"Miss Agatha won't be impressed if I yell down instructions to you. Just tell her what's in your heart and pray that'll be enough to get through to her."

Zayne opened his mouth, intending to ask Piper more questions, but the carriage began to slow and then came to a stop. A groom opened the door almost immediately. He helped Piper out and then extended Zayne a hand. Before he had an opportunity to take that hand though, the groom disappeared, replaced with Zayne's mother who was looking decidedly agitated.

"Where have you been?" Gloria demanded.

"In the carriage, and before that, getting ready. It does take me a little longer to dress these days, Mother, and you should be thankful my valet is so talented with a needle and thread or else I'd be at this . . . ball with one of my trouser legs completely cut off."

"I do sometimes forget you're not quite normal yet, darling," Gloria said before she accepted Zayne's crutches from the groom and thrust them at him. "And I see Piper told you about the dinner party changing into a ball."

"Something *you* conveniently neglected to reveal," he said as he climbed down from the carriage and got his crutches into place.

Gloria blinked far too innocent-looking eyes at him. "My memory isn't what it used to be, but you're here, and that's all that matters. We need to get inside."

"Why?"

Taking hold of his arm, even though he was trying to maneuver his crutches, Gloria began pulling him forward as Piper walked a few feet ahead of them. After stumbling on an uneven patch of sidewalk, he stopped, causing Gloria to do the same. "I realize that something dastardly must be occurring, Mother, which is why you're forcing me to gallop up to the house, but I'm afraid I'm not up for more than a casual stroll."

"Good heavens, do forgive me, Zayne. Perhaps you should set our pace—although if you could make it a slightly rapid pace, that might be for the best."

Refusing to move, even when Gloria began tugging his arm, Zayne arched a brow. "What's the matter?"

"Quite a bit, actually, but I'm afraid I don't have time to go into all the pertinent details. What you need to know is that Agatha clearly took your words yesterday to heart—the ones about resuming *only* your friendship with her—and Mr. Jeffrey Murdock is dancing attendance on her even as we speak, as well as Mr. Blackheart."

She released a sigh. "I would love to think those gentlemen are not quite up to snuff, but Mr. Murdock has turned far too attractive of late, what with his distinguished demeanor, and Mr. Blackheart has taken to treating Agatha as if she's made out of spun glass, which I must admit is incredibly appealing to ladies and . . ." She stopped and drew in a gulp of air. "Drusilla is trying her best to appear nonchalant about the situation, but she looks as if she longs to bash Mr. Blackheart over the head with the first available object."

"What's wrong with Drusilla?"

"Zayne, open your eyes. She holds Mr. Blackheart in affection, and while I don't believe he's in love with Agatha, his protective instincts have been stirred, and he's a distinct threat to you at the moment." She pushed him into motion again. "What do you intend to do about all this?"

"Piper came up with a plan for me."

"You're going to use a plan Piper came up with?"

"It's an ingenuous plan. I haven't worked everything out yet, but Piper's given me some pointers, so I think I'll be fine."

"You'd better tell me what you're intending to do."

"Grandmother," Piper said as she turned, a clear sign she'd been eavesdropping once again, "you're just going to have to trust us. The last thing Uncle Zayne needs is too much advice thrown at him. It'll just make him nervous."

"I hope you know what you're doing," Gloria grumbled right before a lady wearing an enormous amount of feathers on her head called out a greeting, and Gloria, after sending him a look of warning, went off to speak with her friend.

Maneuvering up the steps, Zayne and Piper joined the receiving line. Apprehension stole over him the closer they moved toward Mr. and Mrs. Watson. He had no idea what type of reception he would receive from them. After all, he was once again responsible for hurting their daughter, and they might not be as forgiving this time. When the couple in front of him stepped aside, he found himself facing Cora, who looked him up and down for a moment and then smiled, although her smile didn't quite reach her eyes.

"How lovely you're feeling well enough to join us, Mr. Beckett. Agatha will be thrilled that her *dear friend* was able to attend her dinner party tonight."

Cora hadn't called him Mr. Beckett in years, which meant she was clearly annoyed with him, and he was suddenly thankful he didn't see her trusty shotgun lying within her reach. Summoning up a smile, he hobbled closer to her and took her hand, raising it to his lips. "You're looking delightful this evening, Mrs. Watson, and I do appreciate your invitation."

"I wanted to take you right off the list," Roger exclaimed, although he did step forward and shake Zayne's hand. "I had high hopes we'd finally join my soap business with your railroad business, and don't even get me started on the plans I'd made for dealing with all those miners you'll probably be hiring soon. Why, think how much soap they'll need, and—"

"Roger, this is not the time to berate Zayne about a lost business opportunity," Cora whispered, her face turning pink. "You agreed with me that it was time for us to get our expectations in check regarding Zayne and Agatha, so I'll hear no more about soap deals, if you please."

"Uncle Zayne's got a plan that might help you with those expectations, Mrs. Watson," Piper said, peering around Zayne's side. "It's a good plan too, just like something you and my grandmother would have thought of if you'd had more time, and . . . I think you're going to like it."

"A plan?" Cora breathed, her eyes suddenly glimmering in a way Zayne had seen often over the past few years. "You need to tell me all about it." With that, she stepped forward, took Piper by the arm, and began walking away, leaving Roger to handle the receiving line on his own. "I'll just take Piper up to Lily and Grace, dear. You don't mind, do you?" she asked over her shoulder before she increased her pace and disappeared a moment later.

"You'd better have a really good plan, Zayne," Roger muttered. "These ladies have been driving me mad of late. I'm warning you right now, if you hurt my darling Agatha, or botch matters up further than they've already been botched, I'll get out Cora's gun—or better yet, I'll let her get out her gun."

"I won't botch it this time, sir. I promise."

"See that you don't," Roger warned, turning to the next waiting couple but turning back a second later. "She's in the ballroom."

Smiling his thanks, Zayne slowly moved toward the ballroom, struggling up the flight of stairs until he finally reached the second floor. He was soon surrounded by friends he hadn't seen in over two years, and after exchanging the expected pleasantries, he excused himself and began to make his way through the crowd of guests, stumbling to an immediate halt when he caught sight of Agatha.

She was more than exquisite this evening, dressed in a shimmering gown of deep purple, her inky-black hair piled on top of her head with delightful wispy curls teasing her face. Even from the distance that separated them, he could tell her eyes were sparkling, and she seemed to be having the time of her life as she laughed at something the gentleman standing next to her whispered in her ear.

The man looked up, and Zayne recognized him as Mr. Jeffrey Murdock, one of the men he'd put on the ridiculous list he'd made, but the man he'd also scratched off. Jeffrey leaned closer to Agatha to whisper something else in her ear, and right there and then, all logical thought disappeared.

Starting forward, his only goal was that of reaching Agatha's side to pull her away from the dastardly Jeffrey, a gentleman up to that point Zayne had always liked, but a gentleman he now believed was entirely too attractive for his own good. Why, Jeffrey didn't suit Agatha in the least, and he certainly shouldn't be whispering anything into her delicate ear, and . . . was he holding on to Agatha's arm a bit too intimately?

Zayne made it all of five feet before his crutches suddenly shot out in front of him, most likely because the ballroom floor had been polished to a high sheen and was remarkably slippery. He watched them clatter to the floor, realized he was beginning to lose his balance, and flapped out his arms in a desperate attempt to right himself. He got his one good leg in place and was just about to breathe a sigh of relief when someone brushed against him from behind and he felt himself spinning as he fell, his body stiffening as he plunged toward the floor. A flash of purple met his gaze, and then he landed on something soft.

A loud *woof* met his ears, and then a breathless laugh followed. He suddenly came to the uncomfortable realization that the flash of purple had been Agatha, and he was now stretched right out on top of her.

It was a rather peculiar place to find himself in, especially since they were in the midst of a ball, and honestly, would there ever come a time when she wasn't racing to his rescue? It was a touch unnerving at times, but instead of being annoyed, as he seemed to have been much too often of late regarding her rescuing him, he found it rather endearing and . . .

"You're squishing me."

Pushing up enough so he could see her face, he looked down into her familiar blue eyes and lost himself for a moment in their clear depths. She had wonderful eyes, expressive and sparkling and . . .

"I can't breathe."

He blinked. "Good heavens, Agatha. I do beg your pardon."

"Apology accepted, but you might want to consider getting off me sooner than later since your cast is beginning to cause me to lose feeling in my legs."

"Right, ah, yes, of course." Rolling off Agatha, he landed on the hard floor and found himself staring up at Eliza, who was peering down at him with wide eyes. She leaned closer to him.

"Is this part of the plan Gloria told me you and Piper hatched up?"

"Well, no . . . " he admitted as Hamilton appeared beside Eliza and got him back on his feet in a flash. Accepting his crutches from Mr. Blackheart, who was glaring at him, he mumbled a word of thanks, stuck the crutches under his arm, and looked around for Agatha.

She, unfortunately, was on Mr. Murdock's arm and was allowing the gentleman to help her straighten out her gown, and the sight of that had fury rushing through Zayne's veins.

Having come to the conclusion that Agatha was the love of his life, he couldn't stand by and wait another second to tell her of his love because . . . well, he just couldn't.

He wanted everyone to know how he felt about Agatha, wanted to do anything to make her happy. In fact, he'd even go so far as to buy Matilda a friend, which would surely make Agatha love him just a little, but . . . no, that was insane thinking. Matilda was enough trouble on her own, and—

"Are you all right, Zayne?"

Blinking out of his thoughts, he realized Agatha was speaking to him, and she was no longer holding on to Mr. Murdock's arm, something that pleased him to no small end. He took one step forward and smiled. "I should be asking you that question."

"I'm fine, although it really is amazing how heavy that cast of yours is."

"You look exquisite tonight."

Agatha bit her lip. "Did you hit your head when you fell?"

"No, you cushioned my fall."

"Oh, well, thank you, then—not for falling on me, but for the 'exquisite' description. That was a very nice thing to say."

"You're welcome, and . . . ah . . ." His heart began pounding in his chest, but it slowed ever so slightly when, from out of the corner of his eye, he saw Jeffrey Murdock throw up his hands in obvious defeat and disappear through the crowd.

"Was there something else you wanted to say?" Agatha asked.

"I'm not sure where to begin."

Agatha released the smallest of sighs. "I really need to get back to the other guests, Zayne."

"I've been a complete and utter fool in regard to you," he said quickly.

"I'm sorry?"

"You have no reason to be sorry, but I on the other hand . . . Agatha, can you ever forgive me?"

"I'm not certain I understand where you're going with this."

Zayne couldn't help but notice the room had gone remarkably quiet. He took a step closer to Agatha. "You've always been there when I needed you most, and yet I have never once told you how very dear you are to me."

"Yes, you have. You told me I was one of your dearest friends."

"I misspoke."

Her eyes widened. "You don't want to be friends with me?"

"It seems I just misspoke again. Of course I want to be friends with you, but . . . ah, hmmm . . . You see . . ."

"Your pocket, Uncle Zayne, your pocket," he heard Piper yell from somewhere in the midst of the crowd.

His niece was probably more than a little annoyed with him since she'd been forced to step in even though she'd wanted him to do this completely on his own.

"Was that Piper?" Agatha asked.

"Yes, and I don't think she's pleased with me. I'm forgetting our plan."

"You have a plan?"

"Indeed, but I probably shouldn't have told you that. I don't think Piper wanted you to know she's been helping me."

"Uncle Zayne, just get on with it," Piper yelled.

"Ah, right. I should get on with it." Fumbling in his pocket, he retrieved the ring he'd stashed there before he'd gotten out of the carriage. He looked up and found Agatha watching him warily, although there was also a trace of something that almost looked like excitement in her eyes.

"I know I've gone about this in a horrible fashion, Agatha. And I know that everyone has made excuses for me because I'm shockingly naïve when it comes to matters of a romantic nature, but . . . this was my grandmother's ring, and she told me, when she gave it to me, that I was only supposed to give it to—"

"To me. You're supposed to give it to me."

The whispers began immediately, even as dread settled in his stomach. Slowly maneuvering his crutches around, Zayne found himself facing none other than Miss Helena Collins.

She was dressed, not for a ball, but for traveling, her light hair looking untidy underneath a huge hat with some type of bird attached to the crown. Two bright patches of pink stained her cheeks, and her expression was decidedly agitated.

Even though she'd been the lady he'd thought he was going to spend the rest of his life with, he felt the most uncommon urge to shake the woman since she'd just ruined what should have been one of the greatest moments of his life.

"Surprise," she said through lips that barely moved.

"What are you doing here, Helena?"

"I've come to marry you, of course, like you promised me." Her eyes began shooting sparks. "What I'd like to know—given that you are *my* fiancé—is why it almost seemed as if you were about to propose to someone else."

Before he had an opportunity to address that bit of nonsense, a loud squeal pierced the air, and Matilda charged into the room. She set her sights on Helena, and then . . . chaos erupted.

17

Hardly half an hour after the humiliating fiasco in the ballroom, Agatha snatched up the handkerchief she'd placed on the seat of the carriage and dashed another annoying tear away. She held up a hand when Francis opened his mouth. "I'm fine."

"Of course you are," he murmured in a very soothing, very un-Francis-like tone. "And might I add that you're looking quite lovely in that revolting frock of pink. I must say, you're one of the few ladies I know who could pull off that particular shade."

A snort took her by surprise, even as Drusilla rolled her eyes and continued tucking her hair underneath a dark wig that had seen better days.

"She'll *be* fine," Drusilla said, bending over to take a mirror out of Agatha's black traveling trunk. "But she doesn't want, or need, coddling. Both of you should remember that."

"I haven't tried to coddle her at all," Jeffrey Murdock said from his place beside Francis.

Agatha caught Jeffrey's gaze. "And I thank you for that, Jeffrey, and also thank you for the use of your carriage."

Smiling, Jeffrey shrugged. "Well, I didn't really see that I had much choice in the matter, considering you jumped in it as I was pulling away from your house. I decided it would be less than chivalrous to throw you out."

"You could have gone on your way after I went back into my house to get my disguises."

"True, but given the trying situation you've just been made to suffer, I thought you might be in need of a shoulder to cry on."

Wiping another tear away, Agatha forced a smile. "You should save that shoulder, Jeffrey, for a lady who'd appreciate it more. I'm done with gentlemen . . . for good this time. And I'm done with tears." Her smile wobbled when a single tear dribbled down her cheek. "Or I will be soon."

Jeffrey released a dramatic sigh. "It seems to be my lot in life these days to discover interesting ladies only to then discover they're incapable of returning my affections."

"I'm not really that interesting."

"I beg to disagree," Jeffrey argued. "Why, it seems to me we're currently off on a lovely adventure, not that I've been given any particulars on exactly what type of adventure it may be, but that, my dear, makes you very interesting."

"We'll probably end up in jail," Francis said.

"Really?" Jeffrey's eyes went wide. "How, um, delightful."

Francis shook his head. "Believe me, jail is not delightful, which is why I'm going to suggest you consider simply dropping us off at the brothel and finding your way home. I'll make certain, if we don't land in jail, that the ladies are returned to their respective residences when we complete our business this evening."

"I don't remember anyone saying we were on our way to a brothel," Jeffrey said slowly. "I thought perhaps, given that you and I, Mr. Blackheart, have disguised our features with whiskers, and Agatha and Drusilla have changed into somewhat questionable gowns and put on wigs, that we were on our way to some type of costume ball."

"Sadly, no," Francis replied before he brightened. "Although, I suppose if we searched hard enough, we'd find a costume ball, and that would be great fun—wouldn't it, ladies?"

Agatha lifted her chin. "Nice try, Francis, but I'm in no mood for another ball. I need to work."

"I understand that, Agatha," Francis began, "but we haven't had time to plan this adventure. All we have is a message from Dot saying that Mary might be hiding out at this brothel. We have no backup, no clear idea what we'll find tonight, and I fear—given your distress over Helena's untimely appearance this evening—that you're not thinking rationally."

"You don't have to come with me."

"Right, because I always abandon you in your hour of need."

Agatha leaned forward. "Forgive me, Francis. I'm not being very fair to you or anyone else tonight. You must realize though that, since we have no idea how long Mary will stay in this brothel, if she's even still there, we have to move now."

"Who is this Mary person?" Jeffrey asked.

"She's an assassin who has been hired to kill Agatha," Drusilla said.

"An . . . assassin?"

"Indeed, but not a very good one, since she's tried to kill me twice now but hasn't met with much success," Agatha said. "Now then, I need you gentlemen to turn your heads, because I have to put my pistols under my skirt."

Jeffrey blinked. "Did she say *pistols*?"

"She did," Francis replied, "but look out the window, because her skirt's going up."

Waiting until the gentlemen had turned their heads, Agatha yanked up her skirt, attached a pistol to her left leg and another to her right. She snapped her two garters to make sure they'd hold the weight and then settled her skirt back into place. Diving into her trunk, she pulled out some makeup and began to smooth some of it over her eyes, wincing when the carriage rolled over a rut. "How do I look?" she asked a moment later.

"Deranged," Drusilla said, even as Francis and Jeffrey said "Lovely" at the same time.

Drusilla sighed. "Stop coddling her. It'll only make her weepy, and then that paint she just smeared all over her eyes will run, and then we won't be admitted into the brothel, and . . ."

For some odd reason, Francis got a very unusual look on his face, just as he began shaking his head. "It was truly deplorable, the way Helena showed up this evening, and I'm so very sorry you had to deal with that, right as Zayne seemed about to propose to you."

"Francis, good heavens, when I said don't coddle her, I certainly didn't intend for you to infuriate her by reminding her of events she probably wants to forget," Drusilla snapped.

"But if she starts crying again, maybe we really won't get admitted into the brothel, and then, well, we can actually make a plan before we proceed with the information Dot gave us and we won't end up in jail."

"I like the way you think," Jeffrey said, earning a nod from Francis and a glare from Drusilla. "What? If you ask me, we're behaving rashly, and I know that I called what we're doing a lovely adventure, but now that I've been apprised of where we're going and that there might be an assassin there waiting to kill poor Agatha, well . . ." He squared his shoulders.

"We should turn the carriage around immediately and return Agatha to her mother. Mothers are known to be experts at dealing with broken hearts, at least my mother seems to be quite knowledgeable on that topic. Besides, poor Cora is probably even now roaming the halls of her house, searching for Agatha and growing more frantic by the moment since Agatha's not there."

"I talked to my mother before I left," Agatha said. "And yes, she did seem worried about me, but she understands that I'm not one to hide away and sulk when life throws a disaster at me. I told her I was leaving the house because I needed some air to clear my head."

"I don't believe it would occur to her that you're on your way to find that air in a brothel though," Francis pointed out.

"Well, no, probably not, but I certainly wasn't going to tell her exactly where I was going. She'd only worry more."

"I hate to be the lone voice of reason in the midst of what seems to be insanity, but"—Jeffrey glared at Francis—"Agatha and Drusilla are ladies, proper ladies, and they're not equipped to deal with assassins—something you, Mr. Blackheart, should know. I truly believe you're going to have to put an end to this before someone gets hurt or, worse, killed."

Francis blew out a breath. "While I appreciate your concern, Mr. Murdock, Drusilla is not your average lady. She's a highly competent investigator who used to work for the government before she began working for Theodore. She's quite handy with a pistol, uses the fact she's a lady to lethal advantage, and I wouldn't dream of telling her I'm putting an end to anything, especially since I'm fairly certain she'd shoot me."

Drusilla's eyes widened, and then she smiled a lovely smile. "Why, that's the nicest thing you've ever said about me, Francis."

"Don't let it go to your head."

"Fine, Drusilla's competent," Jeffrey said, "but what of Agatha? I find it hard to believe she's lethal."

"I can be lethal," Agatha argued. "I'm a great shot, if I'm not trying to shoot something off a man's head, and I have wonderful instincts. Don't I, Francis?"

Before Francis could answer, the carriage began to slow. Agatha peered out the window, her nerves beginning to hum as they always did right before she was about to plunge into investigating. "I think we've arrived."

Jeffrey joined her at the window. "I must say, this isn't an area my coachman normally delivers me to."

"He did seem surprised when I gave him the address," Francis admitted right before the door opened and a groom stuck his head inside.

"Begging your pardon, Mr. Murdock, but I think we might have delivered you to the wrong place."

"Unfortunately," Jeffrey said as he stepped out of the carriage, "you didn't."

The groom's eyes turned huge before he gave Agatha his hand, helped her out and then did the same for Drusilla. Francis climbed out last and surveyed the building in front of them. "Seems like your typical brothel to me." He nodded to the groom. "Have the coachman pull the carriage to the other side of the street and . . . are you armed?"

"We have a shotgun."

"Keep it handy," Francis said before he turned to Agatha and offered her his arm. "This is your chance to turn back."

"Honestly, Francis, when have you ever known me to turn back?"

"I can always hope there'll be a first time."

Taking his arm, she walked with him toward the brothel, pausing for a moment when a shiver slid down her spine.

"What is it?"

"Nothing—just a shiver."

Francis glanced behind her, his grip tightening on her arm. "The last time you felt a shiver we soon found ourselves chased by that tribe of Indians."

"True, but if you'll recall, that was brought about because I was riding one of their horses—although, I truly didn't know that it'd been stolen from them."

"My point is that something bad always happens when you shiver."

"Maybe I'm just cold. It's begun to snow, if you haven't noticed."

"Are we leaving?" Jeffrey asked, looking hopeful as he guided Drusilla to a stop right next to Agatha.

"Apparently not." Francis tightened his grip on Agatha's arm, helped her up the steps, and then paused when the door opened before they even reached it. A heavily made-up woman, wearing a vivid gown of blue, her dyed black hair at distinct odds with her pale complexion, smiled at them from the doorway. "Darlings, don't linger out there in the cold. Come in, come in." Grabbing Francis, she yanked him through the door, causing Agatha to hustle in after them since Francis hadn't released his hold on her.

"I'm Madame Bellefonte," the lady proclaimed as Francis took the hand she thrust out to him and brought it to his lips.

"And I'm enchanted," he returned. "Mr. Brown at your service."

"How absolutely scrumptious you are, Mr. Brown." Madame Bellefonte turned and eyed Agatha up and down. "And who would you be, dear, and why would you desire to come to my humble establishment? We don't normally see lady visitors, unless they're looking for a . . . position."

Agatha swallowed. She hadn't thought about that. Normally when she visited brothels she did so as a servant. Summoning up a smile she hoped came across as somewhat vapid, she giggled. "I'm Daisy Mae, ah . . ."

Glancing around, her gaze settled on a picture filled with scantily dressed ladies with a dog by their feet. "Hound, Daisy Mae Hound, and we're out this fine night looking for amusement. My friend, Mr. Brown, thought that bringing us here, to a, er, establishment of your type, would be just a great lark." She forced another giggle. "I'm hoping you offer gambling, because I just *adore* rolling the dice."

Madame Bellefonte narrowed her eyes. "Do you now?" she asked before she set her sights on Jeffrey. "And who is that?"

"That's my very good friend, Mr. Quinto," Francis explained. "He's not from around here, and he's rather shy, which is why he doesn't care to participate in conversations."

"Hmm, interesting," Madame Bellefonte said as she glanced at Drusilla, who was gazing around with unusually wide eyes, even as a silly smile stretched her lips. "And you would be?"

"In need of a good drink," Drusilla said, not bothering to give Madame Bellefonte the courtesy of a name.

"We serve drinks in the next room, but gambling is up a floor." Madame Bellefonte smiled. "I'm afraid we don't allow ladies in the gambling room—unless they work for me, of course—which means you two lovelies will have to wait outside while the gentlemen play."

"But I adore the dice," Agatha said, keeping her smile firmly in place. "I'll be so disappointed if I can't have a turn."

"Life is filled with disappointments, dear. You'll need to get used to them," Madame Bellefonte said before she took Francis by the arm and began tugging him away. "Allow me to escort you to the gambling room." She looked over her shoulder and nodded at Jeffrey. "Come along, Mr . . . ?"

"Quintino," Jeffrey supplied before he winced.

Madame Bellefonte turned around. "I thought it was Quinto."

"Exactly right," Jeffrey said weakly. "I-I-I st-t-utter when I-I-I'm nervous."

"I didn't hear a stutter when you said your last name."

"Ah . . ."

"I told you he was shy," Francis said even as he casually removed his arm from Madame Bellefonte's grasp. "I think we'll wait on the gambling though, my dear. Since the ladies are barred from that room, I believe we'll repair to a secluded table and enjoy your lovely atmosphere while we have a drink. The night is far too young for me to disappointment Miss Hound, but perhaps later she'll be more disposed to want to part with my company."

"Very smoothly said, Mr. Brown." Madame Bellefonte considered them with eyes that had, unfortunately, turned contemplative. "And you're quite right about the evening being young. Why, it's barely ten, and you'll have hours left to gamble, if *Miss Hound* decides that's permissible." She smiled a very odd smile. "If you'll excuse me, I must get back to business." Releasing a laugh that had the hair standing up on the back of Agatha's neck, Madame Bellefonte patted Francis's cheek and glided away.

"That was close," Jeffrey mumbled. "I was afraid there for a minute we'd have to abandon the ladies."

"That would have never happened, but I have a bad feeling about this," Francis said. "Something's wrong. I have no idea what it is, but we're going to leave as inconspicuously as possible, but as quickly as we can."

"I'm not arguing," Agatha said, taking Francis's arm and strolling with him in the direction of the door, Drusilla and Jeffrey following only a few steps behind.

Unfortunately, when they reached the entranceway, the door was blocked by four burly men, all of whom were standing with their arms crossed over muscular chests, and none of them seemed willing to move out of the way.

"Leaving so soon?" one of them growled.

"I'm afraid Miss Hound had her heart set on gambling, but since we've just discovered she won't be permitted to do that here, we're going to move on to another establishment," Francis said.

"We strongly encourage patrons to stay for a drink," another man said, his eyes hard. "Madame Bellefonte expects certain funds to be spent once someone steps foot through her door." He pointed behind them. "You'll find the bar in the next room."

Jeffrey stepped forward and handed the man a wad of bills. "I'm sure that should cover what we'd spend in the bar."

The man smiled, pocketed the money and pointed again. "The bar's that way."

"And we'll be simply delighted to find it," Francis said, turning Agatha around even as Jeffrey's brow wrinkled.

"He's just going to keep my money."

"He is," Drusilla agreed, "which makes this situation all the more concerning."

When they reached the room the man had indicated, Francis steered Agatha to an empty table. He helped her into a seat even as he looked around, slowly sitting down in the chair next to her although he didn't stop scanning the room. She glanced down and discovered he'd taken out his pistol and placed it on his lap.

"Do you think we're going to need that?"

"Perhaps," he said, smiling when a buxom lady sauntered over and gushed over Francis and Jeffrey for a moment. Then, with their drink orders scribbled down on a pad of paper, she turned and sashayed away.

"Why do you think we're not being allowed to leave?" Jeffrey asked, leaning forward across the table in order to be heard over the noise of the other patrons.

"That is the question of the hour, isn't it?" Drusilla replied, her eyes constantly shifting from the left to the right as she surveyed the room without moving her head. "Do you think we've landed ourselves in a trap, Francis?"

Agatha frowned. "You think Dot set us up?"

"She's not exactly reliable, Agatha, and someone might have learned she was asking questions about Mary and paid her handsomely to tell us that woman might be here."

"Dot does have a sketchy past, but I don't believe she'd set us up, not intentionally."

"You might be right," Francis agreed, "but we have a more pressing concern than wondering if Dot sold us out. We need to find a way out of here."

Agatha bit her lip as she glanced around. "Is it my imagination, or are there more brawny men than necessary mingling around this room?"

The serving lady suddenly appeared again at their table, her tray heavy with drinks, which she set down as she smiled at Jeffrey and Francis, making certain to bend over all too frequently, thereby drawing attention to her low-cut gown and charms.

Francis, being the consummate professional, played along with the woman, extending her outrageous compliments, even though Agatha couldn't help but notice his eyes never once lingered on her cleavage. After the drinks had been passed around, the lady straightened and smiled again, but then she froze as she looked across the room.

Swiveling her head ever so slightly, Agatha saw Madame Bellefonte standing across the room, surrounding by even more burly men. She was whispering something to them, and then . . . she turned her head, caught Agatha's eye, and . . . smiled.

"We have to go," Agatha said, finding her arm taken by Francis a mere second later, as Drusilla did the same to Jeffrey, who was looking incredibly alarmed.

"The back door?" Francis asked.

Noticing the line of men now blocking the way to the front door, Agatha nodded. "I don't think we have any other choice."

Francis tightened his hold on her as they began walking, but before they'd been able to move more than a few feet, their progress came to an end when Madame Bellefonte's voice rang out. "Leaving so soon, are we *Miss Hound*?"

"I'm not feeling very well."

Madame Bellefonte looked at her for a long moment and then snapped her fingers. "Seize them."

Francis shoved Agatha behind him as he brought up his pistol right as someone fired at them. "Get her out of here," he yelled to Drusilla before he fired off a shot of his own.

Drusilla was by her side in a flash, pistol in hand and expression hard. "Come on."

"I need to get my pistol."

"There's no time."

Pushing through the panicked patrons who were trying to get away, they made it to a hallway and headed down it. "Drusilla, we can't just leave Francis and Jeffrey."

"You're the target, and yes, we can." Drusilla suddenly stopped moving when the hallway began filling with men, all of them holding pistols pointed in Agatha's direction.

Drusilla shoved Agatha behind her right before she fired off a shot, but it didn't slow the mob racing toward them even though one of the men crumpled to the ground. "Run!" Drusilla yelled as another shot fired, and then . . . Drusilla was falling, the men were closing in on her, and . . . Agatha was suddenly hefted over a man's shoulder. He turned, ignored the fists she was pounding against his back, and ran with her out of the brothel and into the night.

18

Tension radiated through Zayne as he sat staring at Helena, still unable to comprehend what the woman was doing back in New York or why she seemed to be under the impression he'd be willing to marry her.

After Matilda had charged through the ballroom, complete and utter insanity had taken over the Watson house. Guests began fleeing for the doors while Matilda had gone straight for Helena, forcing the lady to turn on her dainty heel and flee, her screams of terror mingling with the shouts of the guests. She'd sought refuge in the Watson library, after Matilda had taken a few bites at her stocking-clad leg, and she'd barricaded herself in that room, refusing to open the door even for him.

Servants had been forced to break in through a window, and when he'd finally gained entrance, he'd found Helena sitting on the floor, sobbing hysterically, although she'd been coherent enough to proclaim, numerous times, that she expected him to remember his pledge to her and that they needed to get married without delay. After wailing for a good five minutes, she'd suddenly slumped motionless to the floor and refused to open her eyes, even when he'd threatened to dump a glass of water over her face.

Hamilton had come to his rescue and picked Helena straight up off the floor, causing one of her eyes to open. When she'd gotten a look at Hamilton's furious face, she'd evidently decided fainting was a prudent option because she went limp in his arms and didn't move another muscle, even when Hamilton carried her outside and practically tossed her into Zayne's carriage. After seeing Helena settled, Zayne had hobbled back into the house and began to search for Agatha, but she'd disappeared.

Cora had found him standing in the empty ballroom. She'd shaken her head rather sadly, told him her daughter had needed some air, but then her eyes began to glint and she'd told him to "Go take care of that woman, and, dear, take care of her *well*," before she'd turned and marched out of the ballroom, leaving Zayne alone again. In no particular hurry to see Helena, he'd looked for any and every excuse not to leave the Watson home, but eventually he accepted he had no choice but to deal with Helena.

So here he was, back at his house, with Helena stretched out on the settee, more irritated than he'd ever been in his life, yet worried as well since he hadn't spoken a word to Agatha after Helena's surprising and untimely interruption.

She had to be furious with him. Once again, she had to believe he'd chosen Helena over her, although that wasn't the case at all. He had no intention of giving in to Helena's demands, didn't feel the slightest compulsion to even humor her, and couldn't, quite frankly, believe the woman had the audacity to show up in New York after she'd left him for another man.

"Zayne, be a dear and fetch me another cool cloth," Helena purred.

Zayne looked at his leg propped up on the table, looked at Helena who was sitting right next to a pitcher of water and a stack of cloths, and crossed his arms over his chest. "The pitcher is right next to you, Helena. Get it yourself."

"Why are you being so hateful?"

He could think of numerous answers to that particular question.

She'd left him without a second thought when he'd needed her most, left him for another gentleman.

He'd been in the middle of proposing to the woman he now knew he loved more than life itself, when she'd burst into the room and ruined everything.

She'd kicked poor Matilda, although to be fair, the little pig had been trying to gnaw on her leg, but still, Matilda was just a small creature. It wasn't as if she could have done any major damage to the leg.

"What are you doing here, Helena?" he settled on asking.

Helena released an overly dramatic sigh. "I'm feeling faint."

Since he'd gotten remarkably adept at faking that particular symptom, he let out a snort. "Your face is blooming with color, my dear, which means you're not feeling faint in the least. So again, what you are doing here?"

She plopped the back of her hand over her forehead. "I came to my senses and realized you're the man I truly long to marry. Isn't that wonderful news, darling?"

"Not particularly."

The hand fell from her forehead as Helena abruptly sat up. "You promised you'd marry me."

Zayne narrowed his eyes. "Have you gotten yourself into some type of . . . trouble?"

Helena's mouth dropped open. "Of course not . . . Well, perhaps," she admitted as she smiled a little too slyly.

She'd never been a lady who'd mastered the whole poker-face business. Annoyance caused him to drum his fingers against the arm of the chair. "What type of trouble are you in, Helena?"

"Oh, let's not get into that just yet, darling, but about that cool cloth?"

"The water pitcher is right beside you, Helena," Gloria snapped as she stormed into the room. "I finally caught Matilda with Piper, Lily, and Grace's help, but it wasn't an easy feat by any stretch of the imagination. The poor dear was completely beside herself, especially after the horrendous treatment she suffered at your foot, Helena."

Helena sent Gloria a glare. "That beast was attacking me. And I cannot believe you have the audacity to chide a lady who has just suffered the indignity of watching the man she's supposed to marry almost propose to another lady and then get set upon by a mad pig."

"Helena just claimed she might have gotten herself into a little trouble," Zayne said, drawing Gloria's attention.

Gloria advanced farther into the room. "Am I to assume this trouble might just demand you find yourself a husband before you start getting a little . . . round?"

Helene's face turned pink. "Ah, well . . ."

"I realize you're probably not the type of lady who has a mind for math, but you haven't seen Zayne for over a year. If—and I stress the *if* part—you are in trouble, Zayne had nothing to do with your condition."

"He'll still marry me though."

The annoyance he'd been feeling turned to anger. It boiled through his veins and caused his skin to heat.

The woman smiling so very smugly in front of him might have just cost him everything—not that she would care about that. She was manipulative, selfish, and downright mean, and he'd had quite enough of her.

They'd been friends for years, since childhood, but friends didn't abandon a man when he was at his lowest. They also didn't put their needs, and their wants, and their problems, before everyone else's, specifically those of the gentleman they intended to marry.

Helena wasn't his friend, certainly wasn't the love of his life, and never had been—that was very clear.

Agatha made him laugh, wanted what was best for him, and had never, not once, demanded a cool cloth be fetched for her.

Hadn't Helena noticed his leg was encased in plaster?

She certainly hadn't inquired about his health.

"You claim you've gotten yourself in trouble, dear, and if that is the case, I'm afraid you're going to have to prove it," Gloria said, pulling him rather abruptly back to the situation at hand.

"I beg your pardon?"

"When are you expecting?"

"Ah, January?"

"Then that would make you about seven months along, but you don't look to be seven months along. In fact, you're looking remarkably svelte."

"I'm not svelte at all," Helena protested, although she unconsciously smoothed down her gown as she protested, drawing attention to the fact she was, indeed, rather svelte.

His temper edged up a notch. Leaning forward in his chair, he smiled. "Let me see."

"What?"

"You're apparently attempting to pass yourself off as an expectant mother, so I need to see proof of that."

"I don't need to prove anything to you. You once promised me you'd marry me, and I'm here to hold you to that promise whether I'm in trouble or not."

"So you're not in trouble?"

Blowing out a breath, Helena rolled her eyes. "Well, fine then, I'm not in that type of trouble. Can't you just believe that I've come back because I still love you?"

"You never loved me, Helena."

"That's not true, I'm sure I must have at some point."

He wasn't certain, but he thought he heard his mother let out a grunt.

Helena seemingly heard it as well, because she swung her attention to Gloria and sent her another glare. "I don't think you need to be here. This is between me and Zayne. Besides, you never liked me."

"God forgive me, but you've got the right of that." Gloria began advancing toward Helena again, her eyes blazing. "You took advantage of the fact Zayne is a true gentleman. You used his sense of honor against him, and I never said much, believing he'd come to his senses, but then . . . you left him when he was at his weakest. Even though God expects me to forgive you, I'll never like you, ever, and hear me well, dear, you'll never hurt my son again."

Zayne felt the oddest urge to jump to his feet and applaud his mother, but the cast on his leg prevented any jumping. Also, since Helena was now bristling with indignation, he didn't think it would really help the situation currently taking place in front of him.

"I didn't come here to hurt your son. I came to allow him the pleasure of my hand in marriage."

Zayne cleared his throat. "I don't believe either of us would find any pleasure being married to each other, Helena. Why don't you just tell me why you're really here?"

Helena looked as if she wasn't going to reply, but she then took a deep, dramatic breath, slowly released it, drew in another, released that one more slowly than the first, and finally opened her mouth. "I need you to marry me before my parents get back to town and force me to marry Gilbert."

Of anything he'd been expecting her to say, that hadn't even crossed his mind. He simply sat there, stunned, unable to find his voice. Luckily for him, his mother didn't seem to have a shortage for words.

"I always knew there was something horribly wrong with you, dear, but may I presume this Gilbert is the gentleman you took up with after you abandoned my son?"

"Honestly, Mrs. Beckett, I take offense at the term *abandoned*," Helena said with a sniff. "You, of all people, considering you've known me forever, should know that I certainly couldn't have nursed your son back to health, especially since it appeared to me he was never going to fully recover." She shook her head. "I am a lady of tender sensibilities, and those sensibilities do not allow me to cater to the needs of others. I am too delicate, too refined, so I had no choice but to part ways with your son, even though it pained me to no small end." She turned to him and smiled. "You understood though, didn't you, darling?"

Zayne blinked and realized that he understood only too well.

A great weight lifted from his shoulders, and he sent up a silent prayer of thanks to God for allowing him to see that Helena had never been meant for him.

She was too shallow, too self-consumed, and she would have

never made him happy, nor would he have been able to make her happy, no matter how many cool cloths he fetched for her.

He shifted in his seat, surprised to feel a smile tug the corners of his lips. "What did Gilbert do to you to make you run away?"

Helena began to pout. "I don't care to discuss Gilbert."

"I'm afraid I must insist, since you've gone to great lengths to get away from him and done a fairly nice job of ruining my life."

"Your life isn't ruined, Zayne."

"If you've caused me to lose Agatha, yes it is."

"That's the lady in the purple dress? The one you were about to give my ring to?"

"It was never your ring, but getting back to Gilbert—what happened?"

"I told you, I don't care to discuss him."

"Then I can't waste any more time on you." Reaching for his crutches, he pulled himself out of the chair and headed for the door.

"Where do you think you're going?" Helena demanded.

"I need to find Agatha and make matters right with her."

"You can't just walk away from me."

Moving forward, he looked over his shoulder. "I think you'll find out soon enough that I can." He'd almost made it to the door when Helena let out a loud wail and dissolved into a fit of weeping that could have earned her a role on any stage.

It was one of her favorite ploys to get her way, and he'd humored her over the years by giving in to her. Those days, however, were long gone, and he had more important matters to attend to, mainly getting to Agatha and begging her forgiveness.

"I say, sir, what have you done to Miss Collins?"

Zayne froze as a man suddenly hustled through the door and brushed past him in a blur, obviously intent on getting to Helena. Turning, Zayne felt his mouth drop open when Helena's sobs came to an immediate end right as she jumped up from the settee and plopped her hands on her hips.

"What are you doing here, Gilbert?" she demanded.

Zayne knew his mouth was still gaping open, but he didn't seem to have the presence of mind to snap it shut. He'd never seen the man Helena had left him for but had conjured up an image in his mind. This man, however, was nothing like that image. He'd expected Helena's love to be tall, broad-shouldered, and incredibly handsome, but Gilbert possessed none of those qualities. He was short—shorter than Helena—had not a single hair on his head, wore gold-rimmed spectacles, and his clothing was rumpled and ill-fitting, although, to give the man credit, he had a very nice smile.

The pale green eyes behind the spectacles held a trace of amusement as the gentleman gazed rather fondly at Helena, even as he continued to smile.

"I've come to fetch you back, my darling," he crooned.

"How did you get to me so fast?" Helena shot back.

"I was on the same train as you, although I was careful to never allow you to see me."

Helena narrowed her eyes. "I don't need fetching. Zayne's the gentleman for me now, and I'll have you know, *he's* never been mean to me. . . . Well, except for today, and he almost always grants me my dearest wishes."

Zayne's mouth finally closed as the reasoning behind Helena's appearance in his life became clear. She'd been thwarted by this unassuming gentleman standing before him, and she was miffed.

"You don't really mean that, dear," Gilbert said. "But I've

been pondering your latest request, and though I find it a bit extravagant to travel over to Europe for our honeymoon, I truly do wish to make you happy. I've taken it upon myself to purchase us tickets, and as soon as we've exchanged vows, we can be on our way."

Helena stuck her nose in the air. "I'm not marrying you. You were horrid to me, as were my parents, and I'm staying in New York, with Zayne." She let out a sniff. "Besides, I didn't simply want to travel to Europe—I wanted you to buy me a house in Paris."

"Yes, I clearly remember that outrageous request."

"And are you willing to give in to that little request in order to win my hand?"

"No."

"Then I'm staying here with Zayne."

"Will *he* buy you a house in Paris?" Gilbert asked, his eyes now clearly brimming with amusement, even though Helena had taken to pouting again.

"Probably not," she finally admitted.

Gilbert tilted his head, his smile never wavering. "I suppose you're facing a bit of a dilemma, then. You can agree to marry me and travel to Europe for our honeymoon, or you can stay here with this gentleman, who doesn't exactly seem thrilled by your presence, and never see me again."

"I didn't say I never wanted to see you again," Helena said slowly.

"You left me."

"Only because I really want that house in Paris."

"It's your choice darling, me or a house in Paris."

"You have enough money," Helena said, her pout becoming more pronounced. "I don't understand why you won't just buy me what I want."

"Because I love you too much to give in to you all the time, and it's past time you, my love, grew up."

Zayne could hear the tick of the clock on the wall as Helena glared at Gilbert, but she finally blew out a breath. "Fine, I'll marry you and you can take me off on a European honeymoon, but I'm not happy about it."

"Of course you're not, darling," Gilbert said, moving to take her arm. "Shall we go find someone to marry us? I'm sure for the right price some minister out there won't mind doing the job."

"Right now? It's the middle of the night."

"Yes, but if we find someone to marry us tonight, we can leave on our honeymoon in the morning."

"And then we'll get to Europe sooner," Helena breathed.

"That's why I adore you, my darling girl—you're so smart," Gilbert said. He sent a nod to Zayne and turned to Gloria but didn't have a chance to nod to her because she was moving toward Helena, her expression furious.

"That's it?" Gloria demanded. "You come waltzing back to New York, ruin my son's life by interrupting his proposal to Agatha, and then you're simply going to run off, marry another gentleman, and go take in the sights in Europe?"

Helena dropped Gilbert's arm, and much to Zayne's surprise, went to meet Gloria in the middle of the room. "Mrs. Beckett, I doubt you really want me to linger, but I do owe you and, more importantly, your son an apology." Helena glanced to Zayne. "You were always too honorable for your own good, my friend, but you're right. We wouldn't make each other happy, and you deserve to be happy. I'm sorry if I caused you some difficulty with that lady in the purple dress."

"Good heavens, darling, what have you done?" Gilbert asked.

Not particularly wanting to watch Helena dive right back into a dramatic performance, Zayne took one step forward. "It doesn't matter, Gilbert." He nodded to Helena. "Go, get married, and try not to drive this nice gentleman insane."

For a second, Helena's eyes turned misty, one of the few times he'd ever seen true tears in them. "I am sorry," she whispered, moving closer to him to kiss his cheek before she returned to Gilbert's side and took his arm. "Shall we go?"

Gilbert chucked her under the chin and smiled. "Indeed we shall." With that, they walked through the door, disappearing from sight.

"I must say, that's one of the oddest scenes I've ever witnessed," Gloria said. "At least you've finally been shown Helena's true character, something I've been asking God to show you for years."

Zayne smiled. "He's been showing me a lot lately."

"Such as the fact you're in love with Agatha?"

Before Zayne could reply, Eliza stepped into the room, looking a bit bemused. "I just saw Helena getting into a carriage with a gentleman I've never seen before."

"That's Gilbert, Helena's fiancé," he told her. "She's off to Europe after they get married."

"Huh, well, good for her, or rather, good for you. One less complication in your life will be wonderful." She stepped closer and gave him a hug. "What are you going to do about Agatha?"

"Once I find her, I'm hoping to extend her an extraordinary proposal."

"Make it good, Zayne. Agatha's my best friend, and you've hurt her, badly this time I think."

Zayne nodded. "I know, and I promise you I'm going to make it up to her, but first I need to find her."

"Cora told me she went out for some air, but I think she went to get that air with Mr. Blackheart and Drusilla."

"At least she'll be safe with them."

"Well, it is Agatha, but . . ." She looked around the room. "Where's Piper?"

"I thought she was with you," Gloria said.

"I thought she was with you," Eliza countered. "Didn't she ride back here in your carriage after the dinner party?"

Gloria shook her head. "The last time I saw her, she was trying to calm Matilda down in Cora's drawing room with Lily and Grace."

"She must still be over at the Watson house," Zayne said. "She adores Matilda, and I can see her losing track of time and forgetting she's supposed to ride home with someone. I'm going there now, so I'll get her and bring her home to you, Eliza."

The sound of running feet had Zayne swiveling on his crutches and facing the door, right as his sister, Arabella, lumbered into the room, her face white and her breathing labored.

"Good heavens, Arabella, what are you doing out tonight?" he demanded. "You're in no condition to be out in the cold."

Arabella drew in a gulp of air, rubbed her incredibly large stomach, and then, with tears flowing down her beautiful face, she opened her mouth. "Theodore just received disturbing news, and since he needed to leave right away, I was the only one around to let you know." She drew in another gulp of air. "Drusilla's been shot, Jeffrey Murdock is unconscious, and Francis has been injured as well."

"And Agatha?" He forced the question through lips that had gone stiff.

"She's gone."

19

The strange thought kept tumbling through Agatha's mind that, instead of being terrified—something she really should be, given her current situation—she was mostly just confused.

After she'd been thrown into a waiting carriage—her hands and feet bound and a gag stuffed into her mouth, effectively cutting off her screams—she'd then been taken, not deeper into the slums, but to a perfectly respectable house right on Park Avenue. If she wasn't mistaken, the house she was currently being held in wasn't far from her own house on Fifth Avenue.

Finding herself dumped in a room painted in soft blue with matching furniture had been confusing in and of itself, but when she'd come face-to-face with Mary only minutes after being deposited in a seat, she thought she'd begun to make sense of everything . . . until it became perfectly clear that Mary hadn't been expecting her.

In fact, that woman was currently ranting at the thug who'd abducted her in the entranceway, and from what Agatha could discern, Mary wasn't the one behind the attack. The biggest question left now was . . . who was?

Eyeing Jessie, who was pointing a pistol her way, Agatha mumbled against the gag that was still lodged firmly in her mouth.

"Stop talking," Jessie demanded, waving the pistol in the air.

"Mmm, mmm, mmm."

"You might as well ungag her," Hannah said from her position by the window. "She might know something."

"What would she know?" Jessie asked.

"We'll never find out the answer to that if she can't talk."

"Oh, right," Jessie said, moving up to Agatha and pulling the gag out of her mouth.

Moistening her lips with a tongue that was incredibly dry, Agatha swallowed. "May I have some water?"

"You want water?"

"If it wouldn't be too much of a bother," she rasped.

"Fine." Spinning on her heel, Jessie moved to a pitcher, poured out a glass, and returned to hand it to Agatha.

"You'll need to untie my hands."

"You'd like that, wouldn't you?"

"Yes, quite frankly, I would."

Tipping the glass to Agatha's lips, Jessie held it there while water sloshed over Agatha's face, but she managed to finally get a sip and then pulled back. "Thank you."

"Humph," was all Jessie said as she stomped away to put the glass on a table.

"Do either of you know what happened to the people I was with earlier?" Agatha asked. "Drusilla was shot, but I don't know how badly."

Jessie and Hannah exchanged nervous glances and then Jessie strode to the door. "Mary, you'd better get in here and listen to this."

"I'm busy."

"Now!" Jessie yelled back.

Less than five seconds later, Mary stormed into the room. "What?"

"Miss Watson just told us some fool shot a woman."

Mary's eyes narrowed before she stepped closer. "Is she dead?"

"I have no idea since I wasn't presented with an opportunity to linger because someone was in a hurry to deliver me to you."

"This complicates matters."

"I'm sure it does, although shooting people is your line of business, isn't it, Mary?"

"I've been rethinking my career choice of late," Mary mumbled, beginning to pace around the room. "Was anyone else hurt?"

"Possibly Mr. Blackheart and Mr. Murdock."

Mary stopped pacing. "Mr. Murdock, as in one of the society Murdocks?"

"The very same."

Rubbing a hand over her face, Mary let out a grunt. "This is a disaster."

"I thought you wanted me dead," Agatha began slowly. "Isn't that why I've been brought to you?"

"As I said before, I've been considering a bit of a lifestyle change, and you'll be relieved to learn I no longer have any desire to kill you."

"That's reassuring, but . . . you won't get paid until you complete the job you were hired to do."

"I have reason to believe I wasn't going to get paid even if I had managed to kill you, and I have little reason to believe that will change now. The man who hired me seems to have no moral compass, and I do believe he might be setting me up right now to take a huge fall." She smiled grimly. "Which is why I won't be killing you tonight."

"Isn't it almost morning?"

"It's approaching one o'clock, so I suppose it is morning. I'll clarify by saying I don't intend to kill you today." She shook her head. "You're remarkably difficult to kill anyway, which has aggravated me to no end, but in an odd way, your unwillingness to die has given me a certain respect for you which is, again, why I can't kill you now."

"You could always just let me go. I don't live far from here."

"Believe me, I'd love to be able to do that, but there's more than one man watching the house at the moment, so I'm afraid I can't let you go. I have a feeling these men would shoot you on sight, even though it's clear someone wants me to do the dirty deed."

Agatha tilted her head. "Who is that someone?"

"I don't know his name, have never met the man face-to-face, since our transaction was done through a common contact on the streets. Most of us, in my business, prefer to handle matters as delicately and as discreetly as possible. Besides, learning a client's name makes our business even more dangerous, especially if that client decides we know too much." Mary began to pace around the room. "It's evident my client believes I'm still interested in killing you, but I can't help thinking, if I were to go through with your murder, a swarm of policemen would soon arrive after the deed was done and take me away."

Agatha nodded. "You're being set up."

"Indeed," Mary agreed as she stopped pacing. "Where did that man find you, the one who brought you here?"

"In a brothel. We'd gotten a tip that you and your girls were hiding there."

"We never hid out in a brothel. I rented this place the moment we reached New York." She smiled. "Mr. Beckett's lovely gold has allowed us to live in style, although that style has been restricted ever since the B. Altman's incident."

"I'm surprised you didn't leave right after that."

Mary released a grunt. "We would have if that annoying Mr. Wilder hadn't been scouring the streets for us. His reputation precedes him, so we thought it best to just lay low here for a while." Mary walked to Agatha's side, pulled out a knife and sliced through Agatha's bindings, freeing her hands. "We're going to have to work together."

Agatha blinked. "I'm sorry?"

"I'm going to have to figure out the identity of the man who hired me to kill you, which means you're going to have to tell me who wants to harm you."

"How much time do we have?" Agatha asked before she launched into the very long list of people who might want her dead, finishing up a few minutes later. She winced when she realized Mary, Jessie, and Hannah were all watching her with wide eyes and looks of disbelief on their faces.

"Maybe we really should just go ahead and kill her," Hannah said. "Might be doing her a favor since we'd do it quickly instead of drawing out her death like some of those people she mentioned might want to do."

Mary's lips curved. "We're not killing her. That's exactly what someone wants us to do, but I'm not going to play his game."

"And because of that, you can just keep Mr. Beckett's gold that you stole from him," Agatha said.

"That's generous of you."

"I'm not really in accord with the man at the moment."

Mary surprised her when she laughed. "I'll be back," the

311

woman tossed over her shoulder as she made for the door. "Don't let her go anywhere. I have a feeling she's safest with us at the moment."

That was a less than comforting thought.

"Who told you we were hiding in a brothel?" Jessie asked.

"A trusted contact of mine."

"She doesn't sound all that trustworthy."

Not willing to dwell on Dot and the idea that she might have been responsible for Agatha's capture and the damage done to her friends, Agatha simply shrugged.

Silence settled over the room, broken only by Jessie tapping her pistol against her leg and Hannah moving from the window to take a seat beside Agatha.

"What do you think Mary's doing?" Hannah finally asked.

"I have no idea," Jessie began as the door swung open and Mary stomped back into the room, shutting the door behind her.

"We're in deep trouble because someone really, really wants you dead, Miss Watson."

"What happened?"

"The men outside the house are demanding to see your body, without breath left in it, I might add, and they want to see it soon." She nodded to Hannah. "You're going to have to sneak out and find Mr. Wilder. Tell him Miss Watson's here and tell him to bring a lot of reinforcements."

"Why don't you just let Miss Watson sneak out and go find him herself?" Hannah asked.

"Because if we do that, the three of us will be dead. Those men out there mean business." She shot a look to Agatha. "Sorry."

"Mr. Wilder's been trying to track us down for over a month now," Hannah argued. "He'll arrest me in a heartbeat if I approach him, and besides, I have no idea where to look for the man."

"He won't arrest you if you tell him about me," Agatha said. "And all you have to do to find him is travel down the streets, ask everyone you see if they know him. I guarantee someone will know him, and someone will get word to him where we are. Theodore has contacts throughout the city. It won't be hard to get to him if you can get out of this house."

Hannah bit her lip, but before she could argue further, the door burst open and a large, intimidating man strode in.

"We told you we're behind schedule, so I'm here to move things along."

To Agatha's amazement, Mary lifted her nose in the air. "We're about to have tea, so your schedule will just have to wait, or better yet, you can take my word for it that I'll deal with Miss Watson and be on your way."

"Your word don't mean much to us," the man snapped, "and there's no time for tea. There's a killing that needs to happen, and serving her tea ain't going to stop that."

"Even hardened criminals are served a last meal. Miss Watson chose tea for hers, so tea she's going to get."

"And ham," Jessie said, speaking rather loudly since the intimidating man had begun to sputter. "She asked for ham."

The odd thought sprang to mind that it was a good thing Matilda wasn't with her.

"My boss won't be happy about this," the man said as he strode for the door, didn't bother to close it, and disappeared from view.

"Hannah, get moving," Mary said before she nodded at Jessie. "You need to go fetch some tea."

"I don't know how to make tea."

"Just do your best, I think water is involved, and tea, of

course, and you might want to make up a nice plate of ham since someone mentioned it. We need to bide us some time."

"Any suggestions on how I should sneak out of the house?" Hannah asked.

"No one is watching this window, and it has some handy bushes hiding it from view."

Agatha's heart stopped beating for just a second as she turned and saw three pale faces peering back at her through the now-open window. Unfortunately, those faces just happened to belong to her two sisters, Lily and Grace, and Piper. Before Agatha could say a word, Grace, followed by Lily and Piper, climbed through the window.

Mary moved across the room, lowering her voice to a mere whisper, her eyes huge as she stared at the children. "Jessie, go get that tea and close the door behind you."

Jessie hurried through the door and closed it softly as Mary turned to Hannah. "You need to get going, and . . ."

"No," Agatha interrupted. "Hannah can stay now." She turned to Grace. "Darling, I have no idea what you're doing here, but you, Lily, and Piper need to leave . . . now."

Grace's expression turned stubborn. "We're not leaving without you, because it's clear you're in some type of trouble."

"I am, but there's no need for the three of you to get involved, and . . . how did you even find me in the first place?"

"Oh, Matilda led us to you. We'd taken her outside for a bit of fun after the whole Helena disaster, but then she turned ornery and ran away from us. We chased her all over Fifth Avenue—for hours. We finally accepted we had no chance of catching her and were about ready to head home to face the wrath of our parents, but then a man rode down the street on his horse and, well, Matilda went crazy. She followed him here, and . . . that's how we found you."

314

"Matilda's here?"

Grace nodded. "She's outside. We'd just gotten up to the window and had started pushing it open when someone mentioned ham, and . . . Matilda's currently hiding underneath the bushes."

A light knock on the door had everyone jumping. Mary placed a finger over her lips, walked over to the door, spoke quietly, and stepped aside as Jessie moved into the room, struggling with a tray that appeared to be holding a variety of cups, one large pitcher filled with a murky substance, and a haunch of ham. Mary closed the door and locked it, moving over to help Jessie with the tray.

"Grace, was anyone guarding the side of the house this window's on?" Agatha asked quietly.

"No," Grace said. "All the men are gathered out front. Quite honestly, once we saw them, we got scared and decided to leave, but then Matilda came scampering back to us, grabbed hold of Piper's hem, and tugged her over to the side of the house. Thinking something might be up, I snuck through the bushes and peeked through the window, and . . . boy, was I surprised when I saw you sitting here, Agatha. I thought you would have been home safe and sound hours ago. Didn't you just go out for some air?"

"Yes, well, since you should be home, where young girls are supposed to be at this late hour, I don't think you should be throwing nasty accusations my way, do you?"

"We'll just be on our way to get help," Grace said before she hurried back to the window, allowing Agatha to give her a hand up before she disappeared.

Agatha helped Lily next and was just reaching for Piper when the doorknob began to rattle. Agatha barely had time to blink before it crashed open and a large man burst into the room. "The boss has arrived, and he . . . Who are you trying to shove out that window?" he bellowed.

"Lily, Grace, go find Theodore!" Agatha yelled before she pulled Piper to the floor right as bullets began whizzing around the room.

20

One thought kept repeating itself again and again and again through Zayne's mind.

Agatha wasn't dead.

She couldn't be.

She was a vibrant, resourceful, extremely intelligent woman, and because of that . . . she'd find a way to stay alive until they could find her. The only problem was . . . they truly had no idea where to look.

Theodore had his men scouring the city, and the police had been called in as well, but time was passing all too quickly, and . . .

"She's not dead," he said out loud, even though he was alone in the carriage. "She's out there, somewhere, and when we find her, I'm marrying her whether she accepts my proposal or not."

Resting his head against the side of the carriage, he closed his eyes, turning to God for what felt like the millionth time that evening, pleading with Him to keep Agatha safe. Feeling the carriage begin to slow, he opened his eyes as the carriage came to a complete stop, and he found Hamilton bending toward the window from his position on top of his horse.

"Theodore and I are going to loop through all the back alleys, but some of them are narrow and your coach won't fit. We haven't gone all the way down Park Avenue yet, so it'll be a great help if you make sure there's no suspicious activity going on there. Meet me back at my house in three hours if we haven't crossed paths by then." Hamilton ran a hand through hair that was standing on end. "We'll find her, Zayne, you have to believe that, and we'll find the younger girls as well—although I'm hoping they were simply out doing whatever it is young girls feel they should do in the midst of disasters and have turned up by now."

Zayne's first instinct was to argue. He didn't want to waste his time traveling down Park Avenue, an area of the city that was completely respectable and probably the last place on earth Agatha had been taken. She'd most likely been taken somewhere deep in the bowels of the stews, or put on a boat, or . . .

Shaking himself out of those less than productive thoughts, he nodded, finding it impossible to speak past the lump that had formed in his throat.

Hamilton leaned closer. "I know this is hard for you, Zayne. I understand your anguish, but with that leg of yours . . ." Shaking his head, Hamilton straightened in the saddle, turned his horse, and galloped away.

"We're going to Park Avenue, Andrews!" Zayne yelled out the carriage window to his driver before he settled back against the seat. He heard the snap of the reins, and the carriage jolted into motion, picking up speed and maintaining that speed because the roads were practically empty since the hour was late. Most people were either still in the midst of their entertainments that would last until the sun came up or were nestled snug in their beds, completely oblivious to the fact Zayne's world had turned on end.

How Zayne wished he were one of those people at the moment. When Arabella had first stated that Agatha was gone, he'd almost crumpled to the ground, thinking she meant Agatha was dead.

When it became clear she'd been taken, not killed, everyone had swarmed into motion. It wasn't too long after that, after they'd stopped by Agatha's house, where Theodore had ordered his men to meet, that it had become known that Piper, Lily, Grace, and Matilda were missing as well.

He was fairly certain they weren't truly missing, just misplaced, but the thought of the children becoming inadvertently drawn into whatever madness was occurring at the moment left him cold and furious.

He was responsible for what had transpired this dark, dark night.

If he'd not gone after Helena but had instead done what his heart had been screaming at him to do—gone after Agatha—she wouldn't have felt compelled to go to some brothel, and wouldn't have put her life in danger.

He didn't deserve Agatha, but even knowing that, he was still going to do everything in his power to convince her they truly were meant to be together forever . . . once someone found her.

The carriage suddenly slowed to a mere crawl, and impatience had him sticking his head out the window. "What seems to be the matter, Andrews?"

"There are some horses blocking the road up ahead, sir. I'm not sure what they're doing there, but no one seems to be around to move them out of the way."

Apprehension had sweat rolling down his back. "Could you come help me out of the carriage?"

"Sir?"

"There shouldn't be horses roaming around the street at this hour of the night, Andrews. I'm going to go investigate, but I'm going to need my cart taken down from the back."

"I don't think that's wise, sir. As you said, horses don't normally roam the streets unattended, and you're in no shape to deal with whatever is happening here. We should turn around and find assistance."

"My cart, if you please."

He heard Andrews mutter something under his breath, but the man climbed down from his seat, moved to the back of the carriage, and reappeared a minute later, his expression decidedly concerned.

"Shall I run along beside you, sir?"

"That won't be necessary. Stay with the carriage and ease up further on the street, but do prepare yourself for a fast getaway." Zayne climbed from the carriage, reached back and snagged hold of his crutches, and held them out to Andrews. "Would you put these on the back of the cart? I might require them if I need to walk somewhere."

Andrews sent him a look that clearly expressed doubt, but he moved to the cart, tied the crutches on the back, and then blew out a breath. "If I may be so bold, sir, I know the situation is dire, but Miss Watson is an uncommonly resourceful lady, and I have to believe she'll somehow manage to come out of this latest disaster just fine." He helped Zayne into the cart and leaned closer to him for a second. "I'll be saying prayers for everyone's safe return."

As Zayne shot forward faster than he'd anticipated, he knew prayers, and lots of them, were certainly going to be needed.

Minutes later, he'd negotiated around the horses but still had yet to find any sign of people who might own those horses. He traveled past darkened house after darkened house, grateful for the sparse light the gas lamps threw out, especially since it had begun to snow. Snowflakes were covering his head at a rapid rate, and he blinked when one fell in his eye and blinked again when something caught his attention, someone charging his way—a lady.

As the lady came closer, he realized it was Agatha running toward him, holding Piper by the hand, but someone else was chasing after her, and that someone had a gun.

"I'm coming, Agatha!" he yelled as he pushed the button that was only meant to be pushed when going uphill. The cart thrust forward, and he realized a second later that he'd lost all control of it. The steering column wouldn't turn, and before he knew it, he was blazing *past* Agatha and Piper and heading directly toward the man with the gun, who jumped out of the way as Zayne's cart zoomed onward. He stomped on the brake pedal, but even though he was pressing it completely against the bottom of the cart, he continued to fly forward.

Looking up, he found an entire group of men running his way, their pace slowing as they caught sight of him. A few of them dove for cover the closer he got, but some weren't fast enough and he winced as the cart bumped into one man after another before he finally came to a stop, directly over a ferocious-looking and profusely swearing man who seemed to be lodged under his front wheels.

"Get this off me," the man rasped.

"Right," Zayne said, reaching around for his crutches, but freezing in place when a pistol suddenly appeared in his face.

"Get your hands where I can see them, Mr. Beckett," the man holding the pistol growled.

Holding up his hands, Zayne lifted his head, but the man leaning over him had his hat pulled low and his collar high. Zayne couldn't make out his features. "Who are you?"

"Why, I'm Mr. Jenkins, of course—reporter extraordinaire for the *New-York Tribune*." Mr. Jenkins released a nasty laugh. "Unfortunately for you, Mr. Beckett, you've just caused me to lose my prey—that being Miss Watson. I really was hoping I could put an end to her once and for all, but she has once again slipped away, and for that, my dear man, I'm afraid you're going to have to pay."

Zayne tilted his head and considered the man. "Why would you tell me your name and that you work at the paper?"

"You asked and it would be impolite not to answer you."

"Meaning you intend to kill me and I won't be able to tell anyone."

"What a bright gentleman you are, Mr. Beckett."

The man still lying under Zayne's cart released a grunt. "Did you call this man Mr. Beckett?"

"I did. You should feel honored that you've been run over by none other than Mr. Zayne Beckett of the illustrious Beckett family."

Zayne frowned. "How do you know who I am?"

"I'm a reporter, Mr. Beckett, and a good one. I know everything about this city."

"I didn't sign up to take on the Beckett family." The man underneath the cart shoved up, and Zayne found himself dumped to the ground. Rolling over to his back, he stiffened as the man loomed over him.

"My apologies, Mr. Beckett," the man said, taking Zayne completely by surprise. "I have no quarrel with you or your family, and I do apologize if you're in any way connected to that lady we snatched tonight who happens to be the same lady we were hired to run over with a carriage. We won't be bothering her again. Now, if you'll excuse me, I'll just be on my way." The man let out a whistle as he dashed down the sidewalk, joined a few seconds later by a group of men, all of whom disappeared into the darkness.

"You haven't finished the job you were paid to do yet!" Mr. Jenkins screamed after them. "Miss Watson is still out there somewhere."

"I don't think they're coming back," Zayne said, earning himself a whack on the head with the pistol in the process.

"No, it doesn't seem as if they are, but no matter. I'll deal with them later."

"You don't truly believe you're going to get away with this, do you, Mr. Jenkins? Theodore Wilder will not rest until he hunts you down, and even though the man has mellowed since he married *my sister*, he doesn't take kindly to men trying to murder ladies."

The man let out a laugh that held what was clearly a note of insanity. "Mr. Wilder has been searching for me for over a year to no avail, probably because he's been centering his attention on the subjects of Miss Watson's articles while I've walked freely under his nose. I'm not that concerned he'll be able to find me once I finish matters with you and Miss Watson. I fully intend to disappear, and I'm very good at reinventing myself, Mr. Beckett. I assure you, I'll succeed once again."

Wanting to keep the man talking in order to allow Agatha and Piper time to get farther away, Zayne struggled for something else to say. "I find myself curious, sir, as to why you're so determined to get rid of Agatha. What exactly has she done to garner your intense dislike?"

"Why, she's a woman, of course."

"That's your reasoning behind wanting her dead?"

"She's chosen to enter a profession she has no business being in, and she was given stories that should have gone to a man. Women have no business traipsing through the slums, or questioning factory owners. They should be at home, raising children, and leaving professions to men, as it's always been meant to be."

"Agatha's a gifted writer. Why should she be expected to abandon that gift simply because she was born a woman?"

Mr. Jenkins waved the question away. "I would have left her alone after she went out west, if she would have stopped submitting stories that were earning her awards. It was beyond frustrating, seeing her win again and again, and it was also frustrating that the paper paid for her bodyguard, which severely limited her chances of getting killed by some random outlaw. That's why I was forced to hire Mary and her small band of idiots. I got tired of watching Miss Watson garner all that praise and decided she needed to be taken care of once and for all. I've now come to the belief, though, that I'm going to have to be the one to kill her if I want the job done right."

"If I'm understanding you correctly, you've done all of this—threatening Agatha with pig heads, running her out of town, and then hiring someone to kill her because of . . . jealousy?"

"I'm not jealous of her—I am her superior. My being able to capture her tonight proves I'm more intelligent."

"And how did you manage to capture her?"

"It was incredibly easy." Mr. Jenkins let out a laugh that had the hair sticking up on Zayne's arms. "I am a reporter after all, and I learned that an old harlot by the name of Dot was asking questions around the city about Mary and her girls. It was an easy matter to feed her information through a drunk on the street. I paid him a few dollars, he went and told Dot where Mary was supposed to be found, and Dot very kindly went along with my plans and gave a message to Miss Watson."

He laughed again. "It was fortunate that I warned Madame Bellefonte this evening to be on the lookout for a lady or two entering her brothel, although asking that favor of the woman set me back a pretty penny. It was all worth it though when Miss Watson actually showed up there. I thought she wouldn't go until the day after her dinner party, but she's always been a bit of an odd duck."

Stalling for more time, Zayne nodded. "Agatha is different, there's no getting around that, but I still find myself a bit curious about something. Did you put that pig's head on Agatha's doorstep or did you hire someone to do that for you?"

"That was personal, so I placed the head there myself."

"And have you placed many heads on people's porches throughout the years?"

"I must admit I have, especially on the porches of editors who don't treat me well. Why, there's an editor in Boston who stayed indoors for an entire month because so many strange things turned up outside his house, and that was simply because he made me do an interview with a lady who made candy. It was a frivolous interview, one I didn't care for in the least, almost as frivolous as when I once interviewed your sister and she showed me the door before I was—"

"I don't remember Arabella ever stating she was interviewed by a Mr. Jenkins."

"Ah, well, enough about that, we need to return to the nasty business at hand. You'll be relieved to learn I've decided to let you live. I still intend to shoot you, just not kill you. You've annoyed me by providing Miss Watson so much time to get away, and so . . . perhaps your other leg, the good one, would be the perfect spot for a bullet."

Mr. Jenkins cocked his pistol, drew up his arm, and . . . flew through the air and landed on the ground, his unusual flying display brought about by the fact someone had hurled into him.

That someone turned out to be none other than Agatha.

She barely spared Zayne a glance as she launched herself at Mr. Jenkins, beating the man with what appeared to be one of her pistols, her black hair streaming down her back as she raised her other hand and slapped the man across the face.

"Agatha!" he yelled, fear coursing over him, "Mr. Jenkins is insane. You need to get out of here at once."

To his surprise, Agatha slapped Mr. Jenkins across the face again. She sat back, leveled the pistol in the man's face, and cocked the trigger. "This is not Mr. Jenkins. He's that weasel of a man, Mr. Horace Pitkin, and he might be insane, but I do believe I'm strong enough to take him."

"Not . . . Mr. Jenkins?" was all Zayne could say until he swallowed and shook his head. "Well, that explains why he didn't want to kill me. He probably wanted to frame poor Mr. Jenkins for the events of this night."

"Don't feel sorry for 'poor Mr. Jenkins,' Zayne," Agatha said. "He's a nasty piece of work, but not, I think, as nasty as Mr. Pitkin." She slapped Mr. Pitkin once again, earning a howl of protest from the man. "May I assume you were the one who brought up the idea about gathering articles from out west to Mr. Chambers in the first place?"

"I might have done that," Mr. Pitkin mumbled.

"You certainly did a wonderful job of acting when I was chosen over you, but . . . if memory serves me correctly, I do believe I remember you seemed almost disappointed when it became known Mr. Blackheart had been hired to guard me."

"You had less chance of being killed in the pursuit of an article with him around."

"I'm very difficult to kill," Agatha said smugly, looking over her shoulder for a second to catch Zayne's eye. "Are you all right?"

"I'm fine, but you shouldn't have come back for me," Zayne said.

"Don't be ridiculous," Agatha retorted. "Of course I had to come—" Her words came to an abrupt halt when Mr. Pitkin suddenly let out a scream, reared up, and pushed Agatha off of him before he sprang to his feet. Agatha's pistol skidded across the cobblestones, leaving her defenseless.

"Agatha, run!" Zayne yelled.

"Not on your life." She jumped to her feet right as Matilda charged into view. "Get him, girl."

Matilda needed no second urgings. She streaked by in a blur of pink and grabbed hold of Mr. Pitkin's leg, hanging on even though he began shaking that leg vigorously.

"Agatha, run. Please, just run," he pleaded.

"And leave you here at the mercy of a madman? Not likely." She dashed around him, grabbed one of his crutches that had fallen off the cart, clutched it in both hands, and charged back at Mr. Pitkin, swinging the crutch like a bat. He heard a loud thud, and then, to his amazement, Mr. Pitkin crumpled to the ground with Matilda still attached to his leg.

"You guard him, Matilda," Agatha said as she dropped the crutch and kicked Mr. Pitkin. She then turned and sent Zayne a smile. "I know it's not well done to kick a man when he's down, but I simply couldn't help myself."

He felt his lips curl into an unexpected smile. "I'd have done just that if I wasn't stuck here on the ground."

"Good heavens, Zayne, I do beg your pardon." Agatha

rushed over to his side and crouched down beside him. "I'm afraid Dr. Gessler is not going to be pleased with this little escapade. You're in for quite the lecture once we get you back to the house."

"I'm not hurt."

She didn't appear to hear him as her hands traveled over his body and then moved to cup his face. "You're bleeding." She reached down, tore a strip of fabric off her unusual gown, and wiped his head.

Loud grunts drew his attention as Agatha continued to mop blood from his face, and he turned his head and grinned as his gaze settled on Matilda.

"Is she trying to eat his shirt?"

"I told her about the head left on my doorstep, and I think she understood what I was telling her," Agatha said with a grin. "She's probably trying to get to his skin to really leave her mark." She dabbed at his head again. "What could you have been thinking, driving Charlotte's invention down this street? The last time you used it you almost killed yourself. Honestly, Zayne, you need to start trying to take better care of yourself."

"I wanted to rescue you."

"Of course you did." She sighed. "While I do appreciate the gesture, you're in no state to rescue anyone at the moment. You could have been gravely injured, or killed, for that matter. I didn't think I was going to get to you in time, and it was only through the grace of God I got to Mr. Pitkin before he shot you."

It struck him then, how completely idiotic he'd been. He'd made the decision that he, being the gentleman, should be responsible for saving her, not the other way around, but . . . it didn't actually matter.

Agatha Watson was an incredible lady. She was bright, funny, annoying at times, and . . . she'd never expected him to be her knight in shining armor. Well, maybe she expected it just a bit, but she was perfectly content for them to share that armor.

What she truly needed was a partner, someone who would participate fully with her in life and share her adventures.

He was that partner, and he was going to do everything in his power to convince her to give him another chance. Hope curled through him when he realized that, since she was currently mopping up his face, muttering dire predictions about his idiocy under her breath in the process, he might still get that chance.

"Agatha," he began, wincing when she touched a cut on his head he hadn't felt before she'd dabbed at it.

"Hmm?"

"I need to say something."

"Can't it wait? You're a mess, and I don't think it's a good idea for you to continue lying on the cold street."

"It can't wait."

She stopped dabbing, although she did so rather reluctantly and caught his eye. "Yes?"

"Well, you see . . ."

"Thank God you're still alive."

Turning his head, Zayne found Hamilton and Theodore racing their way, pistols drawn and looking fierce. They stopped right next to Mr. Pitkin, and Theodore actually grinned. "Good job, Matilda." He looked at Agatha. "You might want to call her off though, Agatha. I'll be hard-pressed to question the man if Matilda gnaws him to death."

Agatha handed Zayne the piece of her dress she'd been using on his face, rose to her feet and walked over to where

Mr. Pitkin, with Matilda standing on his chest, was just beginning to stir. "Come, darling. We'll leave what's left of him to Theodore."

Matilda let out a grunt, stepped off Mr. Pitkin, and moved over to Zayne. She sat down right beside him and gave him a sloppy lick of her tongue before she scooted down on her stomach and let out a snort.

Three of Theodore's men stole quietly out of the shadows, picked Mr. Pitkin up, even though he was trying to squirm out of their hold, and with a nod to Theodore, carted Mr. Pitkin away.

"Take him to jail, gentlemen," Theodore called after them. "I'll meet you there."

"Piper's fine, by the way," Agatha said to Hamilton after the men disappeared into the darkness. "Mary met us a couple blocks down and is taking care of her, but have either of you seen my sisters?"

"They're the reason we found you here," Theodore said. "They were running down Fifth Avenue, screaming at the top of their lungs, and they ran into some of my men." He smiled. "They're safe back at your house, where I'm sure your mother is hovering over them."

"What do you mean, Piper's with Mary?" Hamilton demanded.

"Mary won't hurt her," Agatha said, moving to tug Hamilton to a stop when he started down the street. "In fact, Mary's the reason Piper and I are still alive."

"I thought Mary was in on your abduction," Theodore said slowly.

"She knew nothing about the abduction, although Mr. Pitkin *did* hire her to kill me."

"But since I didn't go *through* with it," Mary said as she

strode into view holding Piper's hand, "I'd appreciate it if you'd stop trying to hunt me down and allow me and my girls to leave town peacefully."

"You're an assassin, Mary. I can't just let you go," Theodore said after Hamilton had Piper in his arms.

For some reason, Mary suddenly looked a little embarrassed. "If you must know, we've never actually killed anyone, not that we didn't try." She smiled. "That's why we weren't upset about tracking Miss Watson out west. Things were getting uncomfortable for us on the east coast. Turns out clients get upset when the assassins they hire aren't very good at their job." She walked over and looked down at Zayne. "Agatha told us we could keep that gold we took off of you, but I thought it would be only right to make sure you don't have a problem with that."

"Not since you apparently helped save Agatha's life," he said.

"Excellent." Mary turned back to Theodore and arched a brow.

Theodore looked at Mary for a moment and then nodded to Agatha. "It's your choice. What do you want me to do with Mary?"

Agatha smiled. "I want you to let her go."

"I won't forget this," Mary said, spinning on her heel and fading into the night, the sound of her calling out to Hannah and Jessie a moment later floating back to them.

Agatha moved closer to Theodore. "Have you any news about Drusilla, Francis, and Jeffrey?"

"They're fine," Theodore said. "Well . . . not *fine,* since Jeffrey has a broken leg, Drusilla was shot—only a flesh wound—and Francis is currently sporting two black eyes and a huge lump on his head. But none of them will suffer from any lasting injuries."

Agatha shook her head. "Poor Jeffrey. He only got involved because I just happened to jump into his carriage."

"But now he has something to talk about for years," Hamilton said as he hugged Piper closer to him and kissed the top of her head. "You have a bit of explaining to do, young lady."

Piper fluttered her lashes at him. "It was Matilda's fault, Daddy. Miss Agatha will vouch for that. And if Grace, Lily, and I hadn't followed Matilda, why, Miss Agatha might not have been able to escape." She gave another flutter. "Because of that, I do think it might be best if you and Mama and Mr. and Mrs. Watson go easy on us with the punishment business."

Hamilton kissed Piper's head again and rolled his eyes. "Why do I have the strangest feeling that you, along with Agatha's sisters, are going to be responsible for giving us white hair way before our time?"

"We're just following in Miss Agatha's, Aunt Arabella's, Aunt Felicia's, and Mama's footsteps, Daddy. You can't claim to be surprised that we'd want to do that. All of them are amazing ladies."

The mention of amazing ladies had Zayne returning his attention to Agatha. She was standing there, swinging her arms back and forth, dirt streaking her face, but she was the most wonderful sight he'd ever seen.

He cleared his throat, which had Agatha moving immediately to his side and leaning down. "Good heavens, Zayne, we need to get you up off of that cold ground. You must be freezing."

"Could you bend down closer?"

Her eyes widened. "Does something hurt? Mr. Pitkin didn't hit you, did he, because if he did, I—"

"Agatha, be quiet."

"There's no need for you to get snippy. I mean, I'm just—"

"I love you."

Her mouth made an O of surprise, and then she sat down, right smack on top of him. "What did you say?"

"I said I love you, but I think you still have a pistol attached to your leg, and it's digging into my side."

"Oh, forgive me." She hitched up her skirt, pulled a pistol out of her garter, dropped it to the ground, and proceeded to settle herself right on top of him again. "You may continue."

"Where was I?"

"You love me."

"Ah, yes, quite right." He looked up at her and smiled. "I love you."

"I know, you said that, but what about Helena?"

He shifted her to the left a bit and then reached into his pocket when he was finally able to find it through the layers of petticoats and silk that covered him. His fingers closed around the ring, and he pulled it out, holding it up so Agatha could see it. "I tried to give this to you tonight, but Helena ruined that moment. I need you to know that she means nothing to me and I never loved her, not in the way I love you."

A single tear rolled down Agatha's face. He raised a hand and captured it. "What I most wanted to tell you, though, is that my grandmother gave me this ring, and she told me that I was only to give it to a lady who could match me wit for wit."

"And that's me?" Agatha whispered.

"Well, yes, but you see, what I've come to realize is that you match me in every possible way. You're my perfect match, and I think I've loved you from the very first moment I truly met you—back in that house you were breaking into with Eliza."

"That wasn't the first time we met," Agatha said, her voice turning a little grumpy.

"I know that, darling, but it was the first time I really saw you. You were feisty and beautiful and annoying and . . . everything I could ever ask for in a woman."

Another tear dribbled down her face, but then she got the look in her eyes that was always followed by some type of argument. "If I tell you I love you, would that mean you're going to continue trying to keep me out of trouble at every turn and racing to my rescue even if you're in no state to do so?"

"I don't think you'll ever be able to stay out of trouble."

"You're right."

"I'm still going to try to rescue you if I think you need rescuing."

"That's fine, as long as you realize I'll be doing the very same thing for you."

He smiled. "I can live with that."

"What else?"

"You're going to marry me."

He winced when she stiffened and remembered Piper telling him he needed to remember the romance business.

"Fine."

"Let me rephrase that, I would be beyond honored if you would agree to become . . . did you say *fine*?"

"Weren't you listening?"

He felt his lips twitch. She was back to sounding grumpy. She was enchanting when she was grumpy.

"I wasn't expecting you to agree so easily."

She considered him for a long moment and then bent toward him until her face was only inches from his. "Why not?"

"Because you never agree to anything I suggest."

"You didn't suggest—you told me I was going to marry you."

"And you didn't like that?"

"I said *fine*. If I didn't like what you said, I'd hardly reply in the affirmative, would I?"

Why was he arguing with her?

She'd apparently agreed to marry him.

He should be quiet before he said something that would have her changing her mind.

"We're getting married tonight." What had prompted him to say that?

"No, we're not."

He really *should* have kept his mouth shut.

"Why not?"

She leaned even closer to him, her breath tickling his face. "My mother has been planning my wedding since before I could walk. You must realize she, along with your mother, would be devastated if they're not given the opportunity to plan a lavish event, so we'll simply have to turn everything over to them and hope they're able to pull a wedding together quickly."

Relief was immediate.

She was going to marry him.

He needed to do something romantic to seal the deal, such as . . .

Soft, smooth lips slipped over his.

The world ceased to exist around him as Agatha kissed him, and even though he'd been hoping to be the one to initiate their first kiss, he suddenly discovered he had no complaints about this odd turn at all. In fact, he was simply going to give in and enjoy the moment.

A sliver of disappointment slid through him when she pulled away.

"We'll have to be diligent convincing our mothers to speed plans along," she whispered.

She wanted to marry him.

His soul began to hum.

"I love you, you know," she whispered, "have loved you for years, and . . ."

He grabbed hold of her head and pulled her closer, this time capturing her lips with his as his hands cradled her face.

When he heard her sigh and her lips went soft, he knew God was smiling down on them, and as he deepened the kiss, he thought he heard angels sing.

Epilogue

CHRISTMAS EVE

Her mother and Gloria had not been able to plan a wedding rapidly.

Here it was, not quite two months since Zayne had told her they were getting married, and finally, she was almost ready to walk down the aisle.

Zayne would be waiting for her, standing on two good legs, his cast having been removed the week before.

That was certainly a nice benefit from having to wait so long, although getting married on Christmas Eve added a lovely touch of something special to the celebration as well.

"Mr. Chambers wanted me to ask you if you have that article done," Arabella said as she strolled into the back room of the church, one of her little darlings, beautifully named Juliet, nestled in the crook of her arm. "I told him now was hardly the time for business, but he says readers are demanding more of your work, so how would you like me to respond?"

"Tell him I sent an article over to the paper this morning, it should be on his desk, and also tell him I'm about to get married and I will not have him pestering me until I get back from my honeymoon . . . in a month."

"I'll tell him," Arabella said with a grin, "and you look beautiful, by the way. I'm so delighted you're about to become my sister."

"Don't start with that kind of talk," Piper warned as she waltzed into the room, cradling Arabella's other baby, Ernest, in her arms—the birth of twins explaining exactly why Arabella had been so huge. "Miss Agatha will start crying, just like Mama was a minute ago, and Grandmother was all last night *and* this morning, and don't even get me started on Aunt Felicia." She rolled her eyes. "She's in the powder room fixing her face, but she did let me hold little Oscar while she mopped herself up." She grinned. "Aunt Felicia's been very stingy with passing around the baby ever since she and Uncle Grayson docked their yacht, but at least she managed to pull off her lovely surprise of making it to the wedding."

"May I come in?" Drusilla asked, sticking her head through the doorway and drawing Agatha's attention away from Piper.

"Yes, please," Agatha said with a smile for the woman who had become a dear friend.

"You look lovely," Drusilla proclaimed, pulling Agatha into a strong embrace.

"I see that arm of yours has healed completely, given the way you just hugged me," Agatha said as she stepped back. "Are you going to go back to work soon?"

"After guarding you for over a year, I think I deserve a bit more of a break."

Grinning, Agatha nodded, but before she could say anything else, a loud clearing of a throat—one she knew only too well—drew her attention. Turning, she found Francis standing in the doorway with a hand covering his eyes.

"Are you decent?" he asked.

"Would it stop you from entering if I said I wasn't?"

His hand dropped as he strode into the room, stopping by her side to kiss her cheek. "You look wonderful."

He turned and smiled at Drusilla. "As do you, Drusilla."

He looked up and smiled right as Jeffrey careened into the room, trying to steer another one of Charlotte's inventions but not having much luck since he bounced off the wall a second later. "I swear I thought the brakes were actually fixed on this thing."

"I can fix them after the wedding," Francis said as he walked over and pulled Jeffrey's cart away from the wall. "I've decided to take an extended leave from the investigation business, which means I'll have plenty of time on my hands. I'm thinking—after I fix your brakes, of course—that I might have to hop on a train and go somewhere warm."

Drusilla bit her lip. "You're leaving?"

"Just for the winter." Francis suddenly turned pink. "You're welcome to come with me, if you'd like. Although you'd . . . ah . . . have to find someone to chaperone you."

Drusilla narrowed her eyes. "I'm a little old for a chaperone, Francis, but I do have an elderly aunt who loves warm places. Tell me though, how will you be able to afford this vacation since you don't seem to have any plans to go back to work?"

"I offered you some relaxation time in the sun, Drusilla, but that doesn't mean I'm ready to impart all of my darkest secrets to you."

"There's hope for the two of you yet," Agatha said with a grin, even though Drusilla and Francis simply looked back at her rather confused.

Charlotte St. James suddenly rushed into the room. "Cora sent me in here to tell everyone they need to take their seats." She stopped in front of Jeffrey's cart and frowned. "Is that a dent?"

"I'm still having some difficulties with the brakes," Jeffrey admitted.

"I'll take a look at them after the wedding," Charlotte said, completely missing the fact Jeffrey's eyes had widened considerably and he was shaking his head even as he backed up the cart and disappeared a moment later through the door.

Drusilla nodded to Francis. "We should go take our seats."

Francis smiled, but then he moved closer to Agatha and gave her one of his famous scowls. "I do hope you'll be able to refrain from causing any mayhem at your own wedding. I would hate to have to pull out my pistol in the middle of the ceremony."

Grinning, Agatha rolled her eyes. "You really are a dear man, and I'll do my best to behave myself, at least during the ceremony."

"See that you do."

She watched as Drusilla, followed by Francis, left the room and then smiled as Eliza and Felicia swept in, both of them carrying babies, and both of them sporting eyes that were suspiciously wet. "This is a happy occasion," she reminded them.

"But it's taken so long that none of us truly thought it would ever happen," Eliza said as she handed Viola to Charlotte and stepped to Agatha's side. "You look beautiful, and I'm sorry for getting weepy, but you were responsible for getting all of the women in this room together with our husbands, and for that we'll be forever grateful. You must know that we want only the best for you."

"Zayne's always been the best for her," Arabella said as she stepped to Eliza's side and sent her a somewhat misty grin.

"They were destined to get married," Piper said as she shifted little Ernest in her arms. "It's been God's plan all along, but it just took them a while to realize it."

"You're very astute, my darling girl," Gloria said as she strode through the door with Cora on one side of her and Matilda at her heels. "It's time. So all of you need to give up your hold on those delightful babies and take your place in line. Fortunately, there are a slew of relatives and friends out in the sanctuary who'd be more than happy to have a turn holding them."

Agatha found herself kissed on the cheek by everyone before the room emptied in a flash, and she stood there alone, except for her mother.

"Don't cry," she said when Cora released a sniff.

"I never thought this day would come," Cora admitted as she dabbed at her eyes.

"On that we're in full agreement," Roger said, coming up behind her before he placed a kiss on Agatha's cheek. "That's a delightful frock you're wearing, Agatha. Is it new?"

Cora huffed. "That's *my* wedding gown and you saw *me* wearing it at *our* wedding. Although we did have it altered to resemble the current style and Agatha's figure."

Her father sent her a wink, took Cora by the arm, and hustled her out of the room, coming back a minute later.

"I thought it best to get her to her seat. She's been somewhat emotional of late, and the last thing we need is for her to start crying," he said blinking rapidly as his eyes filled with tears.

Agatha gave her father a hug and stepped back. "Thank you for everything you've done for me, Daddy. You've been a prince among men for putting up with my antics for so very long."

Roger wiped his eyes and grinned. "Yes, that is true. And unfortunately, I do believe Grace and Lily are following in your footsteps, so it's a good thing I'm getting you married off. I'm getting too old to put up with three of you."

Her sisters took that moment to race into the room.

"Sorry we're late," Grace said. "I was talking to Mr. Daniel Murdock, checking on the health of his brother, and then the time just seemed to get away from me, and—"

"I had to pull her away from the gentleman," Lily explained. "Honestly, you're entirely too young for him, Grace, and you still have several years before you even make your debut. Why, the poor gentleman was probably mortified over the fact you were flirting so . . ."

"Girls, enough," Roger interrupted when Grace began to sputter. "You need to get in place so that Agatha can finally marry her Mr. Beckett."

"Oh, right," Grace said with a somewhat sheepish grin. "Sorry, Agatha, we'll see you at the end of the aisle. And . . . you look beautiful in Mother's dress."

"Shall I fetch Matilda?" Roger asked as her sisters hurried out of the room.

Matilda apparently heard her name, because she pranced over to Agatha's side and stood quite docilely for once as Agatha clipped her leash to the collar. Bending over, she scratched Matilda's ears. "Behave," she cautioned before she straightened and took the arm her father offered her.

"Ready?" Roger asked.

"I do believe I am."

"Then we should go get you married to your Zayne."

Stepping into the church, she felt her heart swell and her

breath leave her as she glanced around and saw all the people she loved, people who had braved the cold and snow to come see her marry the love of her life.

Mary, Jessie, and Hannah were at the very back, waving madly to her and causing her to grin when she realized they'd placed themselves right next to a handy exit. Even though Theodore had kept to his promise and not pursued them, it was clear they weren't taking any chances. She sent them a nod as her father moved her forward and she saw Dot next, beaming back at her and looking completely delighted to have been included in the festivities. The poor lady had been appalled when she'd discovered she'd been played for a fool.

And to make it up to Agatha, she'd taken to the streets, trying to convince as many ladies of the night as she could that there was a better life waiting for them and Dot was more than happy to help them find it.

The friends of her heart—Eliza, Arabella, Felicia, and Charlotte—were watching her from their position at the end of the aisle, all of them dabbing their eyes with handkerchiefs, and she blinked and then blinked again when her eyes began filling with tears.

She was truly blessed to have such amazing people in her life, and she took a moment to send up a silent prayer of thanks, giving God the credit for gifting her with such an extraordinary existence.

"He looks like he wants to race up the aisle and carry you off," Roger whispered with a trace of amusement in his voice.

She blinked again and her gaze found Zayne.

He was leaning forward on his cane, but his legs were steady and his smile huge.

He was going to be fine. The bones in his leg had healed perfectly and even though he still needed a cane because his leg was weak, Dr. Gessler was sure that someday soon he'd be able to abandon that cane and move about freely.

He'd be able to keep up with her now, which was a good thing, since they'd decided to travel out west, once spring hit, and help Willie get the mining venture up and running. Zayne was currently back helping Hamilton with the railroad business, and Agatha knew he was finally and completely whole.

She reached the end of the aisle, and fresh tears stung her eyes when her father pulled away her veil and kissed her cheek before he handed her over to Zayne, taking Matilda from her in return.

Her father might have been after her for years to marry, but the truth of the matter was, she was still his little girl in his eyes, and although he wanted what was best for her, it was obviously difficult for him to let her go.

"I love you, Daddy."

Roger's eyes filled with tears, he gave a watery sounding snort and then turned and quickly took a seat next to her mother, who was sobbing into her handkerchief. Gloria did the same right next to her, as Douglas Beckett, Zayne's father, patted her arm.

"They're a mess," Zayne whispered, causing her to grin.

"We should have known," she whispered back.

"Are you ready?" Reverend Fraser asked.

Agatha felt Zayne squeeze her hand as they turned and began to recite their vows.

Before she knew it, Zayne was sliding a simple gold wedding band over her finger, and then he slipped his grandmother's ring over the band, smiling when she blinked.

"I thought my grandmother would appreciate the gesture, here in the church," he whispered. "And if you haven't noticed, the band exactly *matches* my grandmother's ring—well, your ring now."

"Witty of you, the whole 'match' business."

"I knew you'd understand exactly what I meant."

Reverend Fraser cleared his throat. "We're not quite done."

Zayne grinned. "Oh, forgive us, Reverend Fraser."

Reverend Fraser smiled and raised his voice. "By the power vested in me, it is my great pleasure to pronounce you man and wife."

"It certainly is about time," Eliza called, causing everyone to laugh.

"You are the love of my life and you've made me the happiest man alive," Zayne said right before he dropped his cane, cupped her face with his hand, and claimed her lips with his.

Her heart felt as if it were about to overflow when he drew her closer, and she knew without a doubt they were destined for a life filled with adventure, amusement, annoyance upon occasion, but most importantly, love.

God would expect nothing less from them, and she had no intention of disappointing Him.

Acknowledgments

With each new book I see published, I find myself more and more amazed by the support I'm given by a variety of people. To these people, I give heartfelt thanks.

To my editors, Raela Schoenherr and Karen Schurrer—Thank you for polishing up my stories and getting me back on track when I start going down those rabbit trails.

To the fabulous marketing and sales team at Bethany House—Your diligence in getting my work out to the readers is truly inspiring. I couldn't do any of this without you.

To Paul Higdon and John Hamilton—Thank you for another wonderful cover.

To my brother-in-law, Mike Gibas—I know the family was a little skeptical when you up and married my sister, Tricia, so unexpectedly all those years ago. But, it's been proven time and time again that our skepticism was unfounded. You're a delightful brother-in-law and are simply perfect for my sister. Thank you for reading all of my stories, even the horrible ones, and proclaiming them wonderful. Your encouragement kept me going even when I wanted to throw in the towel and just go back to fashion.

To my sister-in-law, Kristin Turner—I'm so glad you didn't let Dave scare you away with all that talk about his sisters, although I'm pretty sure he wasn't including me when he told you those dastardly tales. You've been such a fun addition to our family, and you've given me two adorable nieces, Meghan and Kaitlyn, whom I just love to pieces.

To Amy Hall, one of my favorite librarians—It's been so lovely getting to know you. Your mad research skills and ability to dig up everything concerning the Gilded Age has been invaluable. Thank you for not getting tired of all my questions.

To all my friends, neighbors, and strangers I just happen to meet on the street—Thank you for allowing me to go on and on about my stories, even when I know full well you have no idea what I'm talking about. I promise that someday, when this isn't quite so new to me, I'll talk about something else, like football, or the latest styles in shoes.

To Al and Dom—Thanks for everything, especially just being my guys.

To the readers—Thank you for picking up my stories and for becoming so attached to my characters. Your letters inspire me, bring me to tears at times, and make this whole writing thing a complete joy.

And to God—for giving me an imagination, an outlet for that imagination, and a wonderful life.

God bless!
Jen

Jen Turano, author of *A Change of Fortune, A Most Peculiar Circumstance, A Talent for Trouble,* and *A Match of Wits* is a graduate of the University of Akron with a degree in clothing and textiles. She is a member of ACFW and lives in a suburb of Denver, Colorado. Visit her website at www. jenturano.com.

If you enjoyed *A Match of Wits*, you may also enjoy...

More Fiction You May Enjoy

BETHANYHOUSE

Stay up-to-date on your favorite books and authors with our free e-newsletters. Sign up today at bethanyhouse.com.

Find us on Facebook. facebook.com/bethanyhousepublishers

anopenbook

Free exclusive resources for your book group! bethanyhouse.com/anopenbook